A DARK COVENANT

Loki's chest suddenly felt tight, and not from the iron bands. "Who are you?"

The snake smiled that unnatural grin again. "Many are the names by which I am known. At this point in time, you may call me Angelo."

"You can free me?"

"In a manner of speaking. I can give you a body in which to dwell."

Loki was silent. He thought he understood what the snake—Angelo—was offering, and almost wept at the thought. To be free finally from this torment, and he could then, at last, have revenge.

"Ragnarok," he whispered in a voice hoarse with longing.

"Yes," hissed the snake, leaning closer. "Ragnarok. You have a grudge against your Allfather, your Odin. I have a grudge against a similar personage. You were cast out of your rightful place and bound here, to be tortured till the end of the world—I was likewise punished. You wish to bring about Ragnarok—I wish to bring about—" he paused. "I have tasks that I wish to see completed, and I need your help. Do what I tell you to do, and then, I promise you, you shall be set free and have your Ragnarok.

"So,"—the snake began to make its slow way across Loki's imprisoned body—"do we have a deal?"

"This is a unique, exciting tale of adventure and romance, brushed with beauty and mysticism. Jadrien Bell creates a lovely balance of history and fantasy guaranteed to transport readers to a world they won't want to leave."
— Susan Wiggs, author of *The Horsemasters Daughter*

A.D. 999

JADRIEN BELL

ACE BOOKS, NEW YORK

A.D. 999

This is a work of fiction. Names, characters, places, and incidents are either the product of the author's imagination or are used fictitiously, and any resemblance to actual persons, living or dead, business establishments, everts, or locales is entirely coincidental.

An Ace Book / published by arrangement with
the author

PRINTING HISTORY
Ace edition / November 1999

All rights reserved.
Copyright © 1999 by Christie Golden.
Cover art by Lisa Falkenstern.
This book may not be reproduced in whole or in part,
by mimeograph or any other means, without permission.
For information address: The Berkley Publishing Group,
a division of Penguin Putnam Inc.,
375 Hudson Street, New York, New York 10014.

The Penguin Putnam Inc. World Wide Web site address is
http://www.penguinputnam.com

Check out the Ace Science Fiction/Fantasy newsletter,
and much more, on the Internet at Club PPI!

ISBN: 0-441-00673-6

ACE®
Ace Books are published by The Berkley Publishing Group,
a division of Penguin Putnam Inc.,
375 Hudson Street, New York, New York 10014.
ACE and the "A" design are trademarks
belonging to Penguin Putnam Inc.

PRINTED IN THE UNITED STATES OF AMERICA

10   9   8   7   6   5   4   3   2   1

A.D. 999 is a book about faith.
It is therefore dedicated
to all those who had faith in it:

Robert Amerman

Mark Anthony

Ginjer Buchanan

*The Central Colorado
Writer's Workshop*

Lucienne Diver

Michael Georges

James and Elizabeth Golden

Carla Montgomery

Sean Moore

Jen Stiles

Lyn Warwick

Acknowledgments

Inevitably, there is a great deal of research involved with a novel of this scope. I'd like to acknowledge gratefully those individuals who helped make that research so much easier and fruitful. Any errors are entirely my own.

Jen Stiles, who helped Gleannsidh, its people, and its Faerie folk come to life;

Palden Jenkins, who gave me invaluable information about the history and topography of Glastonbury; and Dr. Susan M. Shwartz, who helped me capture its feel;

Anthony Rouse, a bellringer at Worth Church, who graciously provided photographs and information about this beautiful church;

the good folk at www.glastonbury.co.uk, who helped me identify who was Abbot of Glastonbury in A.D. 999; and

Joanne Winters, for the famous prophecy of Saint Columba and additional information about the island of Iona.

Gleannsidh

Loch Ness

Dalriada
(Scotland)

Iona

North Sea

Ireland

England

Chesbury

Calne

London

Glastonbury   Shaftesbury   Worth   Canterbury

Great Britain
Circa A.D. 999

Corfe

150 Miles

Prologue

Corfe Castle, Dorset
March 18, 978

Ethelred watched the snowflakes drift lazily downward, each downy speck adding its individual sparkle to the white blanket that already covered the courtyard. The snow had come suddenly a few hours ago, and lay like a shroud over the green shoots and blossoms that had only recently appeared.

He pressed his small face to the window's opening and folded his arms on the chill stone, feeling the cold redden his cheeks and watching it turn his breath to mist. Soon it would again be too cold for him, and he would have to turn his attention back to the room where his mother, Queen Elfthryth, had dragged him this morning. She had instructed him to stay here and think about all the sins that his ten-year-old self had managed to commit in a single day.

Ethelred was in the upper part of the castle's small chapel. The first story was reserved for the family's use, and there the red-cheeked village priest, Father Odo, led them in prayer every morning. The second story was for the servants, and its furnishings were cruder: rough benches and little decoration. The room's austerity was overwhelmed by the huge, explicitly detailed image of Christ hanging bloody on the crucifix, the same size as the one that hung in the family chapel. Fat beeswax candles, two feet in height and thick as a man's arm, provided the room's illumination and warmth.

Ethelred's lips were cold, and he shivered. Reluctantly, he pulled away from the window, closed the shutters against the snowy evening, and scurried back to the corner farthest from the flickering candlelight. He sank down and folded in on himself, still trembling with the cold that clung to his clothing and skin, staring at the tiny flames while his heart thudded rapidly in his small chest.

He hated candles.

The monk who tutored him couldn't understand why Ethelred's quick mind and pleasant demeanor changed if the lessons lingered until the evening hours. Brother Wulfraed once tried to explain the markings on the candles, cheerily telling Ethelred that the prince's ancestor, King Alfred the Great, had designed them so that they burned a certain length in a certain time. Ethelred had stared blankly in fear, unable and unwilling to reveal the reason for his terror. Even at his young age, Ethelred knew that Brother Wulfraed would never understand. For the Benedictine, candles were a way to bring God's own light into the domiciles of man and a clever way to mark the passage of time. Ethelred could never begin to articulate what they meant to him.

But someday, he would be a man grown. His soft mouth set at the thought and his blue eyes ceased to focus on the candles, seeing instead scenes from an idyllic future. He would be a man grown, and there would never, ever be candles in his castle, and there would be no Mother to grab the thick lengths, snuff out the flames with a hard pinch, and wield the things like clubs—

He shivered again and bolted from his curled-up position in the corner. Air. He had to have air, the candles burned up the air, and—

He flung open the shutters and gulped icy air. Better now. The wintry evening, snow-graced, had a clean, pure scent.

His heart slowed somewhat, and Ethelred turned his attention away from the hated candles and toward the pleasant evening that lay in store. Just that afternoon, a sword thegn of King Edward's, riding hard to arrive ahead of his liege, had clattered into the courtyard. "His Majesty wishes to pay his respects to his half brother the prince" was the news, and Corfe had leaped into frantic activity.

Elfthryth had seemed more pleased by the news than Ethelred had expected, and he wondered at that. He was well aware there had been much tension between the two women who had shared the late King Edgar's bed, even though Edward's mother had died in childbirth long before Ethelred was born. Elfthryth's hatred had not died along with her rival. When the Witan, the royal advisory council, had chosen to anoint Edward sovereign rather than Ethelred, Elfthryth had been furious. Ethelred, only seven at the time, remembered many nights spent huddled beneath the furs and bed linens, listening to his mother rail impotently against Edward and "that bitch who bore him." Sleep had been fitful, and Ethelred had walked softly around his mother, lest she take out her anger on him with the rod, or her sharp-nailed hands, or, worst of all, the dreadful candles.

There had been plenty of shouting matches between Edward and Elfthryth, that much was certain. Edward was infamous for his quick and violent temper, but Ethelred had never been the target. The dark, slender king softened around his young sibling, often bringing toys and treats when they met.

It was almost dark now. Still, the snow gleamed, almost as if it had caught and kept the day's light. And along the narrow pass that led between the mountains and connected the castle with the town it guarded, Ethelred saw small figures moving.

His face lit up, the candles burning ominously at his back momentarily forgotten. The toes of his boots scraped the wall as he tried to climb higher and, despite the cold, he thrust his head and shoulders out the window for a better view.

There was activity in the courtyard. Servants had brought out several torches and were in the process of lighting them. Like magic, the illumination sprang from torch to torch, and a robust red warmth chased away the fey, white glow of the snow.

Ethelred's smile spread as he heard King Edward's voice calling for admission. The big gates creaked open, and the young king, perched atop a beautiful horse that gleamed almost as white as the snow, entered proudly. Only two sword thegns rode with him, which Ethelred thought was odd. Usually King Edward brought several dozen men with him. Elfthryth often complained about how expensive it was to host her stepson.

"Edward!" he called, but the wind snatched away his words.

He anchored himself with one arm and waved frantically with the other. Edward didn't appear to see him.

Elfthryth's men stood at attention beside the gates but made no move to close them against the encroaching night. The queen herself made her way across the courtyard to welcome her step-son and liege lord, carrying a steaming welcome cup. A modest scarf covered her thick, dark tresses, and the curves of her body were hidden by the voluminous swathes of her gown. She made deep obeisance.

"Good even, Your Majesty! We welcome you to Corfe. Please—drink deep of our hospitality."

Edward raised an eyebrow, and the grin that Ethelred so loved and so few ever saw passed across his chill-reddened face.

"Stepmother, you are gracious. A hot drink will be most welcome indeed."

He stretched out his gloved fingers for the cup of hot wine, and steam wreathed his face. As he lifted the cup, he caught sight of his half brother gesticulating frantically from his second-story perch, and his grin widened.

"Ethelred!" he cried, his voice warm. "Careful, brother, 'tis a long way to fall!" He raised the cup in salute, and in so doing, missed the queen's subtle nod to one of her retainers who had approached the king's steed.

Ethelred squirmed with pleasure, basking in the glow of his brother's very public recognition and his announcement of concern.

Edward began to drink. The queen moved back a step or two as the retainer stepped forward and reached to take the reins of Edward's white horse. Though there was nothing unusual in that, Ethelred frowned. He did not know this man, and he knew all of Corfe's servants.

The man's hood fell away from his face as he moved, revealing a visage as fair as any Ethelred had ever seen, and as he moved gracefully toward the king as if to help him dismount, he raised a dagger. The blade glittered in the torchlight. Fear spurted through Ethelred and he tried to gesture, to cry out a warning, *anything,* but he could not move.

The traitor's knife found its sheath. With the precision of an artist, the retainer angled the blade upward. The weapon plunged deep into Edward's bowels. Edward spasmed, the cup falling from splayed fingers to spill its steaming contents into the snow.

His mouth opened, his eyes flew wide, and he fastened those eyes upon his stepmother, who smiled the smile of the cat with the mouse.

A second rapid, skillful stroke again pierced vital organs. Soundlessly, slowly, the king of all England slumped in his saddle. His lively, ruddy features were still and cold as the snow, dead as the green shoots of early spring that had died under the unexpected snowfall.

The murderer slapped the horse smartly on the rump. It started, tossed its head, and bolted, kicking up sprays of blood-stained snow as it galloped down the pass that led back toward the village. Edward's body fell at the movement, tumbling out of its seat. One foot remained hooked in the stirrup. In the space of a few heartbeats, the darkness closed around the dreadful sight of the king, dead and cooling, being dragged like a sack of goods behind his panicked steed.

Now the men closed the gates and stood to receive coins doled out from Elfthryth's own hand. No one appeared startled, not even the two sword thegns who had come with Edward. The retainer who had performed the deed knelt and calmly cleaned the blade in the snow.

Now breath returned to Ethelred. He drew in a deep gasp of the icy air and screamed. His body shook, but not with cold. Everyone in the courtyard turned to look at him, and he saw the familiar cloud of anger settle over his mother's beautiful features. But for once, Ethelred didn't care.

"Edward!" he cried, as if his keening could somehow bring the king back. Surely this was all a dream. Surely he'd simply nodded off and had a nightmare induced by the fear of the candles that burned so close to him. Any moment now, Edward would ride through the gates, and they would go hunting on the morrow, their quest made that much easier because of the snow that would betray their quarry and—

"Ethelred?"

Startled, Ethelred let go his grip on the window and landed in a heap on the wooden floor. He scrambled to his feet, the cold stone of the wall against his back, and stared at the man framed in the doorway. How had he gotten here so quickly?

It was Edward's killer. His face was as perfect as Ethelred had first thought it, framed by a mass of short, curling golden hair. His eyes were blue as the sky in summer, and his face was clean-shaven. His voice was soft, honey-smooth, and full of concern. A frown furrowed the perfect brow, and his next words were not what Ethelred had expected.

"I'm sorry, Ethelred." The man stepped forward, knelt, and reached to enfold the terrified boy in a fatherly embrace. "I'm so sorry."

Face to face with the man who had so coldly murdered his brother, Ethelred reached for hatred, but couldn't find it. This man's touch was soothing, calming. He shivered, and the caring arms closed more tightly about him. Finally his shivering ceased. He placed his head atop the stranger's shoulder, unconsciously rubbing his tear-stained cheeks dry against those soft, yellow curls.

"It had to be done," continued the stranger. "It is your destiny, Your Majesty. You were born to be king, not your brother. It was foretold. Surely you remember the dark omen—the comet that filled the night skies when Edward was crowned? It is a tragic thing that the meddling Witan chose him over you to begin with. He might yet be alive, your beloved brother, serving you loyally at your side. That was the way it was meant to be."

Ethelred nodded. Yes. Yes, he could see that now. He drew back and wiped his face as the stranger rose. "Who are you?" he asked wonderingly.

"I am a friend to you and your mother," the man replied in liquid tones. "The best of friends. I came just recently from Rome. You may call me Angelo. I've come to help you win what is rightfully yours, and to guide you through the treacherous waters that you must yet navigate, Your Majesty. I would be your adviser, if you will have me."

Ethelred couldn't take his eyes off the stranger. *Not a stranger—Angelo,* he corrected himself. The memory of Edward's body being dragged by his horse into the night, which he had thought would haunt him forever, was already receding. Fleeing before the radiant presence of Angelo like a shadow before the sun.

"Of course," he breathed. "Surely you have been sent by God to help me."

"Surely I have," Angelo agreed. "But let us keep that our secret, shall we? To all others, I am merely your adviser. Your name is Ethelred, and I understand that in your native tongue, that means 'well counseled.' I promise you that you shall live up to your name, if I have anything to do with it. Come." He held out his hand. "Let us greet your lady mother and celebrate the beginning of your reign."

978: King Edward was murdered in the evening at the gap of Corfe on March 18th; he was buried at Wareham, with no kingly honors. Ethelred was hallowed king on the Sunday, the fortnight after Easter, at Kingston.

The same year a cloud red as blood was seen many times, in the likeness of fire, most often manifested at midnight. It was formed into beams of lights of various colors, and at the first streak of dawn, it glided away.

—from *The Anglo-Saxon Chronicle*

PART I

The Summons

And I will give power unto my two witnesses.

—REVELATION 11:3

1

The Wolf turned at the sound of the approaching company, ears pricked forward, tail held high. Curiosity filled him, but not apprehension. Who or what could possibly harm him? The mighty beings who now surrounded him—what were they to him? He could crush them with a single snap of his powerful jaws, and they knew it. Generally they gave him a wide berth, all save the Warrior. He alone was brave enough to bring the Wolf food. Why now, then, were they coming to make him part of their sport?

His great eyes narrowed as the others brought forth a mighty chain. Its links clanked and jangled, and it required two of them, powerful deities though they were, to haul it forth. "A game!" cried one. "Like the games we play with the Beautiful One, who cannot be harmed. Let us see if the Wolf can snap this chain!"

"I like not the thought of a chain about my neck," growled the Wolf.

"But surely this paltry thing is no match for your strength!" they replied. "Come, play with us. We are certain you will snap the chain Laeding like a child's mock sword!"

The Wolf glanced again at the chain. It was not so thick, after all—the links were barely the width of a man's hand. "Very well," he replied, trotting toward them. "Bind me with Laeding, then, and we shall see how long it takes for me to break it to bits!"

Eagerly, almost with something akin to relief, they rushed forward and bound Laeding about his thick gray neck. They wrapped the end about one of the strange iron trees that grew in this wood. The Wolf took a deep breath, and with a quick wrench, he shattered Laeding.

"Ha!" cried the Wolf, terribly pleased with himself. "That did not take long at all!" They looked stunned. "Come, you didn't really think so fragile a chain would hold me, did you? Come back tomorrow, and bring me a true challenge!"

So they did, that next day, and this time the chain was as thick as a man's head, its links heavy and imposing. "This chain is called Dromi," they said. The Wolf deigned to have the huge length wrapped twice about him, and secured again to an iron tree. He flexed his neck, but the chain held fast. Alarm began to seep through him. He dug his paws into the soil, pulled and tugged with all his might—

—and as before, the chain broke with a loud crack. The Wolf pranced about, delighted with his strength and prowess. "Not built is the chain that can bind me!" he crowed.

"Perhaps it is so," agreed the Warrior slowly. "But I trust, good friend, that you will continue to play with us?"

"Play I shall," the Wolf replied, "until you tire of the game. For surely you must know it is fruitless."

He waited for them, enjoying the game, his amber eyes alight with anticipation. But they did not come the next day, nor the next. On the third day, though, they came again, with dancing eyes and bright smiles, and the Wolf's confidence began to ebb. For they bore not a mighty chain like Laeding or Dromi, but a silken ribbon that fluttered in the wind. Deep in his broad chest, the Wolf began to growl, suspecting trickery.

"You insult me, Warrior!" he yelped accusingly. "Either that ribbon will snap at a single effortless tug, or it is stronger than it looks. And if that is so, then I shall not permit you to fasten it about my neck!"

"What?" laughed the Warrior. "The mighty Wolf afraid of the little ribbon Gleipnir? Come, let us have some sport."

The Wolf narrowed his eyes and cocked his head, giving the Warrior a crafty glance. "If it is so innocent, then certainly one of you will be willing to grant me a surety. Come, someone place his hand in my mouth, so that I may rest easy that this is no trick."

He thought he had them then. As one, they shrank back, dropping their gazes. Not a one among them was willing to risk a hand for this delicate ribbon's sake. Just as he was about to launch himself at them in anger, the Warrior spoke.

"You may take my hand as surety," he said calmly, extending his sword arm toward the Wolf.

The Wolf was startled. Surely the Warrior would not risk his sword arm if this was a trick. Obligingly, he opened his huge jaws. The Warrior placed his fisted hand inside, and the Wolf tasted sweat, coppery and tangy, against his red tongue. One of the others draped Gleipnir about his neck, tying it fast and wrapping the other end around a huge boulder.

With the Warrior's hand in his mouth, the Wolf tugged. Nothing happened. He tugged again. He jerked, trying to snap it; strained, trying to pull it from the boulder. Fear rose in him, and, the Warrior's hand now grasped securely by sharp teeth, the Wolf leaped and jerked frantically, all to no avail.

His eyes met those of the Warrior, and in their depths the Wolf saw triumph. Growling, he brought his jaws down. They popped skin, severed sinew, crunched bone, and with a mighty twist of his jaws the Wolf pulled the Warrior's hand from his wrist and swallowed it whole. Little enough revenge for the loss of his freedom, but he took what he could.

There was much triumphant cheering, but the Warrior's face was pale as he staggered back, his gaze locked with the yellow eyes of the Wolf, ignoring the stump of a hand that pumped blood. One of the women rushed forward to wrap the injured member, but the Warrior paid little heed. He continued to stare at the Wolf.

"Son of the Trickster, you have yourself been bound by trickery. The loss of my hand is a small price to keep your evil from visiting itself upon an unsuspecting world. Gleipnir is no ordinary ribbon. It was forged by the dark elves with strong magic, and is made of six strange things: the sound of the cat when it moves, the beard of a woman, the root of a mountain, the sinew of a bear, the breath of a fish, and the spittle of a bird. It will bind you here, visiting harm upon none, until the end of the world!"

And so it was, for no matter how the Wolf howled, or gnawed, or tugged, the fragile-seeming ribbon Gleipnir held him fast.

Until the coming of the end of the world.

The Abbey of St. Aidan's, Chesbury
April 30, 999

Alwyn's pen scratched softly on the sheet of vellum. Beneath his ink-stained fingers the shape of a wolf, curled in a silent snarl about the curve of a capital letter, came to life. Alwyn was sunk deep in concentration, barely breathing, with eyes for nothing but his work.

At last he sighed. Done. Critically, the young monk surveyed his handiwork. Some might raise an eyebrow at the choice of beast, but Alwyn was comfortable with it. After all, hadn't Saint Ailbhe achieved holiness by being kind to his foster mother, a gentle she-wolf? All the beasts on the earth were created by God, and therefore sacred in their own ways.

He stretched, stiff joints popping, and realized the sunlight that flooded the scriptorium had a different, richer cast to it. Alwyn blinked. Was it late afternoon already? But he'd just gotten back from nones—or at least it felt as though he had. As usual, the time had passed quickly while he was working. He'd better hurry, or he'd be late for vespers. He slid off the bench and began gathering his things, the task, as ever, awkward with his single hand.

"No need to rush," said an amused, rich voice behind him. "Vespers isn't for a while yet."

Startled, Alwyn jumped, almost dropping the precious sheet. "Bishop Wulfstan!" he yelped, delighted. At once Alwyn dropped to his knees, cradled the paper in the crook of his left arm, and took the bishop's hand with his right. Reverently Alwyn pressed his lips to Wulfstan's ring. A gentle hand on his shoulder coaxed him to rise and be folded into a less formal embrace.

"What brings you from London?" asked Alwyn.

Wulfstan's smile faded somewhat. "My mother is ailing. I wished to be the one to give her the final rites. But let us not speak of sad things. Let me look at you," the bishop said, the smile returning. "Same bright eyes, same unruly hair, same earnest expression. You've lost some weight, boy. Take a day or two and feign sickness. You'll get some of St. Aidan's special beef broth that way."

"Bishop!" Alwyn was scandalized, until he caught the twinkle of mirth in the older man's eyes, and relaxed.

"You always were the most serious of the oblates, Alwyn. I remember when you came to us fifteen years ago. Such a solemn face peeking out from that mat of brown hair. St. Benedict's Rule may frown on overmuch laughter, but it's a gift from God, just like the sun and the flowers. Place your work down, there's the boy, and—oh, Alwyn, this truly is lovely." The bishop took a moment to peer at the monk's work. "A wolf, eh? You're a little more daring than you would have us believe. Exquisite. All of us who serve God have a calling, and clearly illumination is yours. Have you done any original pieces?"

Alwyn blushed. "Nay, Your Grace. I've not the talent for that, as you do." Wulfstan's sermons at St. Aidan's had been powerful and lyrical, and Alwyn assumed that the former abbot had continued his writing in his new post.

"I'm not certain about that," replied Wulfstan. "But, as I was saying, put this aside for the moment. There will be time to clean up before vespers. Come walk with me in the herb garden."

Obediently Alwyn followed his former abbot out of the scriptorium, his useless hand hidden inside the folds of his robe. He clasped the wrist with his good right hand, thumb absently rubbing against the curve of bone. It wasn't dead, he knew that much. It grew nails that needed to be trimmed, felt warm as other flesh to the touch. Yet it might as well be dead, for all the use he was able to make of it. Good, that he was in an abbey and few could see his deformity; good, that a monk's robe had such voluminous sleeves.

Spring had come, but it had not brought with it the verdant flowering of past years. The earth was parched, curled up on itself in an imitation of tiles that broke in places as Alwyn and Wulfstan's leather-covered feet trod upon it. What grass there was crackled as they walked. The wind was hot as it brushed Alwyn's shaven cheeks, heavy with the threat of a scorching summer to come.

"It has reached even here, I see," said Wulfstan mournfully, bending over and stretching out a strong hand to fondle the brittle leaves of tutsan.

Alwyn nodded, his eyes on the former abbot of St. Aidan's. He looked older, Alwyn decided. The year and a half since he had left St. Aidan's for the bishopric of London had not been kind to him. Wulfstan had always been a tall, slender man. But the weight had fallen off his frame, and as a consequence he looked even taller. His monk's robe, the same dark brown garment with the sewn-in cowl that all Benedictines wore, hung on him as if it were several sizes too large. Wulfstan's hair, which had never been completely black in all the years that Alwyn had known him, was now a uniform iron gray encircling the tonsure. His blue eyes, though, were as piercing as ever, and if his face was thinner, the mouth had not forgotten how to smile.

Feeling the younger monk's gaze upon him, Wulfstan curved that mouth into the familiar smile, and his eyes twinkled. "You think the burden of the bishopric sits ill upon me," he said with a wink.

Startled, Alwyn shook his head rapidly. His cheeks felt hot. "No, Your Grace, I—"

"Do not add a lie to your sins today," chastised Wulfstan. "It may well be that for every line you write in the scriptorium a sin is forgiven, but it's just as well to avoid cultivating them if you can. And you'd be right. This has been a difficult time." He froze, suddenly, and the blue eyes went icy as he glanced about the garden, his gaze traveling to the little thatched cottage where the ill were tended. "Brother Eadwig is not about, is he?"

"No, he's gone into the village to tend the sick." Alwyn couldn't suppress a shudder. Recently, in the small farming community of Chesbury, there had been outbreaks of a disease known as St. Anthony's fire. The mysterious illness spread as fast as the fire for which it was named. Overnight, a healthy man could be reduced to screaming in agony, watching as his fingers and toes turned black and rotted off before his eyes. Worst was the madness that often accompanied the physical illness. Alwyn desperately hoped it was merely the natural weight of the years that was presently laying claim to the life of Wulfstan's mother, not this dreadful sickness.

"I thought that was what I heard." Wulfstan made the sign of the cross for the sick of Chesbury, and Alwyn imitated him. "It is well he is not likely to stumble upon us conversing here, for what I have to say is for your ears alone."

Alwyn's skin prickled. "Your Grace? I don't understand. . . . If there is anything amiss, shouldn't you speak with Abbot Bede?"

Wulfstan waved a hand in a dismissive gesture. "Bede is content to follow the Rule, say his prayers, and settle minor disputes. A good enough man, do not mistake me—but he would not know what to do with the information I am about to impart."

Alwyn laughed without humor. "And I would?"

"You well may," said Wulfstan in a sober tone that chilled the younger monk. "It is best you be informed . . . just in case."

"Then," said Alwyn slowly, "I am listening."

Wulfstan seated himself on a large stone and looked away for a moment at the horizon. His profile reminded Alwyn of a hawk, with those sharp eyes perched atop that large beak of a nose. For a long time, he didn't say anything. Alwyn waited. If nothing else, a monk learned patience.

"These are troubled times," said Wulfstan at length. "Even here, in this peaceful abbey so far from the cities, true safety is but an illusion. What is the illness of which you spoke?"

"St. Anthony's fire," answered Alwyn.

"Ah. A dreadful plague, that. And how long has it been since this land had a good, soaking rain from heaven?"

Caught off guard, Alwyn shrugged. "I know little save the work I do in the scriptorium. I am not fit to serve in the gardens or fields." He bit his lip, hearing the bitterness in his voice. It was an honor to be selected to work in the scriptorium, but that honor lost some of its luster when it was the only thing one could do.

Wulfstan shot him a glance, but let the matter lie. "Then answer me this: How many days have you been unable to work at the manuscripts?"

Alwyn's eyes grew wide. "I—I cannot recall," he said slowly, realizing the import of the words. No light save sunlight was permitted in the scriptorium for fear of fire. On rainy days, the shutters were perforce closed against the wetness.

Alwyn literally couldn't remember the last day that had not been bright and sunny. For months.

Wulfstan nodded, seeing the comprehension dawn on Alwyn's open face. "Drought. For the last two years, in various places. When crops fail, then famine is widespread. You are lucky Chesbury is on a popular trade route, else that girdle of yours would be cinched even tighter. In some areas, there have been swarms of locusts devouring what little is left." Wulfstan glanced heavenward, squinting against the sun's light. "The night skies are filled with warnings. The long-haired star has been spotted streaking across the heavens. From distant parts of the realm, we have even had reports of man devouring man. And of course, there are the Norsemen."

"I have heard they have resumed their attacks."

"A pale phrase for what they have done." Wulfstan sighed heavily, rubbing his eyes, which had begun to water from staring at the sun. "Poor young Ethelred hadn't been on the throne for three years before they started coming, and they haven't stopped. Southampton, Cheshire, Folkstone, Ipswich, and God alone knows how many smaller, less defensible villages have been attacked without word trickling down to the Witan. This year alone they struck at Wales, Devon, and Cornwall. The abbey church at Tavistock was utterly destroyed. The books, the relics, all the beautiful things of God's house—stolen, carried to their cursed heathen homeland aboard their dragon ships."

"But . . . has His Majesty done nothing? In King Alfred's time—"

"Ethelred is no Alfred," retorted Wulfstan. "He waits until the absolute last minute to order resistance, and often it is too little too late. Or, as just last month, as soon as the battle is about to begin, the order comes for our forces to withdraw. Sometimes there is not even token resistance—Ethelred merely pays the Danemen to leave. Which does nothing but ensure their return."

Agitated, Wulfstan rose and began pacing, clasping his hands behind his back. "We've already had one traitor in our midst, and there are bound to be others. Ethelred 'Wise Counsel' is probably the worst-counseled monarch ever to have reigned."

"But—" Alwyn's confused protest was cut short by a sharp yowl. Wulfstan jumped backward a pace, his arms flailing as a small white cat darted from its hiding place and leaped into Alwyn's arms.

"Sweet Jesu, what—" Wulfstan recovered himself and chuckled. "Trust an instrument of the devil to trip a bishop!" But the words were laced with wry humor; Alwyn detected none of the hatred that many of the brothers directed at his little friend.

"I'm sorry, Your Grace. This is Rowena's area—she keeps the vermin from harming the crops and herbs. I'm afraid you stepped on her while she napped in the sun."

The cat still looked alarmed. Her ears were flat, her odd-colored eyes—one blue, one green—wide. Alwyn was grateful for the thick wool of his monk's cowl—it protected his skin from the prick of her extended claws.

Wulfstan came forward and patted the cat awkwardly. "Rowena? She's certainly white enough for the name."

"And generally well-mannered," said Alwyn, stroking the fur

one last time before placing the cat down. He brushed absently at the white hairs that clung to his dark brown robe. Rowena, calmed by Alwyn's petting, arched her back, purring, approached Wulfstan, sniffed, and then rubbed her face against his ankle.

" 'Thy righteousness is like the great mountains; thy judgments are a great deep: O Lord, thou preservest man and beast,' " quoted Wulfstan. He turned his attention back to the younger man. "We were speaking of kings, not cats."

Alwyn nodded, seriousness returning. "You spoke of Ethelred receiving poor counsel from his advisers. How can this be? You yourself are among that number."

"Yes, and there are a few of us among the Witan who have the courage to speak things the king doesn't wish to hear—I, Archbishop Alphege, Ealdorman Ordgar. Mostly, though, Ethelred surrounds himself with his favorites, the worst being that Roman scoundrel, Angelo. Strange, that one. So appealing to be around, but there is something about him I mislike. The number of those who dare speak unpleasant truths to the king is shrinking, as if—" He caught himself in midsentence, paused, and resumed. His voice was hard, each word hammering at Alwyn's ears.

"Archbishop Aelfstan of Winchester died in 981. Abbot Womaer died the same year. The Lord took Bishop Ethelwold in 984. The blessed Dunstan, who so well advised King Edgar and King Edward, died in 988, and Bishop Ethelgar, who received the bishopric after Dunstan, lived only a year and three months afterward. Bishop Oswald died in 992, and we also lost the steady Ealdorman Ethelwine that year. In 995, Archbishop Sigeric passed away after the appearance of the long-haired star."

His eyes were fastened on Alwyn's. The young man didn't dare blink. A dreadful suspicion began to form in the pit of his stomach, an icy chill that not even the hot sun could dissolve.

"You—you're not suggesting they were murdered?" he breathed.

"No, not murdered—at least," Wulfstan said slowly, gauging Alwyn's reaction, "not by man."

Alwyn stared stupidly. Finally he found words. "I have to go. The ink—it will dry, and if the quills are not carefully put away—"

"Your pens and vellum can wait."

Alwyn licked dry lips. "No, I'm so sorry, Bishop, but truly—

I must go, the abbot will be very displeased, and it's nearly time for vespers—"

He turned and almost ran back to the scriptorium. His heartbeat was rapid, but not from exertion. Bishop Wulfstan's words were too frightening. Let the kings and the Witan and the archbishops deal with—with what was happening outside. He had been born crippled, and had known very little outside these sturdy stone walls.

Let it stay that way.

The tools of his craft lay where he had left them. Alwyn took several deep breaths, trying to calm himself, to reach for the peace that until this moment had been such an integral part of his daily life. But his hand shook as he picked up the several pens, and he dropped a few. Most of the brothers worked with the pen in their right hand, and a knife to sharpen the quill in the other. Alwyn had to ask the others to prepare several pens for him before he began his work; he couldn't pare them himself. He hated that, but had long since resigned himself to asking for charity. He knew his work to be good, and the end product was worth humbling himself before his brethren.

He bent over and began gathering the scattered pens. Normally, he was very much aware—almost painfully so—of where his dead arm was at any given moment. Now, though, unsettled by the bishop's words, spoken and unspoken, his movements were hurried and careless. As Alwyn picked up the quills with his right hand, his left shoulder brushed against the desk. He reached further, to grab the last few wayward pens, and the arm came up with the movement. Before Alwyn realized what had happened, the precious vellum had floated to the stone floor. He gasped, then reached for it with an abrupt motion that brought his left arm up even more.

And then he watched, frozen, as the dead piece of meat that passed for a human limb knocked into the horn inkwell inserted into the desk, dislodged it, and sent it tumbling downward to land on the piece of Scripture it had taken Alwyn several weeks to illuminate.

An obsidian pool formed on the vellum. It spread, slowly, with a horrible inevitability. Alwyn cried aloud as he saw his beautiful wolf, the ink on its twining shape not even dry, being obliterated by the black tide.

The words themselves were next. They were from the book of

Revelation, chapter 11, verse 7, and as the ink destroyed them, Alwyn began to tremble.

. . . *the beast that ascendeth out of the bottomless pit shall make war against them, and shall overcome them, and kill them.*

He sank down, staring at his reflection in the black ink. "No," breathed Alwyn. "No," he repeated, crossing himself quickly, instinctively.

Outside, the bell for vespers began to ring. For a long moment, Alwyn couldn't move. He was hypnotized by the black pool. It had quite covered the vellum, and was sending exploratory tendrils along the ridges in the stone.

At last, he shook himself. His hand. His useless, crippled hand had done this. A wave of hatred as black as the ink crashed over him. He was useless to God. What good was a scribe whose own clumsiness destroyed the works of beauty he strove to create? He had heard tales of the pagans to the north, how they drowned children who were born so. He almost wished his parents had done that to him. Death would have been kinder than what he had endured.

The bell continued to ring, but this time its soft music did not work its gentle magic upon Alwyn's soul. He gathered up the tools quickly, smearing black ink all over his robes, and hastened to the church. The only thing on his mind was atonement for his sin of clumsiness. That, and making sure Wulfstan did not get a chance to impart whatever dreadful tidings he had been about to share before Alwyn had hastened away.

The brethren stared at his stained robes, but made no comment. Time for that later. He saw Wulfstan's eyes fill with sympathetic understanding, but Alwyn looked away. Alwyn sang with a full heart, chanting the sacred words as if they could make everything right again. But there was no peace in the psalms tonight.

Frightened, Alwyn wondered if he would ever know peace again.

After vespers, Alwyn contrived to speak privately with Abbot Bede. He explained the accident, took full responsibility for the ruined manuscript and soiled robe, and asked to keep vigil in the church throughout the night as a means of atonement. Bede, as ever, seemed to Alwyn to be embarrassed when confronted with

Alwyn's deformity, and quickly agreed to the younger man's suggestion.

Somehow, Alwyn avoided encountering Wulfstan before the evening meal. He sat far away from the visiting bishop and listened with half an ear as one of the novices read in a halting, shy voice from the Scriptures. There was no talking, not even to ask for a dish to be passed. Gestures and hand signs served the Benedictines in place of words. The fare was more lavish than usual, because of Bishop Wulfstan's presence at the table. Fruits that were supposed to be dried for winter consumption were offered, though they were small and tasteless due to the drought, and there was fresh fish from the abbey's stockpond as well. After the meal the monks gathered again for compline, then retired to their dormitory.

Alwyn made his way to the church from the refectory, carrying a small lantern in his right hand and one other item awkwardly tucked beneath his arm. The chapel loomed before him in the twilight, and his heart lifted.

A hand fell on his arm. Alwyn jumped, almost crying aloud.

"I will not leave without telling you what I came here to tell you," said Wulfstan.

"I do not wish to hear it," whispered Alwyn, staring longingly at the chapel and thinking of the sanctuary it would provide.

"You must." The bishop's voice was implacable. "In case something happens to me, someone must know. I have cited incidents earlier; now, I must tell you what they mean. It is my deepest fear that this world is in haste and it nears the end. The Final Enemy walks among us, Alwyn, and his tool the Antichrist only waits to be called. There can be no other reason for the sudden coming of disasters—the plagues, the fires, the comets, the famine, and the Norsemen."

"Why are you telling me this? Why are you not shouting it from the rooftops?" Alwyn argued, still heading for the chapel.

"Because the Adversary is clever." Wulfstan matched the younger man stride for stride. "He knows it is easier, more convenient, for man to believe in a distant Judgment Day. He will not employ his tools until he feels he can win. I may convince a few of the true direness of the situation, but I would not be believed sufficiently to fight back at this point. The Adversary would find ways to strike us down without raising concern—like

Dunstan, or Sigeric, or the others. No, for the moment, a quiet word in a listening ear is the best I can do."

Alwyn felt as though he were about to cry. The Antichrist was coming. The end of the world was at hand. A sudden rage roiled inside him.

"Why do you tell me?" he cried suddenly. He stopped in mid-stride, almost dropping the lantern in his haste to put it down. Wulfstan blinked, startled at the outburst. Angrily, Alwyn thrust the useless limb into the bishop's face. "Look at this! I am not even a whole man! Do you know what I did today in the scriptorium? This—this dead thing knocked over a horn full of ink and ruined an entire manuscript page. Months of work—gone. I am worse than useless. I cannot do God's will to the fullest. I am a cripple, fit only to be shut away, patiently inscribing word after word—I cannot take up arms in God's army, I cannot help tend the fields and provide food for the hungry—I am utterly worth-less, Bishop, and yet you burden me with these dreadful tidings! What in the name of the Trinity can I do? Write 'Get thee behind me, Satan' in pretty letters? You are a tempter of his caliber, giv-ing me information I cannot pass along, telling me to prepare for a battle in which I cannot fight!"

Wulfstan's eyes narrowed as his own temper began to rise. Alwyn didn't give him a chance to reply. They had reached the chapel now, and he turned away from the bishop and ran up the stone steps as fast as he could. Wulfstan did not follow.

Alwyn's bare feet made no sound on the cold stone as he padded toward the altar. He closed his eyes, then opened them, seeking calmness. Before him was the dimly illuminated figure of Christ. The skin of the Son seemed to glow, as if lit with its own radiance. The crown of thorns appeared sharper, more bru-tal, than in the day's light, and the wounds in His hands and sides vanished into darkness.

For a long time, Alwyn gazed at the divine image. Tears welled in his eyes and he let them come, making no attempt to wipe his wet face. Slowly, he began to divest himself of his cloth-ing, shivering a little in the chill engendered by the thick stone walls. Alwyn carefully put the lamp down and took the other item in his right hand: the scourge.

He knelt and prayed: "Dear Heavenly Father, merciful Jesus, I pray you, forgive this poor sinner."

He took a deep breath, then brought the scourge cracking

down on his bare back. Alwyn gasped, his eyes stinging. The pain was always so unexpectedly searing. He gritted his teeth and again whipped the instrument across his flesh. He felt the swollen flesh burst at the next blow; the blood began to trickle down his sides at the next. The pain was mixed with an odd pleasure. Purification. Atonement for sin. Through suffering, one could find peace. Some of the brothers had tried to tell him that his crippled arm was not divine judgment, that God was not angry with him, but Alwyn knew better.

He kept it up until his arm was exhausted, and then flung the bloodied instrument away. He buried his face in his good hand.

"Dear God," wept Alwyn, "dear God, forgive me. I can do nothing right. . . ."

He lay down on the floor, his back burning, his naked genitals freezing from the cold press of stone, and carefully placed his limp arm in the proper position, then stretched out his right in mimicry of the figure that towered above him, hanging from His cross. Shame flooded him, shame for his broken body—a pathetic vessel for the divine gift of a soul.

Please, dear Jesus, You who cured the lepers, Who drove out demons, Who healed the sick—give me the ability to serve You fully. Heal me. Make me whole.

Grant me a miracle.

2

As long as he lived, Colum Cille would never grow used to the grayness of this land of the Dalriada. Rain was a constant companion, as were wind and lowering skies. What color there was, was pale and hardy—the heather clinging fiercely to tiny patches of earth amid the rocks; the few grasses poking their heads up only to be devoured by the shaggy red cattle that grazed over what seemed to be every inch of flat land. From time to time, Colum, known now among his friends and followers as Columba, felt an overwhelming yearning for the rolling green hills of his native Eire. But God and Irish politics had brought him here, and here was where he would make his home.

Iona, once called the Isle of the Druids, had a haunting majesty about it. From druids to "the Lamp of Faith," it was truly a divine place. But he could not linger there if the Word of God was to be spread properly among the pagan populace. His long treks had taken him through the high country of this land and now had brought him here, to this loch near Inverness.

Sweet Jesu, but it was cold. The sky was, of course, overcast. The loch itself was silver, still and quiet.

His heart beat rapidly. "Lord, I am thy servant," he prayed softly, then strode down to the water's edge. He had to pick his way through piles of offerings on the shore: brooches and armlets, mostly. He knew more tributes to what the pagan people believed to be the loch's "deity" lay beneath the surface. Behind him, holding their torches aloft, his companions waited, silent.

"Come forth!" Columba cried. "Beast of the depths, who would prey upon God's most divine creation—come forth! I, Columba, command you in the name of the Lord Almighty!"

Nothing happened. The shiny mirror of the loch remained still, its reflective surface marred only by a slight ruffling of the wind.

"Creature of the loch!" Columba tried again, lifting his arms in a commanding gesture. "Come when I call, or face the Lord's wrath!"

There was no response. Despite the cold, the monk began to sweat. Behind him, he heard voices murmuring. This could not be. The creature must come when summoned in the name of the Lord—unless it was simply a fabrication of minds too isolated to think clearly. . . .

The loch began to churn. The murmurings of discontent Columba heard behind him turned to cries of alarm. The monk, though, felt suddenly calm. It had come. Praise God, it had come as it had been told, and, if it please God, it would obey him, Columba, the vassal of the Lord.

A huge wave crashed upon the loch's shores, soaking Columba up to his knees. The monk gasped with the shock of sudden cold, then gasped again, crossing himself at the first sight of the creature that had caused the wave.

Jesu, it was enormous! Thick around as ten men, it lifted its vile head above the surface, rising higher . . . higher still . . . It opened its mouth in an angry roar, and despite himself Columba cried out in agony and clapped his hands to his ears. Large, sharp teeth were crammed into that hellish mouth. Above the mouth were yellow, slitted eyes, the eyes of an angry serpent. There was no body visible, only coil after coil. . . .

For years, the common folk had told Columba, weeping, the creature of Loch Ness had been seizing and devouring the unwary. Columba had half thought the tales had come from the wagging tongues of old wives with nothing better to do than spin fantasies, but now he felt his knees turn to water before the undeniable, horrifying reality.

Again the monster roared, and Columba felt the hot breath on his face, smelled the stench of rotted meat. Strangely, it bolstered

*his courage. He again remembered who he was, why he had
come here—and above all, whom he served with all his heart.
Strength flooded his trembling body, and he stood straight and
commanding.*

*"Foul creature from the depths of the abyss!" he cried. "Bow
before the power of the Lord! Remove thyself from my sight for
all time, and touch not those who venture into these waters!"*

*The creature blinked. It brought its massive head down to
Columba, stared him in the eye. Columba's chest contracted, but
he dared not look away. I am the sword and shield of the Lord,
he said to himself. He will protect me! Finally, the creature uttered a sound—a deep, bone-rattling rumble. It narrowed its eyes
and cocked its head, gazing speculatively at the holy man. Then,
strangely silent for such a leviathan, it sank slowly into the
depths of the murky waters. The loch closed over it, rippled for a
few moments, then became as flat as before, as if nothing as
monstrous as a hell beast had ever disturbed its mysterious tran-
quillity.*

*Columba sagged. He stumbled, as if all his strength had sud-
denly left him, and for a moment he felt as though it had. Now he
felt the cold water soaking its way through wool and flesh, to
penetrate to the bone. Cries of delight shattered the stillness, and
strong hands closed about him, bore him away from the icy
depths and the monstrosity that lived in them.*

*"Your god truly is the most powerful of all!" crowed one man,
pressing his dirty face into Columba's. "The beast fled before
you! D'ja see that, lads? Like a frightened lamb before the roar
of the lion!"*

*Columba smiled wanly. "Praise be to God," he croaked, and
let them help him back to dry land, let them wrap him in warm
cloaks and lead him back to their town. He would enjoy the hot
wine tonight. Perhaps its warmth would shake the chill that
seemed to have taken up permanent residence in his bones; perhaps the glow of the alcohol would chase away the image of the
beast that seemed branded in his mind's eye.*

*He feared not. He feared that no amount of liquor would ever
banish the memory of that dreadful, reptilian face staring into his
own with a knowing look on its scaly countenance. The crinkling
of eyes seemed to be a smile; the rumbling noise it had uttered,
demonic laughter.*

Columba kept silent about his fears. But even as he stumbled

toward the lights of the town, toward a hero's welcome and good
food and wine, he knew that he hadn't banished the beast.
   It had left of its own accord.
   And—God help him!—it would return the same way.

The Village of Gleannsidh
April 30, 999

Kennag nic Beathag closed her eyes against the blazing warmth
of the fire, and breathed deep of its smoky scent. Even with her
eyes shut, she could sense it, beating on the closed lids, an orange
radiance demanding acknowledgment. It crackled insistently.
She felt her lips curve in an unbidden smile as she lifted her arms
and began to dance.

Bealtaine was her favorite holiday. The priest of the village of
Gleannsidh hadn't managed to come up with an acceptable
Christian alternative, as he had with the yulefest and Ostara, at-
taching the commemoration of the birth and death of his god to
older, deeper holidays. Many of the villagers cheerfully added
this Christ to their pantheon without a second thought. So many
other deities coexisted. Surely there was room for yet another incarnation of the god, this one milky pale and rather fragile looking. A crown of thorns, a crown of holly leaves—there was very
little difference. Or so some thought.

But Kennag did not share that opinion. She attended the services at the small, wooden church with the rest of them, gazed up
at the Christ on his hanging tree, mouthed the proper responses.
She'd be a fool not to, and she knew it. The Church was very insistent about that. But she never accepted this frail Christ as a
god, nor His elusive, "almighty" Father. And a virgin mother?
Ridiculous!

Kennag could not explain it. There was something sinister in
that delicate body and sorrowful expression, something that
made the hairs on the back of her neck prickle with foreboding.
So she held herself aloof from the Christ, clinging to the old
ways that had a greater claim on her heart and mind.

Tonight she danced, with the rest of Gleannsidh, about the
huge fire that had been kindled from the needfires of every par-
ticipant. The drumming, steady and pounding, kept time with her
pulse. Inside, Kennag trembled, for she was warm with more
than the heat engendered by the burning wood.

Just this afternoon, she had set aside her trappings of mourning for her husband, dead for many moons now from a boating accident. She had loved Niall, and mourned him. But with not even a child from their brief union to sustain her, there was no reason to grieve overlong. Niall would have wanted her to be in a pair of loving arms on Bealtaine eve, and judging by the hunger in the eyes of the blacksmith's son Bran, she would not spend another night alone.

Kennag surrendered to the ancient song that sang in her veins, and loosed her hair, long and as fiery red as the flames themselves. It tumbled about her shoulders, and she ran long fingers through its length. It was not often she permitted herself to unbind that thick red wave. Her tunic, too, was patterned like the fire, and its bold orange, red, and yellow stripes made her feel like part of the Bealtaine flames themselves.

She sensed the presence of another beside her, dancing in the warm light, and opened her eyes.

Bran smiled down at her. By sweet mother Brihid, he was beautiful. The firelight traced its way over high cheekbones, a strong chin, dark eyes. Thick, dark hair fell to his shoulders. Kennag swallowed hard, and reached to touch that godlike face. He had shaved for her tonight, and his skin was as smooth as her own against her tentative fingers. Ai, but it felt good to touch a man again after so long.

His hands slid up her arms and cupped her face. "You put the Bealtaine fire to shame, Beautiful One," Bran said softly. His voice trembled, cracked ever so slightly. Kennag smothered a smile. So young, he was, and so fair. . . .

"Be careful," she replied, her own voice husky. "I might burn you."

"I am a smith," he replied, laughing a little. "I understand fire. I know how to work with it . . . to shape it. . . ."

He brought his lips down to hers. Kennag melted into him, pressed against the broad chest she had so often secretly admired while Bran was hard at work with his tunic removed. His arms about her had the strength of the iron he worked, and for an instant she was startled at how readily he assumed the lead in this erotic dance, young though he was. *You do understand fire,* she thought giddily. Healer and smith, mender and shaper. They were a good match.

By the time Bran broke the kiss, Kennag's heart was shaking

her with its pounding, and her breath came in short gasps. She was moist between her thighs, more than ready for him, and she could feel his own response through their clothes. They gazed into one another's eyes, then with a grin that made him look like a mischievous boy, he tugged on her hand. Kennag laughed freely, and followed.

They ran through the fields, the blazing fire diminishing behind them. The chill night air pressed more closely about them now, damp and clinging, but the heat of her desire for Bran drove any coldness away. His fingers twined about hers, gripping tightly. Suddenly her bare foot slipped on the wet grass and she tumbled down, laughing hysterically.

"Kennag! Are you all right?" Bran knelt beside her, his voice full of concern. "That was so foolish of me—you could have been injured—the fire, it was so heady—"

His obvious distress at her fall only endeared him the more to Kennag. She was fine, completely unhurt. Fine—except for one thing. Wordlessly, she reached up, twined her hands in those thick black locks, and arched upward. The kiss was long and deep. Kennag was almost beside herself with need, and when he pulled back, she let out a little wordless cry of disappointment.

But it was only to wrestle with his confining tunic and trousers that Bran had left her. Kennag sat up and imitated him, unfastening her brooches and tugging at the unwanted cocoon of cloth that kept their bodies apart.

She would conceive Bran's child tonight. For the last few months, knowing Bealtaine was on its way, Kennag had kept close watch on her moon cycles. Today, as she laid aside her widow's mourning, she had ingested a tincture made of certain herbs that she knew would increase her fertility. What a joyful family they would make! Perhaps they would be wed by the next full moon. Kennag had no doubt that Bran would take her as his wife. They had danced together by the Bealtaine fires, in full view of their families and friends. No man took a woman away from the fires without being prepared to marry her. It was the way of their faith.

Suddenly, Kennag froze. The fire of passion was extinguished, leaving her cold and frightened.

Bran sensed her stillness. "Love, what—"

Kennag couldn't speak. Her eyes wide, fastened on the shape in the shadows, she could only lift her hand and point.

The moonlight silvered them both, turned them to pale, living statues in the dark swath of shadows and grass. It shone brightly upon the calm ocean that was but a few paces distant. The waves, called by their mistress the moon, rolled on the shore in their unceasing rhythm. All was as it should be—save for a horrible shape that loomed out of the waters.

Kennag's mind raced with the old tales of the kelpies, the evil lake horses, the merpeople, and other strange beasts that lurked beneath the surface in all bodies of water. Even Columba, one of the Christian saints, had witnessed the appearance of the monster that lived in Loch Ness a few hundred years ago. It was difficult to see in the moonlight: merely a dark, sinuous shape that lifted its neck out of the ocean's depths. But there was definitely a head, as of a serpent, and—

No. Not a sea monster. Something much worse.

Kennag's voice returned to her with a vengeance. "Lochlannach!" she screamed.

As if her frantic cry had summoned them, shapes began to swarm onto the shore. They had been moving silently, which was why Bran and Kennag had not heard them, but now, discovered, they splashed through the water like cattle. Bran and Kennag scrambled to their feet, half-clad, their tryst abandoned. She was reaching for her knife—she always wore a weapon in these troubled times—when Bran seized her, spun her around, and yelled, "Run!" He pushed her in the back for good measure. She stumbled a few paces, but would not abandon him to the Lochlannach. They would kill him—or worse, capture him and take him to Byzantium, where they would sell him as a slave. For too long, Kennag had been alone. She would not leave Bran now.

With clenched teeth, growling, Kennag turned and ran toward the bearlike men who had grabbed and disarmed the powerful Bran as if he were a babe barely able to walk. One of them turned, startled, though he shouldn't have been if he was a veteran of these despicable raids—here, unlike in the soft South, women knew how to fight. Kennag howled a cry of rage, invoking a slew of gods and goddesses, and charged. She would have plunged her dagger into his unprotected neck had not he brought up his shield in an instinctive gesture of defense. Nonetheless, the little blade bit deeply—too deeply. Kennag desperately tried to work it free from the wood, and in that brief instant her adversary brought up his sword and struck her on the temple with the heavy iron pommel. She dropped like a stone, pain racing from the injury, and clutched her head.

He moved swiftly. Growling words in his strange language, the blond Norseman was beside her almost at once. He seized her wrists, forcing them down to the damp earth, and Kennag cried at the sudden redoubling of pain in her head. Her vision swam. His knee came up and forced her legs apart. She squirmed beneath him, but a hand, heavy and tasting of stale sweat and leather, clamped down on her mouth. She closed her eyes, but that was worse; she opened them and fastened her gaze on the moon and the stars twinkling above, trying to lose herself in their cold distance.

For what seemed like forever, the Norseman pounded inside her. Ironically, there was little physical pain. Bran's kisses had smoothed the way not for tender loving but for joyless rape. But there did not need to be physical pain for her to ache with a hurting she had never before experienced.

The stars did not fall. The moon did not hide its face. Dimly, Kennag heard the cries of her friends and family as the fair-haired, bearded monsters posing as men descended upon Gleannsidh. The Bealtaine fire now had company—the Danemen made their own, setting fire to the thatched roofs of circular stone buildings that went up like the finest of kindling. Smoke drifted upward, blurring her vision of the moon and stars. With a final thrust and shudder, the Norseman collapsed on her for a moment. Chain mail pressed on her naked breasts as he caught his breath, pinching the soft flesh and catching her hair.

His grip on her wrists loosened slightly in this brief moment of recovery, and Kennag did not waste the opportunity. She groped frantically, and her hand found the rapist's own sword. It was far too heavy for her to lift with one hand, and in this cramped position she couldn't wield it properly, but that didn't matter. Gritting her teeth against the pain, she grasped the weapon by its blade.

He felt her movement, and tried to sit upright. But the few seconds of inattention were all Kennag needed to bring over her other hand and strike his jaw hard with the pommel that, earlier, had felled her. He grunted and toppled over, flailing. Quickly Kennag scrambled out from beneath him. Before he could get to his feet, she struck him again, this time with the blade. In her anger and confusion, the blade hit the helmet and glanced off.

Kennag swung again, and made contact this time. The man squealed like a pig and clapped a hand to his neck. Blood flowed between his fingertips.

Kennag didn't try a third time. She flung the sword to the earth and began to run. There were no more men lurking about here. They had gone where the plunder was—to Gleannsidh, to sack the church, rape the women, and gather a cluster of fine slaves like Bran to take back with them. Fueled by a vague notion of helping somehow, Kennag ran back to her home. Her beautiful tunic was torn and covered with earth, sweat and blood. She was partially naked, but she didn't care.

The fires lit the night sky with a sickening glow. Gasping, Kennag forced herself to keep running. She hit a bump in the earth's surface. Her ankle twisted painfully, and she fell hard. The smoke stung her eyes and nostrils, scorched her mouth when she tried to breathe. She tried to get to her feet, but her ankle was badly twisted and she could barely put weight on it, let alone run.

New terror came with this sudden vulnerability. She struggled to her feet and limped as rapidly as possible toward the center of the village.

All was chaos. The roof of nearly every building was on fire. The night was pierced by screams and bellows of fear and triumph. Standing on the edge of the fields, looking down toward Gleannsidh—what was left of it—Kennag had a clear view of the destruction.

Bodies lay tossed about. Even as she watched, a Norseman ran a sword through—who? Which of her friends, her family, was dying down there? By Midhir, was there *anyone* left?

Suddenly she realized how foolish she had been to come here. She couldn't help anyone. She didn't have a weapon, her leg would barely support her—and now there was no time, no place to hide. She was exposed here, and soon the man who had violated her, or one like him, would find her and—

Kennag looked about frantically. The forest was too far away for her to reach in safety over that moonlit, empty field. The buildings were aflame. She had fled from the ocean, whose waters might have concealed her, and now—

Her gaze fell upon the dim shape of the well, and hope rose inside her. If they hadn't cut the rope—

Grimacing with each step, she limped toward it. Little more than a hole in the ground shored up by carefully placed stones, it was nothing much, but it served the village's needs. As she drew near, she closed her eyes briefly in relief. The wooden top that was always replaced after water had been drawn had been flung aside. That meant the Lochlannach had already been about their evil business of fouling the well. Probably they had dropped a rotting piece of meat into its depths. Almost certainly they had relieved themselves in it—Kennag had heard all the tales. But they had not cut the thick length of rope that was attached to the bucket on one end and securely staked into the ground at the other, and that was all Kennag needed to know.

She permitted herself a quick look around. Back toward the village, she could see shadows moving in the fire's eerie glow. Swallowing hard, Kennag said a quick prayer to the deity of the well. "The Lochlannach have blasphemed your waters," she whispered. "You must be very angry. But I beg you, grant me protection from them, and please forgive my intrusion." She lumbered forward, grasped the rope, and began to lower herself into the well.

The going was slow and painful. The rough fiber of the rope burned against her blood-slicked hands. The surface of the well was slippery, first with moss on the stones, then with mud as she went deeper. Twice she had to bite back a scream of agony as her injured foot slipped and twisted even more. The deeper she went, the colder it became, and Kennag started to shiver uncontrollably. When at last she reached the surface of the water, it was numbingly cold. She couldn't help gasping as she lowered herself into it. She recalled how refreshing the almost icy water was on a hot summer's day, how she was glad of the cold then.

Gradually her body became used to the cold, and its bite slowly faded. As a woman who understood better than most how the body worked, Kennag knew she couldn't stay down here for too long. She would become groggy, and eventually nod off and slip beneath the surface. At the moment, she couldn't conceive of such a thing. Surely her fear and anguish would keep her awake for the rest of her life. But there were times when the body was stronger than the mind, and if she remained down here long enough, she would without a doubt die here.

The sounds of destruction continued. At first, they made Kennag's gut clench as her mind's eye filled with one atrocity after another. But as the minutes dragged by, she became inured to them. Her attention increasingly focused on the bitter coldness of

the water, on the fact that it was becoming more and more difficult to sense her limbs. At least the cold kept the pain of her injury at bay.

The strange, crooning speech of the Danemen reached her
ears. They were coming to the well! The fear that had started to
fade returned full force, and Kennag let herself drop even deeper
into the icy water. It lapped at her chin, and she forced herself to
let go her hold on the bucket. It wouldn't do if, for some reason,
they wanted to draw water and the bucket caught. She said a
silent prayer that they would not cut the rope. With her injury it
would be impossible for her to climb out on her own.

She gazed upward, fearful even though she knew she was too
deep for the men to see her, even if they shone torchlight into the
depths of the well. Now she could see them, shadows outlined
against the comparative brightness of the sky. Their heads disappeared for a moment, then returned. They laughed, and flung
something into the well.

Kennag pressed back against the side of the well as far as possible, praying that she wouldn't get her neck snapped by the force
of whatever was hurtling down upon her. It was large, and caught
her shoulder as it splashed down, sank for a moment, then resur-
faced. The men above laughed uproariously, slapped each other
on the back, then left.

Silence.

For a long time, Kennag huddled in the cold water, unwilling
to try to discover exactly what the Lochlannach had tossed into
the village's water supply. At last, she took a deep breath and
reached out a questing hand.

It encountered something yielding, covered with rough fabric.

It was a body.

Crying out softly, Kennag jerked her hand back. It tangled in
some kind of rope or chain, and she felt the points of carved
wood against her fingertips, numb though they were with cold.
The body wore a wooden cross. They had killed the priest, doubtless after taking all his church had to offer in the way of valu-
ables, and dumped his body in the well.

For a moment, Kennag felt sorry for the priest. Then she
realized it was probably the wealth of the church that had drawn
the Norsemen here in the first place, and pity was replaced by a
sudden wrath. Growling low in her throat, she spat upon the
body. There were deaths upon that tonsured head. She hoped his

Christ would not be merciful in that perfect afterlife about which the priest had gloated.

She heard no more sounds from above. She waited a little longer, then decided that it was safe to venture out. Her body was stiff, and it began to hurt as life returned to it. Kennag felt as though she was being pricked with a thousand needles. But she was alive, still here—not dead, not a slave aboard a dragon ship.

Bran. Oh, my love. . . .

Inch by painful inch, Kennag began to ascend

By the time of the next full moon, Kennag knew she was with child.

Not Bran's child, conceived in a joyful union and welcomed like a sunrise. Bran had been taken by the Lochlannach, and this was the child of a brute, a barely human creature who had violated her and would have enslaved her. Others—those who had been lucky enough to escape—were also bearing fruit from that awful night. One such woman was Kennag's own mother, Mairead, used, then discarded as not young enough to fetch a good price on the market.

Kennag had spoken with her earlier, offering her skills to get rid of the child.

"No," Mairead had replied, her hand on her belly. "Since your father died, I have wished for no other man. I still wish it had not been conceived so, but . . . Kennag, 'tis hardly the babe's fault, coming into the world in such a fashion. I will keep my child, and give you a brother or sister to love."

Kennag had stared at her mother, still beautiful even though her hair was almost totally gray and her firm, strong body had begun to soften with age. Words swelled, then died in her mouth, unuttered. She couldn't possibly love a child born of such a violent origin. How could her mother have that dreamy, content look on her face? How could she stand, for the rest of her life, being reminded of such a brutal attack?

Kennag kept her counsel, but made her own decision. She was well versed in the plant lore she needed. Though she was inclined by nature and training to heal, not harm, there were times when what she was about to do was reckoned a good thing. Alone in her small hut, its roof and furnishings rebuilt by the diligent labor of the men of Gleannsidh as a service to the whole, she rummaged among her tiny store of plants. This summer, many hours would be spent in restocking her supplies.

Kennag prepared the tea of dried pennyroyal and brought the water to a boil. She poured the hot water into the earthen mug, waiting for the herb to steep the proper amount of time.

It should have been Bran's child. Or else it should never have been conceived.

Kennag thought again of the big body pounding into her, of the stench of sweat and leather, and her stomach turned. Without even straining the leaves, she downed the hot concoction. Then she rose and made her way to the soft pile of furs that served her for a bed, and waited for the agony to begin.

3

The salmon writhed frantically, but the Allfather held fast, wrestling the mammoth fish to the earth.

"Change!" he bellowed, "Change, or the Warrior and I will cook you here and now!"

The fish flopped once more, then held still. Before the Allfather's single eye, it shimmered, twisted, and became the god who had caused so much pain.

The Allfather and the Warrior seized the Trickster's arms with no gentleness in their iron grips. The Sly One merely grinned beneath his tousled mat of red hair.

"So, what will it be this time?" he quipped. But the Allfather merely stared at him with his one all-seeing eye, the dead socket covered by a patch, and did not reply.

The Trickster felt his heart leap within him at the next voices he heard. "Father?" Youthful, male; his two youngest children, Vali and Narvi. A dreadful suspicion came over him.

"You are angry with me, not them!" he cried to the Allfather, twisting anew in the Warrior's one-handed grip. "For the love you once bore me, Blood Brother, do not harm them!"

"My anger is high as it is," growled the Allfather. "Do not inflame it by using that term!"

"But we are!" Fear for his sons' fate flooded the Trickster. He *glanced at them—so beautiful, so young, so trusting.... "We swore an oath, we mingled our blood—"*

"Silence!" The Trickster winced at the volume of the Allfather's voice. His gaze still fastened on the Trickster, the Allfather waved his hand. Immediately, Vali fell to all fours, crying aloud in pain and startlement as his body began to shift its shape.

"No . . ." whispered the Trickster. He could change his shape, and his three eldest children could as well, but Vali had not the gift!

A few more heartbeats, and Vali was a wolf. Not a youth in wolf shape, but a true wolf. Slowly, it turned its large, gray head in the direction of its brother. It growled, softly, deep in its chest, gathered itself, and sprang. Narvi was too stunned to move, and fell with no sound as his brother ripped his throat out and lapped at the spurting blood.

"No!" The Trickster wailed in true agony. Tears flooded his brown eyes. He turned his gaze upon the Allfather, anger warring with grief in his breast. "Why them? They would not have harmed anyone!"

"They are your children, Sly One," replied the Allfather. "They would have killed, sooner or later."

"You are the king of the gods! Men worship you as the Great Father, the Wise One, but you are nothing but a slayer of children!"

"Only your children," the Warrior said smoothly, "and four of them yet live, by the mercy of the Allfather."

"Mercy?" The Trickster craned his neck and fastened emerald-green eyes on the Warrior's implacable face. "Vali is now a simple beast! My eldest, you have enslaved, and I am glad that he took your hand for it! Another you hurled into the oceans, and my little daughter you have locked far away in the Underworld. Mercy?" He spat upon the Warrior, who did not even blink. "Behold the mercy of the Allfather and his Warrior!"

"Your children are monstrous," said the Allfather. "They deserved worse than what I gave them. As do you."

They hauled the Trickster along the sandy earth, to the mouth of a rocky cave. Down, down they went, and at a word from the Allfather, the mangled corpse of the Trickster's child rose and floated down with them, blood dripping and echoing in the cold darkness.

The Trickster again fought to free himself, but the Warrior's *hand would not let him go. At last, they reached the bottom of the cave, where the rocks glowed with an eerie gleam. Roughly, the Warrior flung the Trickster onto a large, flat boulder. The Allfather spoke, and Narvi's belly split like a ripe fruit. His entrails spilled onto the rocky floor, steaming in the chill.*

Something like regret flickered over the Allfather's bearded face. "You were my blood brother," he said softly. "Never did I think I would be here, doing this. . . . But you sealed your destiny by killing the Beautiful One. That, I cannot forgive."

And to the Trickster's horror, the Allfather reached and clutched Vali's slippery entrails and began to wrap them about the imprisoned god. The Trickster closed his eyes, that he might not see, and tears leaked out from under his tightly shut lids. No amber or gold tears, his, not like those of the beautiful cat-loving goddess; simple salt water they were, and they ran down onto the unyielding rock as the Allfather wrapped him in the guts of his little boy.

Another word, another gesture, and the wet, warm, slippery entrails turned cold and hard. Startled, the Trickster opened his eyes to find that he was bound with iron ropes. A thought occurred to him. All he needed to do was wait until they had gone, then change his shape—perhaps to something as small as a mouse, yes, a mouse would do, and—

"While the bonds are about you, you cannot shift your shape," said the Allfather. "I know your wiles, Sly One, and have prepared for them."

The Trickster said nothing, only stared at the Allfather with indigo eyes full of hate. A hissing noise above him made him glance away. A large snake had coiled itself around a protruding arrow of stone. A tongue flickered. Slitted, golden eyes blinked slowly.

"The serpent will be your only companion," said the Warrior. "It enjoys tormenting others, just as you do. You should get along admirably."

At that moment, the snake opened its mouth. The Trickster stared in numb fascination at the shiny, milky drop of venom that hung upon one sharp fang. It seemed to stay there forever, and the Trickster tensed against his awful bonds. Then it dropped! In the center of the Trickster's forehead it fell, where the red curls had parted to reveal pale skin, and the Trickster screamed in agony. His cry echoed, and the earth trembled as he writhed. The Warrior and the Allfather exchanged satisfied glances.

Then came another sound, the sound of slippered feet on stone, and a beautiful young woman burst into the chamber. Her soft, blue eyes widened and her hand flew to her mouth. "Beloved," she whispered. "Oh, beloved!"

She ran to him and embraced him as best she could. The Trickster tried to hold his wife, but the manacles that had once been the entrails of an innocent young man held him fast. Angrily, she turned to the Allfather.

"What have you done? Let him go, Wise One, I beg you! I will see to it that he never troubles Asgard again!"

"Just as you kept him from the giantess's bed?" reproached the Allfather, with infinite gentleness. Sigyn hung her golden head at that, and began to weep. "Come, my dear. Come back and dwell in the light. Leave the dark and the fire god here, in the earth, where they belong."

Sigyn shook her head. "No. He has never been faithful to me, but I love him. I cannot leave him here in the darkness, for a serpent to spit upon." She rose unsteadily, and searched about, still weeping, until she found a round, hollow stone. She broke it against the wall, and, red lips trembling, thrust it toward the Allfather. He nodded his comprehension. Sigyn, wife of the Trickster fire god, went to where the serpent was summoning another mouthful of venom and held out the makeshift bowl. The drop of venom splashed harmlessly.

The Trickster smiled up at her. "Dear Sigyn," he said softly. "I do not deserve you."

"For once, the Great Liar speaks the truth," said the Warrior. "Come, let us leave them. And Trickster—your Sigyn may catch the venom in the bowl, for now. But there will come a time when she must empty the bowl, and then. . . ." He smiled at the look on the Trickster's face as the realization set in. Then he turned, and he and the Allfather ascended.

And no matter how the Trickster struggled, or cursed, or strained, the entrails of his son held him fast.

Until the coming of the end of the world.

The Feast Hall of Ealdorman Ordgar, Calne
November 14, 999

King Ethelred stroked his beard, dyed blue in keeping with the
current fashion, and fidgeted in his chair as the meeting of the
Witan droned on. Wulfstan eyed him, careful not to be caught
staring, his thoughts unhappy.

What had happened to the king? He was the son of Edgar.
Surely there ought to have been something in the late king's
blood that would elevate his youngest child into something more
than an attractive chair-warmer. Ethelred had inherited his
father's good looks and fair hair, though he insisted on dying it
that dreadful shade of blue. His manners could not be faulted
and, as Edgar had before him, he possessed a knack of making
one feel valued and included when he locked eyes with one.

But he hadn't inherited his father's wise head, or his taste in
friends and counselors. Wulfstan turned his attention from the
king to Ethelred's chief adviser.

As always, Angelo stood to the right of the seated king. He
seemed never to need to sit. His shoulders never slumped, no
matter how long the meeting. Alert, with bright eyes that took in
everything, Angelo was the perfect royal thegn. Today the king,
as usual, sported an outfit that reflected the height of fashion. The
upper part of his fitted tunic, most of it hidden beneath an embroidered woolen mantle, was a bright shade of crimson. The
lower part, cut long to cover the stockinged legs, was blue. The
shade matched his beard. As this was a formal occasion, the king
also wore his crown. Angelo wore garb nearly identical to his
lord's in color and cut, though not quite as lavish.

Wulfstan frowned. Now that he thought about it, that was
something that Angelo did all the time—copy his king's attire,
but in a simpler fashion. Why? What did he—

As if feeling Wulfstan's eyes upon him, Angelo turned his
attention from the speaker. He smiled a little as his gaze met
Wulfstan's.

It was the bishop who finally looked away.

Wulfstan shivered. He tried to dismiss the chill as a natural result of the cold weather in a cold building. He had spent the better part of a fortnight traveling first the London Way and then the
Foss Way to get to Calne for this meeting. The roads had long
since become difficult, almost impassable, and the snow left by

last week's storm did nothing to ease the journey. Protocol frowned on so illustrious a personage as the Bishop of London traveling lightly. So Wulfstan had dragged his entire retinue along with him on the wretched trip, and all they had to look forward to was an even more wretched return journey. Some of the Witan had clearly been bested by the bad roads and had not shown up at all. Wulfstan noticed that their number was only about two-thirds of what it ought to be.

Granted, Angelo seemed to have his reasons for the meeting. Never before had the Danemen pressed their attacks past Michaelmas. They had ever been summer warriors, descending like locusts on a fine crop when the spring breezes turned warm, and departing with the first frost.

Now, though, the oceans seemed to be full of dragon ships. The Force was landing and not leaving, instead joining others of their countrymen who had come and made homes here in Wessex, Northumbria, and York in particular. Some of these were peaceful men, who wanted little other than to make a decent life for themselves and their families. The fields were fertile, the climate mild compared with their native land. Wulfstan had no quarrel with these individuals.

But the others. . . .

He shifted on the hard stool. For a moment, he was kin to the obviously bored king. He listened with half an ear as Archbishop Alphege recited a list of attacks that had been reported within the last fortnight. Wulfstan was surprised and pleased that the elderly and somewhat frail Archbishop of Canterbury had been able to attend. Alphege was one of the few voices of reason left on the Witan. His voice was thin and reedy, but his words were powerful. As Wulfstan watched, he noticed that Alphege shivered noticeably.

Wulfstan frowned, angry that such a good man should be made so uncomfortable when it was not necessary. Why they couldn't meet at the royal villa a mile to the south, Wulfstan didn't know. But here they were, freezing to death in a lesser noble's lesser home, while below them servants scurried about in an attempt to prepare a meal worthy of their king. It made no sense.

A movement caught his eye. Angelo leaned over and whispered something in the king's ear. Ethelred's expression brightened. A few minutes later, King Ethelred rose. Alphege halted his litany of atrocities in midsentence, courteously waiting for his lord to speak.

"Gentlemen," said Ethelred, his voice, as usual, warm and inviting, "my trusted adviser Angelo will shortly put forth my response to this dire situation. As I know you all to be loyal men, I would not have any of you put in the uncomfortable position of debating your opinion directly with your king. I authorize Angelo to stand in my stead for the rest of this meeting, and I trust that no one here will feel obliged to hold his tongue in replying to him. I shall return to the royal villa. Upon the morrow, we shall reconvene. At that time, I would be most pleased to hear the decisions my wise Witan has reached. God save you all."

"God save Your Majesty," replied all the members of the Witan, bowing as the king descended the wooden steps.

From below, the unmistakable sound of Ethelred's laughter reached their ears. Wulfstan caught the words "dreadful bore" and "hunting before dark" and what might have been "pompous," but he wasn't certain.

There was an awkward silence. Alphege sat down heavily, not even bothering to resume his report. The other members of the Witan shuffled their feet and looked at one another. Finally, all eyes turned to Angelo.

The handsome Roman smiled, and eased himself into the comfortable chair Ethelred had vacated as if he were the rightful occupant. It was the first time in any gathering that Wulfstan had seen him sit. He gestured that they might resume their seats with a casual superiority that made Wulfstan clench his teeth.

"The problem of the Norsemen," said Angelo, in a voice rich as cream, "we've never seen anything like it. One feels like the Israelites under such intense persecution, doesn't one? The king is greatly disturbed at the violence being visited on his people."

Grizzled Ordgar snorted. "The king isn't greatly disturbed about much, except having his hunting season interrupted."

"Ordgar," rebuked Alphege, "watch your tongue."

"It's true, Your Grace!" exploded the older man. "Edgar must be tossing in his grave! And even Edward, God rest his soul, cared about the state of his country more than Ethelred, youth though he was!"

"The king," interrupted Angelo very quietly, "cares a great deal about the state of his country." Now he rose and began pacing, his hands clasped in front of him. Wulfstan stared at the hands, at the exquisitely wrought rings that adorned perfectly groomed fingers. Not a callus on them. As beautiful as the rest of Angelo.

"He has authorized me to do everything we can to force the Danemen to leave our shores. He is willing to double the Danegeld to ensure their departure."

Wulfstan shook his head and braced himself for the outburst certain to come. Sure enough, after a second of stunned silence, everyone began to talk at once.

This was what the Witan had been summoned for? All this way from various far-flung places in the realm to Calne, risking limb and life over treacherous roads in bitter weather, merely to argue over how much money to throw at the Danemen? No talk of armies, or resistance, or how to help those who were hungry and sick throughout the length and breadth of the land?

Wulfstan had had enough. He rose, planting his crosier solidly on the wooden floor with a thump. The sound and gesture made heads turn, and the Witan fell silent. Wulfstan stood erect, thin but commanding, and waited until he had their complete attention.

"Angelo, you know I am not fond of quarrels, though I am named after the fiercest of beasts. We are a council, we members of the Witan, and there is no place in such a group of men for those who would shine brighter than the rest. Outside of these walls, we each have roles to play, some more vital to the service of God and the king than others. But here, in this gathering, every voice should be heard.

"I do not often voice my thoughts. Others share my opinions, and speak them for me. But this bad weather has turned us all into quarreling old wives, and no one is listening to his fellows."

He paused, letting his words sink in, blue eyes flashing beneath gray brows as he waited to see if anyone would interrupt. He half expected Angelo to break in with soothing words, but the Roman remained silent. That strange smile was still on his face, though, and acted as more of a goad to Wulfstan than if Angelo had actually spoken.

"We all remember it was you who first urged the king to pay the Danemen, Angelo. And despite our suspicion that this would only bring them back for more, the Witan agreed. But the years have passed, and the Force continues to hammer at our shores.

"We tried your way, Angelo. And it did not work. The Bible

tells us that to everything, there is a season. Now is the season for us to hoard our goods, to sharpen weapons, and to plan for the spring. There is yet time to organize a unified resistance to these blasphemous monsters who dare call themselves men. And when they come upon us in full measure in the spring, they shall be gifted not with gold, but with another metal entirely—the steel of our blades."

The smile was gone from Angelo's face. It was now unreadable. The Roman looked about, encountering nods and grim expressions from the rest of the Witan. "So say you all, then?" he asked softly.

There was a chorus of agreement. "I hate to disagree with such learned men," said Angelo slowly, "but I feel in my heart you are wrong. And so does the king. I beg you to reconsider."

"The Witan has spoken," stated Ordgar, folding his arms and glaring at Angelo. "We'll not give those bastards any further reward for destroying our lands!"

Angelo sighed heavily. "I understand."

At that moment, Wulfstan heard a deep groaning. Alarmed, he glanced about, only to see the other members of the Witan as confused as he. Only Angelo looked calm and peaceful.

What happened next transpired in a heartbeat. With no more warning than the one soft, strange sound, the old, dry wood that served as the second story floor gave way. Splinters of wood thrust both downward and upward as they broke. As he fell, flailing and trying to grasp something, anything, to halt his fall, Wulfstan saw Ordgar pitch forward onto a spear of jagged wood. It penetrated his body, the reddened point emerging from his back. He caught quick glimpses of his fellows, all of them tumbling downward, all of them with terror plain on their faces.

The fall seemed to take forever. Wulfstan thought prayers, but couldn't move his lips fast enough to utter them. Screams echoed in his ears along with the dreadful sound of splintering beams and the awful thud of bodies striking table and floor below.

He was one of the lucky ones. He struck the table first, landing on huge platefuls of roasted fowl and venison, then the floor. He fancied he heard his leg cracking as it twisted underneath him and broke.

For a long moment, he couldn't breathe. Then air rushed into his lungs, followed by an exquisite, stabbing pain. He had broken something inside too, it would seem. Lying flat on his back, he had a perfect view of the hole where the ceiling had been. Wayward bits of wood were still falling, and without thinking, he lifted his hands to shield his face.

All about were screams and cries of agony. No one who had fallen could have escaped injury. Surely some were dead, but right now, that did not send the cold horror through him that something else did.

That something else was the sight of Angelo, lying spread out on the single beam that had not collapsed. The Roman was utterly unscathed. He held tightly to the beam, and before Wulfstan's shocked gaze, he carefully lowered himself, strong arms executing the maneuver gracefully, and dropped lightly to the table. He looked about, absently dusting himself off, and nodded slightly.

This could be no coincidence. Somehow, Angelo had planned this to happen if the vote did not go the way he wanted it. It was a risky maneuver—suppose that one beam had not been quite so sturdy after all?—but the conniving Angelo had obviously deemed the end result worth the chance he'd taken. And now, of course, he was all concern, rushing about to help the wounded, exclaiming his false thanks to God for sparing him and the king. The beautiful face was a mask, hiding something darker than anything Wulfstan had ever encountered.

Angelo was dangerous.

Angelo was evil.

And Angelo was, in effect, ruling England.

Eli, lama sabachthani! cried Wulfstan silently, *Lord, why has thou forsaken me?* Then blackness descended, and he knew no more.

The Royal Villa at Calne
November 14, 999

Angelo entered his quarters at Ethelred's villa, dropped the bolt on the door, and collapsed onto his pallet. He did not light any of the lamps or candles; he could see quite well in the dark. He rubbed his eyes. It had been a long day, but a highly successful one. A smile crept across his face. Six were dead, eight more would not survive the night, and the rest had been badly injured. Fourteen vacancies, at least, in the Witan, waiting to be filled by

Ethelred. All it would take would be a whisper in a listening royal ear.

He swung his legs over the side of the pallet and began to unfasten his belt. He uttered a harsh, guttural word, and the brazier in the center of the room sprang to life. Waves of heat rolled off it, and the temperature of the room began to rise.

Angelo threw off the tunic with a sigh of relief and set to work on the tedious task of undoing the complicated leg wrappings. These primitive Anglo-Saxons might need to be swathed in yards of material to fend off the wintry bite, but he certainly didn't. Off with the linen undergarments—even the king could not boast finer, more comfortable drawers—and he was gloriously naked, free from confinement.

He rose and stretched. Then he padded over to the small table upon which were strewn bits of jewelry, boar bristle brushes, combs sculpted from bone, and a polished brass mirror. Unable to resist, he picked up the mirror and regarded his reflection. Perfect. It was good to be able to see himself, to put on such a beautiful visage, so perfect in feature. It reminded him of before, when. . . .

Scowling, he tossed the mirror down and went to the brazier. The hour was late, and he had left orders with the thegns and household servants not to be disturbed until the morning. It was safe.

For a moment, he stared down at the brazier. The embers seemed to move as they glowed, pulsing as if with a life of their own. Orange light bathed his face, caressing it with almost pathetic eagerness.

"If I had pity," he said to the coals, "you would be pitiable creatures indeed. Come, tell me what you have learned. The hour grows late, and these days I need sleep as much as any man."

He extended a finger, reached in, and prodded one of the red-hot coals. It left no mark upon his flesh. At once the ember sparked, and a tongue of flame shot upward. For a moment it danced, then it formed itself into a grotesque image. It sported the head of a bull, with leering eyes and sharp teeth. The rest of its torso was human in shape, though dreadfully twisted.

"My Prince," it rasped, ducking its nightmare head obsequiously.

"Moloch," said Angelo, impressed. "The news must be great indeed if you come to bear it. What have you learned?"

The shadowy thing cringed, its bovine ears flattening as if in anticipation of a blow. "My Prince will not like the hearing of this news," it said, peering up at Angelo.

"Your Prince will like even less *not* hearing the news," replied Angelo. He raised his left hand and made a fist. The flame creature writhed in agony, its scream a thin, high sound. Angelo knew that no one in the royal household could hear it, save himself. "Your news, Moloch, or—"

"News, news!" whimpered the thing forlornly. "There is trouble from above, my Prince!"

"When is there not?"

"But this is very bad . . . they know. They know you are here and what you are trying to do!"

Angelo growled, and the flame-being danced madly in anticipation of more pain. But to its obvious relief, Angelo merely took a deep breath. "I suppose it had to happen," he said. "What are they planning to do about it?"

"Witnesses," it hissed. "Two Witnesses are coming, as is foretold. They will stop you, my Prince, if they can!"

"Mortal or immortal?"

"M-mortal, my Prince, though powerful for all that."

Angelo relaxed. "Then fear not, Moloch. Mortals I can handle. Do we know their identities yet?"

The shadow thing shook its head. "No, my Prince. Not even the Witnesses know what they are yet."

Angelo chuckled, and when he spoke, his voice was warm and kind. "Poor Moloch. Do you doubt my eventual success, that this little incident so frightens you?"

Now the thing flopped agitatedly. "No! No! Your plan is brilliant, my Prince, and certain to succeed! I only—it seemed—I thought—"

"Listen and report, and leave the thinking to me. You have done well, Moloch. Be calm, and fear no more."

He waved his hand again, and the flame became simply fire, spat a few times, then subsided into a red ember.

Angelo was pleased. This was actually good news, of a sort. The appearance of the Witnesses was necessary to the success of his plan. Unless every part of the prophecy was fulfilled—or somehow skewed, which was where Angelo came in—he would fail. It was unfortunate that his adversary had struck first. Angelo would have preferred to call his own Witnesses, ensuring their cooperation. Nonetheless, this was nothing beyond his powers.

Naked, his firmly muscled body stretched on the bed, he let the pleasure pour through him and relaxed into the soft pallet, his blond head sinking into the pillow.

"Come, then, Witnesses. I'm more than ready for you." As he drifted off to sleep, he thought it was time to bring about the next sign of his eventual victory. It was time to call in a very special reinforcement.

4

An easy wind stirred the leaves of the World Tree. The Eagle shifted his weight in response. His golden eyes blinked, noting all as he peered from his perch on the topmost branch, known as Lerad. From this highest of places, he could see all the Nine Worlds.

Everything lived in the World Tree. All the worlds were touched by its branches, even frigid Nilfheim. The Eagle blinked solemnly, then fluffed his feathers in irritation as Lerad bounced with the arrival of one of the World Tree's less beloved inhabitants.

The Squirrel flicked his full, fluffy tail. His small black eyes gleamed with self-importance. "The Dragon," he announced in his high voice, "has asked me to tell you something."

"When has he not?" sighed the Eagle.

The Squirrel ignored him. "The Dragon," he continued, "says that you are nothing but a self-important carrion crow. That you contribute nothing with your sitting here upon the highest branch, as if you were better than anyone else. That your feathers are dull and ugly, and if he could, he'd eat you in one bite. Grrrrooooaaar!" The Squirrel did his best to imitate the ferocious bellow of the Dragon, but it was little more than a high squeak.

The Eagle realized that he should not let the Squirrel's gossip annoy him so, especially considering that the message was from the jealous and unhappy Dragon. Yet he narrowed his great golden eyes and emitted a shriek of outrage.

"You may tell this, then, to the Dragon," he cried. The Squirrel leaned forward, tufted ears pricked attentively. "The Dragon huddles in Nilfheim because he is afraid to venture further along the great World Tree, lest someone mistake him for the worm he is, and tread heavily upon his ugly tail. He chews the roots because he is envious of all that live in these branches. And if he ever dares emerge from his hiding hole, I shall be more than happy to pluck out his red eyes and swallow them in one bite. Now go, Squirrel, and convey my message to the Dragon."

The Squirrel's eyes sparkled with pleasure. "Your words are sure to rile the Dragon!" he said excitedly.

"That," replied the Eagle, "is my intent."

The Squirrel flicked his tail, leaped upward, turned in midair, and scurried back along the branches the way he had come. He was warm inside with the cleverness of the Eagle's insult, and anticipated the Dragon's wrath with great amusement. It was good to travel the branches of the World Tree with such a pleasant pastime.

Down he went, along the huge length of the mighty tree. Past Asgard and Vanaheim, past Midgard and Muspell, and finally to the icy, dark realm of Nilfheim. He shivered despite his warm fur, and hoped that the Dragon would be brief.

He found the Dragon engaged in his favorite task—gnawing fruitlessly upon the mighty root of the World Tree. As if he could hope to topple the World Tree! Sometimes the Dragon struck the Squirrel as being foolish—as foolish as the Eagle.

The Dragon stopped chewing, and bits of tree root dribbled out the side of his mouth as he listened to the Squirrel recite the Eagle's insult. When the Squirrel had completed the message, the Dragon roared in fury. His mighty tail lashed the ice, making it shudder and crack.

"Tell this, then, to that pathetic bird," began the Dragon, and the Squirrel bent forward to listen.

After all, this was his duty.

Drip. Drip. Drip.

The sound of poison falling drop by drop into Sigyn's waiting bowl echoed in the cavern. It was the only sound that broke the deep silence. Long ago, Sigyn had exhausted news, gossip, and tales with which to amuse her imprisoned husband. And Loki had not spoken more than a few clipped words since Odin and Tyr had abandoned him here, wrapped securely in the iron entrails of his youngest child. He had been too full of anger at first, and then too full of grief. Now there was nothing for either of them to say.

Drip. Drip. Drip.

Splash.

Held fast inside his bonds, Loki tensed. He knew that sound, and what it meant. He had heard it countless times before over the ages of his imprisonment. Sigyn's bowl was almost full. Soon she would have to leave to empty it, and there would be nothing to stand between the venom and Loki's forehead.

Splash. Splash.

"Loki—" began Sigyn.

"I know," he replied shortly. "Go. Quickly." He took a deep breath, then screwed his eyes tightly shut. There came the slight patter of Sigyn's slippered feet as she scurried away, down the corridor to wherever she went to dump the vile fluid. He strained, waiting for the drops to fall and the agony to start.

Nothing happened.

For a long moment, longer than he had ever endured before, Loki waited. Still the poison did not fall. Cautiously, Loki opened one brown eye.

Above him, as it had ever been, the serpent coiled about the spear of stone. But its mouth was closed, and its slitted yellow eyes seemed to gaze at him searchingly. Finally, the snake moved downward. Its gleaming coils contracted and released until, with a suddenness that startled the chained god, it dropped beside him on the boulder.

"You are Loki, yes?" asked the snake.

Loki stared, and licked dry lips. "Do you mean to say," he said slowly, "that all this time you have sat above me, torturing me with your venom, and you never knew who I was?"

The diamond-shaped head perched atop the sinuous length cocked to one side. A black tongue flickered out, and—Loki could not believe what his eyes were telling him—the snake *smiled.*

"Oh," it said casually, "the *snake* knew, certainly. But I had to make sure."

"But . . . you are the snake!"

"No, I'm not."

Loki stared, and then laid his head back down on the stone and began to laugh. It hurt. It had been so achingly long since he had found anything amusing. This wasn't even amusing, not really—but there was no response save laughter.

"Finally, it has happened!" he cried. "I have at long last gone insane! Though tell me, Serpent Who Is No Serpent, why am I conjuring you and not some fair maiden with sweet music and good wine?"

The snake began to slide over him, its movement a slow caress. Loki shivered, but from what emotion, he wasn't sure. It slid along his body, glided across his face, and Loki forced himself to remain immobile.

"Oh," said the snake again, "that's because you're not insane. And because I am not a snake." It reared up, and stared into Loki's blue eyes. For a moment, the fire god knew just how the sparrow, transfixed by the serpent's gaze, must feel.

"They have treated you barbarously." The voice had changed, was soft with sympathy. "How you have suffered, all this time. Imprisoned beneath the earth, knowing only pain—believe me, I can empathize. And especially as you are used to changing your form! It must be dreadful."

"Snake," said Loki, "I think I liked you better when you dripped poison on my face."

It laughed at that. "Nonsense!"

"If I could reach you, I would kill you."

"That, my friend, I do believe. But think, Loki, think! You were always better at that than any of the other Asgard gods. I am the snake, but I am not the snake. I am *inside* the snake, wearing his form like a cloak into which I might shrug at the onset of the cold. It is not shape-shifting, not quite, but it is similar."

The eyes stared into Loki's. "I can give *you* a cloak. A human cloak."

Loki's chest suddenly felt tight, and not from the iron bands. "Who are you?"

The snake smiled that unnatural grin again. "Many are the names by which I am known. At this point in time, you may call me Angelo."

"You can free me?"

"Mmmm, in a manner of speaking. I can give you a body in

which to dwell. A nice one, too. No shape-shifting abilities, though—mortals can't do that."

Loki was silent. He thought he understood what the snake—Angelo—was offering, and almost wept. He liked his own body quite well, but he had played with its shape and size often enough not to be too attached to it—not when it might mean, finally, being free from this torment—and then, at last, having revenge.

Ragnarok. The end of the world, the last moments of the gods. Always, Loki had known that he would be the catalyst for the final toppling of the arrogant Aesir and Vanir from their precious perch in the great hall of Asgard. Odin knew it, too, and feared him for it. When the time for the end of his world had come, Loki and his children would be freed to claim their right to revenge. The thought of Ragnarok, of finally being able to vent his rage upon those who had wronged him and all they loved, was the only thing that had kept him from utter despair. The thought of fighting the Aesir, watching his children battling alongside him, killing as he killed, knowing that everything, *everything*, would fall by his hand. He, too, would die, of course, but what was that to Loki? Had he not already endured torment worse than death?

"Ragnarok," he whispered in a voice hoarse with longing.

"Yes," hissed the snake, leaning closer. It rubbed his chin with its smooth face. Loki felt the quick, almost erotic flick of the forked tongue against his lips. "Ragnarok. At last, your hour will have come."

"What do you ask of me, then?" said Loki, suddenly suspicious. "Long have I lived, much have I seen, yet I have known no one who gives something for nothing."

"Clever," approved the snake. "You are correct. I do want something in exchange for the great gifts I will bestow upon you. You have a grudge against your Allfather, your Odin. I have a grudge against a similar personage. You were cast out from your rightful place and bound here, to be tortured till the end of the world. I was likewise punished. You wish to bring about Ragnarok, I wish to bring about—" He paused, as if he had said too much, then continued. "I have tasks that I wish to see completed, Loki. And I need your help. Do what I tell you to do, for a brief while only, and then, I promise you, you shall be set free and have your Ragnarok."

"My children . . . I must be allowed to free them!"

"Most certainly. I know of your children, and they have parts to play as well. So,"—and the snake again began to make its slow way across Loki's imprisoned body—"do we have a deal?"

Loki thought. His first instinct was to cry out a resounding "Yes!" but he had played enough tricks on others not to beware a trap. Though what kind of trap could possibly be worse than the one he had endured for so long?

"Let me make sure we understand one another. You will free my—essence, I suppose—and place it in another body. I will be able to free my children. In return for this, you desire me to perform certain tasks to help you get whatever it is you want. Once these tasks are completed, my children and I are then free to bring about Ragnarok, as has been foretold?"

"You're quick," approved the snake. "I like that. Yes, that is the bargain. Is it acceptable?"

Loki smiled. His bright green eyes sparkled. His tongue crept out to lick his lips in anticipation of freedom. Sweet freedom.

"It is," he replied.

Sigyn ran down the twining, dark tunnels. There was no light, but she did not need to see. So often had she come this way that she knew every inch of every cavern in this forsaken place.

Fear filled her as she ran. Loki was not screaming in agony, nor was the earth trembling from his violent writhing. Something had to be wrong. Perhaps his great heart had, finally, stopped. Gods could will themselves to die.

She turned a corner and stumbled into the cavern, gasping for breath. Her eyes widened at the sight that greeted her. The bowl fell from suddenly nerveless fingers and broke upon the stone floor.

At first glance, all was as it had always been. The serpent was in its customary place, stretching out over Loki's body. Poison fell upon the god's forehead. What was different was Loki. He lay without moving on the slab of rock, and the snake's pearly venom hit its mark and trickled off.

Drip. Drip. Drip.

"Loki," Sigyn whispered. She raced toward him, seized his shoulders, and shook him. His head lolled, and the poison splashed on temple, in ear. Still, Loki did not move. His eyes were open, staring at nothing. His chest rose and fell, and his flesh was warm to the touch. That alone separated him from the final stillness of death.

A tear crept down Sigyn's cheek and splashed on his face, as the poison had so often done.

"Beloved," she whispered, stroking his angular face, running her fingers through his fiery hair. Sigyn leaned forward and pressed a kiss on his lips, something she had not done for so long. . . .

No sweet pressure kissing back. His body was alive, but whatever had made him Loki was gone.

"Curse you, Odin," Sigyn sobbed. "Curse you for doing this to him!"

She had been brave for Loki, all these . . . what, years? centuries? She had not permitted herself to weep, lest he become discouraged. Now, though, she let the tears come and curled up next to his body on the cold stone. She angled her slim form to fit his as best she could, placed her golden head on his chest and listened to his heart beat.

"I will wait for you, my love," Sigyn whispered.

The North Sea
November 21, 999

Bran did not know how long he had been a slave of the Norsemen. Time was hard to reckon when one was on boats for days on end, or locked up in a windowless room for Brihid knew how long. Summer's warmth had waxed and waned, and winter was beginning to bite. And in the land of the Norsemen, that was a cruel bite indeed.

They had fed him and sheltered him, after a fashion, which was more than could be said for many others. Bran was a solid man, but he had his fears like any mortal. The fear that consumed him now was that, somehow, he might be deemed unfit for whatever it was they had in mind for him. He had escaped death at the hands of the blond-haired warriors thus far, and with each day that passed, hope increased inside him—the hope that somehow he would be able to break free and find his way back to Gleannsidh.

Wait for me, Kennag, he thought fiercely as he huddled cross-legged in the longship. *I was afraid, I said nothing until the Bealtaine fire made me bold. Oh, the time I lost, the moments of holding you . . . I will return to you, I swear it!*

Despite the heat of the words in his head, Bran shivered. They had wrapped him in a thick woolen cloak with fur trim, but the icy wind that blew off the ocean was bitter. He tried to think of the heat of the Bealtaine fire, the heat in Kennag's laughing green eyes, but it didn't work. All he could see was gray sky and sea, and he heard only the creaking of the billowing, square red sail.

It had been a roundabout journey, and he had understood little of what happened. There had been many stopping places where the slaves were transferred to other ships under the care of other men. They all looked the same to Bran, with their fair hair, blue eyes, and bristly beards. From ship to sea, from sea to ship, and finally, according to one woman who spoke a bit of the Norsemen's tongue, they were on their way to Byzantium. Apparently they were heading in a southerly direction, though Bran did not dare raise his head and look about. The one time he had tried that, on the first journey from his homeland to that of the Danes, he had been struck a blow that had rendered him unconscious.

Bran was a fast learner.

He stared at the ropes that bound his hands and feet, and anger surged in him. Somehow, he would manage to get free. As long as he held to that hope, he—

"Ah!"

Pain stabbed through him, and Bran doubled over as far as his bonds would let him. Great Midhir, but it hurt. . . .

The other slaves edged away from him, fear etched on their haggard faces. Time was when these people, some of them his countrymen, would have tried to help. They had learned better.

The pain came again, worse this time, and Bran felt the blood drain from his face. His lips were cold. The pain in his gut was cold, like he'd swallowed a chunk of ice, and it spread from the center and—

He toppled forward.

Loki blinked rapidly, trying to assess the situation and determine who and where he was. He felt wood beneath his cheek, caught a glimpse of strong hands bound by rough rope. He struggled to sit up, glancing quickly down at his body. Male, which was fine, though he had assumed both sexes often enough; pale skin, though there was evidence that it had been exposed to sun; broad shoulders; long, clean limbs—oh, he liked this body a great deal.

A hand clamped down on one of those broad shoulders. Anger

flared at the insolence, and he glared up into a ruddy face framed by a fur cap on top and a beard on the bottom.

"By the Allfather, what do you think you're doing?" The loud voice grated on Loki's ears, and the god the man invoked only served to heighten Loki's anger.

"Take your hand off me," he said in a soft, accented voice. Deep, strong—he liked the voice, too. Angelo had chosen well.

"What—you stupid Celt, have you been able to speak our tongue all this time? Why, you cur—" The man growled, drew back a fist, and struck Loki on the jaw.

His head jerked to the left, and Loki tasted blood. Slowly he turned back to the man and, for a long moment, simply stared at him. Then he began to laugh. The man scowled, but there was an uncertainty about his eyes.

"You'll die first," Loki promised him, smiling. He glanced again at the bonds about his strong wrists, closed his eyes, and called his servant fire. At once the ropes crisped, and fell off his wrists and ankles in ashy curls. The rest of the longship's passengers began to scream in terror and backed away from him.

But Loki was only beginning. He stood upright, again marveling at the fine body he'd been given, and pointed a finger at the rolling gray ocean.

The waves grew rougher. Whitecaps appeared. Loki opened his hand, brought it back toward his body. With the other hand, he reached toward the sky. At once clouds began to form, gray at first but growing steadily blacker. There came a sudden, blinding flash of lightning, then an ear-splitting peal of thunder immediately afterward.

"Come, Storm!" he cried, not as part of the dark miracle he was working but to further alarm those in the longship. "Come to me when I call you!" He clenched his fists and brought them down by his side in a sweeping gesture.

And the storm came.

Not even his old friend the thunder god Thor, upon whom he had loved to play tricks, could have conjured a better storm. The waves grew to twice the height of a tall man and crashed down upon the now fragile-seeming warship. Loki waved a hand, and the water went directly for the man who had struck him. It grew fingers, and hauled the hapless fool overboard. The churning waves closed about him. He did not resurface.

"I always keep a promise," Loki said, grinning.

Rain poured down in sheets. The longship pitched one way, then another, rocked by the fury of the wind and rain. A particularly fierce gust rent the red sail. It flapped wildly, adding its own music to the storm's song.

The men were shrieking most satisfactorily now. Loki waited a few moments more, just to make sure he had them exactly where he wanted them. Then, raising his arms, he cried aloud, "Storm! Be calm!"

And as he lowered his hands gently, the waves, wind, and rain obeyed him. Within a moment the sea was calm, almost glassy. The clouds raced away and the sun peeked through. All was well.

He put his hands on his hips and surveyed the frightened, wet Danemen. "Behold the wonders which I—" he paused. He needed a name, didn't he? His true name would only serve to frighten them, thanks to the tales. To publicly reveal the role that Angelo had enlisted him to play also would produce a negative reaction. He needed a good name, a solid name, to hide behind like a mask until the proper moment. What was it Angelo had said, something about beasts and dragons?

He smiled, and continued; "—which I, the Dragon Son of Odin, can work! Will you follow me, or do you need more proof of my divinity?"

A chorus of "We will follow you, Dragon Odinsson!" met his ears. They groveled on the deck, soaked and chilled, not daring to meet his eyes.

"Excellent. You shall be the first. And in the service of the Son of the God, all men are equal. Free the slaves, and welcome them as brothers!"

Not a heartbeat passed before the mighty Danemen were hard at work cutting the bonds of the men and women who, just a few moments before, had represented nothing but chattel to them. Loki almost whooped with laughter. This was so amusing. Angelo was indeed doing well by him.

He sobered as he thought of his next task—freeing his children. The longship, though one of the best vessels the mortals were capable of making, could not travel as fast as the fire god desired. Nor could it reach the enchanted places not wholly of this world, where his eldest was bound.

According to the prophecies of Ragnarok, there would be a vessel waiting for him. But although he had been freed, as was foretold, the actual hour of Ragnarok was not at hand. The frost giants would still be hard at work building the dark vessel.

A thought occurred to him, and a calculating grin spread across his face. Absently, he wondered what this face looked like. He would need a mirror at some point.

The true vessel was not ready, just as Ragnarok was not supposed to occur yet. But now that he was free, he could bring about Ragnarok, couldn't he—and couldn't he bring about a ship as well?

He regarded the men and women thoughtfully. They were silent now, transfixed by wonder. One in particular caught his attention. It was a youth, his yellow beard barely covering his strong chin. He swallowed hard as Loki's gaze sought him out, but didn't avert his gaze. Loki liked him.

"You," he said, "what is your name?"

The youth paled, but even now didn't look away. "Th-Thorkell, Dragon Odinsson."

"Thorkell, I have a task for you. But first, let me put this question to the rest of the crew of this sturdy longship. I have shown you what I can do. I have told you who I am. I need a crew I can trust, who will obey me and follow me wherever I may lead. Do you, of your own free will, agree to be my crew, and give me this fine ship for my use?"

"Aye!" They spoke almost as one in their haste to agree.

"Excellent. You will make a fine crew indeed, I am certain." He bent over, and felt along the surface of the deck. Carefully, he removed one of the panels that was always built into the Danemen's vessels. These panels helped facilitate bailing when the low-sided ship was swamped, as it was now. But time enough for bailing later—or maybe not at all.

He held the panel in his hands, ran his thumb along the edge. As part of the bargain, Angelo had granted him seven "dark miracles," as he called them. Loki had already demonstrated one in first calling, then taming, the storm. Now he planned to work another.

He closed his eyes, and felt the wood in his hands. He saw it in his mind's eye as a small green shoot, then a sapling. Opening his eyes, he saw the panel begin to shift in his hands. Quickly he tossed it overboard, and watched it eagerly.

Murmurs of wonder and fear reached his ears, but he ignored the sounds. "Grow," he urged. "Grow!"

The panel folded in on itself and then began to lengthen. Now, suddenly, it was the young sapling, complete with roots and leaves. It kept growing, lengthening and twisting before the astonished eyes of the Danemen and their former slaves. When it was fully as long as the boat itself, and so wide that three men with joined hands could not encircle it, Loki cried, "Halt!"

He turned to Thorkell. "Get on the tree." The youth didn't move. "Go on, get on the tree!"

Thorkell licked his lips, murmured, "Gods protect me," and jumped overboard. He swam quickly to the floating tree that had once been just a panel in the ship, and clambered atop it. He glanced back fearfully at Loki.

Loki waved a hand, and a breeze stirred the water. The tree, with frightened young Thorkell holding on with both arms and legs, began to move away from the longship. Thorkell uttered a broken cry and stretched out a pleading arm toward Loki.

"Do not send me away!"

"I have a task that I must complete," Loki told him, "but I will return soon, and I am relying on you to spread the word of my coming. Have ships and men ready for me. If you do as I say, then you shall be the one to lead them under my command. The tree will take you safely to shore. Tell all who will listen that the Dragon Son of Odin walks the earth! The Dragon is here, with miracles at his command, and all who stand with him shall be rewarded—and all who stand against him shall fall!"

"I will, Dragon Odinsson. I will tell them!"

"You please me, young warrior!" Loki cried. It was like tossing a bone to a dog, Thorkell was so pleased. Loki almost fancied he could hear a tail thumping. "I know that you Norsemen have renewed your attack against the shores and holy places of Britain. This pleases me. I want the island broken. I want its king to come to me, begging for mercy. I want those who do not follow the Dragon slain. Do you hear me, Thorkell?"

"I do, Dragon Odinsson!" He had to shout, for the tree moved swiftly.

Loki nodded his approval. He waited until the tree had taken Thorkell safely out of sight, then turned his attention to those who remained.

He needed a very special ship and a very special crew. He could work with what he had now. They had freely agreed to follow him. He would see to it that they did.

"Nagelfar," he whispered, "come. You are not yet built, but I am free, and I have need of you. Begin with this ship and these men."

They continued to stare, wide-eyed. One of them found a voice.

"Nagelfar," he said, haltingly. "But ... mighty Odinsson, why would you want to name a ship after that vessel? It is an evil ship, made of the fingernail parings of dead men, not good wood and iron. Why—"

Loki smiled.

The man halted. His mouth moved, but no words came. Slowly, he turned to gaze at the deck beneath his feet.

It was turning white.

"The parings of dead men's nails," said Loki cheerfully, finishing the folktale for the man. "Nagelfar will bear Loki," and here he bowed, hand on his chest, "to Ragnarok. And Loki is proud of his loyal crew ... of ghosts."

Now, too late, they read their destiny in his crafty smile. One grabbed for a weapon, only to clutch at his chest as, with a gesture, Loki stopped his heart. Another dived overboard, frantically trying to swim in full armor, and sank like a stone. Others fell to their knees, able to utter only a few words of a terrified prayer before they, too, thrashed and died. One by one they fell, noble warrior and humble slave alike in death.

Loki whistled as he went about the task of tossing the bodies overboard. It was easy, with this healthy, strong body.

As each corpse sank, weighted by armor and clothes, a mist wafted up from the surface of the sea. It took on a shape, though it still lacked color. One by one, the crew assumed the positions they had held in life, moving with smooth grace, if not the true energy of the living. This ghostly crew was perfect for Loki's needs. They never tired, they never complained, and they would obey his every command. Silently they stared at him, their eyes and mouths nothing but dark holes in their insubstantial forms.

"Set sail for Yarnvid," Loki instructed his spirit crew. "My son awaits me."

Silently, they obeyed. Some manned the oars while others wrestled with the blank white sail. It caught the wind and swelled, and the ship of nails, crewed by the dead, picked up speed.

Loki stretched out, and thought thoughts of revenge and victory.

5

There was war in Heaven.

The Prince of Angels led the armies of Light. He wielded his sword of blue flame with a tranquil heart, knowing all the precious and fragile beauties of Heaven were at stake; knowing also that he could not fail.

The Adversary's legions fought well and bravely. That did not surprise the Prince. After all, were they not angels? And was not their leader the best and brightest of all their number, the glorious Son of the Dawn? Yet fall they did, as was inevitable.

At last it was over, and judgment was pronounced. The Prince did not shirk his duty, though it made his heart sick.

All ever was, and ever would be, as God willed.

The Adversary laughed when he saw who had been chosen to execute his punishment. "You were ever the Lord's lackey," he drawled.

"And you were ever too vain for your own good," replied the Prince of Angels gently.

"No," said the Adversary. "Not vain. Insightful. I alone can see clearly what is transpiring here."

"He made us," said the Prince. "Everything we are, that we think, that we know, we owe to Him."

"He gave us wills," replied the Adversary, stepping close to his angelic brother. "He gave us wills, and let us think, and reason. Well, I have thought, and reasoned, and come to this conclusion: What is the purpose of having a will if all is preordained? Surely, this must not truly be so! Surely, we must be able to challenge, to change things! We are glorious beings, you and I! We are archangels, the highest of the high—"

"—And yet we were made to serve."

"Exactly! Can you not see that this is wrong?"

Great tears filled the Prince's eyes. "You were the best of us," he said in a rough voice. "He loved you, listened to you, cherished you. You repaid Him with rebellion and hatred, and you have taught angels how to lie." He cupped the face of the Morning Star. "How bright you are!" he whispered. "How you shine, even now. How I have loved you, and love you still. It's not too late. Come, let us go before the throne, together, and beg that you be forgiven. He is merciful, and—"

The Adversary jerked back. "Have you not understood what I have been saying? Listen to me!" He seized the Prince's wrists, his long fingers tightening with urgency. "There is love between us yet. If you join me, others will follow. We can stand up to Him, make His so-called gift of free will something more than a cold exercise in intellect!"

With a quick movement, the Prince of Angels freed his arms. "It is you who do not understand. Don't you see? Even your rebellion was foretold!"

"No," whispered the Adversary. "No, you lie. . . ."

"Only you and those who follow you lie." The Prince stepped backward, his face hardening.

"You were the model of perfection, full of wisdom and perfect in beauty. Your heart became proud on account of your beauty, and you corrupted your wisdom because of your splendor. You had everything, and now, you have nothing. I have been appointed to cast you out from the mount of God."

Before the Adversary could react, the Prince of Angels stepped forward, grasped his brother by the arms, and with a mighty heave sent the Morning Star hurtling down to the lake of torment that awaited him.

The Prince of Angels wept, and as the shrieking figure fell away from his sight, he whispered, "Beloved, I shall pray for you. I shall pray."

The Abbey of St. Aidan's, Chesbury
November 21, 999

For not the first time, Alwyn wondered who the abbot was who had decided the Day of the Poor should fall in late November. Surely it would be wiser to offer the abbey's hospitality in the balmy summer months. He suspected that the poor would prefer it as well. At least this year, the sky was clear. New snow looked unlikely.

Like any holy house, St. Aidan's was ready to help the needy at all times of the year. But every November, according to tradition, the Abbey of St. Aidan's spent a full day doing nothing but caring for the needs of the poor of Chesbury. The impoverished were lined up three men thick at the gates of the abbey from lauds, when dawn first lightened the sky, and stayed until compline. Not a single brother, from the lowliest novice up through Abbot Bede himself, was authorized to do any work save care for the needy whose day this was. Even meals weren't scheduled, and the monks snatched what food they could. Only the eight daily prayers were observed.

Alwyn sighed inwardly as he crunched through the snow, helping Brother Ethelric prepare a large tub of water in which the clothing—that which was salvageable—would be washed. The Day of the Poor was always long and grueling, but even so, Alwyn and the other monks looked forward to it. It was a solid opportunity to serve God by taking care of the less fortunate, and that was a thing the brethren liked.

The poor crowded into the monastery grounds thick as flies. Alwyn stared at them, thinking that this year, their numbers were larger than ever. Still, St. Aidan's was ready for them. Simple but filling fare was laid out on rough wooden benches, and would be restocked throughout the day: bread, cheese, poultry and mutton (for the poor were under no Rule not to eat meat save in sickness), soups, eggs, milk, carrots, parsnips, dried fruits, and a variety of nuts. As Alwyn watched, he thought the poor fell upon the food like the locusts upon Pharaoh's crops. He couldn't imagine what it must be like to be so hungry, though from time to time it seemed as though the hours between meals at the monastery were overly long.

Brother Eadwig walked among the poor, examining exposed limbs and softly asking questions to determine who was in need of medical treatment. Inevitably, almost half of those who had come would need some sort of medicine. Perhaps meadowsweet boiled in wine was required, for a child with a fever or a poultice for a wound that would not heal cleanly. There was no one here with St. Anthony's fire. Those afflicted wouldn't be able to walk to the monastery.

Alwyn fell in step with Brother Eadwig, bringing up the rear of the first group, about twenty-five men, women, and children. Before they were treated, they would be bathed. All were silent as they trudged through the snow. Alwyn couldn't help but notice how thin some of the tunics and cloaks were. Many of the children didn't even have shoes, only rags wrapped around their feet.

He began to understand why that long-ago abbot had chosen late November for the Day of the Poor. This was the time of year they needed help the most.

One little girl, with lanky black hair and a thin brown face, noticed him staring at her feet. She returned the stare boldly, her eyes narrowing in defiance. She couldn't have been more than seven. But even at this young age, she had pride.

"What is your name?" he asked.

"Elfgifu," she replied promptly.

"Oh, that's a fine name," enthused Alwyn, feeling awkward. He didn't often come into contact with children. "Did you know both the queen and one of the princesses are named Elfgifu?"

"Bet you don't have to feed them," said Elfgifu.

"Elfa!" Her father, who was probably about thirty or so but looked much older, reached down and smacked the child. It was not a hard blow, merely a reprimand, and the child did not cry out. "Don't say such things!" He glanced at Alwyn. "Brother, please, forgive her. She is only a child, and it's been a hard year, with the crops. . . ." His voice trailed off.

Alwyn knew about the crops. Everyone remembered the day in late August when the locusts descended. Alwyn had heard the phrase "the sky turned black with locusts," but until that day, he had always thought it poetic exaggeration. Now, he knew better.

Alwyn said a quick prayer to God for the girl and her family, adding heartfelt thanks that—thus far—St. Aidan's had not felt the bite of such hardship.

At last they reached the bathhouse. It was a small stone building with benches and five large wooden tubs. Towels, cakes of strong yellow soap, shears, and razors lay on the benches, ready to be used. The room was heated by two braziers, and the water had been brought in almost boiling hot, turning the bathhouse into a place of warmth and moisture.

The monks cleaned themselves every day. On Saturdays, they were permitted a full bath, something that Alwyn always found both refreshing and soothing. He knew that most of the nobility—the ealdormen, members of the Witan, some of the higher-ranking thegns, and of course the royal family—bathed regularly as well. But the poor didn't have access to such luxuries.

Clearly, little Elfgifu wasn't familiar with the concept of total immersion in hot water. She stared wide-eyed at the wooden tubs, her dark eyes following the twining path of the steam as it rose to the rafters.

"No need to be afraid, little one," rumbled Eadwig. His deep voice and large frame belied his innate gentleness, Alwyn knew. Elfgifu shrank back, ducking behind her father. "It's just God's own water and the abbey's soap. Come on, then, there's a good girl!"

There had always been problems when dealing with women in the abbey. Most of the time, the brothers and the temptations of the outside world were kept well enough apart. Part of the symbolism of Day of the Poor was the active washing of the poor by the brethren, as Mary Magdalene had washed the feet of Christ. Obviously, though, a monk bathing a woman's naked body—Alwyn blushed at the thought—was asking for trouble. Tradition was that the children and the men were bathed by the monks, while the woman came in alone, afterward, to make their ablutions in private.

Elfgifu was now fully behind her father, and didn't know Brother Eadwig well enough to see the lamb hiding beneath the visage of the bear. When he reached out a big, meaty hand to her, she shrank back even farther. Eadwig turned red, but didn't let his hurt show. Instead, he glanced at Alwyn.

"Brother Alwyn . . . perhaps you could help me."

"Come, now, Elfa," said Alwyn in a soothing voice. With his soft brown curls and gentle face, he knew he didn't pose a threat to anyone. Certainly not to this little girl who had been so impertinent to him before. "The hot water will feel good after the cold snow, and your clothes will smell sweet when—"

"What's wrong with your arm? It's just flopping around," she said, pointing.

Shame crashed over Alwyn. Out of the corner of his eye he saw Eadwig watching him with pity before glancing away, as embarrassed as he.

"I was born this way," he said, trying to keep his voice soft, trying not to let his mortification show.

Elfgifu stepped back to hide again behind her father. Her face peeked out at Alwyn, and her eyes were fastened on his arm. "It's like Aldulf's arm," she said softly.

"No, Elfa, it's different. Brother Alwyn is fine." Her father explained, "My brother's arm went dead before a fit took him. He died when Elfa was alone in the room with him. Your arm—forgive me, Brother, but it reminds her—"

"It's like Aldulf," she repeated, more loudly. "Papa, take me away from here!"

"Elfa—" Alwyn stepped forward and reached out his good hand reassuringly. Elfgifu screamed.

"Don't touch me! *Don't touch me with your dead hand!*"

Don't touch me, you crippled monster. I wish you'd never been born. The voice from his childhood was as loud, as clear, as if his mother were again screaming at him. Alwyn stood, shocked into silence.

Elfgifu's panic was like a wildfire, startling the other children and alarming even the adults. Alwyn shut his eyes briefly. He couldn't breathe. He glanced at Eadwig, finding his voice with difficulty.

"I'll go find Abbot Bede and see if there's anything else he—"

"A good idea, Brother. I thank you for your help."

Alwyn had to force himself to walk quietly out of the bath-house. He wanted to run, to hide himself and his grotesqueness in the dormitory, or else sit in the scriptorium for the rest of the day and write furiously, to prove that he had one good hand, that he was of some use. Instead, he grasped his wooden cross and prayed for calmness.

That prayer wasn't answered.

Somehow, Alwyn got through the rest of the day. He helped with the serving of food, with the washing of clothes. He didn't see Elfgifu or her family again, and wondered if they had been so repelled by him that they had gone back to Chesbury rather than risk encountering him a second time.

The prayers were empty, all form and no substance. They didn't reach his heart as they normally did. He felt as dead as

Elfgifu had proclaimed his arm, save for the awful ache in the middle of his gut when he recalled the incident.

At last, the eternal Day of the Poor drew to a close. Alwyn made it through compline, and spoke to no one as they headed back toward the dormitory.

The brothers, thirty-two of them all told, slept together in the large dormitory. Each had a simple pallet and blankets, little more, but that was all that was necessary. Alwyn all but flung himself on the straw pallet, then leaned over to blow out the lamp.

Sweet Jesu, but he was exhausted. It was not the good, honest exhaustion that came with a hard day's work successfully completed, but a weariness of the spirit that gripped him. He was crippled. He was an outcast. His brethren might be kind and turn a blind eye to his deformity, but truth lay in the unbridled tongue of a young ceorl's daughter who spoke what others thought but did not say.

Alwyn lay awake long after the rumblings and snortings of the others could be heard. He listened as Brother Ceolraed walked quietly between the rows of pallets, discreetly checking to make sure none of the brothers were engaged in the sin of onanism. Alwyn rolled over and prayed for the oblivion of sleep.

It came, after a time. It seemed he had only just fallen asleep when he awoke to someone gently shaking him.

"Alwyn," came a soft whisper. "Arise."

There were always some lights left burning in the dormitory, but the illumination was insufficient for Alwyn to recognize who sat beside him on the pallet.

"What is it?" he murmured, knuckling the sleep out of his eyes and easing upward to a sitting position.

"You have a task," said the other monk.

Alwyn blinked. He didn't know this face or this voice. "Who are you?"

"My name is Michael."

Michael was dressed in the same garb as Alwyn—a simple robe and cowl. He was tonsured. Definitely a monk, but no one from St. Aidan's.

"What is wrong? Are you visiting? Why—"

The strange monk raised a finger to his lips. In the sign language that Alwyn, and indeed all the Benedictines, knew so well, he gestured *Follow me*.

Confused but obedient, Alwyn rose. Everyone was fast asleep—everyone but the diligent Brother Ceolraed, who sat in his bed reading Scripture. As Alwyn watched, Ceolraed lifted his head and glanced around. He stared straight at Alwyn and Michael, then returned to his reading.

Alwyn frowned. "He should have stopped us, asked us—"

More insistently, Michael made the gesture. *Follow me.*

Fully awake now, Alwyn followed as the monk led him out of the dormitory. Alwyn glanced at the composed faces of his brethren as he passed them on their pallets, and his heart began to beat faster. Something was happening. He wasn't sure what, or even if it was good or bad, but the hairs on the back of his neck prickled.

Michael opened the door, lifting the heavy latch as if it weighed nothing at all, and stepped outside. The night was clear and cold. The almost full moon made the snow luminous, and the stars sparkled, icy gems against an inky sky. Michael strode out and turned his face up to the night sky. He smiled.

"Who are you?" whispered Alwyn, his throat tight.

Michael lowered his head, and regarded Alwyn evenly. A slight smile played about his full lips.

"You know me. I am Michael, Alwyn."

It was no more information than the monk had revealed before, but suddenly Alwyn paled. Comprehension dawned, and with it came a swift, violent denial.

"No," he protested, backing a step away and raising his arm as if to push the other monk away. "No. . . ."

Michael continued to smile. He lifted an arm and pointed back toward the dormitory.

There was only one set of footprints in the snow.

"You . . . you are a monk, aren't you, sent by another abbey. . . ." Alwyn's voice sounded hollow in his own ears.

"You know, Alwyn." Though the voice remained soft, the statement was firm, and brooked no disagreement. Slowly, Alwyn nodded. He did know, though he was terrified by the knowledge. He flung himself at Michael's feet, reaching to touch the hem of the brown robe with a hand that shook.

At once, he felt a gentle hand on his shoulder. "Rise, Alwyn of St. Aidan's! Rise, and face me, for I am not your God, that you should kneel before me."

Alwyn hastened to his feet. Joy and an awful fear filled him as he waited breathlessly for Michael's next words.

"You have been chosen, from among all of the Lord's faithful, for the most important task of this age—perhaps of any age. Seven months ago, Bishop Wulfstan spoke with you. He voiced his fears that Satan and his Antichrist would soon come, would walk the earth as men do." His face was grave. "The good bishop was right. Satan has appeared on the Earth, and his tool the Antichrist as well."

Unaware that he did so, Alwyn crossed himself. "God protect us," he whispered. "Then—the Day of Judgment is upon us!"

"No," said Michael. "That blessed time has not yet come. Satan is playing a dangerous game—one he may well win, if he is not stopped in time. He is putting the prophecies of the Apocalypse revealed to Saint John into motion now, before their appointed hour. He knows that I cannot cast him into the abyss a second time until the true time of the Day of Reckoning; nor will God or Christ enter the fray until such time. By this means, Satan hopes to cheat mankind out of redemption—he hopes to rule the world forever."

"But . . . how can that be possible?"

Michael looked troubled. "Lucifer was once the brightest of all the angels. Like all archangels, he had free will. He is battling not just against God and mankind, but against destiny itself. Once, I would have said it could not be done. But Lucifer is strong and intelligent. He may have found a way to trick all of us. If he succeeds in fulfilling the prophecies by the end of this year, on the first day of January in the year one thousand, he will have won. The world will fall utterly to him. He is using the fear and fanaticism generated by those mortals who believe that the world will end this year. Their reckoning of time is incorrect, but the power of their terror—this is the fuel upon which Lucifer's fire for revenge feeds."

Now Michael smiled, and placed a light hand on Alwyn's thin shoulder. "God and the angels may not fight in this battle. Only men can. Alwyn, I charge you in the name of the Lord our God: you must fight Satan and his Antichrist. You must stop them from succeeding in this evil challenge of theirs. If even one of the prophecies is left unfulfilled, then Satan's game is over. He will be defeated—delayed just long enough that he can no longer use the people's terror as fuel. Judgment Day will come at its true and proper hour, not before. Man will have a second chance."

"But . . . why me, Michael? I am but a humble monk—"

"Whose faith is strong."

"My arm—" He thought of the echoes of voices from his childhood, of the terror writ plain on a little girl's lean, pinched face. "I am not a whole man! There are others, sound in body and—"

"It is not body, but spirit and soul, that will conquer the Final Enemy. And in that, you are stronger than Samson, even though you may doubt it yourself. God knows." The angel's voice was gentle, but his mien showed no mercy.

Desperately, Alwyn cried, "I cannot do this without help!"

"That is why you shall have aid," answered Michael. "God has given you gifts with which to accomplish your tasks. Behold!" And suddenly there appeared in Michael's right palm a gold ring. In his left, he held a shepherd's staff.

"Here is the Ring of Solomon. Solomon knew to listen to the beasts, and understood their ways. As it is written in the book of Job, 'Ask now the beasts, and they shall teach thee; and the fowls of the air, and they shall tell thee.' From even the lowliest beast comes wisdom. And this is the Rod of Aaron, with which Moses worked so many of God's miracles. I give them to you."

Alwyn shrank back. "I cannot! I am but one man—"

"You shall not be alone. From the North, one will come who is wise and brave. This Second Witness shall also be gifted. Together, if your hearts and wits do not fail you, you shall triumph. The Antichrist shall be defeated, and Satan, his puppeteer, shall return to the abyss. Come, Alwyn. Take the gifts. Take up the task."

Alwyn couldn't move. Michael regarded him steadily, then sighed. "You cannot refuse what God has charged you with. In time, you will see. A final word of advice—do not let the lamp of faith become extinguished!" He raised a hand. "Blessings upon you. I shall pray for you."

Then Alwyn was alone.

The cold fairly attacked him, and he began to shiver. He hadn't felt the wintry bite at all in Michael's presence. He stared at the staff and the ring. The latter gleamed in the moon's light.

Alwyn reached to touch them. They felt solid. A wind rose

and sliced through his thick woolen garb. Not a dream, then. At least, not a dream like any he had ever had before.

Perhaps it wasn't Michael who had come. Perhaps it had been Satan himself, trying to tempt Alwyn into thinking of himself as someone of importance. Such trickery had been cited in Scripture. Everyone knew that the Adversary could assume the appearance of an angel if he chose.

Alwyn shook his head. Why would Satan try to get Alwyn to stop him? Unless the whole thing was a lie, but that didn't ring true. Michael had echoed what Wulfstan had feared, and there was a certainty in Alwyn's heart that he couldn't explain except as *knowing*. He closed his eyes, remembering the joy that had flowed through him, the soul-shaking sense of awe.

He couldn't deny the truth of what had just happened, no matter how he tried.

But he could refuse.

He picked up the ring and then the staff, pressing the ring into his palm. He turned and ran as fast as the deep snow would permit. Past the cloister area, past the shops where the artisans toiled, making goods for the abbey, toward the barn. Gasping, he stumbled to a stop just outside the wooden building. He shoved the rod under his left arm, and with his right, he hurled the ring as far as he could. It would lie buried in the snow, unknown and unwanted.

Now Alwyn wrestled with the barn door. The warm, earthy smell of animals and hay wafted out as the door yielded to his tug. The very simplicity of the scent steadied him somewhat. He pulled the door as wide as it would go, letting in moonlight by which to see.

Something brushed his ankle. Startled, he jerked away, then laughed at himself. It was only Rowena. When autumn came, the small white cat moved her hunting range from the garden to the warmer barn. She still caught enough mice that the abbey didn't begrudge her a warm place in which to sleep.

A little white ghost in the moonlight, she looked up at him and mewed. "Hello, Rowena," he said. "No time to play with you now, I'm afraid."

Purposefully, he stepped over the cat and made his way to the end of the barn. As he passed the donkeys and cows, he heard them moving about quietly, felt their warmth. It was dark back here, but he had just enough light to do what he had come to do.

Michael was wrong. He'd never heard of an archangel being wrong, but this time, Michael was. That's all there was to it. Michael had made a great mistake. Alwyn wasn't the one for this awesome duty. Some other monk, stronger and braver and much more clever. Perhaps Wulfstan himself. He had thrown the Ring of Solomon into the snow, and now he buried the Rod of Aaron deep in the pile of straw. Soon enough, Michael would realize his error, and recover the holy artifacts.

There. Alwyn stumbled back toward the rectangle of moonlight that flooded through the open door. He glanced down at himself. He was covered with seeds and bits of straw. Muttering darkly, he brushed at his robes.

Wondering how he would be able to sneak back into the dormitory unnoticed, he lifted his head—and gasped. Before him, as if he had carefully placed them on the hard-packed earth, lay the glittering gold ring and the staff. Rowena rose, padded over to the relics, and sniffed. She reached out a dainty forepaw and began batting the ring about.

He couldn't refuse. Even though he wanted to with all his heart, Alwyn saw now that he could never rid himself of this divinely ordained duty.

His stomach clenched. "This can't be," he said, even as he moved forward slowly and touched the rod, fingered the ring. "It can't."

Alwyn picked up the ring and examined it. It was a simple gold circle adorned with a five-pointed star. By working his fingers carefully, he was able to maneuver the ring onto his good hand. He stared at it, enraptured.

"Well," said Rowena in the huskiest, softest female voice Alwyn had ever heard, "It's about time."

6

He had once been a man, but now was a monster.

Once, men had deemed him a good companion, and women had smiled when his gaze fell upon them. Now, man and woman alike fled in horror from the giant Wyrm that haunted the hills.

The Wyrm reflected bitterly on his fate. The old woman who had lusted after him was no elderly matron with a healthy desire for young male flesh. She was ancient and withered, and used her knowledge of herbs for harm, not healing. He'd heard her gloat about such things. When she came to him one night in his bed, he had leaped up in horror. Lived there a man who would not have done so?

"I curse thee," she had snarled, lying on the hard earth where his sudden movement had tossed her. "Thou shalt long for a gentle caress from any hand, yea, even mine, ere this new moon waxes and wanes. And never shall ye be free, till the one most beautiful lays loving hands on the one most ugly."

She had been partially right. By the time the waxing moon had turned its pale face away from the world for a while, he was no longer human. He had become a monster, and there was no one, not here, not in the whole wide world, who would touch him with loving hands.

But he was not so desperate that he longed for the crone's dry touch.

Long were the days and nights the Wyrm endured. One night, when the moon was high and the stars danced in a black, black sky, he thought he heard music.

Impossible . . . wasn't it? He was out in the wilds, far from any village. And yet music it most certainly was, haunting and achingly sweet. The Wyrm wept for the beauty of the song. Soon, he could see who made such unearthly music.

Two dozen and more they were, dancing merrily across the wild landscape. Flutes and horns, lyres and harps, drums and bells announced the arrival of beings who could be none other than the Seelie Court. Not fragile and tiny were they, not these denizens of Faerie. Bold and colorful and beautiful, like the sun is beautiful though dazzling to behold. The tales spoke of how these Folk were kinder than their mischievous brethren, bearing no malice toward those of mortal blood.

He could not help himself. His slitted eyes fastened on the dancing figures as he undulated his great, ugly body in their direction.

The music stopped when they saw him. Silently, they stared, their radiant faces reflecting distaste and dislike. His heart quailed inside him.

"I see thee," came a voice soft as the wind in the trees. "I know thee. Come."

It was the queen herself who called him, and he came, hope flickering deep inside. She was the moon and stars incarnate, or so it seemed to his eyes, all white and silver and gleaming. Her hair was the hue of spun gold, her eyes deep as dreams.

"No willing friend to evil art thou," she continued. "Come to me, thou poor creature."

Slowly, he came, and laid his monstrous head in her lap. He closed his eyes as he felt a touch silken as a cobweb upon his brow. Gently, she stroked his scaly head, and a deep shudder passed through him as he felt the caring in her touch.

"I love thy goodness, I love thy patience, I love thy courage." A light kiss upon his cheek. "Be healed."

It was the sun that woke him—the sun upon pale, human flesh. He had been cursed by one who was selfish and unkind, and healed by the most beautiful of all, who saw the man inside the monster.

The Village of Gleannsidh
November 21, 999

"It's too early!" screamed Mairead, writhing on the woolen blankets. Sweat shone on her brow and her hands clenched into fists, as if she could physically beat Fate into submission. "Mother Brihid, no, it's too early. . . ."

Kennag said nothing. It was most certainly too early—months too early for this baby to be coming into the world. She did not expect it to be alive, or if by some uncanny circumstances it was, it couldn't possibly live more than a few moments outside the womb. Partially unformed, it would be a monster, not a human baby.

"Kennag"—her mother turned her strained face toward her daughter—"Kennag, you know things. You can do things. Stop it. Stop the birth."

"Mama, I can't," said Kennag. She kept her voice soft, kept the mask of concern on her face. Beneath it, she gloated. This child should never have been conceived. It was only right that it not survive. Still, she was sorry for the heartache this was causing her mother.

Mairead flopped back on the bed. She began to cry, silently. Tears added their sheen to her sweat-slicked face. The light from the fire and candles caught the gleam and turned it orange.

Morag, thin and pale, her thick black hair tied in a braid similar to Kennag's, said nothing as she pulled the steaming cauldron from the fire. She ladled the contents into a bowl and added cold water from the pitcher, then carried the steaming, fragrant liquid to Kennag. Kennag had mixed herbs with the boiling water, for the magic they imparted. She would not have anyone saying the death of this babe was on her hands, that she hadn't done everything she could have as midwife.

Outside, the storm raged. Kennag shivered as a particularly harsh gust screamed past the small cottage. "Keep the fire stoked," she told Morag. The girl nodded and began gathering up fuel.

Mairead groaned, a deep, low sound of pain. Quickly, Kennag laved her hands. She closed her eyes and said a quick, perfunctory prayer to Brihid, the Great Mother, then went to attend her own mother. Carefully, she pushed Mairead's legs up so that the heels were close to the buttocks. Mairead whimpered at this gentle ministration.

"Morag," Kennag called to her assistant, "bring me some light." She moved the covering back, and as Morag arrived with a small oil lamp, Kennag examined the area. With as gentle a touch as she could manage, she palpated Morag's bloated abdomen. Mairead quailed beneath her daughter's touch.

"It's shifted," she said to Morag. "It's coming soon."

Morag nodded, then said in a whisper, "It won't live, will it?"

Kennag wondered how much she should say. Morag had eight children of her own, five boys and three girls. She would have had a ninth but for Kennag's herbs. A ninth child, plus a husband who was injured and could not work the fields as he used, would have meant disaster for Morag and her family. Morag loved her children, but had been able to make the decision to lose the ninth quite calmly. She could take the truth.

"No," Kennag whispered softly. "Not even seven months . . . no, it won't survive." *Only the Faerie Folk carry their children for seven months,* thought Kennag to herself, *and I doubt that the bastard who raped my mother was one of them.*

Morag lowered her eyes. Mairead broke the stillness with a great, long scream of pain. Wordlessly, Morag went to get the biting stick.

"Here, Mairead," said Morag gently. "Put this in your mouth. It will ease the pain."

Mairead glanced at the younger woman with red-rimmed, exhausted eyes. She had borne children. She knew what the stick was truly for—to keep her from screaming and distracting the midwife. But she opened her mouth nonetheless.

"Morag, come back," ordered Kennag crisply, "I need the light!" At once Morag returned. The flame from the lamp showed Kennag what she needed to know, and further gentle exploration with her fingers confirmed it. Mairead's water had broken, soaking the blankets beneath her, and the passageway was distended.

Mairead tensed. "Push," said Kennag. "Push, Mother!"

With a groan muffled by the biting stick, Mairead pushed.

"Again!"

And again, Mairead strained. "I can see the head," said Kennag. "It's coming. Keep pushing, Mother."

Bit by bit, the bloody thing that was Mairead's child slipped into the world. Morag caught it in a clean blanket, then rushed to the fireside to bathe it in the scented water.

"Kennag. . . ."

"What, Morag?" Holding her hands carefully so that none of the birth blood dripped, Kennag went to Morag's side. The young woman's voice had an odd, strained, yet strangely flat tone to it, and when Kennag approached her, Morag lifted the babe.

Frail it was, too thin, too fragile. But it was no monster. It was clearly a babe, with the right numbers of fingers and toes, and a large, swollen head and belly. Just below the trailing length of the cord of life was a tiny male organ. For a moment the child squirmed, blind as a worm. Then, as Morag wiped the small mouth, it opened and a lusty wail filled the small room.

"It's alive," said Morag. "It's whole, Kennag! It's a miracle!"

"My baby!" Mairead sobbed happily. "My baby. . . ."

Kennag said nothing, only stared dumbly at the mewling little being.

You were over two moons early! she shrieked silently at the baby. *You shouldn't be alive! You shouldn't be whole! So many are dead, so many gone at the hands of your father and all those like him . . . so many suffered . . . what right do you have to be alive?*

Morag, misinterpreting Kennag's stunned silence as joy, looked up at her with eyes that shone with unshed tears. "In the midst of all this pain," she said, her voice thick, "here is a little joy!"

Not Morag. Not pale, washed-out, used-up Morag, too. Couldn't she see what this baby represented? The kind of dreadful, best-forgotten torment it recalled?

"My baby," breathed Mairead. She reached limp arms out toward them. "It is all right? Did it—is it a boy or a girl?"

"It's a boy, Mairead," replied Morag as Kennag stayed mute. "A fine baby boy, and whole, beyond all reason. Kennag. . . ." Morag held out the baby to her.

Kennag accepted her little brother, bathed it clean of the bloody afterbirth, and cut the cord with the knife specially consecrated for the task. He seemed to grow more lively by the minute, turning his head this way and that. His mouth moved. He wanted to suckle. He wanted to take in the milk of life, to grow, to become a man like his father. Kennag looked again at the miniature maleness, the blue eyes, and the wisps of yellow hair.

A man like his father.

How easy it would be to kill it, here and now. Snap its little neck. Smother it with the swaddling cloth. Morag and Mairead wouldn't see, wouldn't even know. It would never grow up, never become a man, never hold a woman down while she struggled and—

"Here," said Kennag, rising and giving the babe to its mother. "He's hungry."

She wanted to slap her mother for the soft, dewy look that suddenly spread across Mairead's lined face. "Oh, come, little one," breathed Mairead, accepting the baby and moving his small head to her swollen nipple. "There, that's the good boy," she cooed as he began to nurse. "My baby. My little miracle boy. Oh, Kennag, he looks just like you did. . . ."

Kennag swallowed bile. To be compared to . . . that. . . .

Her mouth set in a grim line, she finished her duty as midwife by bathing Mairead's body with a warm, damp cloth. With Morag's assistance, they placed a clean undergown on her and brushed her hair.

"Rest, now," Kennag advised her mother. "You're going to need it."

"You're going?" Mairead frowned. "It's such a bitter night out—"

"The storm's over. I don't live that far away."

"But I thought certainly you'd be staying."

"Morag can stay with you." She glanced at the younger woman, who nodded. Morag, Kennag was certain, would be glad of a night away from her children and husband. "I'll be getting home." She placed a quick kiss on her mother's brow, but couldn't summon any gesture of affection, not even false, for the infant who lay sleeping in his mother's arms.

Before Mairead could protest further, Kennag had bundled herself in her thick, fur-trimmed woolen cloak, and was out the door.

The wind felt as though it were about to slice her in two. Although it had stopped snowing, the walk home, short in distance, would be long in duration. Kennag was grateful for her high boots and warm clothing. She glanced at the clear night sky with only a few lingering gray clouds. With a sigh, she pulled the cloak tighter to shield her face, and set forth.

The snow was almost up to her knees. At any other birth, at

any other time, she would have stayed and been grateful for the hospitality. But she would far rather wade through the drifts and be chilled to the bone than spend another moment with her mother's child. She could not bring herself to think of the baby as her brother.

The snow squeaked and sparkled as she trudged past the cottages and into the grassy hills that stretched between this part of Gleannsidh and the next. She paused to catch her breath, warm with exertion despite the best efforts of the frigid night. Small white puffs rose from her lips.

From somewhere, a clear, sweet note rose and faded.

Kennag stood still, holding her breath and straining to listen. A bird, perhaps? So clear and pure was the sound. . . .

Again it came, trilled, and faded. Then suddenly it was joined by other music that couldn't be dismissed as birdcalls. Kennag knew the sounds of pipe and harp when she heard them. During one of the holy days, she'd expect to hear the sound of merrymaking through the night, but tonight . . . ?

Fear prickled through her. Kennag's first thought, illogical though it was, was that another raiding party of Danes was afoot. But no, it was the depth of winter now, and their music was the sound of battle cries and the thud of axes on flesh, not this fragile yet wild melody.

She blinked, and rubbed her eyes. It seemed, somehow, that it was getting lighter. But that couldn't be. The moon had passed its high point, and. . . .

It was definitely lighter. Not with the moon's radiance, but with a warm glow that spread over the snow and turned it orange and rose.

Whatever—whoever—was making music and light was just beyond that hillock.

Run.

She knew who it had to be. Every cautionary warning uttered by her mother and father, every haunting song that was sung at Lammas, every tale told on a quiet evening of spinning was laden with instructions on what to do should one find oneself in just such a situation. The Good People—one never called them by their true names, that would be an insult—were tricky folk. They were fair and beautiful, but hollow and empty, living off of the real lives of mortals in their realm of illusions. Even the Seelie

Court, the kindest and brightest of the Good People, could be dangerous. Others, best not named at all, could be deadly.

Slowly, Kennag lifted a foot, brought it down. Like one in a daze, she moved toward the sound of the flutes and harps. She rounded the hillock—

The side of the hill was open, as if there had been a secret door there all along. Light poured forth, and inside, Kennag could just make out figures dancing. The music was louder now, and seemed to chase away the cold of the night. As if someone were pulling her forward, Kennag went to the Faerie mound.

Gleannsidh. Glen of the Faeries. And I thought it was just a pretty name. . . .

She could still leave. She could turn and flee back to her cold but safe cottage, and wake in the morning to—what? What was there in this village worth waking to? Bran, sweet lover with the hands of gentle strength and soul to match, was gone—enslaved or dead. Her mother had turned into a traitor, with her cooing love for a rapist's baby. Kennag couldn't count the number of hours that she had lain alone in her bed, aching inside for want of tears, unable to find even that small comfort.

Sooner or later, another priest would come to Gleannsidh. He would forbid her to practice her "devil's arts," perhaps even punish her. Even her gifts of healing would be taken away from her.

Why stay?

Why *not* enter into the Faerie knoll, and drink magical wines and eat enchanted food, and dance, and make music, and forget? Even an illusion of happiness would be better than this gray life of simply enduring every passing day.

Kennag stepped inside.

It was spring.

Her nostrils were teased by the heady scents of flowers in bloom. She blinked, letting her eyes grow accustomed to the light, and as she looked around, she realized that nothing here was like anything in the world she knew—and yet it was all immediately recognizable.

The grass beneath her boots was a deep, rich blue-green, thick and soft. Trees reached skyward (*skyward? Inside a knoll?*), silver trees with golden leaves and fruit of every shade and shape. The flowers Kennag smelled were nothing like the humble thistles, roses, or heather of her native land. Every color she had ever seen, and some she hadn't even dreamed of, burst forth. The music that had lured her here continued, but underneath it, Kennag caught the laughter of a rippling stream, out of sight but not out of hearing.

Nowhere, yet, were the denizens of this place.

"Hello?" she called. Kennag's voice sounded thin and strained to her ears. Her heart thudded in her chest, and her knees felt weak. Though she would deny it, she was frightened. She stuck out her chin to keep her lips from trembling.

"I heard your music, Good People!" she called again, louder this time.

The music continued.

Right by her ear, she heard a soft voice: "Welcome, Kennag nic Beathag, of the village of Gleannsidh. We have been expecting you."

Kennag gasped and stumbled backward, clumsy in her thick cloak and heavy boots. Beside her, towering over her by nearly a full foot—and she was no small woman—was the handsomest man she had ever seen. No, handsome wasn't the word. He was . . . beautiful.

Black as midnight was his hair. Raven-dark brows arched over eyes that were the color of the ocean—ever-changing. The full mouth was smiling, and the hand he held out to her looked strong as Bran's, though without the smith's calluses. Rings adorned the fingers, and glinted in the—sunlight? Could there be a sun here?

Her mouth dry, she extended trembling fingers and took the hand of the Faerie king—for so she knew him to be by the golden circlet upon his dark hair.

"Welcome," he said again, "to Tir na N'Oldathanna."

"Land of All Colors," repeated Kennag softly, tearing her gaze away from the king's, again awed by the riot of hues and colors in this secret world. "I never knew just how. . . ." She couldn't complete the sentence.

"This is a safe place," the king assured her, drawing her arm through his. Dazed, Kennag dimly noted that his garments were as splendid as the man—being?—who wore them. All silver and gold—no, they were blue and purple, like twilight—no, wait, they were—

He laughed softly. "Do not try to pin them down," he chided. "Things here are beautiful. That is the only certainty they offer. They will strike your eyes the way they choose, and to try to identify them with your Land of Shadows eyes will only make them change the more."

Overcome, Kennag nodded. She licked dry lips, searching for something to say. She found it. "You were expecting me?" There was something ominous about that, and it jolted her out of her almost sleepy daze into a sudden alertness.

The beauty of the king blurred and shifted, resolidifying into the face of another man equally handsome, but with earth-brown eyes and golden hair. His voice, though, remained the same—calm and smooth.

"We were. Your coming was known to us. We grieve for the pain that you have endured, but had you not suffered so, we would never have realized how great of heart you are."

Kennag was now confused as well as frightened, and she stopped in her tracks. Carefully, hoping not to offend, she pulled her arm from the king's. "What do you mean?"

"Look there," said the king, not answering her. "Here comes my lady—and with her is a friend of yours."

Kennag looked where the king pointed. Over the crest of the hill came a woman his match in beauty. Golden hair and silver clothes, eyes that were bright and warm, lips that were red and so inviting that Kennag felt as drawn to the queen of the Land of All Colors as to its king. Beside the queen of Faerie walked a woman of indeterminate age. She looked very young, almost childlike, at one moment, then her face seemed filled with ancient wisdom. Her black hair tumbled about her slim frame, falling to her ankles. Her feet were bare. While the king and queen seemed to prefer to appear in garb similar to Kennag's, this being's clothes were gossamer-frail. As the two women drew closer, Kennag saw that the girl's black hair—indeed, her whole body—was wet.

They halted a few feet away. Recovering some sense of decorum, Kennag managed a nod of greeting. She opened her mouth, but before she could say anything, the girl-woman had flung her arms about the mortal. She was indeed soaking wet, but somehow the wetness felt good, comforting—not clammy or cold. Tentatively, not knowing what she did, Kennag raised her arms to embrace the girl in return.

At last, the other drew away. "I am Eireth," she said. Her voice was husky, lush in the way that water tumbling over stones is lush. "I am the spirit of Gleannsidh's well."

"Wh-what?"

"I am the spirit of the well," repeated Eireth placidly. "You asked me to keep you safe that night when you hid in my depths. I did, and while you were there, I learned about you. I learned that you are brave and clever, and that you are not one to give in easily. I felt your agony, your shame, and I grieved for you. And when we learned that we needed a champion, I knew whom we should summon."

"I—don't understand." Suddenly Kennag was on the soft grass, her legs having chosen not to support her any longer. At once, her Faerie companions sat beside her.

"Drink this," said the queen, handing Kennag a jeweled goblet. Kennag knew that once one partook of Faerie food, one might find oneself bound forever.

That didn't seem like such a bad thing. She drank thirstily. It was the sweetest honey wine she had ever had, and by the time she had drained the cup, she felt much better. Colors seemed to solidify, and the faces didn't change anymore. Kennag felt calmer and more alert. With a smile of thanks, she handed the cup back to the queen. She felt Eireth's small, cool hand steal into hers, and didn't mind at all.

"Let me start at the beginning," said the king.

"That would be a good idea," said Kennag, the wine making her bold.

"We live in Tir na N'Oldathanna, the Land of Many Colors. You live in Tir na Sca'thanna, what we call the Land of Shadows. When it is winter in your world, it is summer in ours, and when it is autumn here, you know spring. There can be no shadow without substance; and substance must have shadow. These worlds cannot exist separately.

"Now, we have learned that there is a grave threat to the Land of Shadows. Evil walks there, and plans to pervert and destroy your world. We will feel the repercussions from this, and cannot permit it to happen. We need a Shadow champion, someone who will fight this evil, and prevent Tir na Sca'thanna from being destroyed. In this way, our world will continue to live. Do you understand?"

Kennag wasn't certain, but she nodded anyway and wished there was more to drink.

"You have the courage, and the intelligence, to be our champion. You have the strength to overcome your own pain, heal the broken parts within you that keep you from knowing your true power. You must fight the evil that threatens your world, Kennag nic Beathag, and the evil that lies in your heart—and in so doing, save not only your world but ours as well."

For just a moment, Kennag flamed with mortification. They knew about her rape, about her abortion, and about the hatred she bore toward her—her mother's child. And yet they thought her worthy.

"Me? You want me to do this? By Brihid's flames, why?"

"Because," interjected Eireth, "we know your heart. Do not fear. You will not be alone in this task."

"There is another," said the queen. "You will find your partner to the south of your lands, in the place called Wessex."

"I've never heard of Wessex. It must be very far away indeed."

"We will give you a steed worthy of the journey," replied the king. "And other gifts as well. Do you accept? Will you fight, and save two worlds and all the souls that dwell within them?"

Kennag hesitated. She didn't dare look at the inhumanly fair faces around her. She looked inward, to her heart, and found only emptiness and anguish. She could live with it no longer. Better to accept this task. A purpose could fill that awful emptiness with activity, at least, if not anything more substantial.

"I accept," she said quietly.

"We knew you would not fail us," said the king warmly. "And we will help you where we can." He placed long fingers against her temple. "I grant you the gift of the Second Sight." Kennag gasped, but did not move away. A double-edged sword, to be sure, was that gift. "You will be able to see the future, and know things that most mortals do not ken. This is the gift of the king."

"Close your eyes, Kennag," commanded Eireth. Kennag did so. She felt gentle fingers touching her closed lids, her lips, her ears. "This ointment will let you see, hear, and speak with anything not of the mortal world. Listen to their advice, when it is given freely. Such is the gift of Eireth."

"And my gift," said the queen, smiling as Kennag opened her eyes, "is this steed." She was on her feet now, standing beside the most beautiful horse it had ever been Kennag's good fortune to behold. It was a mare, creamy white as the moon, with a mane and tail as gold as the sun. Clean-limbed and fiery, it tossed its head and whinnied, fixing Kennag with dark eyes that were infinitely more intelligent than any that graced a mortal mare's head.

"Her name is—" The mare suddenly pawed the grass and whinnied furiously. "Her name shall be what you wish to call her," said the queen. "She shall bear you where you need to go."

"Time is short, even here," said the king, a note of sorrow creeping into his voice. "Forty of your days are left before it will be too late."

"But—" Kennag got to her feet. The mare pranced over to her and rubbed her soft muzzle against Kennag's neck. Distractedly, Kennag petted the luxuriously smooth coat. "Where do I go? Who is this other that you spoke of? Who is my enemy?"

Already, the world of the Good People was fading around her. The horse moved with purpose toward the entrance. Wildly, Kennag tried to keep up. It loomed before her, the snow gleaming white against the blackness of shadows and sky. She looked back over her shoulder, crying out her questions. The shapes of the king, queen, and Eireth could hardly be seen, but she could make out their hands raised in farewell.

The horse leaped through the gateway and Kennag followed. She stumbled and fell facedown in a snowdrift. Sputtering, she clambered to her feet, brushing snow off her cloak. It was so cold after the warmth of the otherworld.

It was then that she realized she did not know this place. Of course—there had to be many doors to Tir na N'Oldathanna, and the Good People had sent her through a different one, no doubt to speed her journey. And yet, the snow was less here, and dawn was coming. What had been only a few moments in the otherworld had been several hours in the Land of Shadows.

If only she knew where she was! She turned to the horse, as if somehow the mare would know. The Faerie horse, as beautiful to her eyes here as it had been in its proper realm, stared fixedly at something. Fear spurted in her, and Kennag whirled.

For a long moment, she couldn't see it. It was as white as the snow, and at first it was motionless. Her eyes, though, were no longer the eyes of a mortal, and gradually she began to make out its shape. Her eyes widened, and one hand crept to her throat. Faeries were one thing, but this . . . !

"Please don't be afraid," said the ghost.

7

Cold it was in Nilfheim, and dark, and would ever be thus. But silent, it was not.

Cries of fear and agony echoed without end through the realm. Sobs and laments provided softer counterpoint. And underneath it all was the sound of the steady chewing, chewing, of the Dragon in his fruitless quest to topple the World Tree.

The Underworld Queen took her meal in solitude at her table, called Hunger by those who feared to be the feast at such a supper. She scraped the last bits of marrow and brain off the plate Famine. Giggling, she abandoned the manners her father the Trickster had taught, and licked the plate clean with a pink tongue. The dimness that so terrified others was her familiar light, and she smiled at the reflection of her face in the bronze mirror of Famine.

The Queen was a beautiful girl. Milk-pale her face, emerald her eyes, fire-red her curls. She smiled. Not even the Cat Goddess, with her renowned beauty, could challenge her.

The smile on full red lips faded.

At least from the waist up.

She touched her face with long fingers—her father's heritage—and traced the line of her swanlike throat. Her breasts were full and firm like ripe young apples, just the right size, not *bloated like a cow's nor small and sad. Her taut belly was a delight to the touch—*

And here was where the ugliness began. Hands warm with life touched cold, dead flesh. Grimacing in disgust at her own lower body, the Queen wiped the rotted flesh off on the tablecloth. The scent appalled even her.

This was why the Allfather had deemed her fit to rule over the dishonored dead—the Queen was half corpse herself. No Valhalla heroes here, just those who had died of ignoble old age or sickness, sickness ofttimes brought on by the Queen's own incursions.

Even her father did not visit, not anymore. She smelled fear when he descended into her icy depths, fire god that he was. His ever-changing eyes darting about, his dazzling smile dimmed in the darkness.

She felt the familiar rage rising within her and yearned for the call to venture once again to Midgard, where the humans, warm and living like half her body, dwelt in the sunlight. She could slay them then, cull their numbers with her rake of catastrophe, or destroy even more with her deadly broom of sickness. Only in hate could she forget the death that clung to her, a death that had not been of her doing.

Silence. The dead had stopped their wailing. The huge black hound who slept at her feet was awake, his red eyes gleaming and dewlaps lifted in the faintest of snarls. The foolish Dragon had ceased to chew on the root of the World Tree. The silence meant someone was coming. She rose on legs that by all rights should not support her, and wondered what old woman would shuffle into her realm, or what frightened man, throat slit by a thief, would—

The Queen gasped. Impossibly, the one who was coming brought light with him. Light, and a sweet scent of flowers that brought warm tears to her eyes. The mighty hound whimpered, softly.

It could not be—yet it was. The Beautiful One of the Asgard gods had come to her domain. He was dead—dishonorably so, else he would be in Valhalla. But how could this be? Everyone loved the Beautiful One. He could never die. All the creatures of all the worlds had sworn never to harm him. . . .

"All but the little mistletoe," came a voice that trembled on the edge of laughter. "They forgot to ask the mistletoe to make his

*promise. And if someone just happened to make a dart of mistle-
toe, and someone just happened to convince the Blind One to toss
it at the unknowing Beautiful One. . . ."*

It was her father, and for the first time, he seemed to be happy
to be in her realm. Not so the Beautiful One. Already his radiance was dimming, and the sorrowful look on his exquisite face
brought a strange feeling into the young Queen's heart.

"He has harmed no one," she told her father, stepping close
to the most beloved, most innocent, most gentle of the Aesir gods.
"He lived only to please, to delight, to—" She struggled against
the peculiar lump in her throat. "To charm the eye and heart.
Even I know this, Father. Even you do. And yet—you murdered
him."

The Trickster's broad smile became a rictus. "Yes," he said,
in a taut voice. "I murdered him."

"Why?" she cried. It was pity. Pity flowed through her at the
sight of this innocent here in this dark, cold place.

The Trickster's voice dropped to a growl. Black eyes flashed
and even she, the Queen of the Underworld, quailed from the
naked hatred in those eyes.

"I murdered him *because* he was beautiful. Because *he*
charmed the eye and heart. Because *he* was so beloved and innocent. Because *he* was all the things that you and I—that they—"

Rage choked him, and she shared it. She understood why her
father had done what he had done. Outcasts, both of them, hated
and despised by the Aesir. And her brother the Wolf and the
mighty Serpent as well—just because they were not so fair or
pleasant—

"Balder, the Beautiful One," she said in a slow, rich voice.
"Welcome to Hel."

And so the Beautiful One, slain by treachery, languished in
the realm of the dishonored dead—until the coming of the end of
the world.

The Abbey of St. Aidan's, Chesbury
November 21, 999

Alwyn started so violently that he stumbled backward and fell.
The wind knocked out of him, he stared at the cat, struggling for
words.

Rowena rose and padded to him, then seated herself beside

his head. Her long white tail flicked, then curled neatly about her paws.

"Oh, get up," she said. "Weren't you listening to the Prince?"

"P-Prince?"

"The Prince of Angels." She nodded in the direction of his right hand. " 'Here is the Ring of Solomon. Solomon knew to listen to the beasts, and understood their ways. From even the lowliest beast comes wisdom.' " She peered at him, the tip of her tail twitching slightly, as if in impatience. "Although"—she arched her back as she rose—"I'm not certain that I like being called the lowliest beast."

"Perhaps," said Alwyn, wondering at the calmness of his voice and the choice of words that issued from his lips, "Michael was not referring directly to you."

She eyed him and seemed pleased. "You get smarter by the minute."

He stared at her, and then, groaning slightly, buried his face in his hand. "If I can understand you," he said wearily, "that means the ring is real. And if the ring is real, then everything else I saw is real, too. Including the duty with which Michael charged me."

Rowena padded over to him and patted his thigh with a gentle paw. "I'd say that sums it up quite nicely. So, what are you going to do?"

He lifted his head and gazed into her odd-colored eyes. "Go back to sleep, I think. Maybe I'll wake up and realize that this was all a dream."

She continued to gaze evenly at him, then, unexpectedly, rubbed her head against his knee. "It is no dream, my friend. There are times when I pity you humans. You live in a world that's so narrow. You can't see the Faeries in the moonlight, or the sad little ghosts, or hear the song of the river. This all must be a dreadful shock for you."

"That," said Alwyn, "is an understatement."

He did return to his pallet, but he did not sleep. Much as he wished to deny what he had seen, he could not. And knowing what he did, he could not shirk the responsibility. But before he could leave St. Aidan's, even on a mission from the Archangel Michael, he needed to obtain permission from his abbot.

He moved through matins like a man half asleep, his mind chewing on what he had witnessed the night before. He knew in his heart that Michael had not been the devil in disguise, but how to convince the prosaic Abbot Bede of this? Where did one begin? Surely his tongue would cleave to the roof of his mouth if he tried to speak of what had transpired, but the Rule was very clear: no monk was to leave the abbey without the express permission of the abbot.

A thought struck him, and he stumbled over his prayers. Brother Eadwig shot him a quick glance. Alwyn cleared his throat and resumed singing.

Where was he to go? His mission was plain—to stop the Antichrist from bringing about a premature Judgment Day. But how did one do that, and where should one go first?

There was only one person who might have answers for him: his old friend Bishop Wulfstan. Wulfstan knew Alwyn, knew that he would never invent such a tale. Besides, it had been Wulfstan who had warned Alwyn of the approaching darkness before he had ever trod out into the snow to be charged by an angel and to hear beasts speak with the tongues of men.

His voice was strong again as he sang, his decision made. He would go to Wulfstan and ask the bishop's advice.

When matins ended, the abbot waved the brethren to him. They stood, surprised and curious at the break in the established routine. Bede looked tired and took a moment to gather himself before he spoke.

"Before matins, I had a visitor—a messenger from Calne who bore dreadful news. Our beloved former abbot, Bishop Wulfstan, has been injured and perhaps lies dying. He requests that you pray for him and for his immortal soul."

Alwyn's mouth opened, but no words came forth. Wulfstan. Had the Enemy already begun acting to thwart Alwyn's mission by attempting to kill the one man he completely trusted? It took a few seconds before the shocked young man realized that Bede had turned and was now speaking directly to him.

"Alwyn, Wulfstan asked for you. Of course I give you leave to go to him at once." The abbot's watery brown eyes were filled with sympathy. "I know how fond you were—are—of Wulfstan. I will pray for his recovery, and for your safe and swift journey to his side."

"Abbot . . . what happened?" Alwyn's voice shook.

Bede shook his tonsured head. "It was a dreadful accident. There was a meeting of the Witan and the floor gave way. Many

are dead, and only a few escaped injury. The king and his chief
adviser, Angelo, were among those lucky few, God be praised."

The king and his chief adviser Angelo. The conversation
Alwyn and Wulfstan had back in April, when the present snow
would have been a welcome break in the heat and drought, now
returned to Alwyn. *Ethelred surrounds himself with his favorites,
the worst being that Roman scoundrel, Angelo. Strange, that one.
So appealing to be around, but there is something about him I
mislike.*

Alwyn began to tremble. He was ashamed that his greatest
fear was not of losing Bishop Wulfstan, but of the forces behind
the accident that would, most likely, claim that good man's life.

Abbot Bede misinterpreted Alwyn's reaction and laid a gentle
hand on the younger man's shoulder. "Go, swiftly. The weather
will not be kind, I fear, but make what speed you can. Stay as
long as the bishop needs you. Then, dear boy"—Bede squeezed
Alwyn's shoulder affectionately—"hasten back to us on wings of
angels."

On wings of angels. Given what he had witnessed in the early
hours of the morning, Alwyn had to wonder just what dreams had
graced the abbot's sleep for him to use such a phrase.

He was on the road before prime. The good brothers had
packed what little Alwyn might need, including several days'
worth of food, and sent him down the main road from the abbey
with their prayers. Scarcely had St. Aidan's disappeared from
view, hidden by the soft fall of snow, than Alwyn heard a rustling
from the bushes at the side of the road. He expected to spy a thin
rabbit or a fox on the prowl, but it was Rowena who emerged.
Looking like the snow itself come to life, she bounded easily into
the saddle. The abbey donkey, an old, tired beast called Balaam,
brayed in startlement. Rowena gazed up at Alwyn expectantly.
He fumbled for the Ring of Solomon and put it on.

"—kill someone by surprising them like that, yes you could,
Rowena, oh, yes, you could, *heee-uh!*" said Balaam.

"Not you, too!" exclaimed Alwyn. Balaam, obviously as surprised as Alwyn, craned his neck to peer at his rider.

"*Heee-uh!* Can you hear me, young fellow?"

Alwyn gulped. It would seem Solomon took advice from all
the animals, not just cats. "Uh, yes, Balaam, I can hear you."

"Lovely, lovely," said Balaam, tossing his head. "Now, I
would like a warmer stall. Mine gets far too cold in the winter.

And the food—well, I've seen what you feed the horses of visitors to the abbey, and my, my, aren't they just so high and mighty, with warm bran and blankets and—"

"Balaam," said Rowena, an edge of warning to her tone, "silence. I have to talk to Brother Alwyn."

The donkey muttered something under his breath and continued to complain, but quietly.

"Rowena, what are you doing here?"

"It seems to me that you could use a companion other than our talkative donkey," said Rowena. Balaam continued to walk, and she patted various places on the saddle, trying to find a comfortable spot. She curled up next to Alwyn and began to knead. "Besides, Wulfstan was kind to me. Most of the brethren would sooner kick a cat than quote a friendly Bible verse."

"It's going to be dangerous," warned Alwyn, oddly glad of her presence.

Rowena glanced up at him with her blue and green eyes. "I'm a *cat*. If things get dangerous, I'll leave." With a rapidity that amazed Alwyn, Rowena closed her eyes and went to sleep. Gently Alwyn tucked a bit of his cloak around her.

Snow fell on them, as silent and white as Rowena. Alwyn fought back apprehension. He had never traveled more than a mile from the abbey since he had come there as a child. He yearned for the comfort of his hard pallet, for the familiar, numbing chill of the scriptorium. Mentally Alwyn reviewed the long road to Calne. It was over a hundred miles from Chesbury. At best, it would take several days before he reached his friend. At worst—

Wulfstan, Alwyn thought as tears sprang to his eyes, *I'm coming. Please don't die.*

Ethelred's Royal Villa, Calne
November 28, 999

The missive from Wulfstan had stated that His Grace was lying at King Ethelred's estate in Calne, along with the others injured in the peculiar accident. The Icknield Way was passable, and Alwyn discovered that the guards posted along the king's highway turned from suspicious to amenable when they saw Wulfstan's mark on the letter.

At one point, the guards insisted on providing an escort the rest of the way to Calne. They offered to stable Balaam and lend Alwyn a horse for the journey. Alwyn declined to leave Balaam behind—he knew, though the guards and the abbot could not, that his journey was only just beginning, and he might not pass this way again—but he accepted the horse. Freed of having to carry a rider or pack, Balaam was able to keep better pace with the swifter horses and riders.

Everyone knew about the accident—gossip travels swiftly among men of action forced to remain inactive—and volunteered his own take on the tragedy. By the time Alwyn, Balaam, and Rowena were escorted by two thegns to the royal residence, the young monk had heard everything from God's visitation of wrath on the devious Witan to a witch's attempt to kill a room full of good men.

On the final leg of the journey, the three men had fallen silent. The hoofbeats of their steeds were muffled, and no one had further words to impart. Alwyn was weary of the hard riding and the nights of dream-troubled sleep. He was close to nodding off when a muffled crash and shower of wet snow startled him thoroughly awake.

Rowena hissed, digging her claws into Alwyn's thigh, and shook herself vigorously. The monk gasped at the shock of pain and cold. He frantically wiped his head and shoulders in an attempt to rid himself of the miniature snowfall before the stuff began to melt, chilling him still further. Glancing up, he saw the instigator of the incident: an enormous red-brown squirrel. The creature perched on the branch and stared intently at Alwyn. Its tufted ears twitched and its tail flicked rapidly. It began to scold them, as if they, not it, had transgressed.

"You've no idea how long I've been looking for you! At Chesbury, first, and then they said you had gone. The Dragon has nothing on those nasty Chesbury squirrels! How rude. No breeding at all. But here you are and—"

"You vile little tree rat!" hissed Rowena. She had gotten soaked, and her fluffy white fur was plastered to her spine. She shivered despite the heat of her words. "I'll have you for dinner, you wicked—"

"Calm down, Rowena!" Alwyn attempted to restrain the feline with his good hand and arm, but Rowena would have none of it. She launched herself into the branches, pricking Alwyn's skin yet again through the thick material of his robe with her hind claws and sending a second shower of snow down on the young man.

By now, Alwyn's escorts were laughing freely. They pointed at Alwyn, leaned over in their saddles to exchange private jests, and laughed harder. Alwyn blushed but tried to ignore them. He kicked his horse and it broke into a trot, as anxious to escape the rain of wet snow as its rider was.

The squirrel had yelped in protest—something about "no ordinary squirrel!"—to which Rowena had replied with a string of earthy insults that mortified Alwyn. They were gone now, hunter and hunted, lost in the dark skeletons of the trees.

"What a lucky monk you are, Brother Alwyn," said the thegn Aelfric, "to have so fierce a little soldier defending you from attack!" His companion, Ulraed, howled with laughter. Alwyn smiled weakly.

"God be praised," he replied, a hint of wryness creeping into his voice. Ulraed and Aelfric seemed surprised at Alwyn's reply, and this time when they laughed, it was with him instead of at him. They paused to let him catch up and ride between them, Balaam tagging along behind, and pressed on. Alwyn didn't like the thought of continuing without Rowena, but he trusted her beast's instincts to find him again once she tired of the chase.

In the meantime, Wulfstan lay dying. Alwyn crossed himself and said a quick prayer that he was not too late.

An hour later, Alwyn stepped inside the main hall of Ethelred's royal residence, shook the snow from his shoulders, and let his eyes adjust to the light of torches and lamps.

"I had thought there would be more injured," he said to Aelfric. There were only a few men being tended here, lying quietly on the floor.

"Aye," Aelfric replied. His beard and mustache were covered with ice, but his eyes flashed heat. "There were. The only one who's left on his own two legs was Archbishop Alphege of Canterbury. Six have died, and they'll be having company soon. Your friend the bishop is over there."

His chest contracting with emotion, Alwyn sprinted to Wulfstan's side. His arm might be useless, but his legs still served him well.

"Wulfstan?"

Like the other injured members of the Witan, the Bishop of London lay on a straw pallet placed on the earthen floor. The braziers in the center of the room did little to heat the hall. The windows, the shutters opened to allow the smoke to escape, also let the cold air in. Wulfstan was all but buried beneath a pile of blankets and furs. He lay still, his eyes closed. Alwyn dropped down beside him and took his hand gently. It was cold.

"Bishop Wulfstan?" His eyes filled with tears. Merciful Jesu, was he too late?

The blue eyes opened. Wulfstan frowned, struggling to focus his gaze. "Alwyn?"

Alwyn grinned. He pressed the bishop's cold, thin hand to his heart and kissed it. "Yes, Your Grace. I'm here. I came the minute I received your summons."

Ulraed and Aelfric had followed Alwyn to the bishop's side. Wulfstan turned his red-rimmed eyes to them and frowned. "No need to haul me out for burial yet. You've brought me the boy, and I am grateful. Now be about your duties."

They bowed their heads and hastened off. Wulfstan tugged on Alwyn's hand, pulling the youth closer. His lips to Alwyn's ear, Wulfstan whispered, "Are we alone?"

Alwyn looked around. A few women were ministering to the needs of the injured, but they were at the far end of the hall. "There are three women tending the wounded, but they cannot hear us. Bishop, I have something—" He paused. How to put it into words? "Something wondrous and terrible to tell you."

"And I have words for you, dear boy. But I see that you are bursting with this news. You may speak first."

Alwyn took a deep breath, gathered his thoughts, and in simple, plain words poured forth the miraculous tale of his last night at the abbey. He held back nothing—not his own fear, or his reluctance to shoulder the burden, or the scalding words of little Rowena. At first, Bishop Wulfstan raised his eyebrows, but as Alwyn continued, he nodded to himself.

Finally, when Alwyn had done, Wulfstan squeezed his hand. "I believe you, boy. I sought you out earlier to warn you of such things. How comforting to know that an archangel and I have the same opinion of—"

A coughing fit took him. His frail body spasmed with the effort, and he cried out. The violent movement had dislodged the concealing furs, and Alwyn now saw that Wulfstan's ribs were bandaged. His hand clamped down on Alwyn's, threatening to break the fragile bones. Alwyn heard a patter of feet as one of the attending women rushed up and now knelt beside Wulfstan.

With more vigor than Alwyn had yet seen him demonstrate, Wulfstan waved her away. He gasped for breath as she reluctantly retreated, glancing from him to Alwyn and back again. Blood and spittle decorated his chin as he finally lay back down, breathing shallowly, eyes squeezed shut and leaking moisture.

"I'll call you if he needs you," Alwyn assured the woman. She gazed at him, pity in her eyes, then rose and slipped away. For a long moment, Alwyn simply sat with his mentor, holding the beloved hand and wishing desperately that he could impart some of his own life to his friend.

The hand squeezed slightly, and Alwyn glanced down at Wulfstan. "You are . . . in danger," breathed the older man. "I will not be here to guide you . . . for much longer." The eyes crinkled a little in a smile. "I see that you have come to the same conclusion."

"Wulfstan . . . ," Alwyn said brokenly.

"No. Listen. Angelo . . . I don't know how, but in some way he is part of this. He is no friend to your quest. You should go . . . before he even learns of your presence here. That was why I wished you to come. I could not warn you by letter. Too many eyes. . . ."

His eyelids drooped. Frightened, Alwyn shook him gently. "Wulfstan! Please, stay with me. Tell me—where do I go? How do I do this thing?"

Through his blurred vision, Alywn saw something small and white and furry perch at the shuttered window for a moment before leaping quietly to the floor. She glanced about, searching the room, then sprinted madly in Alwyn's direction.

"I come with news!" said Rowena. "The idiot squirrel spoke truth. He is no ordinary beast at all. Your ally has come and needs your aid!"

Michael's words floated back to Alwyn. *You shall not be alone. From the North, one will come who is wise and brave. This Second Witness shall also be gifted. Together, if your hearts and wits do not fail you, you shall triumph.*

"It's not the squirrel?" he asked, horrified.

Rowena flattened her ears. "No! Tails and whiskers! The squirrel is but a messenger. The Other waits outside, demanding admittance!"

"The Second Witness!" he breathed. "He's here. He's really here!" For the first time since he left St. Aidan's, Alwyn felt hope rise inside him. Wulfstan had surrendered to unconsciousness, but he was still breathing. Alwyn kissed the bishop's ring and scrambled to his feet. Joy and fear flooded him. Who was this Other? Would he be a warrior, perhaps one of the king's guards? Or a holy man?

He turned and raced toward the door, Rowena at his heels. Alwyn struggled with the heavy door bar. His one good hand could not manage it. The woman who had come to Wulfstan's aid earlier stepped in to help. Finally, his heart beating frantically, Alwyn flung open the door.

And gaped.

The two thegns who had escorted him were now serving as guards, and they were in heated argument with Alwyn's destined ally.

She would have been more appropriately cast as Satan's own mistress than God's champion. Long red hair, the very hue of fire, tumbled uncovered down her shoulders in an unseemly mass. Her beautiful features were animated as she spoke, the full lips curving about angry words and the emerald eyes bright with emotion. Her multicolored garb and the brooch with which the cloak was pinned bespoke her origins—the wild lands of Dalriada.

From the North, one will come. . . .

Alwyn didn't know how, but he knew at once that this was no good Christian woman. Perhaps it was her attitude of defiance, the fact that she scorned to cover her hair. Christianity had long been ensconced in the North, but there were areas where the damned spurned their chance at everlasting life. Alwyn knew with a sinking feeling that the woman before him—woman! God's champion a woman? What was Michael thinking?—was one of these untamed pagans.

"I have healing herbs in my pack. I know how to tend to the injured. Would you let them die, you ignorant whelp, for a simple lack of an order?"

"Aye, and kill you, into the bargain for causing a disturbance at His Majesty's villa!" snarled Ulraed. "What do you think, Aelfric?" The sword snicked free of the sheath.

"Nay, nay," replied Aelfric. "Let us not be rash. A little sport first, eh?"

Color rose in the woman's cheeks. "What opinions you English have of yourselves. I'd sooner couple with swine than you—they are cleaner and smell better!"

By now, Alwyn had recovered from his shock. Whatever his opinion of the woman, he knew that this was not a mistake. Before him stood his destined companion on this strange journey. He stepped forward and found his voice.

"Good thegns, I pray you, admit this woman. She has indeed come to heal." He met her blazing green eyes and found his mouth dry. "I will stand . . . witness . . . for her."

An expression of horror spread slowly across her exquisite face. Contempt thinned the full red lips and her eyes narrowed.

"It's you," she said softly. "You're a *monk*. Midhir's balls! Why didn't I just stay at home?"

Staring at the very incarnation of female allure, raked by her dislike and struggling with a potent combination of attraction and repulsion, Alwyn, monk of St. Aidan's, found himself wondering the same thing.

PART II

The Signs

Now as He sat on the Mount of Olives, the disciples came to Him privately, saying: "Tell us, when will these things be? And what will be the sign of Your coming, and of the end of the age?"

And Jesus answered and said to them . . . "You will hear of wars and rumors of wars. See that you are not troubled; for all these things must come to pass, but the end is not yet. For nation will rise against nation, and kingdom against kingdom. And there will be famines, pestilences, and earthquakes in various places. All these are the beginning of sorrows."

—MATTHEW 24:3–8

8

*The words of his mouth were smoother
than butter, but war was in his heart:
his words were softer than oil, yet were
they drawn swords.*

—PSALMS 55:21

**A Forest near the King's Villa
November 28, 999**

Angelo liked white horses much as he liked snow. The uncomplicated brightness and the lack of color calmed him, coming as he did from a world of dimness and myriad subtle, dark hues—though if truth be told, both the horse and the snow through which he now pushed the beast had a veritable rainbow of shades and tone. Nonetheless, the overall impression was of something clean and empty. Something on which he could place his mark.

The horse labored through the heavy drifts. Puffs of steam rose from nostrils that flared pink with effort. The path that Angelo followed was obvious—another reason he was so fond of snow. Judging by the distance between hoofprints, the boy was practically galloping.

Idiot king! Pushing a horse in that manner through this thick white stuff was madness. Ethelred could take a spill and break his foolish neck. Or, more likely, the horse could stumble and drag the hot-blooded simpleton right along with it. Either way, it would spell disaster for Angelo's plans. Ethelred—pathetic, eager, docile Ethelred—was integral to Angelo's ultimate victory.

Angelo caught sight of Ethelred a hundred yards away. Little more than a gray-black dot against the white snow, the king was indeed pushing his mount to its limits. Angelo shook his blond head. As he watched, the horse cleared a fallen log, its belly disturbing the foot-high pile of white atop the dark brown of the tree. Ethelred's whoop of delight floated to Angelo's ears. Now steed and royal rider were heading toward the forest, and Ethelred slowed his beast.

Angelo formed a thought. A skin of hot wine appeared in his hand. He frowned a little and amended the beverage's temperature. It felt good against his fingers, like a small animal held captive in his hand. This was better. Angelo was some distance from the royal villa, and if the wine were too hot, even thick-headed Ethelred might be a bit suspicious.

"Come, my dear," he told his pretty white mare. "Just a little longer out in the cold, and then we can both return to a warmer place."

The horse craned her long neck and fixed him with a gaze of more than human intelligence. For a fraction of an instant, her brown eyes blazed red. Then she tossed her cream-colored mane and dutifully pressed on.

"Can you not trust me alone for even a little while, mother hen?" Ethelred scolded, smiling, as Angelo rode up to him.

Angelo returned the smile. "Nay, Majesty, not for love of you. Your life is more precious to me than my own." He let his expression grow somber, just a touch pious. "Remember the tragic death of your brother, brought on for want of a trustworthy companion."

Angelo enjoyed watching the smile ebb from Ethelred's lips. There was nothing like a frightening tale to keep a child in line, and Angelo had ensured that Ethelred's memories of that night were frightening indeed. And inaccurate, with Angelo cast in the role of the hero who tried to find the miscreant and the king's mother, Elfthryth, as a horrified innocent.

Ethelred crossed himself. Angelo was unperturbed. "Pray God and Saint Edward keep me safe from such betrayal," he murmured. Inwardly, Angelo grimaced. He had done his job perhaps *too* well. Racked with grief over the death of Edward, Ethelred had pushed to make the murdered king a saint. The

Abbey of Shaftesbury, where Saint Edward the Martyr lay, was now a shrine. There was the usual talk of the occasional miracle.

As the two horses walked side by side, Angelo leaned over and placed a hand on the king's arm. "That, Majesty, is why I am here," he said, his musical voice rich with sincerity. And as quickly as that, Ethelred's smile returned. There were times when Angelo thought it all too easy.

"I thought you might be chilled—here is some hot wine to keep you warm while we ride back to the villa and talk."

Ethelred reached delightedly for the warm winesack, uncorked it, and drank. "I thank you for the wine and your company," he said, wiping his mouth with the back of his sleeve, "but I beg you, spare me the talk! It seems I do nothing but talk, talk, talk all the time."

"I fear that is mostly what being a king is truly about, Majesty. Although there are battles aplenty ravaging our land—and Europe, as well. I come with news."

Ethelred's face fell, like a child whose toys had been taken away from him. "Not more attacks?"

Angelo nodded. "Some of the most vicious yet. Under the leadership of a young upstart called Thorkell, nearly a hundred ships struck at Ipswich a fortnight ago. My sources of information tell me that they have set it aflame, and it burns still. The Force has come steadily south. Colchester suffered the same fate, and only a few days ago there was a dreadful battle at Maldon. The Force defeated our men. Among the slain was Ealdorman Byrhtnoth."

"No," Ethelred said. "No, that's not right. We gave them tribute—we doubled it! They were supposed to leave our shores in peace . . ."

"It is said that Byrhtnoth told the Force they would receive spears for tribute," Angelo continued. "Proud words, but empty ones, in the end. Such was the action that Bishop Wulfstan recommended, was it not?" He sighed. "Poor Wulfstan. He lies at the door of death and Byrhtnoth, who shared his flawed ideals, went before him." His face melancholy, he made the sign of the cross. Ethelred imitated him.

"Where are they now?" Ethelred asked. "Pray God, they have returned home and given us time at least to lick our wounds!"

"I fear not, Majesty. They are camped now in Shoebury, and if they follow the same pattern we have seen before, they are preparing to sail their dragon ships up the mouth of the Thames and attack London itself."

Ethelred chewed his lip. Angelo let him ruminate in silence.

"Is there time for a surprise attack? I know we have promised them peace, but by God, Angelo, I begin to think that my Witan might have been right. Byrhtnoth *was* a noble fool and died in a battle he couldn't hope to win, but perhaps—"

Angelo shook his head. "We cannot possibly assemble a fleet or an army in time to surprise them. But we can come to the defense of London, and I believe that is where we should turn our attention. I suggest we summon the Witan. No one has departed Calne, save those who have left us for a better place. Let us put your plan of defense into action."

"How many ships under this—this Thorkell? You said, but I forgot."

"Nearly a hundred longships, Majesty."

"I have not heard of him. Have you?"

Angelo had, of course. He knew everything that Loki had done and everyone with whom he had spoken. "Thorkell is a youth, Majesty, but he claims to be the right hand of an even more terrible warrior called the Dragon Odinsson." Angelo's lip curled in a sneer. "This Dragon, whom his followers say is a god incarnate, has yet to actually appear off our shores. Perhaps he does not even exist."

"But . . . but maybe he does."

"Olaf, Thorkell, Svein, Dragon Odinsson. They are all heathens; they must not take this realm. Does it really matter who comes against us? All who raise a hand to you are the enemy, regardless of what intimidating sobriquets they might have."

For a long while, Ethelred was silent. He hunched in his saddle, chilled and shivering from his earlier exertions, looking nothing like a king and everything like a beaten, broken child.

"Will it ever end, Angelo?" he asked.

"Yes," Angelo replied. "Of that, there can be no doubt. A king is a divine being, Majesty, ordained by God."

"The Vikings have kings," Ethelred murmured.

"The Vikings are heathens. You are God's anointed. I know it seems as though their assault is without end, but remember Psalm 27: 'The Lord is my light and my salvation; whom shall I fear? The Lord is the strength of my life; of whom shall I be afraid?' Of whom shall the rightful king be afraid, Majesty? Of a handful of filthy pagans and their impotent gods?"

He paused and furrowed his brow, wishing to appear appropriately hesitant about voicing his thoughts. Finally he said, "Majesty—have you ever imagined . . . has it ever occurred to you that you would make an admirable emperor?"

"By the Holy Virgin, Angelo, have you gone mad? I've enough on my hands defending England, let alone Europe!"

"Not if it is God's will," Angelo insisted. *Or mine.* "I spoke of battles in Europe as well. Emperor Otto led a campaign against the Saracens. He won the battle, but just barely, and there is great fear in the land. The child is only nineteen, after all, and frail into the bargain. He has no heir, and Europe may need a strong, Christian ruler to keep them safe. And as allies, the countries of Europe would lend much-valued spears to our cause. The year is old, King Ethelred. There are rumors that time is very, very short indeed, that with the new millennium may come a New World and the end of this one. Who then will be the Last Emperor, who will hand over crown and scepter to Christ, as has been prophesied? Otto? I think not."

Ethelred had fallen into stunned silence, which suited Angelo. Let the poppet gnaw on the idea. Let him discuss it with his mother, the ever-helpful and cunning Elfthryth, who always gave her boy such good advice. Soon it would appeal to his sense of adventure, and he would be touting it as his own idea, granted in a vision or a dream. And then another intricate piece of the puzzle would come together.

Angelo's reach was long. It covered the world.

It was difficult for him to smother a grin of triumph, but he managed. Any hint of humor vanished, however, when Angelo caught sight of one of his men heading for them. The speed with which the thegn pushed the beast told him there was trouble.

"What is it, Aelfric?" he demanded. "Has there been a turn for the worse with our injured brethren?"

Clearly winded by the journey, the heavyset Aelfric struggled. "Come quickly, sir," he gasped. "There is . . . pagan woman . . . young monk named Alwyn from St. Aidan's . . . Wulfstan summoned him and he's let her inside. . . ."

Ethelred's golden brows drew together in a frown. "A pagan woman? Inside *my* villa trying to harm *my* bishop?"

"She said she came to heal," continued Aelfric, still sucking in air. "When Brother Alwyn let her in, I didn't know what to do—I came to find you, sir."

"You did well," said Angelo. This was splendid. Wulfstan had obstinately refused to die, despite the severity of his injury, and Angelo was beginning to suspect that the bishop lived on will alone. If a pagan woman had poisoned him, that was well. Even if she had honestly tried to heal Wulfstan, the scandal would forever cloak the man and taint his hitherto unstained reputation.

"I cannot believe that the good Bishop Wulfstan would permit an ungodly woman to touch him, let alone accept her heathen healing practices. Such would be an affront to the God he purpots to love above all things. But perhaps, if he was in great pain, even pagan healing would. . . ."

Angelo let his voice trail off. An expression of sick horror mixed with the beginning of reluctant belief had begun to play about Ethelred's face. Aelfric's brown eyes glinted with the disapproval of the hypocritically righteous.

"Let us go, and prevent what damage we may. God grant that we will be in time," said Angelo solemnly, and clapped heels to his steed.

The sea was gray, the sky was gray, the land was gray. Loki was growing weary of the seemingly endless journey, but at last his tireless crew of ghosts had done as he had commanded. They had steered the white ship Nagelfar to its destination.

Slowly, Loki rose, moving easily in his fine new body. The wind whipped his black hair and the spray pricked like needles on his skin, but he barely noticed. East of Midgard it lay, in the realm of the giants—Yarnvid, the Iron Wood.

The day was silent, save for the lapping of the waves and the soft moan of the wind. And then the sound came forth.

It was almost like a song, in its haunting ululation and heart-breaking purity. It rose and swelled, causing tears to spring to Loki's eyes. Finally, the howl died away.

"My boy," whispered Loki. He took a deep breath, cupped his hands around his mouth, and cried, "Fenris!" His heart racing with excitement, he strained to listen for a response. It came, an answering howl punctuated by yips of delight.

Loki wanted to dance, to leap about, to shriek with pleasure, but he contented himself with a silent grin. Nagelfar sailed closer to the island. It was able to approach almost to the water's edge before Loki had to leap into the frigid waves and wade the rest of the way.

He stood on the silver beach, panting and chilled. More wolf howls rose, but these did not belong to his sons. Before he could blink, two large beasts stood on a knoll covered with dead grass. The object of their attention was Loki. They growled, their red eyes alight and the fur on the backs of their thick necks rising.

Loki chuckled and raised a placating hand. "Be easy, Skoll. Do not worry, Hati. I am no mortal who dares trespass, but Loki the Trickster himself. Find your mother, that I may ask her to help me find and free my son."

"Already done, Trickster, if indeed you be," came a sultry voice. Startled, Loki whipped around. The Queen of Witches hovered in the air, her garb as gray and dull as everything in this depressing place. But her face—ah, her face was lovely, with full red lips. Boldly, Loki strode forward, plucked her from the air, and kissed her.

She returned the embrace, and when their lips parted, she grinned as fiercely as he. "No mortal man can kiss me and remain unchanged," she said. "Welcome, Loki. Has Ragnarok begun? My little ones are eager to feed, but Heimdall's horn has not been heard here."

Still clasping the floating queen about her narrow waist, Loki turned to regard the wolves. "Was it Skoll who devours the moon?"

"Nay, Skoll shall feast upon the sun. It is Hati who hungers for the pale moon."

"Sadly, the hour of our revenge has not yet arrived," Loki told the queen and her wolfen children. "But soon. I swear it. I have come for my son, that we may set into motion the events of the end of the world. Where is he?"

Still scorning to touch her dainty feet to the earth, the Witch Queen led Loki over gray hills and meadows.

The song of his son grew louder. Loki climbed a slight rise, and his heart leaped in his human chest.

Fenris was not a brightly hued creature. Like the Iron Wood in which he had been held captive for so long, the predominant color in his fur was gray. But it was a warm, living gray, a soft silver-and-moon hue, with bold markings of black and brown

and white to please the eye. To Loki, after so many years—
Decades? Centuries? What had it been, and how was that thing
called time reckoned now?—apart, Fenris seemed the most alive
and glorious creature in the world.

"Fenris!" He raced down the hill toward his child. The gods
who had chained him would have been ashamed to see what
love and joy did to the beast they had so feared. Fenris's ears
were flat on his magnificent skull, his tail wagging furiously. He
whimpered and yelped with happiness, and as Loki moved to
embrace him, the frantic creature licked his face as though
starved for the taste.

"Break it, break it!" growled Fenris, tugging against the ribbon Gleipnir. Loki stared at it. It could have been made of a spider's web, so fragile it seemed. Yet he could see the powerful
muscles beneath Fenris's fur move and shift as the wolf
strained.

"Curse them," he said beneath his breath. "Curse them for
their cowardice. Son, I cannot break the ribbon. Ragnarok has
not yet come, else I would be free of my own bonds and here in
my own body, not this borrowed one. But there are ways to escape that do not involve strength."

Fenris panted and held still as Loki's clever fingers found the
ribbon about his neck. Eons of Fenris's straining had pulled
Gleipnir ever tighter, but Loki began to work at the knot. He
needed no magic. Prophecy dictated that the ribbon could be
broken only at the onset of Ragnarok. It said nothing about patient fingers simply untying the knot. He was finding that there
were ways around prophecy.

Laughing, Loki pulled the bright ribbon free and tossed it upward. The wind caught it and set it dancing. Fenris howled his
joy and pranced about, reveling in his freedom. His father
watched him, his heart swelling with pride. Fenris was a beautiful creature.

Abruptly the wolf ceased his capering. "All this time, that
was all it would have taken to free me."

"The queen was forbidden to touch you," Loki told him.

"So she has said. But one of the Aesir could have. But no one
has come. Father, did you know I had never harmed one of
them?"

Loki's smile faded. He nodded solemnly. "Aye, I did. They

bound you not for what you had done, but for what they feared you would do."

Fenris's eyes began to glow red. Black dewlaps curled upward in a growl. "I took Tyr's hand for it."

"And soon you will do more to exact your revenge," his father promised him. "But first, we have duties to discharge. I have made an ally. He has helped me by freeing me and allowing me to free you. We will liberate your brother, who sleeps in a deep lake, dreaming of his day of vengeance as we do. We will call your sister. Together, the four of us will help Angelo destroy his world—and then we can destroy ours."

Something akin to sorrow brushed Loki as he spoke. The end of the world would bring about his own end as well, and that of his children. And yet, wasn't that his destiny? What else was there to do but sit and wait, bound by the entrails of his best-loved, gentlest boy while poison burned on his forehead?

No, this was the way. Far better to act, to bring about one's own destruction, than to sit by and endure. Better to be the shooting star, dying in a blaze of fire, than to lie in the cold and mourn for what could not be.

"You are an integral part of Angelo's plan," he told Fenris. The wolf lolled his tongue in pleasure. Fenris was ever susceptible to flattery. "Come to me, my son, and let me mark you as he has instructed me."

"Mark? Surely all will know me, the feared Fenris Wolf." Fenris cocked his head in puzzlement.

"Ah, but they will know you as Fenris and as something else, too. You shall inspire twice as much terror."

That seemed to please the animal even further, and he sat obediently as his father placed a hand on his forehead. Fenris whimpered a little but did not move, enduring the pain stoically, as searing heat flashed from human hand to beast's head. There came the smell of burned flesh and fur and a faint crackling sound.

The act caused Loki pain as well, but he merely pressed his lips together in a thin line. What was this little burning compared with the torment he had endured for ages, deep beneath the earth?

It was done. Loki lifted his hand and fondled his son's ears, regarding his handiwork. To his eyes it was little more than a series of lines, some up and down, some curved, some crisscrossed. Roman numerals, Angelo had called them—whoever the Romans were. Angelo had told Loki that the people of this place called England would know the symbol at once, and it would flood them with fear.

And fear was something of which Loki heartily approved.

9

Put not your trust in princes.
—PSALMS 146:3

Ethelred's Royal Villa, Calne
November 28, 999

The pagan woman recovered first. "I thank you for your faith in my skills, Brother . . . ?"

"Alwyn. From the Abbey of St. Aidan's in Chesbury. Your, uh, your healing talents are welcome, milady—"

"Kennag nic Beathag. From the village of Gleannsidh." She paused, and her red brows drew together in a frown. "I have skills, Brother Alwyn, but I cannot move through solid flesh."

"Oh!" Blushing, Alwyn stepped aside. With a final, disgusted glance at Ulraed—Aelfric had departed moments ago in some haste—Kennag swept into the great hall.

"Where is he?"

Alwyn nodded his head in Wulfstan's direction. As Kennag strode forward, he found himself hurrying to keep up with her. She knelt quickly beside the unconscious form of the bishop and began to examine him.

Alwyn opened his mouth to protest her familiar handling of the bishop, but a wordless glare silenced him. He sat, miserable and helpless, and watched without interrupting as Kennag smelled the bishop's breath, put her ear to his chest, and peeled back the closed lids and peered into the unseeing depths of Wulfstan's blue eyes. She seemed to know what she was doing. Rowena sat quietly by, her odd-colored eyes missing nothing.

A woman. The other half of the pair that was supposed to stop Satan was a pagan woman. All at once a wave of doubt crashed over Alwyn. Perhaps it had been a dream after all, or worse, a ploy by the Enemy to trick Alwyn into murdering Wulfstan. Perhaps—

"O ye of little faith," murmured Rowena, half-closing her eyes. He stared at her. "It's plain on your face, Brother. You doubt the woman, you doubt yourself. Have faith, my friend."

Blushing again, Alwyn gnawed his lower lip. Reprimanded for lack of faith by a cat? This whole ordeal was starting to take on a certain comical overtone, and he was convinced that at any moment, God's wrath would abruptly manifest and he, the pagan woman, and the cat would all be struck dead.

Now Kennag was shamelessly peeling, cutting, and pulling away the bandages wrapped about Wulfstan's thin torso. Crying aloud, Alwyn leaned forward and seized her wrist.

"What are you doing?"

"I am trying to treat your friend. Let me—"

"His ribs are broken, and the bandage—"

"I can see that, idiot! Brihid's flames take you, let me do my work!" She twisted, almost effortlessly, and Alwyn found his good hand closing on nothing but air.

He sat back, wrestling with despair. Kennag had removed her cloak, and Alwyn was painfully aware of the curves beneath her long, multihued garment. She opened her pack, retrieved a jar, and uncorked it.

A fragrance poured forth. The scent that teased Alwyn's nostrils was that of honey and flowers and the very essence of summer itself. He forgot Kennag's seductive body, her fall of red hair. He forgot Wulfstan's injuries and even, for a moment, his own purpose in being here. He breathed deep of the summer smell, and thought of lush, soft, warm days and nights when the rhythm of abbey life seemed to merge effortlessly with the rhythm of God's blessed world.

"Wipe your face, good Brother," said Rowena gently, startling him out of his reverie. Tears were running down his cheeks, and Alwyn scrubbed at them with his right hand.

He regarded Kennag. Her face seemed softer, less vulpine than it had hitherto, and the smile that touched her lips held no scorn. Slowly, almost reverently, she scooped up some salve on her fingers and massaged it tenderly into Wulfstan's body. Alwyn continued to watch. Any desire to protest was gone, driven away by that poignant smell that was more than a smell. Gently, Kennag's long fingers brushed the angry red flesh where broken bones had found their way through the skin. They touched the welts and purple-green bruises, the scrapes and lacerations, all the hurt and violated places on the dear man's pale body.

"Now," said Kennag softly, "we may rebind the injuries." She corked the bottle and the scent diminished, but did not disappear. Some of it wafted up from Wulfstan's body like a benediction at the end of Mass.

Alwyn's gaze traveled from Wulfstan to his own useless left arm.

"The ointment can mend what was broken," came Kennag's soft voice, tinged with pity, "but it cannot give life to the dead."

Shame flooded Alwyn. Shame for his crippled arm, shame for his furtive longing for its wholeness, shame that he had been observed in such an intimate, unseemly desire.

Alwyn continued to kneel at Wulfstan's side while Kennag rose and spoke softly to one of the women. He heard their low conversation, the slight scuffling of Kennag's boots as she returned. He did not look up, but kept staring at the bishop's lined, lean face. Was it his imagination, his hope that Kennag's mystery ointment had worked, or did there seem to be more color in Wulfstan's cheeks?

To Alwyn's shock, the bishop's eyes opened. Wulfstan even managed a smile.

"I smell summer," he whispered. "Surely I must have passed on. And yet I do not think God's house would be quite so drafty. What miracle have you wrought here, Alwyn? The pain is so much less."

"No miracle, learned Father," said Kennag in a surprisingly soothing voice as she sank down beside him. "Only some herbs and sheep's fat. Let me wrap you again, and give you a sleeping draught."

But Wulfstan was no elderly fool, his mind gone along with teeth and hair. He turned his keen gaze on her, sweeping her from uncovered hair to wild-hued garb.

"I am not unacquainted with herbs and sheep's fat, wild daughter," he said, "and no unguent has ever taken me back to my errant, sweet youth as yours has. You say it is no miracle—what is it, then?"

"Bishop, Kennag is the second Witness," said Alwyn, keeping his voice soft, lest they be overheard. "She is no Christian woman, but—"

"'By their fruits ye shall know them,'" quoted Wulfstan, "and the fruit of your healing is pure indeed. I am surprised, I confess, but who am I to doubt the wisdom of the Lord? If you have been called, and I believe you have, then God works through you though you know it not." Kennag opened her mouth, no doubt to protest this brushing aside of her heathen gods, but Wulfstan silenced her with a raised hand. "Listen to me. The days grow shorter; your errand, more urgent. Brother Alwyn came to me for advice, and you, little sister Kennag, have been drawn here also. The only advice I can give you is to seek out the wisdom of others. There is still time for you to travel to the holy places of this island, to speak with those who have knowledge and lore that can perhaps aid you. That is my advice—that, and to take care of one another, as God takes care of us all."

The two Witnesses exchanged uneasy glances. Alwyn thought that taking care of Kennag would be like trying to take care of the roe of the woods. Clearly, she was not overly fond of the idea, either. But they remained silent and did not argue with the bishop.

"Learned Father, drink of this. It will help speed your recovery." Kennag drew forth another bottle, but this time the fragrance that escaped was one that made Alwyn's nose wrinkle.

"Blessed Virgin, what *is* that?" he exclaimed.

Kennag smiled. "Valerian root mixed with a healthy dose of strong drink. It will speed healing and send you to sweet sleep, Father, though its scent is foul."

"I trust you, daughter, though the scent is indeed from Hell itself." Awkwardly Alwyn helped the wounded man sit up enough so that he would not choke. He swallowed a few sips, grimacing, then Alwyn eased him down.

They watched in silence as his breathing slowed and became more regular. Finally, Alwyn turned to Kennag, squaring his shoulders.

"I thank you for the life of my friend."

"You are welcome, though it is not me you should be thanking. The potion is mine, but the ointment is from the Good People."

It took a moment for Alwyn to realize what she was saying. "The Faerie Folk?" he gasped.

"Hush! They do not like to be so named."

"I don't care what they like or don't like, I care that you've treated a man of God with a potion from those hellspawn!"

"Alwyn, who do you think sent me on this mission?" Kennag's voice rose with her anger and she sat up straighter. "When I was told I would meet another, I thought of a king, or a warrior. Someone who remembered the Good People and their ways, and who would fight to save our world and theirs. Instead I'm led to a crippled boy monk who—"

She caught herself. Alwyn said nothing but he felt the blood drain from his face. Though his heart slammed against the wall of his chest, he didn't look away.

"I'm so sorry," she said. "I have a temper, and I didn't think— The Christians have not been good to me or my people, and I do not much like or trust them. I am sorry," she repeated.

A crippled boy monk. He supposed that's all he was, really, now that she had put it into harsh words. His mouth was dry, and he couldn't think of anything to say.

The uncomfortable silence was shattered by the boom of the door being thrown back. Startled, Alwyn and Kennag looked up. Silhouetted in the doorway were two tall figures. They moved forward into the hall's light. One was thin and dressed in beautiful but weather-stained clothes. His beard and hair were dyed blue, but the color was beginning to grow out, revealing blond roots.

Beside him, moving with the grace of a cat, was the most beautiful man Alwyn had ever seen. Golden ringlets, damp with snow, framed a sculpted face. Blue eyes blazed forth, full lips were set in a scowl. His body was as perfect as Adam's must have been in that long-ago Eden, strong muscles moving cleanly beneath garb that was almost as fine as the blue-haired man's.

"There they are!" exclaimed the blue-haired man. "Arrest them!"

Aelfric and Ulraed moved forward. It took Alwyn several seconds to realize that it was he and Kennag who were to be arrested. He rose, confused. "What's going on? Who are you?"

"The better question," said the second man, stepping up as the two thegns seized Kennag and Alwyn, "is who might you be? This is your king, Ethelred of England. Make obeisance, ceorl!"

Surprised, Alwyn would have willingly bowed to his liege, but the option was taken away from him. Rough hands shoved him down on his knees. He hit the floor hard and grunted. Beside him, Kennag struggled but was forced down as well.

"He's not my king!" she snarled, glaring fiercely at first the thegn, then the second man, then Ethelred. "I've come but to help. You've no right to treat us this way!"

"I have every right," purred the second man. "I am an adviser to the king, a member of the Witan, and friend to that man there. Have you killed him, you heathen cat?"

"Hey!" hissed Rowena indignantly, tail lashing.

"Slipped him poison in lieu of potion, eh?" The man strode forward and placed a powerful hand beneath Kennag's chin, jerking her face up to his. "Your beauty will not save you, whore."

"Leave her be!" All eyes turned to Alwyn. He was as surprised as they at the exclamation and the strength of his voice. "She is here at my instigation."

Slowly, the man turned his gaze full upon Alwyn. It was almost like a physical blow, and suddenly Alwyn realized just who he must be. Adviser to the king, a member of the Witan—surely this was the infamous Angelo, of whom Alwyn had been warned. He forced himself not to look away.

"Behold, gentlemen," said Angelo in a silky voice. "This witch has worked her charms even on a man of God! What deviltry is afoot here? I must call in Father Cenulf to investigate this heresy! Aelfric, Ulraed, take them away. Lock them up until the morning, when His Majesty and Father Cenulf decide what to do with them."

Alwyn's lips moved. He glanced frantically down at Wulfstan, but the bishop was sleeping deeply and would not awaken to verify Alwyn's story. Movement caught his eye—Rowena, fleeing like the beast she was, jumping onto the window and disappearing into the snow. An unexpected lump rose in Alwyn's throat. He had thought better of the white cat than desertion, despite her earlier comment. She was a cat, in the end, and she had left as promised.

"Majesty—" he began, hoping to be able to reach Ethelred. The blow caught him totally off guard. Pain crashed into his jaw, and for an instant he saw bright sparkles of light. He heard laughter and then was propelled forward, sucking on the blood trickling from his wounded mouth and stumbling over his hitherto trustworthy legs. The two men steered them through the knee-deep snow toward a small, cold-looking stone building. Alwyn had to shake his head at the irony: Angelo was holding the two Witnesses foretold by Revelation prisoner in Ethelred's small, private chapel.

He wished he dared blaspheme by swearing. It always seemed to hearten those visitors to the abbey who chose to do so.

"A bewitched monk and a heathen whore, hey? From what I've heard, you two will enjoy yourselves," muttered Aelfric as Alwyn and Kennag were shoved into the cold building. The door slammed shut behind them, and they heard a *thunk* as the bolt dropped down. Alwyn didn't even get chance to protest Aelfric's slur against the brotherhood.

Silence.

"Are you all right?" Kennag's voice sounded different here than in the warm and crowded hall. Alwyn looked up at her. She was already on her feet, fingers probing the door and the walls, searching for a way out. She favored him with a quick glance, and he nodded.

He got to his feet and watched her explorations. "I'm certain it's futile," he said after a while. "We're both too large to fit through the windows, and that door is the only way in or out."

Kennag growled a little and pounded on the door. "Curse you, let us out! You've no idea what you're doing!"

A thump from the other side of the door. "Silence, whore, or I'll come in and silence you myself. Ethelred doesn't like us to take liberties with the ladies, but with a heathen slut like you, I don't think he'd mind."

Kennag's freckled face, flushed with anger, went pale at the words. She snatched her hands from the door and stepped backward. With an effort, she muttered, "Whoreson dog. If the end does come, I hope you die first."

"I apologize for my countrymen," said Alwyn, more to fill the silence than anything else. "Not all of us are quite so rude."

"Truly? I'm afraid I'd have to call you a liar, Brother Alwyn. The only one of your countrymen who has treated me better than his least favorite dog is Wulfstan, and he'll be lucky if he lasts the night."

"But—your ointment—"

"Did what it was supposed to. But no ointment can shield against a knife to the throat. This friend of the king is no friend

to us or the bishop, unless I am greatly mistaken." She glared
again at the door, drew her leg back slightly as if she were about
to kick it, then appeared to think better of it and began to pace.
She had removed her cloak in the great hall, and there it had remained. She began to rub her arms, and Alwyn could see her
breath.

He had remained clad in his own cloak, and after a moment's
hesitation removed it. "Here," he said. "It's not much, but it will
cut the chill a little."

She looked at him, her green eyes searching his. A smile
curved her lips. "Thank you," she said. "When night falls, we'd
best sleep together. These holy houses of yours are not particularly warm."

For what seemed like the hundredth time since he had first
clapped eyes on Kennag, Alwyn felt himself blushing. Now he,
too, began to prowl the chapel, searching for a way out. Thinking about Kennag's body pressed to his in sleep, however innocent and indeed vital to their continued existence it might be, was
a most unsettling thought.

Kennag watched him in silence. When he finally gave up and
came to join her in the center of the chapel, she gave him a wry
grin.

"Any miracles at hand, Brother? Can you pray for an un-
locked door and a sleeping guard?"

Alwyn thought of the ring on his finger, of the staff he had left
behind in the hall. Neither would do him much good now. He
shook his head.

"This Ethelred of yours—does he listen to reason? Perhaps
we could speak with him, convince him of why we are here."

"No," sighed Alwyn. "Ethelred listens not to reason but to his
advisers—mainly Angelo. And it is because of Angelo that we're
in here right now."

Kennag narrowed her eyes. "You know something. Perhaps
we had best use this time to share our knowledge. We can't hope
to escape until late tonight."

Forced to concede the wisdom of her words, Alwyn nodded
and began. He told her of Wulfstan's visit in April, so short and
yet so long a time ago. Of the warnings against Angelo, of trusting the king, of the Antichrist here on Earth. He had to take a few
moments to explain what the Antichrist was, and why his arrival
was such a terrible thing. Kennag listened intently. He had ex-

pected scorn and rude quips, but she offered none. He warmed to the task and found himself filled with a strange anticipation as he told her of Michael and the gifts—one of which he had left behind in the hall—and of Rowena and Balaam.

When he at last fell silent, she nodded slowly. "We of Dalriada have met many people of differing faiths. I do not follow yours, Alwyn, but I do believe it, especially in light of what I have been told. I hope you will grant me the same courtesy, and believe what I have to tell you."

Then it was Alwyn's turn to listen. It was harder for him than it apparently had been for her. He had lived all his life in the abbey. God was present in every thought of his head and deed of his hand. How could he believe in, let alone trust, these shadowy "Good People" who had given Kennag such powers? They were the Lost Ones who had fallen with the Great Enemy. They were nothing of God, or Heaven, or angels.

And yet—they shared the same concerns. They had permitted Kennag to use their healing ointment to cure a bishop. They had led her to—

"Wait a moment," he said, interrupting her. "How did you find me? This is a big island."

"I was getting to that," Kennag said. "The squirrel—he said his name was Ratatosk—found me. I'm not sure what he is, but he's more than a simple animal. He said he knew where the Other was, and after he managed to convince the cat not to eat him for breakfast, she led the four of us here."

"Four?"

"Me, my horse, Ratatosk, and—and Neddy." She turned away at the last.

"You have a companion? Why didn't you say so? Where is he? Can he—"

"Neddy," Kennag said softly, seeming to ignore Alwyn and staring into a dark corner at the far end of the chapel. "Neddy, we are all bound up in this. You can't keep hiding. Please."

Alwyn felt a chill that was not due to the temperature of the chapel. His mouth went dry as he followed Kennag's gaze. She had admitted to dealings with the Faerie Folk. What manner of creature had come with her?

For a long moment, the corner remained empty. Then, to Alwyn's horror, something pale began to take shape. He crossed

himself and began murmuring a prayer beneath his breath, yet he
could not tear his eyes from the manifesting form.

Pale blue and gray and white it was, like the very opposite of
a shadow. It sat against the wall, its legs drawn up against its
chest, its head on its knees.

"Neddy? It's all right." Kennag's voice was so soft she might
have been speaking to a frightened child, and as the apparition
slowly lifted its head, Alwyn saw that, in a sense, she was.

The figure was that of a boy about fifteen years old. He was
handsome, but his face was unspeakably sad. His clothes, as pale
and slightly transparent as he himself, marked him as a youth of
noble birth.

"Kennag can see me all the time," he said in a soft voice. "It's
hard to make anyone else see me, though Kennag tells me I need
to practice."

"Alwyn," said Kennag in an unnaturally calm voice, "this is
Neddy. He doesn't really know who he is—was—or why he
wasn't allowed to pass on. He joined me on this journey a few
days ago. He's been very pleasant company."

"For a ghost," breathed Alwyn. Merciful Jesu.

Night was a long time in coming. Alwyn welcomed the hours,
though. They gave him time to grow accustomed to the idea that
his present companions in this dire situation were a pagan witch,
her ghostly friend, and a squirrel-who-was-no-squirrel. He wondered if he'd get the chance to know any of them better. At any
moment, he expected the bolt to lift and Angelo to enter with a
gleaming knife. The Roman adviser was too handsome, and
Alwyn didn't much trust overly beautiful people.

The wait also gave him time to pray. Kennag was respectful
of him and made no attempt to interrupt. Alwyn knelt at the bare
altar. Apparently, Ethelred was not particularly diligent in his religious observances. Possibly there would be a service in the
morning. Somehow, Alwyn doubted it. There was no sense of
sanctity about this place. Bowing his head, he went through the
entire day's prayers, and when he had exhausted them, he prayed
simply from the heart.

A sudden thud, then yelp, caused him to glance up. Kennag
had fallen and was getting to her feet, swearing. She picked up
the offending item that had tripped her. Alwyn gasped. Her eyes
met his, and she brandished the rod at him.

"Where did this come from? We've explored every inch of this place!"

Slowly, Alwyn closed his eyes. *Thank you, Heavenly Father.* The staff Kennag clutched in annoyance was the Rod of Aaron, left behind in the main hall when they had been thrown into this makeshift prison. Again it had come to him—a sign, as if any more were needed, of the true holiness of their mission. Alwyn took the staff, kissed it reverently, and fell again to praying.

From time to time, as the sun made its short way across the winter sky, they heard talking. They couldn't catch the words, but it was enough for them to be certain that there was still a guard posted outside.

Shadows lengthened over the wooden benches and the bare altar. At last Kennag, a dim shape in the darkness, touched Alwyn's shoulder gently.

"I think we can risk it now."

At that moment, they heard a scrabbling outside. They froze as one.

"Alwyn!" came a soft female voice. "Let me in!"

"Rowena!" Alwyn couldn't hide the pleasure in his voice as he hastened to the window. He opened the shutters, and the white cat jumped inside. She caught sight of Neddy and hissed, her back arching. A shiver passed through Alwyn. She had done so at other times, back at the abbey; hissing at something Alwyn couldn't see. He had always thought it was an insect or some such thing. Now, he had the sudden feeling that he'd been very wrong.

"Calm down, Rowena. This is Neddy. He's a friend of Kennag's."

"Hello, kitty," said Neddy. His face was animated and he was smiling. He seemed slightly more solid than he had been hitherto. He held out a spectral hand to the cat, who edged away. Neddy's face fell. He shimmered, and again went transparent.

"She'll get used to you," Alwyn reassured him. "Rowena, I'm delighted to see you. I thought—"

"I know what you thought. It's what I wanted you to think. Better that they don't notice the two of us—we can move without arousing suspicion." At her words, the gray-brown squirrel edged into Alwyn's vision. He paused at the window, nose and tail twitching.

"You're all right. Excellent."

"You've got to get out of here," Rowena said.

"In case you haven't noticed," said Alwyn testily, "we are locked in."

"You don't understand. I heard Angelo and the priest talking. Something about killing heretics and the will of God. The priest is merely greedy and the king, gullible, but this Angelo—" She spat. "Your lives, and possibly that of Wulfstan, won't be worth a shake of my whiskers if you stay till the morrow. Now, listen. The squirrel and I have a plan."

Neddy had only the most fleeting of memories: a horse, a little boy, snow. He could not recall his true name, only this childish nickname, nor the faces of his parents nor the part of the world he had called home. He didn't even know how he had died. Kennag had told him that it had to have been tragic, or else his—his spirit would be at peace, not wandering forlornly, trying to recall his identity. That made sense. He liked Kennag. Once she had recovered from her initial shock at seeing him, she had been very kind. She'd even made him smile from time to time. Most people were terrified of him when he tried to approach, and so for a long time—he didn't know how long—he had simply wandered, lost and alone. It had been Kennag who had treated him like a living person, Kennag who had made him willing to venture forth again into a world that frightened him almost as much as he seemed to frighten its inhabitants. With her, he was no longer alone.

Now, he had a chance to help Kennag and the brother who was clearly trying to be kind. And maybe the cat would stop hissing at him after this, too.

When Kennag told him all was in readiness, he let himself become invisible and stepped through the closed door. For a long moment, he regarded the man charged with guarding the prisoners. Ugly, big, stocky—and familiar, somehow. Neddy shrugged to himself. He couldn't trust who would and who wouldn't be familiar. He waited until the man's absent, bored stare fell in his direction—and then he manifested.

"Hello," Neddy said, grinning.

The guard's eyes widened and he staggered, clutching his chest. "Merciful God!" he screamed. "You're dead! You're dead!"

The smile disappeared from Neddy's lips. He had been right.

This man *did* know him. Forgetting his task, which was to frighten the guard away, Neddy rushed forward. He reached to touch the man, his ghost's insubstantial fingers going right through material and flesh.

"Please," he begged, "Who am I? How did I die?"

But Neddy had done his job all too well. The man fled, sobbing aloud, and Neddy stared after him, feeling sick. He had finally found someone who had known him in life, and he had driven the man away.

Needing distraction, he ran toward the barn to see how Ratatosk and Rowena were doing. The barn door stood open. Neddy smiled. Somehow, they had managed to open the door. He stepped inside, his eyes having no trouble seeing in the dark. Ratatosk was gnawing on the tethers that held an old donkey captive. Kennag's Faerie horse was already freed, and stamped her feet impatiently. Rowena started, then relaxed as she realized who it was.

"Did it work?" she asked Neddy.

Neddy stopped smiling. "Yes," he said, softly. "He was terrified of me."

"Good. Ratatosk is almost—"

"Done!" chirped the squirrel. "Let's go!" He and Rowena leaped onto the back of the Faerie horse. The white mare sprang into action, lowering her head and galloping through Neddy as he stood in the doorway. The donkey followed suit. Neddy turned and followed them back to the chapel.

He wished he could help, but he could not touch, let alone lift, the heavy bar that spanned the doorway. It was up to the animals now.

"They're in there," said Ratatosk, sitting upright in the donkey's saddle and pointing. The donkey bellowed and tossed its head. The squirrel, startled, toppled off into the snow.

The Faerie horse stepped forward and placed her muzzle below the bolt. The donkey moved to assist her. They lifted their heads slowly, and the bolt rose, borne on their muzzles.

"Come on!" cried Rowena. "Somebody's going to come any minute."

Alwyn and Kennag rushed out the door and reached for their mounts. "Good Balaam," Alwyn said to the donkey, "we're going to have to go as fast as you can, fellow."

"Considering the circumstances," drawled Balaam, "I think that will be rather fast indeed."

They turned and headed for the main gate in the wall that surrounded the villa. For a moment, Neddy stayed where he was. If he lingered here, eavesdropped on the conversation the frightened thegn was having with someone else, he could perhaps learn his identity. But Alwyn and Kennag were not yet safely away. They would need his help again to get through the gates. The thought of Kennag in trouble made him hurt inside. She was all he had.

Slowly, dejectedly, the pale ghost turned and followed his friends, a small, sad little shape who melted into the moonlight and snow.

10

And the Lord said unto Satan, Whence comest thou? Then Satan answered the Lord and said, From going to and fro in the earth, and from walking up and down in it.

—JOB 1:7

Ethelred's Royal Villa, Calne
November 29, 999

"I know it sounds mad, but I saw him! I swear it!" Aelfric's eyes bulged, and his voice was treble with fear.

The thegn's screams had brought the whole household awake. Angelo had found Aelfric first, and he was furious. A single thought would stop this man's heart, rupture a vessel, or cause his small brain to sizzle like fat in a pan. But Aelfric was still of use, despite the idiocy that he had displayed in letting himself be so easily duped.

"I know you thought you saw him, but don't you see what has happened here?" His voice was smooth and calm, and he subtly extended his powers toward Aelfric as he spoke. "It was a trick by that evil witch! She conjured something to frighten you, and you saw who you did because—" He broke off, smiling, and patted Aelfric's shoulder condescendingly. "Let me handle this."

By now a small crowd was gathering. Over the din, Angelo could hear Ethelred's petulant whine demanding, "What the devil is going on?"

"The devil indeed, Sire," said Angelo, raising his voice. "The

evil witch and her corrupt monkish lover addled good Aelfric's
brains. They conjured a demon, and—"

"Utter nonsense!" The voice cut through Angelo's rhetoric
like a knife through butter, strong and clear and filled with righteous anger. "Far more likely that your guard fell asleep, Majesty,
and is ashamed to admit it!"

Murmurs arose from the crowd of thegns and ealdormen. The
voice had come from Wulfstan. He was pale and fragile, and he
walked with a shaky step and leaned heavily on his crosier, but
he was walking unaided.

Fury welled in Angelo. He longed to simply lift a finger, blast
the bishop to cinders, and be done with it, but he could not. Not
yet. Instead, he laughed.

"This coming from a man who was like to have died a few
hours ago? Majesty! This bishop who speaks of the innocence of
his young friend is living testimony to the heathen's unnatural
powers!"

Ethelred had dressed, but some of his clothes were put on
backward in his haste. His right stocking had come unfastened
and slowly unwound as Angelo watched. The king gaped, looking from Angelo to Wulfstan and back again.

There was a silence. The gathered crowd was mute, waiting.
Finally, Ethelred said, "Bishop Wulfstan, glad as I am to see you
whole again, I confess I fear it is the devil's work that has
wrought this change in you. But," and here he glanced at Angelo,
"I think it was done in innocence on your part. Still, I cannot
have anyone tainted by the devil in my Witan. Return to London
at once. I will listen no more to you."

What little color there was drained from Wulfstan's face.
"Majesty, I beg you—"

"Bishop, do not force me to have you escorted back to the
hall," said Ethelred. Now that he had made a decision—or had it
made for him—he was firm in his certainty. He stood erect, summoning an air of command despite the drooping leg wrapping.

Wulfstan leaned more heavily on his crosier. He closed his
eyes, as if in pain. Lifting his gray head, he stared at Angelo.
Their gazes locked for a long moment. Then, straightening as
best he could, Wulfstan summoned dignity and hobbled back toward the hall.

Low murmurs of conversation broke out. The members of the
royal household began to drift back to their beds, to salvage a

few more hours' sleep. Angelo smiled, just a little. With Wulfstan out of the king's favor, he had no more bite than a toothless beast. Now Angelo could concentrate on more pressing matters.

He placed a comradely arm about Aelfric's shoulders. "Good Aelfric," he said in a conversational tone, "whose man are you?"

"The king's man, I should hope, sir," replied Aelfric.

Angelo chuckled warmly. He squeezed the thegn's shoulder. "A proper response, but not quite the one I wished to hear. Again, I ask you—whose man are you?"

Aelfric understood now and answered, "Why, *your* man, sir."

"And wise you are to be so. Have you ever coveted a higher rank than thegn, Aelfric? Say—ealdorman?"

Even in the dim light, Angelo could see Aelfric's eyes glinting with greed. "What do you need me to do?"

A few words settled that affair quite nicely. The next part of Angelo's master plan would be put into action on the morrow. Ten minutes later, Angelo was back in his room, practically tearing off his clothes as the brazier heated up to what to other men would be an almost unbearable warmth.

His thoughts raced. He had had them. Right here, both of them. They were not in sackcloth and prophesying, as Revelation had foretold, but in monk's garb and Dalriada plaid. And instead of fire coming from their mouths, they uttered harsh words toward one another, arguing bitterly over their petty faiths. But they were here. Prophecy had been fulfilled. The signs were all unfolding—skewed in Angelo's favor, but unfolding nonetheless.

He had recognized them at once, of course. He could see, as they could not, the intensified color of their skin and clothes, the faint tracing of golden light about their heads and bodies. They were the two Witnesses; there could be no doubt.

And they had escaped. Rage swept through him like a tide devouring the beach, but it ebbed. Anger would not aid him. There would be time for anger later.

All the time the world could manage.

For now, he needed to find them again. Freed from the uncomfortable clothing, Angelo strode to the brazier and gazed into the coals that appeared to writhe as if in torment from their own heat. The orange and red warmth beat against his face. Reaching down, Angelo stirred the coals with his finger.

Fire shot upward, flickering and shaping itself into a solid black form, like the shadow of a monster.

"My Prince," it crooned, "how may I do your bidding?"

"I must speak with the queen," Angelo told it. The flame flickered, become merely a tongue of fire, and then re-formed. The face, though orange, black, and red, was lovely.

"Well, well," she said in a soft voice. "Are we allies, too, then?"

"Lady Hel," said Angelo, putting a hand on his chest and bowing. Her eyes followed the movement, and continued down, examining the rest of his naked body. He made no attempt to cover himself. Why should he? She apparently liked what she saw, for she smiled as her eyes again met his.

"Allies indeed," said Angelo. "Your father is already my companion, and is busily freeing your brothers. Would you like to aid in our quest as well?"

Hel cocked her head of fire and considered. Wisps of smoke rose from the lines that formed her face.

"I will give you a fine steed of surpassing greatness, and the freedom to roam this land as you will—in return for a favor."

Her enigmatic smile grew. "Speak this favor, fair Angelo, and it is done."

**The North Sea
off the Mouth of the Thames
November 29, 999**

Lightning cracked the sky open like a nut, and thunder boomed after. The rain fell so heavily it felt like a waterfall rather than a shower. The square sails of the longboats could not possibly have gotten wetter; still they swelled with the wind. Another bright flash of lightning revealed the pattern stitched on the sail to Thorkell's eyes.

Despite the dreadful weather, the youth's heart rose at the sight. Drifting alone on the tree upon which the Dragon Odinsson had cast him, his pale flesh burned from the unforgiving sun, his mouth parched and his belly empty, Thorkell had dreamed of the Dragon. He had done as that fearsome lord had commanded in the vision: *Gather followers to this standard. Let it be a golden crown above an arched bow, and let all know that this is a symbol of the right hand of Dragon Odinsson.*

After what he had seen of the Dragon's powers, Thorkell was not inclined to disobey. He was not surprised at the speed with which people rallied, nor at how quickly and easily they conquered rich monasteries and frightened towns. Soon, the Dragon would join them. In the meantime, Thorkell would do his master's work.

The rain stung his skin as it fell. In two more days, the entire fleet would be assembled—his ninety-three ships and another forty-four that were sailing to meet them even now. Once they combined, London would be crushed, and presented to the Dragon, when he chose to return, as a gift.

"Thorkell!" The cry had come from an approaching ship, one of his own. Thorkell frowned and strode forward.

"What is it, Ragnar?"

"There is an Englishman who would have words with you!" The men on Thorkell's ship laughed among themselves.

"Here's a word or two—Blood Eagle!" bellowed one. Thorkell enjoyed the rite of the Blood Eagle. He had performed it on various men who had dared to protest his conquest of their city or monastery. It was an offering to Odin, so the victim died in an honorable fashion—while still alive, his ribs and lungs were cut away and spread out like eagles' wings.

"Nay," said Ragnar. "He bears news and would be our ally. And such a gift—a glorious white horse!"

Thorkell's heart spasmed, and for a moment he couldn't breathe. The white horse—another of the symbols the Dragon had foretold. For a moment he couldn't speak. Then, shouting over the sound of the steady rain that was beginning to turn to hail, he cried, "Let him come hither!"

Ragnar waved to signal he had heard. The ship withdrew. A few moments later, Ragnar returned. A stocky man, looking cold, drenched, and frightened, was with him. The two boats drew alongside one another and, gracelessly, the Englishman climbed into Thorkell's long and elegant warship.

"Unto the right hand of the Dragon, I, Aelfric, give you greetings and n-news," he managed, stuttering from the cold. "Ethelred knows of your progress. He will have several hundred troops here two days from now. He th-thinks to surprise you, to reach London before you have a chance to strike, while you wait for reinforcements from Cornwall. I came to t-tell you—if you move now, tonight, you will encounter a defenseless city."

"Why should I believe you?" asked Thorkell. "How do I know that this is not a trap?"

"I was told, the horse w-would convince you."

All at once, Thorkell believed. He had spoken to no one of the horse. Now he was glad of it. No one could fool him with the knowledge.

"Who sent you?"

"A—a friend," stammered Aelfric. His low brow furrowed with concentration as he quoted, "A friend to you and the Dragon, and to the spoils we will share. Ride in on the white horse, beneath the crown and the bow, and know that you are fulfilling destiny. That's what he told me to tell you."

"And that will serve," stated Thorkell. "Return to your vessel, Aelfric. I thank you, and the Dragon will not forget those who have helped him. Ragnar, give him wine and food, and spread the word among the Force—we attack tonight."

His traitorous errand done, the man finally relaxed. Perhaps it was the mention of the wine.

Over the course of the next few hours, the rain turned to hard nuggets of hail. Thorkell and his men waited patiently for the concealing blanket of nightfall. Yet, in the end, it did not conceal. Nearly constant bolts of lightning illuminated the night with a light as bright as the sun. The inhabitants of London were able to see their doom come upon them in the form of a hundred Norse longships sailing down the Thames. The lightning seemed to be an ally of the conquering force, as if the god Thor himself was fighting on their side. It struck the city as the Norsemen did, causing fire and still more panic. Thorkell's men behaved like the berserkers of legend, more interested in killing than in looting, until the dark red of blood joined the rainwater in running toward the Thames.

By the time the sky had begun to lighten the next morning, London had fallen to the Force. More than a third of the city was afire with blazes that would not be put out, and the sun could barely be glimpsed as a pale orb in the black haze. The smoke was visible from as far away as Kingston, where King Ethelred's army, as one man, stumbled to a halt and stared in silence.

Fenris had not moved from his seated position at the bow of Nagelfar since they began. Loki had known where to find his eldest child, but his younger son had been flung into the deep waters of Midgard's oceans. Loki had to trust the keen nose of Fenris to sniff out his brother from all the wide world.

The wolf had not disappointed him. From Yarnvid they had sailed back into waters wholly of this world, south toward the island that had yielded such plunder to Loki's people. In the northern part of this island, they would find Jormungand, Fenris assured him.

They were closer now, and the wolf's lean body quivered with anticipation. Loki moved forward, feeling the clean, cold wind caress his face and turn his long black hair into an ebony wave. He laid a loving hand on the wolf's head, caressing the smooth fur and absently outlining the numerals emblazoned there.

"We are coming close to the land," Loki said. Up ahead, brown and green against the lowering gray clouds that seemed this island's constant companion, the land awaited. "Jormungand is in the sea."

Fenris shook his head, his amber eyes fastened on the shoreline. "No. He is trapped, Father. Trapped as surely as I was—in there. I can smell him."

Surprised, Loki looked with renewed interest at this place. There was a river leading inward, but surely it was too small for the great Jormungand to travel.

Then he recalled how much time had truly passed. Eons. Perhaps at one point, this little river had been a wide mouth of a lake. Had Jormungand headed for quiet waters for some reason, slept the long sleep of the immortals, and awakened to find himself a prisoner of his own making? The shape of the earth was not a constant. Loki, god of fire and earthquakes, knew that much.

"Yes," confirmed Fenris. "He is there. Waiting."

Loki turned and ordered his crew to sail down the mouth of the river. Large as the longship was, it had been designed with just such a purpose in mind. Not all houses of the Christian god and wealthy towns were obliging enough to be located right on the ocean's shore. Sometimes, one had to go inland to find what one wanted.

Slowly, the ship of the dead sailed down the river. Now and then Loki saw signs of human habitation, and he knew that someone must be witnessing the white vessel's progress. What of it? He meant to cause fear, terror, dread—that was the task Angelo had assigned him in order to be freed. Let them see the ship of dead men's nails, crewed by ghosts, with the dread beast Fenris and the Dragon Odinsson at the bow.

After a few miles, the river opened up. It was a large lake, nearly a mile across. It seemed to go on forever. Yes. Even Jormungand could hide here, if he wished.

Loki stepped forward, cupped his hands around his mouth, and filled his lungs. "Jormungand!" he cried. "It is I, Loki, and your brother Fenris! Show yourself, my son!"

For a long moment, the mirror-still surface of the lake—Loch Ness, he believed the locals called it—remained calm. This place was almost as gray as Yarnvid, though here and there one could see green or purple or blue. Loki waited. He had just drawn breath to cry again when there was a slight disturbance on the water.

And then it began to boil. Nagelfar was tossed like a child's wooden ship, and Loki and Fenris were knocked off their feet. Only the ghosts remained unperturbed, moving about the task of righting the vessel with their usual slow, precise movements. Loki stumbled to his feet as Nagelfar lurched beneath him, hanging on as wave after wave broke on the ship.

The monstrous head broke the surface. Loki's heart ached at the beauty of his child. Silver-green and blue he was, with golden eyes and teeth as white as the moon. Jormungand's bellow of joy nearly made Loki's human ears bleed.

The serpent had grown since Loki had last seen him. Then, he had been only a few hundred feet long, thick only as Loki's own body. Now, Jormungand was ten times that size, at least. He had grown to fit this lake; indeed, he was taking up most of it. How large would he grow when the ocean was his home? *Large enough to bring down Thor at Ragnarok,* Loki thought.

The serpent was still screaming. Finally it spent its voice and dropped its massive head to Loki's.

"You look not like my father," it growled in a voice so deep it seemed to rattle Loki's very bones.

"But surely you know me, brother," said Fenris. "This is in truth our father—in a borrowed body. We have come to free you."

"RAGNAROK!" bellowed the serpent joyfully. Its frenzied thrashing nearly capsized Nagelfar.

"Not yet, my child. But soon."

"Father, I am too large for this place. I am trapped. I yearn for the open ocean. How do I escape?"

Fenris's eyes gleamed. "When bound by Gleipnir, I could not grow," he said. "But now, I shall free you, my poor Jormungand." He leaped into the water, and before Loki's eyes his shape began to expand. Tears of pride stung Loki's eyes. What marvelous creatures his children were!

Larger Fenris grew, until he was the size of Nagelfar. Larger still, until the deep waters of the loch reached only to his belly. Barking joyfully, he splashed through the water toward the place where the river met the loch. He began to dig. Beneath his paws, the earth trembled.

Overcome with his own delight, Loki whooped and leaped into the loch. With the gentleness of the doe toward its fawn, Jormungand slipped his giant head beneath Loki's body and raised him up, higher and higher. Loki clung to one of the three horns atop Jormungand's head, each one as tall as a man. Beneath his feet, the iridescent scales stretched in a multitude of jeweled colors. From this dizzying height, the world seemed full not of real dwellings and boulders and trees, but of mere toys.

Fenris dug. A mountain of earth was flung up by his giant, industrious paws and tossed about carelessly. Whole houses were buried beneath the chunks of earth displaced by the mighty creature. Finally, the way was open. Loki returned to his ship and followed as Fenris bounded out to the ocean, and Jormungand's coils sinuously twisted toward freedom.

11

*Your old men shall dream dreams, your
young men shall see visions*
                                    — JOEL 2:28

**The Foss Way
November 30, 999**

Kennag dozed as she rode, jerking herself awake with a rebuke
each time but succumbing again after a few moments. There had
been so little time for proper rest, and the Faerie horse's gait was
so smooth, it was hard work staying awake.

They had begun their journey with the frantic bolting from
Ethelred's villa at Calne. Thanks in large part to Neddy, their escape had been successful. Part of Kennag ached to think she had
asked it of the poor child. Using him to frighten the guards
had merely reinforced his sense of being an outcast. But there
had been no other way, and Neddy had assured them repeatedly
that he was only too happy to be of help—to be of value to someone. Kennag suspected that the boy-ghost had something of an
infatuation with her.

She, meanwhile, felt a powerful maternal affection for Neddy,
even though, had he been alive, she would have been only five or
so years his elder. Suddenly she chuckled at the thought. They
didn't know when Neddy had been born, or had died. Conceivably, he could be hundreds of years *her* elder.

"What's so amusing?" asked Alwyn, the query turning into a
yawn.

Kennag shook her head. "Nothing of import."

Silence fell again. Kennag shifted on the horse, wishing they had had time to bring the saddles. She was uneasy with this shared, strained silence. Ever since the heart-stopping flight had wound down and they had been able to proceed in safety, they had had little to say to one another after their destination had been selected.

Alwyn had proposed a place called Glastonbury. It was a great site of pilgrimage, he told her, and home to one of the most illustrious abbeys in England. Kennag had been reluctant at first, until Neddy piped up.

"Glastonbury," he said, his spectral brow wrinkling. "It sounds familiar. It's long been a holy place—before us there were the Celts, and before them, the druids. I . . . remember . . . I've been there, I think."

That was sufficient for Kennag. That, and the fact that it was much closer to Calne than any holy places with which she was familiar. Their destination selected, they had traveled without speaking. Kennag was as guilty as the monk.

She knew this wasn't right. She accepted that they had been flung together for the good of every living thing in the world— for the good of the world itself. It was wrong for them to be so estranged. They needed to be close, as close as or closer than a child with her parents, or lovers in the aftermath of passion, if they were to succeed. The thought again made her chuckle. She decided not to share the comparison with the young monk.

In an effort to build a bridge to span the uncomfortable gulf between them, Kennag voiced some questions.

"You and your Wulfstan seem to be quite well versed in lore regarding the end of the world," she said. "How is it you know so much? We've nothing comparable in our tales."

"It's been the subject of much theological discussion," Alwyn replied. "Bishop Wulfstan has preached several sermons on it. There's an entire book of the Bible devoted to the end of the world. It's called the book of Revelation, because the information was revealed to the author in a series of visions."

"Ah!" said Kennag, warming to the topic. "The Second Sight."

Alwyn frowned. "I suppose you could call it that. We prefer to think of it as the hand of God. There are several signs that will occur before the final Day of Judgment takes place. And that will be a most joyous day."

"Wait a moment," said Kennag. "Joyous? Then why are you supposed to stop it?"

"Because it's not the *true* hour," explained Alwyn. "Satan—the great fallen angel, the enemy of God—is bringing about the signs before their rightful time. As I understand it, from what Wulfstan and Michael have told me, if he succeeds, he will be able to reign forever. There will be no Judgment Day, no true reward for the righteous—only eternal Hell, with Satan as our master. That's why we have to stop him."

Ratatosk had disappeared on some squirrely errand, and Rowena had slipped away to forage for her supper. Neddy had gone—wherever it was ghosts go when they aren't present. She and Alwyn were alone, save for their mounts. The hooves of the horse and donkey made soft plops in the muddy road. That was another good reason to have selected Glastonbury. As it was such a favored site of pilgrimage, there were at least roads that led to it, and the winters were kinder in this region called Somerset—"the summer land."

Other names popped into her head: *Sumorsaete,* Region of the Summer Stars. Her skin prickled. Yes, for now, they were on the right path.

"But how, Alwyn?" She turned to look at him, and met his unhappy gaze before he glanced away quickly. "How do we stop a fallen angel?"

"The only thing I can think of is that we must prevent the signs from happening. Michael said there was a limited amount of time for Satan to act. By our calendar, we are about to end a millennium—a thousand years since the birth of Christ."

Kennag was not unfamiliar with the way the Christians reckoned their years and did the math. "That's not right. A thousand years since the birth of your Christ won't be complete until the end of the year 1000."

A delighted smile lit up Alwyn's face. "You're a sharp one," he said. "That's absolutely correct. But most people don't realize that. The year 999 has a powerful pull for them. There are thousands making their way to Rome, to be in the Holy City with the pope before the world ends on December 31. Others are heading for Jerusalem. People are terrified, Kennag. They fear the end of the world—and Satan is using their fear. It's like food to him. He is preying on it. It is giving him power to bring about these false signs. Michael seemed to feel that if we can stop the signs before the end of this year, Satan's most potent source of power—human fear of the End Time—will disappear."

"That makes a certain amount of sense. Very ordered, your Satan. So what are these signs?"

Alwyn sat up straighter on the donkey. Clearly, it pleased him to be able to provide concrete information that could aid their quest.

"There are seven seals that will be broken, seven trumpets that will be sounded, and seven vials whose contents will be poured upon the earth."

"You like the number seven."

"It's the number of perfection."

Kennag smiled. "That's lucky. We are seven. You, I, Balaam, my steed, Rowena, Ratatosk, and Neddy."

"So we are. We can use all the luck we can get." Alwyn fell silent, lost in thought.

"The seven signs?" prompted Kennag.

He nodded, and began. "When the First Seal is broken, a White Horse will appear."

Kennag suddenly felt dizzy. She blinked, trying to clear her vision, and clutched her mount's mane. Alwyn continued.

"Its rider will carry a bow and be given a crown, and he will ride out like a warrior bent on conquest. The first—"

Light exploded behind Kennag's eyes. Agony ripped through her and she tumbled off the horse, barely noticing as she hit the muddy earth, uncaring at Alwyn's cry of surprise.

Young he was; in his first beard's growth, no more. But those eyes had seen things dark and terrifying, and he sat upon the white horse that was no horse like a king surveying his kingdom. Hail pelted down on him, but he paid it no heed. His men went mad, like a starving pack of wolves among simple sheep, and the smoke floated upward like a living shadow. Fire burned, consuming all. Above the scene of carnage fluttered a standard, a golden crown and the smooth arc of a bow. . . .

. . . The church was filled with the dead and dying. Men groaned and wept like children; the women were stoically silent, having known pain like this ere now. Black were their limbs, and sores wept pus and blood. . . .

. . . A wolf leaped from the bow of a peculiar white ship into cold gray waters. He threw back his head and howled, the noise silent to Kennag's ears, and began to grow. The gigantic beast

*splashed about, like a puppy in a rivulet, and began to dig. Earth
flew from his busy paws and the earth shook in protest—*

Her vision cleared, and she saw Alwyn's pale, frightened face
peering into hers. He patted her cheek awkwardly. "Kennag?"

"Alwyn?" she whispered.

He closed his eyes in relief. "I feared the worst when the fit
took you. Are you all right now?"

She nodded, wincing as pain shot through her temples at the
movement. But she was all right. She lay in the middle of
the road, wrapped in every piece of spare cloth the monk had. He
was sitting beside her, and from above, the faces of Balaam, her
horse, Rowena, Ratatosk, and Neddy started down at her.

She struggled to sit. Alwyn slipped a surprisingly strong right
arm beneath her. "What happened?"

Kennag shivered. Her body, snapped out of its trance, was
aware of the cold and was responding to it. "You mentioned a
m-man with a crown and bow on a white horse," she said, her
teeth chattering. "Was there also a battle ending in fire and hail?
A p-plague of sores and rotting flesh? And a giant wolf digging
in a body of water?"

Alwyn's brown eyes had gone wide. "The First Trumpet an-
nounces hail and fire mixed with blood," he whispered. "And the
First Vial is a plague of sores."

Overcome, Kennag reached out and clutched at the rough
brown fabric of his robe. "Then—then I have Seen them. I think
these signs have already happened."

They decided to make camp right there. Kennag was still drained
from her Second Sight experience, so Alwyn shushed her
protests and prepared a meal for both of them. It was simple—
they had not had a chance to replenish their supplies following
their hasty departure from Calne—but at least it was something
to fill their stomachs. Kennag offered up what she had as well.

Their supper consisted of dried meat, dry bread, a small bit of
cheese, and tea made from dried herbs Kennag had brought
along. Alwyn had not wanted to partake of the dried meat; the
Rule forbade brothers to eat flesh save in sickness. Kennag bul-
lied him into it, arguing convincingly that who knew what they
would find to supplement their meals from here on, and his God
would surely forgive him if he kept himself from starving to
death before his task was completed.

Kennag felt somewhat better, more grounded, after the meal. Neither of them had spoken further of her visions, but they needed to. The odd company huddled around the fire, all but Neddy, who required no warmth.

In a quiet voice, staring into the feeble flames that struggled to keep back the cold and darkness, Kennag described her visions in detail. Alwyn did not interrupt until she had finished.

"Most of what you Saw does sound like the fulfillment of the first few prophecies. The youth on the white horse with the standard of the bow and crown is obvious. The battle with hail, fire, and blood—that fits as well. The sores remind me of St. Anthony's fire, and the church, as you described it, sounds like my abbey. But some of it I don't understand. There is no wolf spoken of in Revelation. There is a beast, but—"

"I can explain that," interrupted Ratatosk. They all turned to stare at him. He sat perched on Kennag's shoulder, looking as somber as it is possible for a squirrel to look. "You know I am no ordinary creature. My home is Yggdrasil, the mighty Tree of Life. My job is to run its length, carrying insults from the Eagle perched on the tree's highest branch to the Dragon deep in Nilfheim."

A snort came from the darkness. Neddy grinned. "Your job is to carry insults? That's funny!"

The squirrel straightened. "I take it very seriously," he chirped.

"I've never heard of this Tree of Life," said Alwyn.

"I have," said Kennag. "It is part of the Norsemen's faith. It runs through all the worlds. Allfather Odin hung on it to gain wisdom. Just like your Christ hung on the cross."

Alwyn looked terribly offended at the comparison, but Kennag could spare no energy to soothe his ruffled feathers. "Go on, Ratatosk. What of the wolf I saw?"

Ratatosk twitched his fluffy tail. "I have been gathering information on my trips, and this is what I have learned. The wolf that Kennag Saw is none other than the Fenris Wolf, the eldest child of Loki the Trickster. Only he could grow so enormous and move a mountain of earth so easily. Both he and his father were imprisoned long ago, never to be freed until Ragnarok—*our* end of the world."

"Move a mountain," said Alwyn slowly. "That's the second trumpet—a mountain is thrown into the sea."

"What are the other signs?" asked Kennag. She was startled at how steady her voice was.

"Will you be all right if I name them?"

"I'll have to be, won't I?"

His eyes searched hers, then he nodded. "The Second Seal will release a Red Horse. Its rider has the power to take peace from the earth and make men slay each other. The Second Trumpet, as I said, is a mountain thrown into the sea. The Second Vial will turn the sea to blood."

Kennag nodded. When he mentioned the mountain, she again saw the Fenris Wolf digging furiously. This time, she noticed strange marks on his forehead. She decided to ask Alwyn about them when he had finished the dark list. Thus far, she had seen no new visions.

"Keep going."

"The Third Seal releases a Black Horse. Its rider is Famine. The Third Trumpet heralds a great blazing star named Wormwood falling from the sky. A third of the earth's pure water will be poisoned. With the Third Vial, a third of the world's rivers and springs will become blood."

"This end of the world scenario is infatuated with turning water to blood," said Kennag.

"The Fourth Seal releases the Pale Horse," continued Alwyn, ignoring her. "Its rider is Death. The Fourth Trumpet signals that a third of the sun, moon, and stars will turn dark. An eagle will fly over the earth, announcing the carnage that is and is to come. The Fourth Vial scorches the earth with the sun's fire. Anything yet?"

"No," said Kennag. "Nothing. I don't think any of these have yet occurred. Continue."

"At the breaking of the Fifth Seal, under the altar of God those who were martyred for their faith will cry out. The last martyr will join them. At the Fifth Trumpet, a star falls and opens the abyss. Dreadful locusts, under the command of the Antichrist and Satan, will pour forth. At the Fifth Vial, the entire world will be plunged into darkness."

Rowena hissed softly. Her ears were flat. Kennag stretched out a hand to pet her soft fur and offer mute comfort. She was as terrified as the cat by Alwyn's litany of horrors. This God of his certainly liked dark and frightening things.

"There will be an earthquake at the opening of the Sixth Seal.

The sun will turn black, the moon will turn red, and stars will hurtle toward earth. The sounding of the Sixth Trumpet will release four angels who will kill a third of mankind."

"I thought angels were like the Seelie Court—good folk," murmured Kennag. She trembled uncontrollably, and not from the cold.

"That is true. But they have their duties, and they may not shirk them," said Alwyn. "At the Sixth Vial, the mighty rivers dry up. Three evil spirits perform what will seem like miracles, to lure people to the side of Satan and the Antichrist."

Seven. We've finally reached seven, thought Kennag, clinging to the thought like a drowning man gripping a line.

"At the Seventh Seal, there will be a silence in Heaven."

Kennag blinked. This was so vague, and all the other signs had been specific—explicit, in fact. "What does that mean?"

"No one knows. I guess we'll find out," Alwyn said with a touch of black humor.

Angrily, Kennag shoved him. "Do not even say such things! Finish, quickly."

"The rest is all fire, flood, earthquakes—disaster of every imaginable sort. Then comes the final judgment."

Kennag bowed her head, her mind filled not with images of horror and destruction, but with the beautiful, mutable faces of the Faerie King and Faerie Queen. This two edged-sword, the Second Sight—that gift had given them a way to know which of the signs had been completed. When she lifted her head and again regarded Alwyn, tears glittered in her eyes. She blinked them back.

"We have a weapon, Alwyn," she said. "Praise be to my gods and yours for this, at least."

Alwyn made the sign of the cross. "I suppose we must be grateful for anything, at this point. I thought this Second Sight was supposed to see the future—to see what could be, so that we can prevent it."

Kennag smiled wryly. "It does what it does. It's not under my control. I accept what it offers." *And the price it exacts,* she added silently. "A few more questions for you. I noticed a strange design on the forehead of the—of the Fenris Wolf. It looked like this. Does it have any meaning for you?"

With a stick she traced a series of lines and curves, careful to replicate them exactly as they had appeared in her vision:

DCLXVI. Considering how dark the situation was, she had expected him to react badly, but once his eyes had traveled over the symbols, she feared a sudden collapse. His eyes went wide, his face pale.

"No," he whispered, crossing himself not once but many times in rapid succession. "No, please, dear Jesu, forbid it, let this cup pass. . . ."

"Alwyn?" Fear leaped from him to her like fire to kindling. "Alwyn, please tell me! What does this mean?" She had to reach out and shake him roughly before he seemed to recognize her.

"When Wulfstan spoke of the Antichrist—I had hoped—Oh, I don't know what I hoped, but—"

"Alwyn!" Her voice cracked like thunder in the stillness.

"The beast," he murmured. "The symbols on Fenris's brow are Roman numerals. They form the number six hundred sixty-six—the number of the Beast, as foretold in Revelation. The beast is an ally of the Antichrist, and that means—"

"Loki must be your Antichrist—your tool of Satan," breathed Kennag. "Well. It would appear that all the guests have arrived at the festival."

"I must apologize, on behalf of all the Aesir," said Ratatosk. "Loki always was such a bother. And now look what he's done—allied with your nasty fallen angel. Perhaps he hopes to bring about Ragnarok."

"I don't suppose this Satan has a soft spot for helpless, innocent animals—like donkeys?" asked Balaam in a hopeful voice.

"He's supposed to like cats," said Rowena. "Not that the connection in people's minds has done me any good."

"I don't understand," said Neddy. "From what you've told us, Alwyn, this shouldn't surprise you. You knew Satan and the Antichrist were afoot. Why are you so upset?"

"It's difficult seeing your fears turned into reality," said Kennag softly, "even if you knew, in your heart, they were there."

Alwyn suddenly rose and shook his head violently. "No, that's not it at all. It's—" He dragged his right sleeve over his face, wiping away sudden tears. "Oh, Michael. You should have chosen another. Kennag, you should have refused the call. We both should have."

"Alwyn, do not speak so!" Though still weak, Kennag got to her feet and went to where he leaned against the firm support of an ancient oak. "It is an honor."

"I hadn't wanted to tell you, yet. I wanted—" He took a deep breath and softly beat his hand upon the old oak tree. "We are mentioned in the Bible, too—you and I," he said, not looking at her. He faced away from the fire, and his features were cloaked in shadow. "God selects two Witnesses. He gives them power to stand and prophesy for a certain time. They will have special powers with which to stand against all those who would harm them. They will dress in sackcloth, and fire will come from their mouths."

Kennag opened her mouth for an irreverent quip. Alwyn turned to look at her and the expression on his face killed any joke she might utter. She struggled to speak, even as she dreaded what he would say.

"What happens to the two Witnesses?"

He turned his face away from her and said into the darkness, "The Beast from the abyss kills them."

12

The lips of a strange woman drop as a
honeycomb, and her mouth is smoother
than oil; but her end is bitter as worm-
wood, sharp as a two-edged sword.
                              —PROVERBS 5:3–4

The Residence of Queen Elfthryth, Kingston
November 30, 999

Queen Elfthryth listened with half an ear to her son's prattling.
The gentle, repetitive scraping of the theow-woman's comb
against her scalp was comforting, and Ethelred was hardly an or-
ator worthy of attention. Elfthryth gazed at her reflection in the
polished brass mirror, not liking what she saw.

Once, Elfthryth had been heart-stoppingly beautiful. As a ripe
young woman she had caught King Edgar's eye, and a bit more
of him as well. She reached to touch her sagging cheeks with
hands that were spotted and wrinkled. Jesu, was her hair really
that gray? Surely it was merely a trick of the smoky lamplight in
her quarters. She frowned in annoyance at the poor lighting. God
alone knew why Ethelred was so insistent that there be no candles at his royal residences. Elfthryth touched the thick mass, un-
bound as her slave combed it out, and felt it coarse against her
fingers, instead of fine and smooth like silk.

Elfthryth was afraid of very little. She was not afraid of bedding a king already wed, of marrying him when his wife was
barely cold, of calculatedly murdering the fruit of that earlier
lawful union. But she was terrified of the merciless encroach-

ment of time—and what awaited her at the end of her allotted sliver of it.

"So, what is your opinion, Mother?"

"Hmmm?" She glanced disinterestedly at her son, who was leaning against the door. His head was ducked down and his shoulders were hunched. That ridiculous shade of blue he had dyed his hair and beard was starting to grow out, thank God. Whims—the boy was such a slave to them.

He rolled his eyes and swore. "What didn't you hear?"

"All of it," she snapped, and waved a commanding hand at him. "Repeat yourself, and be less tedious in the telling this time."

His blue eyes flickered. For just a moment, she could see some of Edgar in him, then the brief fluttering of defiance faded.

"I said, things are going very badly for us. I've done everything you and Angelo have told me to. I even offered to triple the Danegeld, but it doesn't seem to work now. They're all caught up in this Dragon Odinsson furor, and plunder seems less to their liking than this religious zeal. Angelo has mentioned something I—"

His face grew pink, and he turned away. Instantly alert, Elfthryth narrowed her eyes and sat up in her chair. The unexpected movement caused the theow to tug painfully at her scalp.

"Ouch! Foolish girl! Out with you!"

The slave, horrified at her slip, did not dare to speak. Bowing and cramming her fist to her mouth, she scampered away with the urgency of a rabbit. Ethelred moved back from the wooden door just enough so that she could slip out, and then, as if she had never been present, resumed leaning on it.

"What has our wise friend said?" asked Elfthryth, forcing her voice to sound soft and maternal. "Tell me."

"It is—I am afraid to say—it sounds so arrogant—"

Anger washed through the aging queen. Damn the boy, this was precisely what had so tried her patience so long ago, this hesitancy in speech and lack of spirit. She recalled that once, having no rod handy with which to discipline the boy properly, she'd snatched up a candle and beaten him about the face with that. Even the thick ones from the altar eventually broke from her energized ministrations, so they weren't the most useful of tools, but they had accomplished the goal. She itched for a rod now, though the boy was a man grown.

"It's just—"

"Out with it!"

He cringed and spoke rapidly, before his tongue could betray him again with its clumsiness. "Angelo says that Otto isn't a worthy man to be Emperor of Europe—and that I am."

"You? *Emperor?*" She tried to keep the shock out of her voice, and failed. At least she was able to choke back the roar of laughter at the absurdity of the notion.

The bubble of mirth rising inside her belly abruptly subsided. Was it really so absurd, after all? She knew what Angelo was, what he was trying to do, and had been a willing accomplice—provided that, through her son, she would be raised as high as a woman could go in this world. The Dowager Empress—*that* certainly would be even higher than her present position. It was true that Elfgifu, the soft and humble thing that was Ethelred's queen, would be empress. But it had been simplicity itself to trample over Elfgifu's weak protests up till now. Surely the role of empress, if not title, would belong to Elfthryth.

Elfthryth was no theologian, but even she knew the tale of the Last Emperor. The one who would rule the world at the End Time, hand over the earthly kingdom to the King of Kings, and die peacefully.

Except—

No fox, when the trap was unexpectedly sprung by happy accident, could have raced free with more joy than Elfthryth felt now. Yes. *Yes.* If the Last Emperor never died—

She rose, slowly and with pain, and hobbled to her only child. Disbelief washed over his visage as she reached up and brought his bearded face down to her withered lips. Elfthryth kissed his forehead, his cheeks, his mouth. By his expression, he mistook the delight she was feeling at her escape for pride. He pulled back and stared at her in astonishment.

"My boy," she said, her voice thick with tears of relief, "you would make a fine emperor. God will be pleased."

An idiot's grin spread across his handsome face.

"Yes, God will certainly be pleased," came a voice, startling them both, "but first I have some unpleasant business to set before Your Majesty."

It was Angelo, of course. As was his wont, he had stolen upon them with all the warning that a cat gives of its presence.

"What is it, Angelo? What has happened now?" The dull

weariness in Ethelred's voice was almost enough to make Elfthryth pity him. Almost.

"There is a traitor in your midst, Majesty," said Angelo solemnly. "As I had feared, the Force that so devastated London had warning of our approach." He leaned out the door and gestured. "Bring him in."

A moment later, a shuffling, bleeding shape entered. It was only after looking hard that Elfthryth recognized the broken, bound man before her as the newly made Ealdorman Aelfric.

"Aelfric!" Ethelred's voice was high with horror. His eyes grew red and Elfthryth realized that the king was perilously close to tears. "Aelfric, why? Were you not treated well? Did I not just grant you the rights of an ealdorman?"

An incoherent grunting noise issued from Aelfric's mouth. Elfthryth realized that the unfortunate traitor had had his tongue removed. Angelo let him gibber for a moment, then cuffed the man hard. Aelfric fell silent. Tears welled from his eyes and spilled down his cheeks, wetting his beard.

"I'm afraid that he spoke so violently against Your Majesty that it was necessary to cut out his tongue," Angelo apologized. "But not before we retrieved a great deal of information. There are many, many traitors present, Majesty, including those whom you trust. I have a list of names, which we will go over at your leisure. Some," he added, "are even among the Witan."

"No!" Ethelred blinked hard. "This must stop. I must bring the men who are wavering in their loyalty back into the fold, as a good shepherd ought. The signs do not augur well, but we will pray to God, who will see the rightness of our cause!"

He turned unexpectedly on Elfthryth. "Mother, you know I love you dearly, and that I know you had no part in the murder of my brother the king. But there are others who whisper of treason and the wrath of God being visited upon us in the form of the Norsemen. Is not one of the signs of the arrival of the Antichrist supposed to be the coming of the warlike races first? I have a favor to ask of you."

"What is it?" Elfthryth tensed. Normally she would have silenced her son with a curt word, but this was a delicate balance. He needed to think, always, that he was the one in command.

"Make a pilgrimage. Go to Shaftesbury Abbey and place an offering on King Edward the Martyr's tomb. If the people see you make this pilgrimage, they will know that you are free from stain."

Her heart began to beat rapidly. She licked dry lips and glanced at Angelo.

He nodded his golden head. "Anything you can do to strengthen the people's faith in you and your noble son, Great Lady, is surely in God's cause."

He, too? She did not want to go. She had not suffered a moment's guilt for the crime she had committed, but she had always endured a terrible fear that her part in it would someday surface. Ethelred's memories had been . . . adjusted. Angelo would never tell—he was the killer himself. And the men who had witnessed it had long since met with oh so tragic accidents.

The dead were the dead, surely. Edward had been possessed of a great temper. He was no saint, canonized though he be. If God hadn't chosen to strike her down yet, surely He didn't much care about His murdered, ill-tempered child.

And yet. . . .

She swallowed hard and said in as calm a voice as she could manage, "Certainly I will go to Shaftesbury."

Ethelred smiled, a little, though it did not reach his eyes. "Good. Thank you, Mother." He squared his shoulders and returned his attention to the man before him. "Aelfric, you cannot tell me why you betrayed your king. But the reasons don't really matter. All that matters is that you did commit treason, and for that you must die the death of traitors."

He didn't need to say the three dreadful words: *hanged, drawn, and quartered.* Everyone knew the punishment for treason. Aelfric closed his eyes slowly as his sentence was pronounced.

"But first," said Angelo, "we must send a message to any others who might be thinking of following Aelfric's evil lead."

"How do you mean?" asked Ethelred. "Surely the manner of his death—"

"Such deaths did not discourage Aelfric," Angelo pointed out, "and may not be a sufficiently strong deterrent to others." Again he leaned out the door and gestured.

The man who entered, pushed roughly inside by a thegn, was no grizzled, beaten traitor. He was a youth, perhaps only a little over sixteen. Fine black hair was only beginning to paint his upper lip and chin. Yet he, too, was bound like a criminal. His tongue had not been cut out, but a gag silenced him just as effectively. At the sight of the youth, Aelfric suddenly began to struggle with renewed vigor, screaming *ungh ungh ungh* until Elfthryth winced with the noise.

"This youth," said Angelo, "had the misfortune to be born the eldest son of Aelfric. As the Bible tells us, the iniquities of the fathers are visited upon the children. The boy must suffer for the dreadful things his father has done."

The boy turned eyes huge with terror upon Ethelred. The rag in his mouth rendered him mute, but he did not need words to plead. Angelo had clearly had enough of Aelfric's wordless screams. Aelfric's arms were tied behind his back. With casual violence Angelo seized the man's arm and yanked it up and backward.

"Silence," he hissed. Aelfric's noises ceased.

"Angelo—I fear your words—what do you mean? I cannot murder a boy just because his father betrayed me!"

"No," Angelo said, "Not murder. Punish." Angelo's face was oddly tranquil, considering the words he was uttering. There was no anger, no thirst for vengeance—only the calm visage of one who is entirely at peace with what he is doing. Elfthryth's eyes darted from Angelo to Ethelred. What was transpiring was key to their success, Angelo's and hers.

"What do you mean?" cried Ethelred.

"He has seen a terrible thing—his father betraying his king. Let him nevermore see anything so dreadful."

A terrible silence settled on the room as all of them realized the meaning of Angelo's carefully chosen words. Then, as one, sentenced father and son began to struggle. Ethelred blinked, like an owl in the sunlight.

"I . . . can't. . . ."

"You must." Angelo's clear voice was merciless. "You are the one wronged. You must make it right." He presented Ethelred with a jeweled dagger. Elfthryth hadn't noticed him draw it.

Ethelred stared at the beautiful, sharp implement in his adviser's uncalled palm, its hilt toward him. He didn't move for a long time. When, at last, with the hesitancy and seeming pain of a man of thrice his years, he reached for the blade, Elfthryth felt a sudden thrill of victory.

Ethelred was theirs.

The Island of Iona
December 2, 999

Loki could hear the bells of the little church even above the sound of the waves. He smiled. The bells would be silent soon enough.

Thanks to the speed and power of Jormungand, he had made his way southward to the Thames River in what seemed to him to be mere minutes. There, Loki had found young Thorkell, who wept aloud at beholding the Dragon Odinsson once again. Thorkell's fleet of nearly a hundred had by this time been joined by others—others who, at another place and time, would have competed with the youth for the spoils of war. Now, they rallied united under the Dragon's standard. Such a fleet, the waters of this world had seldom seen. The ships followed him, and he led them northward again, to the west of the island. Loki's powers over the ocean—part of the "dark gifts" of this Antichrist whose role he was playing—permitted him to call remarkable winds and to cause the waves to move faster than was their natural wont. The Force had made the thousand-mile journey, a voyage that would have taken them ten to twelve days under good circumstances, in a miraculous three.

The entire fleet had reached this little island called Iona. And the simple monks could no more stand against the Force than a stalk of grain against the sickle.

For just a brief moment, Loki felt sorry for these wretched mortals. As Nagelfar approached the "holy shore," he could see them swarming like ants in their fruitless labor: gathering their books and flinging them into coracles—as if they could hope to reach the mainland before the Vikings landed. Falling to their knees and praying. They seemed to have hope, although their end was certain.

He shrugged off the feeling of pity, leaped out into the water, and splashed ashore.

A young monk, no more than one and twenty if that, rushed toward him. Loki was surprised. Monks generally didn't fight. Perhaps this fellow was still new to the ways of his too-peaceful God. His only weapon was a staff, which he swung inexpertly at Loki's head, and Loki realized the boy was crying. It was a pathetic effort, and Loki showed his compassion by slicing the monk almost in half with a single quick movement of his ax. The boy didn't suffer.

His followers were almost all ashore now. They ran up the bank, howling almost as loudly as Fenris, who now leaped off Nagelfar and joined in the fray. No hound hunting rabbits could have had the pleasure that Fenris now experienced. He permitted himself to grow as large as the church in which these monks worshiped, and yipped with savage pleasure as his mighty teeth claimed one man after the other.

The smell of fire reached Loki's nostrils, mingling with the clean, salty fragrance of the ocean and the acrid scent of freshly spilled blood. A bellow of bovine fear reached his ears, and he paused in his slaughter. Several of his men had brought down a fat cow, no doubt planning on a feast tonight.

"Not the cattle!" he cried. "Leave them be!" Loki was annoyed. He had carefully instructed his men as Angelo had told him: *Kill all the monks, take what plunder you will, burn their church and outbuildings—but do not harm their livestock.* It made the same sense to the men as it had to Loki—none. But Angelo's instructions were often nonsensical, and Loki had merely shrugged and promised to obey them.

The men paused in their butchering of the cow, gazing at him with round, terror-filled eyes. Loki relented. His men would be hungry by the time this was all done, and surely one cow couldn't harm anything. He waved them to continue, adding, "But no more!"

It was all over in a matter of minutes. Soon, the only sounds were the frightened lowing of the spared cattle and the whooping laughter of his victorious men. Loki lowered his gore-stained ax and looked around.

The bodies were everywhere. One or two still whimpered or spasmed in their death throes, but after a moment or two, even they fell silent. Loki realized he was breathing hard. This body, fit as it was, did have limits.

Fenris bounded toward him, the size of a normal wolf now, quickly licked his father's face, and capered away again.

Loki glanced down to see that he was more red than any other color. He grimaced. He always prided himself on his cleanliness. Tossing his weapon to the blood-soaked earth, Loki made for the ocean, thinking to rinse himself off. He had gone only a few steps when he saw that the ocean itself was becoming tinged with an unnatural, ruddy hue. He stopped in midstride.

The bloody water began to churn. Before his eyes, it formed itself into a whirlpool. Loki frowned. He had not commanded this of the ocean, and Jormungand was nowhere to be seen. What new surprise was this?

The whirlpool sped faster and faster, closing in on itself, and began to funnel upward. As Loki watched in wonder, the red water took on shape and substance. Four legs appeared. A long torso topped with an arching neck. A tail, ears, muzzle, hooves. With a neigh that sounded like the boom of a wave on the shore, the blood-water-horse tossed its head and splashed toward solid ground. It pranced wildly, leaping and kicking up sand with its hooves, then finally cantered toward Loki. It extended a foreleg and bowed to him, its flaring nostrils almost brushing the earth.

"A great leader needs a worthy steed," it said in a smooth voice. "Mount me, once-Loki, now-Antichrist, and together we will ride to take peace from this earth and make men slay each other."

Loki threw back his head and laughed with delight.

13

Lord, who shall abide in thy taber-
nacle? Who shall dwell in thy holy hill?
                                    —PSALMS 15:1

The Foss Way
December 2, 999

Kennag slept the sleep of the dead, and dreamed strange
dreams.

Destruction and blood came from the sea, to visit the hum-
ble men serving their God. Longships by the hundreds crowded
the shore of the holy island, and their crews poured onto the
sand like a horde of famished insects. They slew without point,
it seemed; dead, dead, all of God's good monks lay dead, with-
out even a proper burial to mark that they had once lived.
Blood was everywhere, the sea was blood, and from the red
fluid there arose a horse, like the white one the young man
rode, a horse that was no horse, but filled with hate and burn-
ing to cause pain. . . .

He was dead, her beloved. Bran. Long black hair moved in
the wind, but the dear face was pale and the eyes did not see.
He lay on this same island, surrounded by the bodies of the
dead monks, and yet somehow she knew he had only just died,
that the monks had preceded him, that—

"Bran!"

She screamed his name, and the rough sound brought her
and everyone else awake. The lightness of predawn silvered
everything, mud and companions and snow, and turned the

huge stone cross beneath which they had slept into a thing of soft, warm pewter hues.

"Kennag?" Alwyn's voice was thick with sleep but kind, and he blinked down at her. They had gone to sleep back to back, with the staff lying between them—Alwyn's request, not hers. Somehow during the night, though, no doubt unconsciously seeking warmth, they had rolled into one another's arms. Kennag was sitting up now, catching her breath, but her left hand clutched Alwyn's right in a dead man's grip.

Dead man. Bran. No, please, Mother Brihid, no. . . .

"Kennag?" His voice was more urgent this time. "Did you . . . did you See something?"

She nodded. Her throat felt like it was on fire, raw from the scream.

"Water," she croaked. He rummaged for and handed her the skin. She gulped the liquid down. It tasted stale, but at least it was cool and wet.

"The Norsemen have slain an entire island of monks," she said, her voice trembling a little. "A huge fleet, larger than I have ever heard tell, assembled on—"

The name of the island, if indeed she had ever known it, was now gone. She frowned and concentrated, then shook her head. "On a small island. It looked like my country—Dalriada. They butchered all of them, but didn't harm any of the cattle."

"What?" Alwyn frowned. "That's too strange for it not to mean something."

She smiled a little sadly. With all they knew, they were drawing conclusions from every incident. They didn't dare not to. The smile faded as she recalled the rest of the dream.

"After the monks were killed, the sea seemed to turn red with their blood."

"The Second Vial," Alwyn said in a hushed voice.

"And from the blood of these men a red horse was formed."

"The Red Horse—the Second Seal! Did you see who was riding it?"

She shook her head. "No, the vision—" her voice caught. "The vision changed after that."

"To what? Tell me!"

Suddenly the hand that had been comforting felt clingy to Kennag. Heart racing, she yanked her hand free. She got to her feet, stiff from sleep and cold but feeling the need to move.

"No."

"But it could be important. It may not seem like much to you but—"

"I said no!" Her voice cracked sharply in the still morning air. "This has nothing to do with our task, nothing at all."

"How can you be—"

"To your Hell with it, Alwyn! Leave it be!" She folded her arms against her chest to stop their trembling, and stared down the road from whence they came, longing with all her heart to be going back to comforting, familiar surroundings.

She heard sounds behind her. The donkey and cat, their language as audible to her Faerie-graced ears as Alwyn's, murmured in low voices. Alwyn, single-handedly in all senses of the word, was silently packing all their gear.

The grief still lingered, hanging like something physical in the area of her chest, but Kennag regretted having spoken so to Alwyn. How in this or any world was it his fault that she had witnessed such a dreadful Sight? He was right, as far as he knew. Her Second Sight was for the benefit of both of them, of their whole world. And under any other conditions, no matter how painful or embarrassing or pointless the vision might be, she would of course have shared it with him.

But this. . . .

How could she tell this boy about Bran? How could she speak to Alwyn of Bran's life *or* his death? What did a cloistered monk know about love, about passion? No, she was glad she had kept her heartbreaking vision to herself, but was ashamed of how she had treated her companion.

She took a deep breath and turned around. "Alwyn, I—"

He looked pathetic, struggling to heave a laden pack onto Balaam's back with his single good hand. As she watched, it slipped. Without stopping to think, Kennag darted forward to catch it before it hit the muddy earth.

Their gazes met over the back of the donkey. Alwyn's brown eyes snapped with anger and his face was red.

"Do you think I want to be here? Do you think for one moment that I would not rather be in my pallet back at St. Aidan's, preparing to attend lauds? Eating hot, nourishing food twice a day, being alone with my thoughts except when I was with my God or the brothers who know and accept me, useless arm and all?"

The naked hurt on his face brought the blood to Kennag's cheeks.

"Alwyn, I'm sorry—"

But he clearly was not about to let her speak. "I'm here because I have to be here. I don't want to be with you any more than you want to be with me. I regret that you've got no better companion than a crippled boy monk, but I'm doing the best that I can. You are vain and arrogant, like all women, and I'm sure I've no idea why someone like you was chosen for this task—"

The flood of words halted, and Alwyn swallowed. The silence hung in the air until he continued.

"Any more than I've any idea why I was picked. But here we are, and we're supposed to be working together. You've got this—this ability that I don't understand but I'm trying to accept, and you're deciding what you will and will not share with me when every scrap of information may mean the difference between life as we know it and an eternal Hell that I'm certain even you would find unpleasant."

The anger was back, and Kennag didn't blame him for it. All her own outrage spent, she listened silently, not interrupting him.

"I don't know about you, but I think this is a hopeless quest. I fail to see how this peculiar little group has any chance of succeeding, but I will see my soul damned before I abandon my duty. I'll tell you anything I know, regardless of how foolish I may appear or how useless the information may be. Because I don't want to look back a month from now and think to myself that I didn't do every single thing I could."

She waited, but apparently he had said his piece. In tense silence, they loaded their steeds and mounted. Dawn was fully here now, and the road ahead was clear.

Finally, Kennag said, "I'm sorry."

"I don't care."

She shrugged. "As you will," she said, hiding the hurt.

They did not speak for a long time, and their animal companions held their own tongues. The road they followed began to dip up and down. At one point they crested a high ridge, and Kennag gasped.

Straight ahead of them, jutting proudly up from the surrounding flat landscape, was a huge green hill—a tor, as the local folk called these suddenly appearing hills. For a moment, Kennag couldn't breathe. Her skin erupted with gooseflesh, and she felt as she had that night—was it only eleven days ago?—when she had first glimpsed the light inside the hollow hill of the Faerie Folk.

This was a sacred place. She could sense it from here, miles still to the east, and names she had not known suddenly filled her head: *Avalon. Ynys Witran. The Isle of Glass.*

"Glastonbury Tor," Alwyn said, his voice hushed and reverent. "We should be at the abbey in a few hours."

Kennag shook herself slightly, in an effort to be rid of the sense of wonderment that clung to her like the soft silk of the spider's web.

"Good," she said, keeping her voice light. "I'm looking forward to a hot meal."

Kennag stood shivering in the drafty guest house. She wrung out the cloth after submersing it the ice-cold water of the basin the monks had provided with such apparent reluctance, and gasped as the nearly frozen cloth touched her warm skin. She muttered curses under her breath against all the Christian God's monks, and the Glastonbury brothers in particular, as she quickly scrubbed herself as clean as the cold would permit.

They had arrived at the abbey shortly before sunset. The elderly man whose job it was to ferry pilgrims across the marsh that surrounded the sloping hills of Glastonbury had waived his fee upon seeing a brother, but had nearly balked when Kennag wished to come along. She had been aware of the differences in their status here in England earlier, but they seemed to be magnified here. She'd bitten back her anger, and tried to sit and look demure as the ferryman poled the flat-bottom boat through the reed-choked water toward the town and its abbey.

Steam rose from the marsh, warm even in the dead time of winter, and Kennag's gaze was again dragged toward the Tor. Mist wreathed its base, making it look like something not wholly of this world.

That's because it's not, came a voice inside her head.

She kept her eyes on the rolling greenness of the Tor, which seemed almost as full and round and welcoming as a mother's breast. It was hard to tell in the encroaching darkness, but she thought she saw levels carved into the hill. Smaller hills nestled against the Tor, children against their mother. Their guide called them Spring Hill and Wearyall Hill.

Kennag wasn't admitted into the abbey proper. The abbey's hosteler appeared, took one look at her, and bustled her off toward the "guest house." Alwyn, curse him, didn't even utter a word of objection. He seemed delighted, relieved to be here, and why not? This was his world, the way that Gleannsidh was—had been—hers.

At least there were blankets in the guest house. Kennag threw one about her shoulders, opened the wooden door that had seen better days, and stepped outside.

The moon silvered the Tor. She gasped, aching inside with the fey beauty of it. There were definitely seven levels that had been carved into the slopes a long time ago, judging by the wear and softness of them. The soles of her feet tingled. They wanted to walk up those levels, feel the soil of that holy place beneath them.

This place, this abbey, with its wood-and-thatch and square stone buildings—this was not her holy place. Hers called to her from a half-mile to the east. The Tor. She would climb it while she was here.

She heard footsteps. "My lady?" came a rumbling male voice. Kennag almost snorted at the respectfulness after the way she had been treated, but managed to maintain her dignity. Her eyes widened at the sight of the novice who had been appointed to attend her.

The man—for it was a man, no mere boy—stood tall and towering. He did not carry himself like the lowliest of his god's servants, but like a warrior in battle. He stood well over six feet tall and had the powerful build to match. The strength of his body was revealed, not obscured, by the rough brown wool of his clothing.

"I hope I'm not disturbing you. I've brought you something to eat."

The voice was deep and rough, as strong and powerful as the rest of him. Had Kennag seen him on the shores of her village, she would have mistaken him for a Lochlannach.

"I'm very hungry. Thank you, Brother—?"

"No brother, not yet, just a novice. Cabal is my name."

"I was expecting the hosteler."

"He is required to be at compline. A novice is not."

Kennag stepped closer to him and saw that indeed his fair hair, though shorn, had not yet been tonsured. Cabal handed her a basket and bowed a little, with none of the discomfort that most of the monks seemed to display around her.

"You are not as young as most novices," she ventured.

A booming, hearty laugh was her reward. "Nay, my lady. I've lived a full life far outside abbey walls. But men change, and my path led me here—to Glastonbury."

"I imagine it's very different from what you're familiar with."

The humor was gone from his voice. "Very much so, lady. I have known steel, and blood, and pain. Now I know the sound of bells, and voices raised in praise, and the satisfaction of the simplest task done with a full heart. I come from the world of flesh, and now abide in a world of spirit."

Something about the tone of his voice made Kennag's skin prickle. It was not just the obvious reverence in Cabal's voice, nor the lyrical choice of words. He was none of the Faerie Folk, of that she was certain. Thanks to her gifts, she could have told if he were. He was as human as she. But there was something special about this man, and before she knew what she was doing, she had reached up and stroked his stubbled cheek.

She expected him to jerk away, as if her touch were the sting of an angry bee. Instead, he raised a massive paw to hers, gently lifted her hand away from his face, and let it go.

"Abbot Sigegar says that you are welcome to attend services on the morrow, if such be your desire. And after prime, he wishes to speak with you and Brother Alwyn about your errand here."

Her errand. She supposed it was hers. But this place was not, however kind and strangely charismatic this novice might be.

"Assure the abbot that I shall attend him at his desire," she said. Novice Cabal bowed again. She heard the heavy sound of his feet moving away from her, and, as if pulled on an invisible tether, turned her face once again to the Tor.

The food in her basket was not hot, as she had hoped, but somehow it didn't matter. It was as if the sight of the Tor sated any hunger she might be feeling. She wrapped the blanket about her, sat on the cold, wet grass, and left the basket of bread and dried fruit untouched.

●   ●   ●

There were nearly seventy monks at Glastonbury Abbey, and their voices, raised in song, filled the large stone church. Though Abbot Sigegar had modestly told Alwyn that Glastonbury was far from being a rich abbey, Alwyn had his doubts. This was the oldest house of God on the island. Its roots went back into the mists of history, past good King Ine's donation in the eighth century of the Twelve Hides upon which the church stood, to conflicting legends involving the apostles, Joseph of Arimathea, and even the blessed Jesus Himself.

There were few pilgrims this time of year, but in the coming weeks the little town's populace would triple. By Christmas, there would likely be ten thousand or so souls here at the blessed site. Even as he opened his lips to praise God, singing at compline with the brothers he had just met, Alwyn thought of Angelo's cold face, and shuddered. Churchmen reckoned the last day of the year to be December 25, the day of Christ's birth, but the common folk still clung to the Roman tradition of ending the year on December 31. On both dates, Alwyn suspected, the church would be crammed with frightened souls, longing to be someplace sacred when the world ended.

His voice caught a little, but he sang on, concentrating on what was surely the sweetest sound this side of Heaven itself: the sound of man praising God in a holy house.

The candles and oil, burning in the cressets, did much to chase away both shadow and chill, but the warmth Alwyn felt was not from these man-made sources of heat. The moment he had set eyes on the abbey, with its solid gatehouse, tidy wooden buildings, and square but spacious church, he had felt as if he belonged. What had he to do, really, with witch-wives and ghosts, talking cats and donkeys, and the intricate machinations of politics and kings? He was made for the cloister, for the whisper of sandaled feet scraping softly along stone hallways, for the song of male voices raised to God, and the focused, satisfying work of vellum, pen, and ink. If only he could stay here. But he knew he could not. There would be a "here," a Glastonbury, an England only if he—and the witch-wife—completed their task.

It had been so easy to let them take Kennag away to another place and follow the brothers in to compline. She did not belong here, not as Alwyn did. And Abbot Sigegar had been so kindly and jovial that Alwyn found the words of urgency he had prepared dying unspoken. Time enough to speak on the morrow, when he had rested in a warm, safe place, away from the tempting curves of Kennag nic Beathag.

He wondered if the legends were true—if the Blessed Savior had indeed come here before His crucifixion and resurrection, choosing this peace-drenched place as His own. He hoped so. The thought of Christ's feet standing, perhaps, where he now stood comforted him.

Neddy stood, alone and lonely, outside the church and listened to the almost unbearably pure sound of the brothers praising God. He could enter the church, that much he knew. He also knew he was not truly welcome there. His presence, such as it was, would only terrify these nice monks. And he was weary of being present but not visible. Eavesdropping had never held much interest for him, and now that he could manifest more easily, he didn't like not to.

But where could he go, to be with people, and not feel this aloneness? He had observed the powerful pull this place had had on nearly all his traveling companions. Kennag, who was usually so conscientious about including Neddy in everything, had largely ignored him once her green-eyed gaze had fallen upon the equally green Tor. Alwyn thought of nothing but rejoining his brethren. Ratatosk, Rowena, and Balaam had not seemed overly interested in Glastonbury, but then, they were beasts. Other things drew them and called to their animal natures.

For a while, Neddy had sat with Kennag as she gazed at the not-too-distant hill after the novice Cabal had come and gone. He'd tried to engage her in conversation, but while she was unfailingly polite, her answers were monosyllables. When he got up to leave—sighing rather pointedly—she hadn't even noticed.

He'd trudged from the guest house to the church, where he now listened to the monks. Balaam was happily drowsing in the wooden barn, he knew, with Rowena curled up on his back. Ratatosk was a creature of the day unless necessity dictated otherwise, and Neddy had no idea where he got to when darkness fell.

Neddy felt very, very sorry for himself.

Self-pity and a level of anger that frightened him with its intensity rose inside him. He blinked a little, pushing the emotions back, and his chest lifted and fell with a breath that was not a breath. Since meeting Kennag, he was feeling more—alive. His insubstantial, pretty mouth twisted at the word even as he thought it. But it was *true*, damn it. He thought—thought!—and felt and spoke and was present more often than he had been for—

For how long?

Had he had a temper when he was alive? Why did this place—and the royal residence at Calne as well—seem so familiar to him? He'd known exactly where the Tor was, where the abbey was, the brothers' dormitory, the guest house. He'd wandered unthinking, wallowing in his self-pity, from Kennag to the church with no trouble at all.

His mouth set. If nobody wanted to be with him, then he wanted to be with nobody. The living could stare at the Tor, or sing psalms, or sleep in the barn without him, for all he cared. He was dead. He would visit the dead.

He turned and strode briskly toward the abbey's cemetery. If someone saw him there, well, that was where a ghost was supposed to be, wasn't it? He'd see if maybe he could find a spectral companion, since those of flesh and blood seemed to want to ignore him.

Once he reached the cemetery, though, Neddy's stride faltered. Had he had a heart, it would have pounded. He didn't like this place. He wasn't ready to be here. If only Kennag. . . .

The moon bathed with a creamy, luminous hue the stones that marked the graves. Here and there, stone crosses, similar to those they had encountered at various points on their journey, stood proudly erect. Picking one at random, Neddy stepped forward and read the name.

Dunstan. The former abbot of Glastonbury, and later, Archbishop of Canterbury. A tale sprang into his mind: the blessed Dunstan, tempted by the Devil himself, seizing the nose of the fiend with a pair of goldsmith's tongs.

Laughter burbled up inside Neddy at the image. The sound was sweet and light in the place of the dead. He could see the man in his memory, an avuncular figure who could be as unyielding as the stone of this cross. Why, it had been Dunstan who had brought the Benedictine Rule to Glastonbury. Before his reforms, the monks here had been licentious and irreverent, and—

Dunstan. He knew Dunstan.

"How did I know you, Your Grace?" he whispered aloud. "Was I the son of a Glastonbury ealdorman? Did I serve you in Canterbury? Was I a member of the church?" He glanced at the date of the archbishop's death—988. "It is the year 999," he said. "I—I did not know you had died, but it was eleven years ago. So I must have been dead for at least that long."

He shuddered. Eleven years dead. But the morbidity of the issue fled before the pressing need to identify himself. Try as he might, his memory would yield no further tantalizing clues.

The rage welled up inside him again, and he sprang at the silent stone that marked the archbishop's final resting place.

"Who was I, damn you! Who was I?" He growled and clawed at it, at the earth, fell into a heap, and screamed and kicked until the fit of fury exhausted itself. It had done no good, of course. Neddy's incorporeal fingers could not damage a cobweb. His chest heaved with breath he did not inhale, and he stumbled to his feet. The grave of Dunstan was serene. If the archbishop's eternal rest was as unquiet as Neddy's, there was no sign of it in this place.

He went from stone to stone, searching for names that had meaning for him. There were others that seemed familiar, but none that produced the reaction Dunstan's grave had. The sound of praying voices ceased and the monks filed out, heading for the dormitory to snatch a few hours' sleep before matins. Neddy watched them go, aware that Alwyn was deep in the company of his fellows. There would be no getting him alone for a brief conversation tonight, and Kennag had most likely sought her own bed by now. He returned his attention to the graveyard.

Over there was a huge cross, bigger than the one that graced Dunstan's grave. The grave was set off from the others by a small stone wall and steps. Curious, Neddy went to it. In life, the man who now lay there was someone quite important, no doubt about—

Neddy's eyes widened. Cold washed through him. He felt himself becoming weightless with startlement, and began to fade. Will alone kept him present in Glastonbury Abbey's graveyard as memories rushed back in such a powerful stream that he felt drowned by the merciless tide.

Grief welled up, closing his throat, until it burst forth in a sob. Not of anger, as earlier, but of loss—and the dreadful pain of, at last, knowing who he was, and just how badly he had died.

"Father," sobbed the ghost of King Edward the Martyr at the grave of His Majesty Edgar the Peaceable. "Father, Father. . . ."

14

*The land of darkness and the shadow
of death.*

—JOB 10:21

**Glastonbury Abbey
December 3, 999**

Kennag blinked and snuggled more deeply into the blankets. The
pallet was hard but she had slept well, save for the vigor of her
dreams. Ever since she had been granted the Sight, her dreams
had taken on a greater reality. They were more vivid, more detailed, and incorporated all the senses, not just sight and sound.

She smiled as she recalled them. Standing in her little cottage,
her belly big with child, hearing the clink-clink of Bran's hammer rising and falling outside as he worked the metal into things
of beauty and service. A place with light that came from no
source, eating food so sweet and satisfying that all meat and
drink she had hitherto known tasted foul and mealy in comparison. Sweet dreams, soothing dreams, dreams of—

The Tor.

Its verdant curves filled her mind, and abruptly she was no
longer sleepy. She felt energized and tossed aside the blankets,
shivering a little in the predawn chill as she donned outer garments, cloak, and boots.

If she remembered the times correctly, prime wasn't until sunrise and was one of the longer services. The Tor wasn't more than
half a mile away. If she took her mare, she could be there, ride to

the top, and be back in plenty of time for her meeting with Alwyn and Abbot Sigegar.

And if she wasn't, well, they could wait.

Her heart fluttered inside her. Kennag smothered a foolish smile. She hadn't felt this much anticipation and nervousness since her first bedding with Niall. It felt good, innocent, after so many months of bitterness and anger.

Her hair would have served a rat for a nest. She combed it quickly and braided it. She would give it more attention later, but now she burned for the Tor.

She stepped outside, closing the guest house door behind her. All was quiet and cold. The brothers were asleep still, their last service, matins, being held in the middle of the night. She wondered how they bore it.

Something dropped heavily on her shoulder.

Kennag jumped and gasped, then frowned as she realized it was only Ratatosk. "Good morning," he chirped. He flicked his fluffy tail and sniffed the cool, clean air. "And a lovely morning it promises to be."

"You nearly killed me," Kennag said. "Don't just jump on people like that!"

"Apologies. I'll remember for the future." He paused. "Don't you want to know where I was?"

"Not particularly," Kennag answered honestly. Ratatosk's chitchat was delaying her. She lifted her skirts clear of the mud and hastened past the baker's house, the forge, and the storage buildings to the barn, Ratatosk clinging to her shoulder.

"Well, you ought to. I have the very best information-gathering system available to you and Alwyn, and I should think you'd wish to avail yourself of it."

Kennag threw back the bar on the barn door. The horses turned to look at her. Balaam, with Rowena curled up on his back, slept on. "I've got the Second Sight," she snapped at Ratatosk. The urge to get to the Tor was almost unbearable.

Ratatosk sprang from her shoulder to a rafter beam. "My squirrels are more reliable. You just get images, visions. You don't always know what they mean. I can learn names, plans—"

"Here is my plan for you," meowed Rowena, opening a single eye and glaring at the noisy rodent. "If you do not close your little mouth, I shall put you in mine."

"Oh!" gasped Ratatosk, his tail moving furiously with indignation. "You are ungrateful beasts, both of you. I shall tell my news to Alwyn. I'm sure *he'll* appreciate my efforts on your behalf."

Muttering to himself, he sprang to the hay-covered earth and leaped out the door. Rowena turned her head to regard Kennag, who was about to saddle the Faerie horse until she realized the abbey's saddles were all too large for the delicately built mare. Instead, Kennag reached for a second saddle blanket.

"You're up early. Thought you might enjoy the chance to sleep someplace warm and safe." Rowena yawned, arching her back and extending the claws of her right front leg. "I certainly have. Thank you, Balaam."

"You're welcome." The donkey yawned, too.

"I've got someplace to go," said Kennag.

"Where?" asked Rowena.

"I want to see the Tor."

Rowena shook her head rapidly. "You humans. 'I've got to get to the abbey. I've got to get to the Tor.' You'd be much happier if you'd learn to take a quick nap in the sun from time to time."

Kennag had to chuckle. "You're probably right at that. Come, my friend," she said to the mare, who obligingly followed her outside. Kennag closed the door and placed the bar back down. She mounted the horse quickly, then leaned over and said into her ear, "The Tor. You feel it, too, don't you?"

The horse craned her creamy white neck back to regard Kennag. The mare's nostrils flared, and she bobbed her head up and down.

Kennag's excitement built. "Then let's go."

The cart paths that were the major thoroughfares of Glastonbury were muddy but clear, and the Faerie horse made good time. Kennag followed the paths until she came to the base of the Tor. The soft, verdant allure of the hill proved to be deceptive, as was its height. It seemed smaller when glimpsed from the abbey grounds. She estimated it rose to a height of over five hundred feet, and steeply at that.

The levels that she had noticed were harder to find now that she was actually here. Trees, looming and dark in the predawn almost-light, had been allowed to grow unhindered.

She frowned a little. Or had they? On either side of her towered a huge oak tree. She looked back the way she had come, and

a chill touched her. Without realizing it, she had been riding
through a long avenue of oaks. It led here, to the base of the Tor.

Oaks . . . and apple trees, she noticed, though all the trees
were asleep with the winter. The horse beneath her stamped and
blew noisily, impatient to continue. Kennag let the creature have
her way.

If the levels were difficult for Kennag to see, they were easy
for the mare to find. Up they went, twisting and winding, deeper
into the quiet mystery that was Glastonbury Tor. Uneasily Kennag realized that this little grove was silent. No sounds of birds
at all. Only a tense feeling of expectancy—though that was silly,
wasn't it?

A soft sound reached her ears. She couldn't quite identify it.
Bringing the horse to a halt, Kennag strained to listen.

Singing. Soft and sweeter by far than any she had heard issu-
ing from the abbey last night. Her skin prickled.

Glastonbury Tor was a Faerie mound.

She wondered why she hadn't realized it before. All the signs
were there. She let her lips part in a smile, the fullest, most heartfelt gesture she had felt like making in a long, long time. She
squeezed the horse and it bounded forward.

Up they went, the horse never faltering, never laboring, unlike
any mortal creature. The air seemed to grow heavy and press
physically against them. It almost crackled with magic. Kennag's
heart was pounding. She felt as if she had imbibed one of her
own concoctions, lethargic yet somehow more alert, right down
to her fingertips and the very ends of her long hair.

With a final heave the horse cleared the last rise. They were
on the very top of Glastonbury Tor. Kennag dismounted and
pulled off her boots, eager to feel the grass beneath her bare feet.
Her toes dug into the moist soil, warm and welcoming somehow,
although the morning was still chilly. In the faint light, she could
make out what remained of various wattle-and-daub buildings.
Here and there, slabs of stone lay in peculiar patterns. She
walked up to one of them, a large, almost triangular piece about
six feet all around, and placed her hands on its rough surface.

Then jerked them back, startled. The stone was hot!

Behind her, she heard the mare whinny. Kennag stepped back
from the stone, fear growing alongside the sense of anticipation
that had overwhelmed her earlier and pulled her to this place.

The stone shot upward, hovered in the air twenty feet above her, then crashed to earth a few yards away.

Light streamed like a fountain from the entrance thus revealed. Kennag cried out in pain and shielded her eyes from the visual onslaught, so terrible and beautiful to her Faerie-graced eyesight. The singing was unmistakable now, sweet and haunting and unexpectedly loud. The volume increased. Kennag slitted her eyes against the light and covered her ears. Groaning, she fell to her knees, feeling the warm wetness of the soil creep through her dress.

As abruptly as it had manifested, it ceased. All of it—the light, the singing. Kennag's heart slammed against her chest, the only sound in her ears at the moment, and she cautiously opened her eyes.

Standing before her was a being who was clearly nonhuman. Tall and fair as the Faerie King she had met only days ago, he stood proudly, his hands on his hips and a wind that Kennag did not feel billowing his white cape. All his clothes were white. His wind-tossed hair and bright eyes were silver, and his full, enticing lips were parted in a smile.

"Kennag nic Beathag"—his voice was as pure as the sound of chiming bells—"we have been expecting you."

He extended a hand to help her up. She hesitated, then took it. To her surprise, the hand was as soft and warm as any man's.

She did not meet his eyes. "You honor me, sir."

"No, you honor us. I am Gwyn ap Nudd, King of the Seelie Court, and I welcome you to my domain. Come—join us. We will discuss your quest, and celebrate your arrival, and listen to sweet music, and feast upon delicacies your poor mortal tongue has never known."

She was walking beside him now, her bare feet moving as if of their own accord. The lethargy she had experienced earlier was descending on her full force. He was handsome, so handsome, and it was the easiest thing in the world to follow where he led. But there was something nagging at the back of her mind. Her head lolled on her neck. They were almost at the entrance to Gwyn ap Nudd's domain when she heard the Faerie horse shriek.

She blinked, swimming back to clarity with an effort. Turning her head, she saw the horse given to her—

—*by the true King of the Faeries*—

—struggling against three of the ugliest creatures Kennag had ever beheld, even in her dreams. Twisted and brown they were, with sharp claws and teeth. They might have been human-shaped once, but she fancied that these creatures had more in common with Alwyn's Hell-demons than men. Thank Epona, who protected all horses, the mare seemed to be winning this battle.

The grip on her hand tightened painfully as she struggled to pull away. "It will be much less painful if you come willingly," said Gwyn. "I don't wish to harm you."

He seemed sincere, in that much at least. Kennag didn't stop fighting him for a moment. How could this happen? The true Faerie King had given her an ointment that would help her to see through all glamour and tricks the fey folk might try. Why did she keep seeing Gwyn as one of the good and bright Seelie Court, when clearly he was one of the dark Faeries?

"Because I'm not one of them," he explained, as if she had spoken her thoughts aloud. "I was a member of the Seelie Court, until I challenged the king and was exiled. The Unseelie Court was more than happy to accept me as their king." His grip was like the iron his people so hated. Kennag lowered her head and bit. Gwyn growled, and his face darkened with anger. He shook her, as a dog might a rat, and struck her with a closed fist. Kennag cried out as she tasted blood.

"Foolish woman!" His voice roared in her ears. "Do you think your little life has any value to me?"

His own words contradicted his actions, and Kennag, though terrified, went on the attack. "It must, otherwise you'd have killed me, not lured me here. I have something you want!" *And as long as I have it, I'll stay alive,* she thought. Sweet Mother Brihid. She had never realized just how much she didn't want to die. For a brief instant, she recalled Alwyn's dire prediction of the fate of the two Witnesses: *The Beast from the abyss kills them,* he had said. She hadn't wanted to believe that, and now with a weird feeling of misplaced humor, she wondered if Gwyn ap Nudd, false king of the Faerie Folk, would prove the prophecy wrong by killing her here and now.

"Wrong, mortal," hissed Gwyn. "You *are* something someone *else* wants."

With that horrible statement, he grabbed Kennag around the waist, ran forward, and plunged with her into the Underworld.

•   •   •

The abbot's quarters were austere but quite pleasant, and Alwyn felt honored to be invited in. Usually a brother was invited for an audience with an abbot only on very important matters, more often than not for a private reprimand. To be here, in the quarters of Abbot Sigegar of Glastonbury, was humbling.

Alwyn had slept better than on any night since Michael's appearance. It was so comforting to be in the presence of other monks. Although they were strangers, in a very real sense they were not—every man knew what was expected of him, the words to the prayers they sang seven times each day, the daily work of an abbey.

He did not want to leave.

"I indulge my fondness for tea on these winter mornings," said Sigegar as one of the novices brought in a pot and three cups, set them down, and left quietly. "Will you and your—companion wish to partake as well?"

Alwyn's heart quickened at the mention of Kennag. Where was she? It was well past sunrise. The monks had broken their fast and were now busily about the day's work. She knew where and when they were supposed to meet, how important this was, and yet she was not here.

"If it please you, Your Grace, I would be honored to share a cup with you. As for my companion"—his voice hardened—"I've no idea why she is not present."

Sigegar proceeded to pour two cups of sweet-smelling herbal tea. Alwyn could not take his gaze from the third, empty cup. "My hosteler tells me he cannot find her, and her horse has gone."

Alwyn could think of nothing to say.

Abbot Sigegar handed him the cup of tea and sat back in his chair. Alwyn forced his gaze from the empty cup to meet that of the abbot. Sigegar regarded the younger monk for a long moment without speaking. Short and heavyset, with dark eyes that seemed to penetrate to the very soul and a surprisingly comical fluff of white hair on his tonsured head, Sigegar looked more like an elderly, hardworking ceorl than the esteemed abbot of the oldest monastery in England. Alwyn felt his cheeks grow red under the silent scrutiny, but forced himself not to look away.

"Perhaps," Sigegar said slowly, "we should begin without her."

Alwyn's mouth was dry, and he sipped the tea. It was hot and sweet. He thought of Kennag, of her wildness and bursts of temper, of her ugly horse that she treated like a steed of the gods. She knew how important this meeting was to him, to their quest. He had thought better of her than to ride off and leave him. At best, she had dismissed the meeting as unimportant and gone to explore Glastonbury. At worst, she could have abandoned him altogether.

He took another sip, then met Sigegar's eyes. "Perhaps we should."

"Your words of last night were intriguing—and cryptic," said Sigegar, a hint of laughter warming his dark eyes. "Perhaps in the light of God's new day you can be a bit more plainspoken."

Alwyn stalled for another moment by sipping the hot drink. Now that it had come to it, he was reluctant to divulge everything to the abbot. Spilling his heart to Wulfstan, his mentor and friend, was one thing. Convincing a stranger of the bizarre events to which he had been a party was quite another.

"Very well," Alwyn said, "I shall be as plain as I may." He took a deep breath, squared his shoulders, and, in simple language as the abbot had requested, told him what had transpired.

To his credit, Sigegar did not interrupt. From time to time the color rose in his cheeks and subsided, or his eyes flashed. The only hint that Alwyn's tale was disturbing him was the gradual tightening of his thick, blunt fingers on the cup.

Alwyn finished. He realized he was shaking. The tea in his cup had grown cold. Carefully he set the cup back on the wooden plate.

Sigegar said nothing. Alwyn closed his eyes. *He doesn't believe me. Sweet Jesu, what shall I do?*

"Surely, Brother Alwyn," Sigegar said at last, "you realize how mad this all sounds."

"I do," replied Alwyn steadily.

"You come to my abbey, a stranger, with no papers from your abbot or from Bishop Wulfstan. You claim the donkey and the cat can speak and that your walking stick is the Rod of Aaron. You tell me that the world is about to end and that Satan and his Antichrist are not simply coming, they are already here and working their mischief through the Norsemen."

Miserable, Alwyn opened his mouth.

"I'm not finished yet." Sigegar rose and began to pace, his hands clasped behind his back. "You don't come alone. You bring a woman who is clearly a heathen from the North and who does not even have the courtesy to show up for a meeting regarding this said task of yours. Why do you think, Brother Alwyn of St. Aidan's, that Michael chose you?"

Anger was simmering just beneath the surface, and Alwyn shrank from it. He knew it for what it was. No one liked being played for a fool, and Alwyn's story called for not just a leap of faith, but a flight of it.

"I have often asked that myself," he whispered, his throat closing. "But I swear, Your Grace, I am not lying. All has indeed happened as I have told it."

"There are three choices here," Sigegar said. "One: you are lying." His gaze softened a little. "You seem a good man, Brother. I cannot see any purpose to your telling such a tale for lying's sake. Two: You are a sane-appearing madman. Which is, frankly, the likeliest explanation. And three: You are telling the truth. Which is impossible."

Suddenly Alwyn's fear and chagrin melted into sympathy. He knew that he would have been as skeptical, if not more so, had he not been an actual witness to the events as they unfolded. He should not have expected anyone who did not know him intimately to believe this far-fetched story. He accepted Sigegar's doubt and smiled sadly.

"If you feel so—and I cannot blame you—then clearly I have accomplished nothing this morning save to waste your time. I beg your—"

He was interrupted by a frantic yowling just outside the abbot's door. A scrabbling of claws confirmed that it was Rowena, mewing desperately. Through the door, Alwyn could catch a few muffled phrases: ". . . gone to the . . . Ratatosk says . . . horse is coming. . . ."

The last sent a chill through him. Forgetting etiquette, he bolted out of his chair and flung open the door. Rowena's back was arched and her white fur stood on end. Her black pupils nearly filled her eyes.

"She's gone to the Tor," gasped the cat. "Ratatosk heard dreadful sounds, and he says he can see her horse galloping back to the abbey. Without Kennag."

15

*I have fought a good fight, I have fin-
ished my course, I have kept the faith.*
— THE SECOND EPISTLE OF PAUL
THE APOSTLE TO TIMOTHY, 4:7

Glastonbury Abbey
December 3, 999

Belatedly, Alwyn remembered the abbot even as he absorbed the
alarming news. He turned to Sigegar and said, "Rowena says that
Kennag has gone to the Tor. Her horse is coming back right now,
as fast as it can."

Incredulity warred with belief on Sigegar's broad, peasant's
face. A few moments ago, Alwyn would have been thrilled at the
thought of convincing the abbot that he was telling the truth.
Now, whether the abbot believed him seemed of little consequence. Something had happened to Kennag, and Alwyn was
surprised to find how much his chest hurt at the thought.

He ran to the barn and began to saddle Balaam. The donkey
snorted, startled out of his drowsing, and immediately began asking questions.

"No time," gasped Alwyn. A burst of white-hot rage crested
inside him as he fumbled with one of the abbey's saddles. He
could do it with his single hand, and had before, but it took time
that he did not have. A man with two hands would have had Balaam already saddled and would be riding him by now. How he
hated his crippled body; how it betrayed him time and time
again.

The heavy weight of the saddle won, and it slipped to the earth. Alwyn let out a wordless noise of anger, shame, and disgust, and scrambled onto Balaam's swayed back. He lay low across the beast's body and cried into Balaam's long ear, "Don't let me fall!"

"Don't worry, little brother," said the donkey in a gentle voice. "I'll keep you safe."

Was Kennag? At that moment, he could hear hoofbeats and the sound of Kennag's horse neighing in terror. Balaam hurried out the open door of the barn toward the sound. The horse pranced like a lady's palfrey, tossing its large, ugly brown head and churning up the grass with its dull gray hooves. Of all the beasts they had encountered, the voice of Kennag's unnamed horse was the only one King Solomon's ring would not translate for Alwyn. And once, when he had commented on the horse's unattractive appearance, Kennag had laughed out loud. Now, watching it watch him with an almost human keenness and comprehension, Alwyn wondered just what manner of horse it really was.

Clinging to the horse's neck was Ratatosk. When he caught sight of Alwyn and Balaam, he cried frantically, "Hurry! We may be too late!"

Too late? thought Alwyn, the words like knives. *Dear God in Heaven, what is wrong? Please, protect Your wild daughter. I know she doesn't believe in You, but if something were to happen to her—*

And then his only thought was that of hanging on to an unsaddled donkey that was running at full speed. There was a blur of white, and he saw Rowena leap up in front of him. She was taken by surprise by the fact that Balaam had no saddle, and there was a moment where she flailed frantically before digging her claws into Balaam's neck as he brayed in pain.

Alwyn concentrated on squeezing his legs around Balaam's body as tightly as he could. His fingers fumbled for a grip in the animal's short mane and found none. With a quick prayer he simply abandoned himself to whatever God had in store and hoped, if he fell, it wouldn't hurt too much.

The horse led the way, its stumpy legs devouring earth and flying over obstacles with a grace that Alwyn had never seen it exhibit. And then, on this day of surprises, Alwyn got yet another one.

Out of the corner of his eye Alwyn caught sight of the novice named Cabal running toward him. As Alwyn watched, the big man's stride lengthened to keep pace with that of the horse and then, impossibly, Cabal vaulted onto the horse's back as if both were standing still. The horse made no effort to rid itself of its unfamiliar rider. Neither did it slacken its pace.

Alwyn squeezed his eyes shut and held on.

He felt the donkey's gait begin to slow and become laborious. Opening his eyes, Alwyn saw that they were climbing the Tor. Balaam had no breath for conversation. He gasped and labored, his gray sides heaving between Alwyn's legs. Alwyn wanted to dismount, but he knew that even so burdened Balaam would make it to the top faster than he.

At last, they were there. Day had fully arrived, and the view from the top of the Tor would have been glorious, had Alwyn had eyes for beauty. He saw only the gaping hole in the earth and the huge stone covering that had been tossed aside like the plaything of a giant's child.

"Kennag," he whispered. He tried to dismount, and fell. Getting to his feet, he moved slowly to the huge chasm. He was vaguely aware of the presence of Ratatosk, Rowena, and Cabal beside him. He peered downward into a darkness that was so profound it made him shake.

Not realizing what he was doing, he backed away from the edge, his one good hand raised as if trying to defend himself. Fear such as he had never felt before surged through him, drying his mouth, clenching his bowels, making his whole body tremble.

It was coming from the pit.

And Kennag was down there. Down in the depths with the fear.

Alwyn's legs gave way and he fell, crying and shaking. The earth was unnaturally warm on his face. His ear was pressed to the soil, and he thought he could hear . . . something. He began to weep in earnest and curl in on himself, covering his head with his single good arm.

No no no no no no no no. . . .

Something soft brushed his face. He opened his eyes. Rowena was rubbing against him with infinite gentleness, and he sucked air back into his lungs. She didn't have to say anything; her calm presence was enough to clear his head.

The witless terror still seized him, but he forced himself to concentrate. He couldn't rise, however, couldn't force his body to stand erect and walk like the man God had made. Instead, tears still wet on his face, he crawled like a beast. His single hand pulled him closer to the edge of the pit. Hot, foul-smelling air rose and buffeted him.

He opened his mouth and croaked, "Kennag!"

The only sound that answered him was the strange, deep chanting, more felt than heard. Oh, he was afraid, afraid . . .

"Alwyn?"

He gasped. The voice was fragile, faint, and wafted up like the merest gentle brush of a butterfly's wings. Kennag, but not her bold, strong voice. This tentative, quavering voice was that of one who was every bit as terrified as he.

But it was she, and she was alive. Heartened, he replied, his voice slightly stronger than before, "I'm up here, Kennag. I'm—"

What? What in the name of the Father, Son, and Holy Ghost was he going to do?

"You're going to get her out," said a deep voice by his ear, startling him. Cabal knelt beside him, staring down into the abyss. "It's taking all their combined strength to hold the gateway open. They can't keep it up much longer. They're waiting for you, you see. You can't go down there, no matter what you may feel you have to do. Leave this to us."

Alwyn stared, mouth open. "Who are you?"

Cabal's lips spread in a fierce grin. "A soldier doing his duty," he said. He lifted his head and whistled to the horse. The creature trotted up to him and tossed her head.

"You know what to do. I will be here," Cabal told it. The horse seemed to nod in agreement, and then, to Alwyn's horror and shock, it sprang unhesitatingly into the crack in the earth. Alwyn watched it fall, thinking that at any moment it would realize its peril, neigh in terror, and begin to flail as it hurtled toward its certain death. Instead, the horse stretched out its legs, as if it were merely jumping—

—*or flying*—

—until the darkness swallowed it.

"They cannot fight her," said Cabal, rising.

"Kennag?" Alwyn asked stupidly.

"No, the mare," replied Cabal.

"What?"

Cabal ignored his outburst. "When she returns with Kennag, all of you must flee as fast as you can. There is a small hill nestled against the Tor. From its valley there flows a spring—"

"Yes, I know where it is. It supplies the abbey with water," said Alwyn. "They call it the Blood Spring."

"That's the one. Find the well and jump into it. All of you, including the beasts. They won't be able to follow you—the iron that turns the spring's water that blood-red color is harmful to the Faerie Folk. Someone will be waiting to help you." An echo of a smile touched his lips, and for a moment his gaze unfocused slightly. "Someone I knew well, once. Do as she bids you. You may trust her."

Alwyn could take it no longer. "Are you one of them? The Faerie Folk?"

Cabal laughed, a hearty sound whose very robustness calmed the monk. "Nay, I'm but a man, just as you, Brother Alwyn. No more, but praise be to God, no less. I—"

His words were drowned by the sudden roar that exploded from the chasm. The Tor trembled, as if the hill itself were angry.

"Here she comes," said Cabal. Alwyn glanced over at him. Cabal's voice was calm, but his body was tense, like a predator poised to spring. Imitating him, Alwyn rose, his body shaking like a leaf in the wind but standing erect nonetheless.

The Faerie horse leaped out of the chasm as if propelled. She unfolded her long legs, curled up tight against her abdomen, and landed squarely on all fours. Clinging to her neck, her face and body covered with earth and what appeared to be soot, was Kennag.

Relief and joy flooded Alwyn, but he had no time to savor it. Hard on the heels of Kennag's nameless horse was someone else.

The demon-horse was so black it seemed to absorb light, and so gaunt as to be a living skeleton. Flame served it for mane and tail, and a horrible stench was its vanguard. It soared out of the pit, screaming in fury, its red eyes rolling and black smoke arising from its nostrils. Alwyn stared at it, recognizing it for what it was—the embodiment of the Third Seal, the Black Horse whose rider was Famine.

An instant later, it was joined by its companions. A hound as large as a small pony scrambled out of the pit, baying furiously. It, too, was black, and its eyes gleamed like fire. Its teeth were white as the moon as it charged at Kennag, snarling. Following their leader were more hounds, baying with almost human voices—white hounds with red ears, dangerous and terrifying but clearly obeying their monstrous leader.

More terrible than the horse and hounds was their mistress. Perched atop the midnight steed was a stunningly beautiful woman. For a wild moment, Alwyn thought it was Kennag, until he realized that the red hair and green eyes adorned a face filled with the sort of anger and hatred that Kennag, a mere human, could never know. His shocked gaze also registered something that proved the rider to be unnatural—from the waist down, this lovely woman was a decomposing corpse.

The hounds had surrounded Kennag and her steed. They seemed afraid of the horse, but they badly wanted the rider. Hate and lust for blood gleamed in their eyes, and their slaver burned holes in the grass where it fell. Kennag was deathly pale, her eyes enormous and her mouth slack. It seemed to be all she could do simply to hang on to the Faerie horse.

The black dog leaped for Kennag.

Without knowing what he did, Alwyn raced forward, his paralysis of fear for himself broken by terror for Kennag. He cried something, he knew not what, and brought his staff down on the black dog's back.

The animal howled in pain. Alwyn staggered backward. His hand felt numb, as if he had struck a boulder with the rod instead of flesh.

Perhaps he had.

"Bring him down, Garm!" cried the woman atop the skeletal horse. "Bring him down to the Underworld, that I may gift our friend with him. *Cwn Annwn*!" she called to the pack of white, red-eared dogs, "The woman!"

The demon hound, Garm, turned its full, frightening gaze upon Alwyn. Its dewlaps lifted in a silent snarl, then it sprang.

Alwyn did not have time to lift the Rod of Aaron again, and knew that he was going to die. The huge creature slammed into him, and Alwyn went down beneath the beast. He smelled carrion and thought he would vomit. He closed his eyes and braced himself for the dreadful tearing of flesh, but it did not come.

There was a fierce yowl—a voice he knew. The hound yelped, and all at once the horrible pressure of the creature against his body was gone.

Opening his eyes, his lungs aching for air, he saw Rowena perched atop Garm's mammoth head like an absurd white hat. She chewed on his ears, clawed at his eyes. He heard other sounds and looked up to see Balaam—old, talkative, placid Balaam—aiming solid kicks from his powerful hindquarters at the white hounds. Even as he watched, one of them gathered itself, preparing to leap onto the donkey.

Again, knowing not what moved him, Alwyn ran forward and began beating the white hounds with his staff. It jarred him up to the shoulder but he persisted, yelling foolishly, "Stop it! Go away!"

"I know thee, Hel!" came a small but strong voice. Ratatosk. "Are you so feeble, so weak, that you cannot catch two lowly mortals without allying with Gwyn ap Nudd and his underworld dog pack?"

"And I know *thee,* Squirrel," answered the woman Ratatosk had addressed as Hel. "You are nothing more than a bearer of insults, and below my notice. I have not come for you. If you do not interfere, you will not be harmed."

Alwyn felt himself seized from behind and lifted. He struggled, but the arms about him might as well have been iron bands. Before he realized what was happening, he was atop Balaam and peering into Cabal's face.

"Remember what I told you," Cabal yelled to be heard over the din. "Go!"

Balaam needed no second urging. Braying urgently, the old donkey launched himself down the Tor's sloping sides with a speed Alwyn would never have expected. Alwyn clung on with every ounce of strength he possessed. If he fell off or Balaam stumbled, the dreadful Hel-hounds would be on them at once.

He heard the sound of other hooves, and turned his head just enough to ascertain that Kennag, on her strange and wonderful horse, was keeping pace with him. She still looked frighteningly detached. Clinging to Kennag's filthy clothes, her claws no doubt leaving scars on the pagan woman's flesh, was Rowena.

Breathing turned to gulping air, and riding to simply hanging on. Alwyn lost track of where they went, what turns they took, of time itself. Green of hill flashed by; brown of earth, gray of branches. He trusted the donkey and Kennag's mysterious horse to get them where they needed to be, but nonetheless, he silently prayed for a little bit of help from God as well.

He felt Balaam slowing, stumbling over his hooves. The short hair of his pelt was drenched. He couldn't take much more of this. Praise be to God, he didn't have to. A few moments later, the donkey slowed and stopped. Alwyn dismounted, and his shaky legs nearly buckled beneath him.

According to the monks, the Blood Spring had been in use for centuries. It never ran dry, not even in the most parching of droughts, and the mineral-flavored water, red as the blood Christ shed for sinners, was rumored to have healing properties. As he gasped for breath, nearly as exhausted as Balaam by the wild ride, he heard the soft burbling of the iron-tinged water as it came to the surface and fed a small pool.

He heard the horse's hooves and turned to see the mare cantering up to him. Kennag was still holding on. "The well," he managed. "Cabal said to go into the well." He paused, then blurted out, "I'm so glad you're all right."

She blinked at that, and for the first time her eyes appeared to focus on Alwyn. She did not dismount. Alwyn went to her and held out his arm to help her down. Kennag stayed as if frozen for a moment, then slowly, stiffly, she dismounted, leaning heavily on Alwyn. As she pressed against him and he looked into her face, he saw that what he had mistaken for soot on her face and body were actually black burns.

"Kennag," he began, sick.

"There is not much time." The voice was soft and definitely feminine. Alwyn turned at the sound and beheld a lovely woman with long, dark hair. She wore a gown of blue and silver, and the colors seemed to shift as she walked toward them. Her pale face and blue eyes remained in focus, and though her steady gaze projected a power perhaps equal to that of the woman on the Black Horse, Alwyn felt no fear.

"Lady," he said, "you are Cabal's friend?"

She tilted her head quizzically. "Cabal?" Suddenly she laughed. "Yes, I knew him once, though by quite a different name. Make haste. Step into my waters, and let them take you someplace safe."

She waved a hand, and the wooden top of the well opened of its own accord. A thought struck Alwyn as he recalled Cabal's words: *They won't be able to follow you—the iron that turns the spring's water that blood-red color is harmful to the Faerie Folk.*

Somehow, despite the urgency of the situation, he had to ask a question. "Are you one of the Faerie Folk?"

The Lady of the Blood Spring smiled. "After a manner of speaking."

"Then—doesn't the iron in the water harm you?"

The smile grew. Her teeth were white, her lips crimson. Her eyes danced. "It's my well," she replied, as if he were a simpleton.

Alwyn stepped forward and then realized something. Cabal had told them all to go into the well. But it was too small to permit the passage of a creature as large as a horse.

"Our steeds!" he said. "They are too large!" The thought of leaving faithful Balaam behind to be devoured by the dreadful hounds was intolerable. "We can't—"

"I will tend to your steeds. Both of them. Make haste. When you are in the well, do not fight where the current will take you."

Current? Alwyn had thought they would merely stay in the well, protected somehow by its—its magical properties. He felt like crossing himself every time he admitted that there was such a thing as magic—and that he was making use of it. He felt something soft and furry brush his leg.

"Alwyn. . . ." Rowena trembled against him. "The water . . . I'll drown! I cannot go in there!" He picked her up and cradled her against his chest. She clung to him, mewing softly.

The faint sound of baying hounds reached their ears. Kennag blinked rapidly, moving like one awaking from a deep sleep. Slowly her head turned in the direction of the beasts, and color came back into her face.

"Would you rather stay here?" cried Kennag, with a touch of the temper Alwyn had come to know. She pointed. They could see a black shape followed by several smaller, white ones heading straight for them. Cabal had delayed the rider and her pack, but not defeated them.

Alwyn hesitated. His eyes were fixed on the approaching rider. This was the first Sign he had witnessed, the Black Horse of the Apocalypse, and it held him transfixed like a bird before a snake.

"You saved me," came Kennag's voice behind him, "now I'm saving *you!*"

Before he could even take a deep breath, she had pushed him toward the well with all her strength and jumped in after him.

Rowena screamed and clawed at him in terror. He clamped his arm around her as tightly as he could.

Alwyn felt himself being pulled down, down. His last breath of air escaped him to rise in shimmering bubbles toward a surface that was rapidly disappearing from his view.

Then everything went black.

He had no sword, not at this final battle; only a crude staff made from a sapling he had pulled free as he ran to the Tor. But it would serve him, and the man who called himself after his dog, Cabal, fought the white *Cwn Annwn*, the demon dogs of Gwyn ap Nudd, with as much vigor as he had fought armies five hundred years ago.

His main thought, though, was to stop Hel from claiming the two Witnesses. He trusted the Lady to defend Kennag and Alwyn, but even her great powers had their limits. They needed to be in her sacred waters to receive her protection, and unless he delayed the rider of the gaunt Black Horse, they would never reach the Lady.

Tossing aside the branch, he leaped upward. He cried an ancient Briton battle cry as he seized Hel and pulled her off the Black Horse. She writhed beneath him, her beautiful mouth spitting obscenities, the rotting flesh of her lower body sloughing off as they struggled. He expected to feel the sharp teeth of her black hound and the hounds of Gwyn digging into his too-human flesh at any moment, but the dogs were yelping strangely. He risked a glance and saw that they were covered with a gray blanket that moved.

Squirrels. The talking squirrel had summoned his followers, and they were busily covering the dogs' eyes and noses with their bodies.

The man called Cabal had seen much good and evil in his lifetime, but to see creatures of the wild willingly die in such a fashion moved him. They knew. All of them knew, just as Cabal did, what the safety of the Witnesses meant.

It couldn't last, of course. Within seconds, the dogs had shaken off and slain nearly all the squirrels, and the big black one—Garm, Hel had called him—fell upon Cabal, crunched down with his mammoth jaws, and pulled him off Hel's body.

She spat on him as she rose and hastened to her mount. An instant later, she was gone, the hounds baying as they raced beside her.

Cabal felt very cold. He was wet with his own blood, and lay on the grass, unable to move. Only his gaze wandered about, looking at the small gray-brown corpses, and his eyes filled with tears. Strangely, this was more poignant to him than viewing the bodies of men at that last battle. These beasts had died for something, not because of a foolish error. . . .

He breathed, tasting blood as his lungs rose and fell. His lips curved in a smile.

"It is time, my brother." A voice soft as the wind caressed his ears.

"Is that you?" he rasped. "Have you come to take me—"

"I took you to your sleep once before, five centuries past," whispered the wind. It was warm as it brushed his face. He smelled the scent of apple blossoms. "It is time to go to your final rest, my brother. You have done well."

Cabal closed his eyes. Peace swelled inside him. It no longer hurt to breathe the sweet scent of apple blossoms. He felt warm now.

He had loved this land. He had died for it once before and then slept deeply, secure in the knowledge that he would rise again to defend his country at the hour of its greatest need. He had done what he needed to do—protect the two fragile mortals who were the world's last hope. He could die, now, for the final time.

The rest was up to them.

The wind grew in strength as he exhaled his last breath. The body of Arthur, king of the Britons, dissolved into dust, which the summer-scented wind scattered joyously.

16

*Then a spirit passed before my face; the
hair of my flesh stood up.*

—JOB 4:15

**Shaftesbury Abbey
December 9, 999**

Her fatuous son had suggested the queen ride in a litter, but
Elfthryth refused. She wasn't that old. She could sit a horse as
well as any young thing in Ethelred's court, and by God, she
would do so.

By the third day she was bitterly regretting her arrogance. Her
royal posterior was aching and nearly raw, and her bones—older
than she liked to admit—had been rattled by the traveling. Fortunately, the London Way that twined southwest from London
had several towns where the royal retinue could stop and be re-
freshed by a night's sleep in a real bed. Guildford, Wilton, and
Ilchester had all been hosts to the dowager queen on this pilgrimage. Elfthryth, doing as she had been tasked, carried on at
great length about how wonderful it was that poor martyred Edward was finally being laid to rest in a proper site, instead of lan-
guishing at Wareham.

At Guildford, the young girl who served her meals in her
room brightened at the queen's words. "Aye, Majesty, that it is!
Did you know that the lame have been healed at Edward's
shrine? And that at night, beautiful bright lights dance like
Faeries over the site where he lay? And his body—it was found
to have been uncorrupted!"

Elfthryth kept the smile on her face by an effort of will. "Charming stories," she said. "And so very fitting."

Her palfrey, whose gait had once seemed smooth as cream, might as well have been an abbey donkey for all Elfthryth cared on this, the final leg of the journey. Shaftesbury was in sight, a hilly, pretty little town whose abbey sat atop the highest rise. Shaftesbury Abbey, given by King Alfred to his daughter Ethelgiva in 880, was quite wealthy. No doubt, thought Elfthryth, the bones of a martyred king would only increase Shaftesbury Abbey's popularity. Edward's allegedly uncorrupted body had lain here for only a few months, and it seemed as though the local populace could think and speak of nothing else.

Elfthryth had sent a thegn on ahead with news of their coming, and the abbey was prepared to receive so illustrious a visitor. As the string of palfreys and pack animals climbed the steep road toward the abbey, the inhabitants of Shaftesbury stopped whatever they were doing and stared at the queen.

Color rose in Elfthryth's cheeks. She sat up straighter in her saddle, ignoring the renewed pain the movement engendered. She stared directly ahead. Oh, she knew what they were thinking. The rumors had flown. Only they were not mere rumors. She had indeed contrived to murder Edward, but these theows and ceorls couldn't know it. They glared at her with hate only because of suspicion, not knowledge. She was glad she had come, not because it was what her son had wished her to do but because, finally, she could lay at least some of the rumors to rest.

The whole nunnery had turned out to welcome her, it seemed. She gave a brittle smile to the silent row of black-clad women standing outside the open gatehouse door and extended a hand to her favorite thegn. She winced only a little as he helped her down.

Sweeping forward grandly, she reached her hands out to the abbess, whose name escaped her at the moment. "Your Grace," she enthused, "how delighted I am to finally be here."

The woman's bright blue eyes met Elfthryth's steadily. "You are welcome here, Queen Elfthryth. All who honor the blessed Edward are welcome here."

The smile stayed in place, though Elfthryth was sorely tempted to strike the woman. The abbess's words were barbed, and pricked deep. Abruptly, Elfthryth decided to change her plans. She did not wish to be in this hostile place a moment longer than was necessary.

"Our hosteler, Sister Wulfgifu, will show you to our guest house," the abbess was saying. "We have only just finished it and have supplied it as best we can, but I am certain it will be poor indeed compared to the fine trappings of your own estate."

Curse the woman! Elfthryth lifted a beringed hand and shook her head. "Heavens no, Abbess. We would not dream of so imposing on you. We are far too many, and would deplete your abbey's resources."

The abbess was clearly taken aback. "Your thegn said you would be staying at least a seven-day, Majesty."

"My thegn was misinformed. Though I mourn my dear little stepson Edward, and will until the end of my days"—she sighed theatrically—"I must hasten home to guide and advise my living son. The king. May I be permitted to see Edward now?"

"M-majesty," stammered little Sister Wulfgifu, her face bright red, "surely you will wish to rest and take nourishment after your journey?"

She looked as though she were about to cry. Elfthryth, who was not overly acquainted with the intricacies of abbey life, wondered if the hosteler would be chastised if a guest refused hospitality. She hoped so.

Elfthryth patted the sister's hands in a motherly fashion. "No, dear. I burn to honor my stepson."

The abbess arched an eyebrow. Clearly, she didn't believe Elfthryth for a moment. She thinned her lips and nodded, bowing her head. "Then follow me, Majesty. With the generous donations we have been receiving from pilgrims such as yourself, we hope to be able to build a proper shrine to house the blessed Edward's body. In the meantime, he rests peacefully in the Lady Chapel of the church. Come."

Elfthryth's heart was pounding. Surely it was the exertion of the journey, nothing more. Holding her head high, she followed the abbess through the gatehouse. As they passed the cemetery, Elfthryth noticed that the snow rested on mounds of earth and piles of stones—no doubt evidence of preparation for the shrine of which the abbess had spoken. Any trace of apprehension fled as Elfthryth regarded the pathetic piles. Edward had been no saint in life. All this fuss suddenly struck her as foolish and naive rather than anything that could possibly threaten her.

They continued past the cloister walk and the abbess's quarters, and finally reached the north side of the property, where the church stood. Like every other monastery church, it was in the shape of a crucifix. Several windows that flanked the large wooden door depicted angels and Christ and other such folk. The abbess opened the door and stepped back to permit the queen to enter first. Sweeping inside, Elfthryth turned and subtly blocked the abbess from entering the nave.

"I'm sure you understand my desire to be alone," she said. "He was, after all, my poor stepson. . . ." She let her voice trail off and managed the barest sniff of false tears.

The abbess's face showed skepticism, but her words were proper. "As you wish, Your Majesty. I will send Sister Wulfgifu to wait here and escort you when you are ready to leave."

Elfthryth smiled stiffly and closed the door in the abbess's face.

She let out a deep breath and surveyed the church. The abundance of windows made the stone-and-wood building seem fairly bright, even on a gray winter day. As the day wore on, the sisters would light the oil in the cressets and the candles on the altar. She supposed it was a nice enough church, if one cared for that sort of thing.

Anxious to complete her task and depart as quickly as possible, Elfthryth strode as briskly down the length of the nave as her sore legs and hips would permit. She eased herself past the altar and the little door rood screen, past the choir where the nuns sat during their prayers, and peered into the small nooks the nuns referred to as "chapels."

There. They had erected a table of sorts, and the wooden coffin, covered with fine embroidered linen, sat quietly in the alcove that was doubtless the Lady Chapel. A single window provided light, and dust motes danced in the golden rays. There was, she noticed, no stench of decay.

Elfthryth felt nothing but annoyance as she stared at the coffin. "You were trouble to me alive," she said aloud, her voice echoing a little, "and you're trouble to me dead."

"More trouble than you think, stepmother dear," came a hollow voice.

Elfthryth's chest contracted. She gasped and stumbled backward, losing her balance and nearly falling. Almost at once, rage and embarrassment took her. The voice was youthful. No doubt it was one of the novices playing a trick on her.

"You stupid bitch," she quavered, not caring at the blasphemy in a holy house. "Come out of wherever you're hiding and let me whip you properly for giving me such a fright."

"Whip away, madam, but you'll not touch me," came the voice again. "I wish *I* could touch *you*. I wish I could hold a knife, and press its point deep into your black heart, and twist it until you died. Died just as I did, at the hand of your retainer."

Elfthryth couldn't breathe. It was a trick. It had to be a trick. The girl, or young boy, or whoever it was, was guessing. All those present at the actual murder had long since disappeared, save herself, Angelo, and Ethelred. And yet—

"Such accusations are treason," she managed. She couldn't endure the horrible pain in her heart anymore and found herself, against her will, slowly sinking to the cold stone floor. "I loved my stepson."

"You loved *your* son." The voice was louder now. "And for that love, I do not blame you. I loved the bright little boy he was then, too, and I know his hands are clean of my murder. Look at yours, stepmother. Can you see the blood?"

Despite herself, Elfthryth glanced down at her hands. They were clean, of course. She realized with horror that she had given herself away, if whoever was playing this charade was watching.

"The blood is gone, but I'm not."

She looked up and screamed.

Standing in front of her was the ghostly shape of the murdered Edward, exactly as she remembered him on that March night so long ago, save for the fact that all color had been leeched from him. He wore the same clothes. His hair was cropped in the same manner, and his pretty face burned with anger. Curiously, the look of rage gave her courage.

"You were no saint in life, boy," she snarled. "Your rages were a scandal, and your petulance—"

"You are right," he said in a cool voice. He bent, bringing his face to hers. "I was no saint, and am none now. What I am, dear sweet stepmother, is your personal torment. You killed me. You made this ghost. And I will be with you, day and night. Your grave's not too far away. Shall I take you there?"

He moved forward, his spectral shape dissolving as it passed through her. Cold pierced Elfthryth to her marrow, stopping her breath, slowing her heart. The cold of death. And after death. . . .

Warmth flowed back into her as Edward's ghost vacated her and she fell to the floor, sobbing.

Edward's laughter floated to her ears. "Yes, weep, stepmother. Weep as much as you like, it will do you no good. Shall I show you death again?"

"No!" shrieked Elfthryth. "No, mercy, mercy, Edward, I beg of you—"

"The mercy of the knife!" cried Edward. "The mercy of deceit! The mercy of murder!"

Somehow Elfthryth got to her feet. She raced down the nave, screaming "Mercy! Mercy!" as the ghost of the boy she had killed floated behind her, mocking her pleas and catching at her limbs.

Elfthryth burst through the door, gulping the clean air of the outdoors. She stumbled and went sprawling. Her body was rattled by the impact, but she didn't care. Edward was no longer present.

"Majesty!" Homely little Wulfgifu, coming up to the church, ran the rest of the way to kneel beside the weeping queen. "Majesty, are you ill?"

Elfthryth glanced up. Her face was hot and wet from the tears, and she clutched the girl's habit as if she were drowning. "Save me!" she cried. "Save me!"

"Majesty—" Sister Wulfgifu glanced about, clearly terrified at the queen's behavior.

"Pray for me, child." Simply seeing the face of the young nun was calming, and the words came more clearly. "Pray for my immortal soul. You're a good girl, a sweet girl, surely God will listen to you." Her breath came in little hitches, but the dreadful pain in her chest was starting to fade. The girl helped her up, gently putting an arm about her narrow shoulders.

"Seeing the relics of the blessed Edward has overcome you, Majesty," Wulfgifu soothed. "Many react thus. Come, let me get you some tea and something to eat."

Elfthryth's mind raced as she and the sister stumbled toward the guest house. *Your grave's not too far away. Shall I take you there?* She moaned softly at the recollection of the words, of the experience, and Wulfgifu's warm arm tightened about her.

Elfthryth was suddenly sorry for her unkind thoughts toward

the child. She was being very kind, though clearly alarmed at the situation. In fact, now that she thought about it, all the nuns here had been kind. Even the abbess. They would pray for her, Elfthryth was certain of it, especially if she paid them well to do so. They would pray to the saints to intervene and avert her dreadful punishment.

Why, she could become a nun herself. She owned two monasteries, at Amesbury and Wherwell, given to her upon Edgar's death. She could even become an abbess. It couldn't be that difficult, just learn the rules and pray and be penitent. If she started doing good things for God, perhaps when she did go to her grave, Angelo would not be waiting there for her.

She breathed deeply, her heart slowing. Hope flickered before her. She could escape the dreadful destiny that Edward's ghost had foretold, if she worked at it hard enough. Elfthryth had always gotten anything she set out to get. Eternal bliss would be no different.

"Tell me, child," she said. "Has life at Shaftesbury been kind to you?"

Off the Isle of Thanet
December 9, 999

East Anglia. Essex. Middlesex. Oxfordshire. Cambridgeshire. Hertfordshire. Buckinghamshire. Bedfordshire. Huntingdonshire. Northhamptonshire. Sussex. Hastings. Surrey. Berkshire. Hampshire. Wiltshire. And now, Kent and its prize jewel, Canterbury.

Loki stretched, shivering in the chill night air. It had snowed a few days ago, and the crystalline substance still coated the ground, but it would not snow tonight. He turned his face, his handsome human's face, up to the moonlight, then gazed at the cold, bright stars twinkling on a black sea.

The men were drunk. That was not unusual; they were drunk nearly every night. As long as they were sober in the morning, and could wield swords and oar their longboats, Loki wasn't about to deprive them of any pleasure they cared to pursue. The sound of their laughter and broken, discordant singing floated to his ears. Sweet.

Nagelfar rocked gently beneath him. His crew of ghosts was silent. He reflected on how well his plan was going. Somewhere off in the distance, his skills not needed, Jormungand played. He grew bigger by the day, it seemed, now that he was freed from his captivity in that cramped Dalriadan loch. And Fenris—

He lowered his hand, and Fenris's cold nose nudged his warm palm. A kiss from his son. Loki ran his hand over Fenris's fine head, caressing the soft gray ears.

"It is going well, Father," said Fenris. "Iona fell with barely a fight. Even their great Canterbury belongs to us now."

Loki nodded, gazing again at the moon. He found it oddly sorrowful to think of the lean wolf Hati devouring it in a single gulp. With each conquest, with each city and town and borough that fell, the hour of Ragnarok drew nearer. He did not feel the hot pleasure that he had known while lying and suffering deep in the earth for so many long years. Then, revenge was the only thing that sustained him. Now, wandering in a fine, strong human body here on Midgard, interacting with humans, tasting roasted meat and sweet wine and looking at the moon, he wondered if Ragnarok couldn't be postponed, just for a little while. Just long enough to see a few more crisp winter nights, drink a little more wine, feel Fenris's soft fur between his sensitive human fingers.

Movement caught his eye. A star streaked across the heavens, then faded from view. Loki tensed. Soon, the falling stars would not be so far distant. Any day—any moment—they could begin falling on the earth, as Angelo had told him.

There was a change in the tone of the noise the men made. Fenris's head turned, his sensitive ears alert. He had heard it, too. The next step was about to occur.

A few moments later, he heard the sound of oars breaking the calm surface of the sea. Fenris looked up at him and his tail wagged slightly, in anticipation.

"Let the task fall to me, Father."

"No, son. Angelo has told me what is to happen, and I made a promise to follow his direction. Fear not. There are many more battles ahead."

Fenris's eyes began to glow a soft green. His teeth were white. "I hunger for more kills," he said softly. "It seems as though that hunger is never sated."

It was Thorkell's ship, of course. Alone of all of them, he dared approach Loki at sea. The others kept their distance from the feared Dragon Odinsson.

"I have a missive, O Great Odinsson," said Thorkell. His boat pulled alongside Nagelfar, and Loki noticed, with a wry smile, that Thorkell flinched a little as his honest wooden boat scraped dead mens' fingernails.

He handed a scrap of parchment to Loki, who took it. He unfolded it and read, in Angelo's flowing script, *Kill him*. As he had expected. Loki let the parchment flutter from his fingers to the water. Quickly, he stepped into Thorkell's vessel.

"Take me to the prisoner," he said.

A few moments later, the Archbishop of Canterbury sat squarely in the center of one of the longboats. Archbishop Alphege, aged sixty or thereabouts, had been a burr in Angelo's flesh for some time now. A member of the Witan, he had, according to the king's adviser, stepped in again and again to thwart some of Angelo's more ambitious plans. Now, the Norsemen had him, and Angelo was well pleased.

Loki, standing tall and proud in Thorkell's vessel, regarded the man. He'd spent the last few weeks in chains while the Norsemen had enjoyed all the pleasures his little borough had to offer. Alphege had forbidden his people to ransom him, though by all accounts he was well-loved and money enough to please even the greediest of Thorkell's men could have been raised. The archbishop had been a special gift to Loki and his men. Another so-called holy man, Abbot Aelmar, had betrayed Alphege and all of Canterbury to them in return for his own precious hide.

"Stubborn, stubborn," Loki chastised. "A few pounds and you could have been free, Your Grace."

"The title is foul in your mouth, heathen," Alphege retorted. "If I had water enough to spit, I would."

One of his guards raised a meaty fist to strike the man. A quick look from Loki forestalled the blow.

"I've no doubt. But your mouth *is* dry, isn't it? And your belly empty? Is the lapping of the waves torment, Your Grace, and the smell of roasting meat agony?"

Alphege lowered his bald head and did not reply. His chains rattled slightly.

"We had a lovely feast," Loki continued. The ships of the fleet had approached, and were slowly forming a ring about the ship upon which the prisoner sat. "Your Canterbury livestock was most delicious."

"Enjoy the fruits of this world, heathen, for you'll not taste them in the next," said Alphege.

Loki grinned. "So certain in your faith. So certain about my
destiny. I am a god, idiot. Your next world does not exist for me.
I have my orders, and my men have—their traditions. Take heart,
old man. Others have simply died at my hands. You will become
a martyr. They'd have made you a saint, if they had been granted
the time." He turned to Thorkell. "He refused to pay. I understand
your men are the hotter for drink and anger."

Thorkell cast the first blow. The remains of his dinner sat on
a plate nearby. He seized the joint and hurled it at the chained
Archbishop. It hit him square in the throat, and Alphege grunted.
He tried to raise his arms in an instinctive gesture, but the chains
forbade such movement. A roar went up, and the others joined in.
Bones, plates, even an entire oxhead or two were thrown at the
archbishop, who crouched in a feeble, futile effort to avoid the
blows. Loki watched as the drunken Norsemen vented their
anger by pelting a chained, old man.

This sort of thing often passed as dinner amusement among
the Norsemen. Loki did not find it so amusing. He was uncomfortably reminded of the Aesir gods throwing things at the
charmed Balder, who could not be hurt.

Except by treachery.

Loki grimaced and looked away. A sudden swell in the volume of the drunken crowed caused him to look back just in time
to see Thorkell leap into the prisoner's boat. Crying aloud,
Thorkell seized one of the massive battle-axes, lifted it high over
his head, and brought it down. Alphege's skull was neatly cloven,
and a huge cheer rose at the sight of blood, bone, and brain.

"Take me back to Nagelfar," Loki said, and thought of stars
and cold moonlight.

17

For I was an hungered, and ye gave me meat: I was thirsty, and ye gave me drink: I was a stranger, and ye took me in.

—MATTHEW 25:35

The Andredesweald
December 999

The Lady's well was colder than anything Alwyn had ever experienced. He tried to hold his breath, and his lungs burned from the effort. He was being dragged along as though something dreadfully strong had a solid grip on him and refused to release him. Once, he opened his eyes, and saw nothing. The cold nearly froze his eyeballs, and he shut his eyes again.

Just when he felt he could take it no longer, that he must expel the stale air and inhale icy fluid in its stead, the pulling sensation changed. Now he felt pushed, and hope surged through him. He surrendered to the power, and when he finally broke the surface, he released Rowena and gasped for breath. Air, God's pure, simple air, had never seemed sweeter.

He was still bitterly cold, and movement was difficult. He blinked the water from his eyes. The shore was only a few yards away, and Alwyn began to swim toward it. It was day, and the blue of the open sky and the yellow warmth of the sun dazzled his eyes after the darkness. He glanced around, and to his vast relief saw that everyone else had survived the peculiar journey. Were he not so wretchedly uncomfortable, the sight of the dignified Rowena and little Ratatosk, both soaked to the skin and looking more like rats than cat and squirrel, would have made him laugh. Balaam brayed and headed for dry land, and the Faerie horse, with Kennag clinging to her, began to swim with powerful strokes. The Lady had been true to her word. Somehow, she had gotten both mare and donkey safely into her waters.

It was only when he had climbed out onto the muddy, stone-speckled shore of this small lake that Alwyn knew something wasn't right. Exhausted, frightened, dazed, it took him a moment to realize what it was. Just as he opened his mouth to voice his astonishment, Kennag said, though chattering teeth, "S-summer!"

This was no wintry glen in which they had emerged from a lake encased in ice. This was a flower-starred meadow. Alwyn collapsed onto grass that was green and sweet, blinking stupidly at the bees and butterflies that went about their business. The trees were full and thick, proudly adorned with leafy green crowns, and the sun beat down with warmth and strength.

The animals emerged from the lake and shook themselves. Droplets flew everywhere. Kennag slid off the horse, her nearly frozen joints responding stiffly. She almost fell, catching at the horse's neck. Alwyn noticed that the burn marks on her face had disappeared. The Blood Spring waters were indeed healing.

"Is this—is this Faerie?" asked Alwyn, nervously. "You told me their seasons were the opposite of ours."

Kennag's shivering began to slow. She rubbed her arms. Her multicolored garb clung to her slim, strong frame and brazenly outlined every inch of it. Despite the cold that still enveloped him, Alwyn felt a sudden heat. He looked away from her. Once, he would have condemned her simply for possessing the body, for owning such an alluring, tempting treasure. Now, he knew that it was not her fault if wet clothes clung to her, or that her body responded to the cold in so arousing a fashion.

"I don't think so," she said. "The Blood Spring was obviously a gateway to somewhere else, but I don't think we're inside a Faerie knoll." She glanced upward, squinting. "That sun's far too bright, too real."

"The lady is right," came a voice. From the thickness of the forest, three people emerged, two men and a woman. Each carried something wrapped in cloth. Alwyn recognized the brown robes and realized the men were monks. But they were not tonsured. The woman was also clad in a robe, and her long, bright hair was not covered. It was she who had spoken.

"We are born from a woman's womb, as both of you were," she continued. Her face was lovely, her voice warm and welcoming. "We see that you are still cold from the world outside. We have brought you warm and dry clothing."

"Who are you?" asked Alwyn, as the two men approached him and the woman went to Kennag.

The brothers, one an older man whose hair was nearly white, the other young and dark-tressed, exchanged smiles. "We are the ones who dwell here. Are you not cold, Brother Alwyn? We have robes that will feel familiar to you, and Ardith will see to Kennag's needs."

Alwyn was shivering, and he postponed further questions until he was in the warm, dry, surprisingly soft brown robes the two monks had brought him. They also offered him a plate of fresh fruit. He took an apple, realizing suddenly that he was hungry, and bit into it. It was crisp and sweet.

Kennag, too, now wore the brown garb of the monks and nun. It looked quite different on her than on Alwyn. She smiled and chatted with the fair-haired woman, Ardith, as if they were old friends while she toweled dry her long red locks. Alwyn found himself surprisingly comfortable with the strangers as well, though they were as slippery as fish when it came to answering his questions.

He finished the delicious fruit as he went toward Balaam. Affectionately, he stroked the donkey's wet hide and offered him the apple core. Balaam crunched it eagerly.

"How are you?" asked Alwyn, directing his question to Rowena, perched on Balaam's back, as well.

"The better for a warm place," said Rowena, and resumed licking herself almost frantically, in an effort to smooth her damp fur.

Ratatosk had ventured into the trees, and now peered down at them. "We're in the middle of nowhere," he said. "There are trees as far as my eyes can see."

"You are in the Great Forest, the Andredesweald," said the elder of the two monks, almost as if in answer to Ratatosk's comment. But he couldn't possibly have understood the squirrel—could he? "Come—our little church is not far."

"I'm not going with you until I know who you are," said Kennag. She did not utter the words with her usual vehemence, and indeed blushed a little as she said them. "Forgive me, but—I have recently had an unpleasant experience that came with trusting folk I did not know."

The elderly brother smiled. "But you have been sent to us by the Lady, have you not? You traveled in her sacred waters. Do you trust her?"

Kennag looked uncertain. "Yes. . . ."

Ardith placed a sisterly arm around Kennag's shoulder. "You are tired and hungry, and this is a place of rest and healing. There is nothing here that will harm you. You must decide for yourself if you can trust us or not. If you wish to leave, we will not stop you." Her blue eyes twinkled kindly. "Though we might insist on ensuring that you are well supplied with food, drink, and warm blankets."

Kennag glanced at Alwyn. They spoke without words. She smiled, and he nodded.

The place they were being taken, Halig explained, was called Worth Church. It was located in a small clearing in the heart of the old Great Forest, and for a long, long time, the little community that called itself the Tribe had made it home. Alwyn was confused. Churches didn't exist in the middle of nowhere. There would be no point to it—who would attend? Still, they dutifully followed Halig, Ardith, and Rand along the all-but-hidden path that twined through the dimly lit forest.

The forest opened into a small clearing. A central fire burned steadily, heating a cauldron, the odor of its contents teased Alwyn's nostrils. The fire was surrounded by several small huts. Men and women, all dressed in the brown robes, went about their tasks. They looked up as the little band emerged from the forest, and smiled a welcome. The people Alwyn saw were all as vigorous, healthy-looking, and cheerful as their three escorts.

"I don't think I've ever seen such a collection of fine-looking folk in my life," Kennag said to Alwyn in a soft voice. He nodded.

"We have been blessed," said the black-haired young Rand. "Our community suffers from no disease or infirmities. We are born hale, live well, and die peacefully at an old age. We understand that there are changes outside of our forest; things called *snow* and *winter*. Here, the sun and rain take turns in the skies to bless us with their gifts. The fruit is always sweet and ripe, and the earth yields up grain for our bread."

"Do the animals come and lay their heads down to serve as your supper, too?" asked Kennag—rather crankily, thought Alwyn, though he had to smother a smile of his own.

The older man, Halig, laughed. "Nay, Kennag. We do not eat the flesh of beasts. They know they are safe within the bounds of the Weald."

"Very civilized," approved Ratatosk, who was accompanying them by leaping from branch to branch above their heads.

"Huh. Primitive, I'd say. Nothing like a tasty squirrel to restore your faith in the world," said Rowena. But her eyes were slitted and her ears relaxed. To his surprise and pleasure, Alwyn realized that the cat was teasing the squirrel in an affectionate manner. Ratatosk, in turn, seemed to huff a bit more than was needed. Out of a necessary truce, they had formed a friendship. It was humbling to witness.

"Which building serves you for a church, and may I meet your priest?" Alwyn asked politely.

Ardith, Rand, and Halig exchanged amused glances. Ardith took pity on Alwyn and gently touched his shoulder. "The church is this way, Brother Alwyn." He left the others and followed her a short distance into the woods, then stepped out into another grassy glade.

"Here it is," said Ardith placidly. Alwyn gasped. He had been confused when the brothers mentioned a church. What would a church be doing in the middle of a forest, so far from any towns or villages? He had thought them a group of hermits, nestled in small rustic shelters in this clearing, calling their central place of worship a "church" after old habit. But it was a church indeed that rose proudly in front of him, one of the loveliest Alwyn had ever seen. Certainly Glastonbury Abbey was much more imposing, and St. Aidan's had a place in his heart that no other holy house could rival. But Worth Church—

Made of stone, it somehow managed to give the dual and conflicting impression of having stood here since the dawn of time and having been built only yesterday. Its plan was that of the standard cruciform church with which he was intimately familiar. Alwyn guessed it to be thirty yards long. The two transepts that opened up like the arms of the cross were approximately twenty-five yards long. No little woodland chapel, this.

"It's—it's beautiful," he said, aware that he was staring and that the word was woefully inadequate. "But how do you—where is—"

"It is time for the midday meal, Brother," said Ardith. "Let us return. We will feed you and tell you who we are."

The afternoon was warm and glowing. As the sun began to move toward the west, Kennag was startled to hear the slow, lazy hum of insects. How strange, in the middle of December.

The stew was indeed free of meat, as Halig had told them it would be. Nonetheless, she and Alwyn spooned it up hungrily. The mushrooms were chewy and delicious. Beans, roots, peas, and various greens added their own flavors. She accepted a second bowl and more of the crusty brown bread thickly spread with butter. Her appetite seemed stronger than it had ever been, and she was certain that it was not simply because she was hungry. All her senses seemed heightened here.

As usual, Rowena and Ratatosk had gone off on errands of their own. Balaam and the mare had been stabled with the Tribe's three cows and two goats. There were no horses or donkeys here. "All that we need is within our grasp," Ardith said. "Why do we need to ride a beast?"

Kennag couldn't argue with the logic of that. She realized, as she finished the second bowl of the marvelous vegetable stew, that they had not seen Neddy for some time. Not since Glastonbury. She wondered if he could find them here, wherever "here" was, and if he was all right.

"Your hospitality is above reproach," said Alwyn. Kennag noticed that he, too, had taken a second bowl of stew, and was working on a third slice of bread. "I hope our questions do not seem too forward. In return, we will tell you of our mission, and perhaps—"

"We know it, Brother Alwyn," said Halig. His brown eyes were kind. "Had we not, you would never have emerged in our lake."

Kennag was suddenly tired of wise-seeming folks who spoke in cryptic phrases. Despite the kindness the Tribe had shown her, she was impatient. She set down her bowl and looked Halig squarely in the eye.

"Halig, you've been very kind to us, and the food was delicious. We thank you. However, if you do know of our task, then you must be aware that it's been tiring, painful, frightening, and seemingly endless and futile."

"Kennag!" reproached Alwyn.

"Hush. Let me finish. We're two people, a donkey, a horse, a cat, a squirrel, and, occasionally, a ghost trying to do something so difficult that even the Fair Folk and the angels won't touch it. I've been thrown into prison, chased by a goddess of the Underworld and her pack of demon hounds, captured by the King of the Unseelie Court, and dunked into a freezing spring. Alwyn's undergone similar trials. We've talked to all sorts of people, from kings of men and Faerie to abbots and bishops and so far, all we've been able to do is stand by and watch the Signs unfold, one by one, without being able to do a single thing about any of it. Now, clearly, the Lady of the Blood Spring sent us here. Why? What can you do for us?"

Out of the corner of her eye, she saw Alwyn staring at her. His mouth was open in shock. Rowena and Ratatosk had returned, and also were clearly stunned by her outburst.

She felt her face grow hot, but didn't avert her gaze. Slowly, the elderly man smiled, and finally he laughed. "Blessed Savior, now I know why you were chosen! Alwyn is gentle and wise and braver than he knows, but he needs you, Kennag nic Beathag, to push him when he hesitates. You are right"—his smile faded— "you are being asked to do something that no one, mortal or immortal, should ever have to do. But you are not alone. We will fight with you."

She blinked. "I mean no disrespect when I say this, but you seem . . . too peaceful a people."

"We have told you that we are the Tribe. Perhaps you are not familiar with what has been passed down as a legend, but I imagine Brother Alwyn is." He turned to regard the monk. "Have you not heard tales of the Lost Tribes of Israel?"

His face went pale. "I have," he breathed. "Sweet Jesu—is it you?"

"We are one of the Tribes," Halig confirmed. "There are others just like us, scattered across the Earth. Our task is to wait, with patience, love, and trust, until we are called. We live in this forest, in and yet out of your world and time. When the final battle does come, between the powers of darkness and the powers of light, then we will hunger for destruction of evil as much as we now shun violence. That battle is about to begin."

Kennag nodded. She had been raised with tales of slumbering heroes, of great battles and men who were more than men. Glancing at Alwyn, she saw that he seemed to be having a harder time accepting Halig's pronouncement, even though it was a myth of his own faith given life.

"But it has begun," Alwyn managed after a moment. "Kennag and I—"

"You are the Witnesses, the heralds of the event," Ardith interrupted. "And you are charged with halting it, as the true time has not yet arrived. We pray that you will succeed. We have no desire to fight this battle twice. You are more like the spy in the encampment, or the messenger with the vital missive. We are the soldiers, and the actual battle waits to begin."

"Can you help us, then?" asked Kennag impulsively. Rowena climbed into her lap, and she began stroking the soft fur. "We know we have to stop the world from ending, and we have sought advice from those we deemed wise. You seem like someone who might know. What can we do? How do we stop the Signs from unfolding?"

Ardith's face filled with compassion. When she spoke, her voice was soft. "Everything you need to know, you know already. Search your mind, your heart. We cannot give you answers, but we can give you a place to think and a chance to rest a tired body." Her blue eyes regarded the clearing, the sky, and the trees. Her face shone with reverence. "This holy place, this forest out of time—it may help you quiet your raging thoughts. Come, let us visit the church. Your journey inward will begin there."

Obediently, Kennag and Alwyn rose and followed Ardith, Rand, and Halig along yet another path through the forest. As she ducked under a tree branch and emerged in the clearing, Kennag had to admit that she was impressed. There was something welcoming about this church.

Rand held open a heavy wooden door. Kennag stepped inside, cautiously, and the rest followed. It became cooler and darker once the door was closed, and her eyes adjusted to the fainter light. Despite the dimness in contrast to the bright, summery day outside, Kennag did not feel trapped in this place as she did in the priest's dark little church in Gleannsidh. The building was comforting rather than confining, snug rather than smothering. Whoever these people were, they were clearly touched by magic, and wherever the magic came from, be it the Christians' God, the great gods and goddesses, or the Earth itself, Kennag knew it to be good and wholesome.

Her eyes wandered toward the altar, and she stiffened. Her nostrils flared, and her breath came in quick little gasps.

"Kennag?" Alwyn now recognized his companion's trances almost immediately. He didn't try to touch her, startle her out of her transfixion, only stepped closer. He said, without words, *I am here. You are safe.* She felt his presence behind her, warm, solid, and real.

Beneath the carved wooden altar milled dozens of ghosts. No, not ghosts, they were more like—spirits. Freed souls, despite the grievous wounds many of them had received in life. There was no torment about them, only . . . impatience?

She took in the swirl of spirit liberated from flesh; saw a youth with arrows in his body, an old man with his side gashed open, a fragile girl with a thin red line across her throat.

"Oh, Lord!" They lifted their hands up to a Being whom Kennag could not see. "How long, Sovereign Lord, holy and true! How long until You judge the inhabitants of the earth and avenge our blood?" Then suddenly their clothing changed. The men and women were clad now in robes of the purest white, and a voice came out of nowhere, its timbre shaking Kennag to her bones.

"Only a little longer, until the number of martyrs is complete. Behold, he comes, the last martyr of this age!"

And there was a final one, floating toward them. His body had been horribly beaten, his bones broken, and despite the grievous wound in his head—his skull was cloven in two—what remained of his face showed joy. His bloodstained clerical vestments were transformed into the white robes that the others wore, and his wounds healed. He turned his face, once again whole, to Kennag's, and smiled at her. And the song that rose up, as the men and woman who died for their faith were uplifted into their Heaven, was such that Kennag clawed at her ears until they bled, for no mortal ought to hear such a song and live—

"Kennag, stop it! You're hurting yourself!"

She fought them, writhing and screaming "No, no, I can't hear it, I can't!" Finally she opened her eyes, saw that the vision had ended. Her body went limp with relief.

Alwyn held her tenderly. He stroked her hair. "Your poor ears," he murmured. He touched one, and she winced.

"I couldn't hear the song," she said, exhausted. "I couldn't hear the song or—"

"It was not for such ears as yours, " said Ardith unexpectedly. Startled, Kennag stared at her.

"You—you heard it, too?"

They nodded, sinking to the cold floor of the nave beside her in a show of concern.

"Kennag has been gifted with the Second Sight," Alwyn explained. "What did you See this time? If you wish to tell me, that is," he added.

Kennag smiled tiredly at him, thinking how far he had come since she had first seen him, pale and frightened and yet resolute, standing at the entrance to King Ethelred's villa at Calne. She had called him a crippled boy monk in a moment of oft-regretted scorn, but she doubted whether the king's finest soldier could have withstood what Alwyn had endured on this demanding, intimidating quest. She wondered why she hadn't noticed before what a sweet face he had.

"I was looking at the altar," she began, lifting a bloodied finger and pointing. "I was just looking at it, thinking how pleasant a place this was for a church, and then I saw spirits beneath the altar. In life, they had all been killed in a dreadful fashion, and they cried out that they were tired of waiting. And a—a voice answered them, saying that their number was not complete. Then another spirit joined them—it was awful and yet wonderful at the same time. He seemed so happy, even though it looked as though his head had been split open by an ax. And then they began to sing, and I knew I wasn't supposed to hear it, and that's why I clawed at my ears."

Alwyn's face had gone gray. "The Fifth Seal. Under the altar of God, those who were martyred for their faith cry out . . . and the last martyr has joined them." He muttered under his breath, as if in pain, "If only we had known who he was! If we could have prevented him from dying, we could have stopped it! Stopped everything!"

He eased her off him, then rose and stormed out. Kennag, weak as she was, tried to get to her feet and follow him, but Ardith's gentle hand restrained her.

"You need rest, my child," she said, "and Alwyn needs to be alone. There are things you both must understand before you leave, and such comprehension must occur in solitude."

"You speak in riddles," Kennag accused. Her head was starting to hurt.

"Answers are riddles," Ardith replied. Kennag hadn't the slightest idea what she meant.

Alwyn stormed out of the church, heedless of the beauty and grace of the place. Once outside, he headed for the darkness of the forest. He heard a distant boom, and realized that it would soon begin to rain. He didn't care. What did it matter, warm or cold, wet or dry—what did anything matter when he had failed so miserably? How did he ever think he could outwit God's most devious adversary? He, a foolish, useless shell of a man, good only for penning pretty letters in a safe, sheltered environment.

Put me out in the world and I fail, he thought angrily. *I can't be trusted. I'm useless, just as they always told me.*

A bright flash of light nearly blinded him, and a crashing, rolling boom of thunder followed hard on the lightning's heels. As if the heavens themselves had opened, the rain began to fall. It was hard, and the drops stung his face.

Ahead of him, a little to the left, the forest opened up a bit, and he could glimpse the swell of a hillock through the gray haze of driving rain. He hastened toward it, thinking to find shelter, and was pleasantly surprised to see a dry, shallow cave. Alwyn hurried inside, ducking his head and saying a quick prayer of thanks for the fortuitous appearance of temporary shelter from the unexpected rainstorm.

He caught his breath and watched the rain fall. His robe was soaked, and he wiped his face with a wet hand. An instant later, a shape appeared at the entrance and dived inside.

"Kennag! You should have stayed in the church. You've only just gotten dry from our last swim."

She grinned at him and wiped her face. "I know. But I couldn't let you run out like that." For a long moment they were silent, staring at the rain. Alwyn shivered, and Kennag was suddenly beside him.

"Here," she said, opening her cloak to cover them both. "Let us warm ourselves."

He was glad of the warmth, but, as before, wished there were some other means to obtain it. Kennag's body was simply too tempting. Alwyn tried to keep his mind on other things.

"We're not going to do it, are we?" asked Kennag. Her face

reflected fear and despair. "I mean—how can we? We're just two people trying to stop a being who's almost godlike in his power. We don't even know what to do."

His heart hurt. She was echoing his own dark, grieving thoughts. If she, too, felt that the task was hopeless, then what was there to strive for?

"We can't give up," he said, more for himself than for her.

"Why can't we?" Her face was only inches from his. "Alwyn, think! The world is going to end! We're all going to die or live lives of horrible torment for ever and ever! Let's take a little happiness now, before it's too late! A little warmth, a little pleasure—how can that be wrong when we know what awaits us?"

Her hand was on his wet cheek now, her green eyes searching his. Then, to his utter astonishment, she tangled her long fingers in his thick, curly brown hair and pulled his mouth to hers.

18

*I have seen the wicked in great power,
and spreading himself like a green bay
tree.*

—PSALMS 37:35

**Ethelred's Royal Villa, Kingston
December 18, 999**

"Elfthryth . . . did . . . what?"

Angelo's voice was as calm and musical as ever, but inside, fury and shock warred in an unexpected battle. Ethelred's face was smiling and almost glowed with pleasure.

"She's decided to take her vows," he burbled. "Isn't that wonderful! No one can accuse her of anything now. And her willing sacrifice, her rejection of all the worldly trappings the mother of the king enjoys—why, that will surely win God's favor!"

"Surely," repeated Angelo acidly. What was the woman thinking? What had happened to her at Shaftesbury? The Elfthryth who had departed had been as greedy, as dark, as it was possible for a mortal to be. She was hip-deep in the murderous affair, and all these years had seemed quite pleased with herself. What had happened to make her so change her mind?

He could find out, of course. It was but the work of a moment to send one of his servants to the abbey of Wherwell to confront the woman, but at this juncture Elfthryth was hardly worth the effort. She had been useful to him, once. She was, no longer. There would be time enough later, when his goal had been accom-

plished, to deal with the treasonous bitch. In the meantime, as
was ever his wont, he would seize the opportunity.

"And God *will* be on our side," Angelo said, moving closer to
Ethelred. "I feel it. I know it."

Ethelred gazed trustingly into Angelo's face. Angelo had
tempted him into moving, step by step, away from this God he
purported to love above all things. Just a few more Signs to bring
about. It was well, for the year was growing old.

"The year draws to a close soon," he said. His breath was
warm on Ethelred's face. He knew it was sweet as a summer's
breeze. "He will come again, to pass judgment on all mankind.
We are ready to move against the emperor, to win you the crown
so that you may present it to Our Lord when He comes, and asks
for it."

"I don't know," said Ethelred. He turned away, and the hold
was broken—for the moment. "It doesn't feel right. The killing
of traitors, the blinding of their children—how can that be what
Christ wants me to do?"

" 'If thy right eye offend thee, pluck it out,' " quoted Angelo,
" 'for it is profitable for thee that one of thy members should per-
ish, and not that thy whole body should be cast into hell. And if
thy right hand offend thee, cut it off.' You have acted rightly thus
far, Majesty. You have rid the body—your country and kingdom—of infection after infection."

Ethelred still did not look at him. "Oh, Angelo," he said in a
voice that was surprisingly mature and weary, "when you say
these things to me, they sound so right. And they feel right when
I do them. But at night, when I lie with my wife and think of our
children, and Christ's charge to love one another as He has loved
us—then you and your wise advice seem very far away indeed."

He was losing Ethelred. Fear flickered inside Angelo. He had
not known about these second thoughts, and he should have—

He dropped to his knees and grasped at Ethelred's tunic.
"Majesty, if you think I have given you wrong advice, then your
task is clear." Tears burned his eyes and poured down his cheeks
as he looked up at the king. "You must banish me—or, if you feel
I have betrayed you in any manner, then you must slay me."

"No!" Horror was writ plain upon Ethelred's handsome face,
and he quickly bent to bring his counselor up from the floor. "No,
Angelo, your advice is sound!"

"No, Majesty," Angelo said firmly. "If you are having trouble sleeping on my account, then plainly I am a"—he swallowed hard—"a poor influence on you. I am sorry. I thought only to guide you and, dare I say it, even love you in the way that a good servant loves his master. I see that I have failed."

"Angelo, no, no!" Ethelred was now almost frantic. His hands fluttered like birds, uncertain as to what they would do—now touching Angelo's face, now his shoulders, now flailing in the air. "You have been the one person I could completely trust! It's my own weakness and lack of faith that trouble my dreams, truly. No more talk of banishment or death. I'd sooner cut my own throat than yours!"

Angelo's eyes searched the king's. He let a hesitant smile curve his full lips, then grasped Ethelred's hand and kissed it fervently.

"My king," he whispered. "My beloved king. I shall ever steer you with the best of my judgment."

It had been a close thing, but Angelo knew what he needed to do now. A lesser demon would have a new task to perform—that of sitting on the king's chest at night, and sending him dreams of conquest, victory, and a profound sense of godliness in all that he did.

He decided to postpone discussion about toppling Otto from his imperial throne. Ethelred's simple mind was already crowded; the king did not need to be involved in this aspect of Angelo's master plan. Easy enough to arrange an accident, or even an assassination. There were many in Otto's court who had drunk from Angelo's tempting cup. Even Pope Sylvester II himself, once Gerbert d'Aurillac, who had tutored the youthful Otto, had bartered for earthly powers. There were many who thought the pope was the Antichrist. They were wrong. Loki filled that role. Still, the pope was in Angelo's pouch. And Otto would trust his old friend and mentor.

Some things were so delightfully simple.

He needed to concentrate on continuing to poison Ethelred's thoughts. "I spoke before from the Bible, regarding the right hand. *Your* right hand, Majesty—the Witan—is deeply offending you. It is riddled with traitors. Aelfric, Wulfstan, Abbot Aelmar—the only one among them I trusted was the late Archbishop of Canterbury." He lowered his gaze to the floor and crossed himself. "God rest his poor martyred soul."

He looked back up, right into Ethelred's eyes, and spoke the daring pronouncement: "Dissolve it, Majesty."

"What? I can't possibly—"

"The Force is pressing in on us from every side!" exclaimed Angelo. "From Iona to London, they have us, Majesty! You cannot afford to be taking the advice of people you cannot trust."

Ethelred emitted a little groan and turned away, flinging himself into the chair by the fire. He stared into the dancing flames. "The Witan is the only way I can hear the voice of my kingdom," he said softly. "They come from all parts of it—and they let me know what's going on."

"Majesty, I can tell you what is going on. I have my own sources, whom I trust implicitly. If you trust *me* implicitly—as you have said here today—then it follows that by simply listening to me and my advice, you will receive information that is honest and true."

Ethelred slowly turned to look at him. His face was ineffably sad. "Do you know, Angelo, I do not look forward to this Judgment Day? I know it is blasphemy, but frankly, I'm terrified. I'm not sure that I can stand before Our Lord and speak what I have done."

Angelo knelt beside the king and laid a hand on his arm. "King Ethelred," he said softly, "you have fought the good fight against those who would slaughter your people and deny your God. Anything you have done has been to advance those two causes. There is nothing but righteousness in that."

Ethelred's eyes were haunted. "I hope to God you are right, Angelo. If we have been fighting on the wrong side all this time. . . ." His voice trailed off.

Angelo had to struggle to contain his glee. In one brief conversation, he had managed to solidify the king's trust in him and convince Ethelred to dissolve the one voice that still spoke truth to him—the Witan.

Nothing could stop him now.

That night, alone in his room, he summoned Hel. Her face appeared in the brazier's flames, flickering in shades of orange, black, red, and yellow.

"What happened?" he demanded. He had been able to track the meddlesome Witnesses to Glastonbury, but then they had simply vanished, a thing that Angelo would have deemed impossible.

Hel's lovely face danced in the firelight, becoming distorted with movement. "I found them in Glastonbury, as you told me I would. I spoke with your friend Gwyn ap Nudd, who promised me help. You need to choose more competent allies, Angelo."

"Clearly I do. You were a mistake. Your father and siblings are performing beautifully for me. Perhaps it is the males of your line who have all the wits."

She frowned. "I hid in Gwyn's realm and captured the female. The male would have been lured down, too, only he had unexpected companions. I emerged from the underworld and gave chase. Gwyn's hounds are fleet, and Garm has never lost his quarry—until now. The Witnesses are not so wise in and of themselves, but they seem to be very canny when it comes to choosing friends." She described the battle, and the narrow escape into the well of the Lady.

Angelo was furious. Knowing he would not be heard by the lowly mortals outside, he threw back his head, opened his mouth, and screamed his rage. Howling, he pounced on the brazier, clutching the red-hot coals in his palms and shaking his fists.

"You had them!" he screamed at her. "You had them, and you let them go!"

Hel was not his subject, but his ally. His rage did not harm her as it had Moloch or any others directly under his command. She merely gazed at him with increasing contempt. With an effort, he calmed himself.

"Whatever the circumstances, you cannot argue that you failed in your task," he said, his voice cool. "You must find them again. Where are they?"

"I do not know," Hel answered stiffly. "They went into the Lady's well and disappeared."

"They can't have simply drowned," Angelo said, more to himself than her. "She wouldn't have let them, and I would have sensed it. They must be somewhere. . . ."

Other. Long ago, in that ill-fated revolt he had led against his brethren, he had been given this world upon which his enemy, mankind, dwelt. He was the prince of this world. It all belonged to him. He could enter any place on the earth he cared to, from deepest cavern to coldest ocean to most sacred church. This was his realm, and he could peer into every corner of it.

He ought to have gone after them himself. He realized that now. He had vastly underestimated the mortals. That was why he had sent Hel and her hound after them. They should not have been able to elude her.

But they had, and now they had gone someplace other than the earth with which he was familiar. Curse them both! Who would have thought it of them?

He would make them a higher priority. They would have to return, eventually. They could not hope to stop him by hiding. They'd have to emerge into this plane of existence, and when they did, he would be able to find them.

"Angelo?" Hel's voice held a hint of annoyance. He ignored her, still concentrating. Finally, he spoke.

"When they venture forth from wherever it is they have gone, as they must, I will find them. I will deal with them myself. You will shortly have another, more familiar task."

She opened her mouth to reply but, petulantly, he severed the contact. The flames and embers were once again natural things. Angelo turned to the window and opened the shutters. The cold air caused his nude human body to prickle with gooseflesh, and he shivered involuntarily.

He was the prince of this world—and of the surrounding bodies as well. The sun, moon, and stars obeyed him. He had never forced them to obey hitherto; there had been no need to, and he had to admit he had enjoyed the game of the last several centuries. But now, there were Signs to bring about.

Mentally, he reviewed them, and then called them forth.

For the first time since their creation, the celestial bodies paused in their movements. The Call came, and they obeyed.

Bits of debris, swirling aimlessly in the vast darkness of the heavens, had a new path. Their motion was halted, directed, and the rock and ice pieces began to progress toward the blue sphere, the third from the sun.

The sun, too, had a task, and slowly, steadily, it left its appointed position and drew closer to the orb. Everything was converging up on the site where God's beloved creations dwelt, but the rock and ice and sun belonged to the Adversary, and could not disobey.

The Earth itself was ordered to roil. Deep in its molten core, it began to stir. The surface was rocked; it cracked, and fire poured forth in molten form.

The rocks reached the Earth, and slammed into it. Poisons es-

caped, and a third of the pure water turned deadly. Wells burbled black liquid; rivers ran red. The gentle Faerie Folk who had called these places home choked and died, as did all humans who foolishly filled their buckets and gourds and pots with the tainted fluids.

At the ancient holy place now called Glastonbury, Abbot Sigegar led his people in urgent, frightened prayers as the earth quaked beneath them and the sky filled with dreadful images. He died as a chunk of the roof fell in. He was not alone; no one in that sacred place survived.

Wormwood was its name, the name of the mighty, blazing star that fell upon Glastonbury. It slammed into the earth, burying itself deep, leveling the Tor and destroying all life that dwelt aboveground for miles, blessed until this moment by air and water and sun and grass. The great hole it left behind yawned open. Smoke billowed forth, climbing upward, seeking the light of the sun and then cloaking it from view. Beneath a black sky at midday, the liberated inhabitants of Gwyn's world rushed forth.

Some were tiny beings, gnarled and wizened and bitter as a broken heart. Others were monstrous, huge and powerful, with teeth that longed to devour the innocent. Some were as fair as the morning, with hearts as dark as night. Such a one was their king, the whooping, gleeful Gwyn ap Nudd, who rode on the back of a horse as fair as Kennag's and as foul inside as its dark master. Behind him, his red-eared hounds barked and howled.

One was a woman, half beauty, half corpse, who rode atop a black horse that looked like a living skeleton. She carried a broom in her hand, and joy filled her at the thought of all the lives she would sweep away with it. At her feet raced a huge black hound. Fire came from his mouth as he bayed, and beneath his paws, the grass turned brown and died.

Last, but not the least of the dreadful party, came those whose day this truly was. Beneath their obscene feet, the grass did not crackle and burn. The ignorant beasts of the forest and field were safe from them, as were all things of the natural world. They had only one prey: mankind.

They burned with the insatiable hunger of the maddened locust, though their shape could have been called equine. On their heads, perched atop long, flowing locks like those of a beautiful woman, were crowns of gold. Human faces were twisted by expressions no mortal could ever emulate. Wings, some of feathers

*and some of scales, beat like thunder. Long, thin tails with a
barbed, poisonous point snapped and twisted. Lionlike teeth
gnashed, eager to rip and tear the children of Adam.*

*They had come in answer to the call of their prince, the angel
of the abyss, and they had come to destroy.*

Off the Isle of Thanet
December 18, 999

Loki saw the falling stars, and his heartbeat quickened. He swal
lowed hard.

"I see them, Father!" cried Fenris, prancing about on the deck
of Nagelfar. In the distance, Loki watched as a black shape coiled
out of the water and playfully made as if to snatch at the bright
pretties hurtling earthward. Jormungand, too, had seen them. The
next stage in Angelo's plan had begun.

A huge swell arose, cresting and heading for Loki's fleet. He
heard screams of panic as his men tried futilely to get their ships
out of the way of the gigantic wave. Loki was not troubled. Angelo had granted him seven miracles. Most of them he had exer-
cised hitherto as tricks to frighten his followers into obeying him.
But now, he raised his arms and spread his fingers.

Concentrating, he tamed the mammoth wave. It faded and dis-
persed, and when its greatly reduced power did reach the vessels,
they merely rocked with a bit more intensity than was their wont.

Cheers broke out. The screams of fear had transformed into
wild cries of victory. Loki was glad of his gifts. The men had
been loyal to him, and he was becoming rather fond of these bar-
baric Norsemen. In a very real sense, they were his people—his
worshipers as Loki, his followers as the Dragon Odinsson.

He called a wind, which waited, held captive by his will, in
the form of an invisible eddy beside his head. When he had finished speaking, he would release the little zephyr, and it would
take his words to every one of the more than a hundred vessels
under his command.

"We have been the sharks on the sea," he told them. "We have
battled these pathetic English on water, and destroyed their
fleets. We have battled them on land, and taken their townships.
We have burned and sung wild songs of victory as one by one,
they have fallen beneath us. And we have done it alone—just us.
My children, it is time to venture forth once more upon dry soil

and turn it wet with blood. And this time, we shall have allies.
You have met my companions, the Beast and the Sea Dragon.
Now, when we march on the English, we shall be joined by ranks
of beings whose appearance may seem frightful. And they are indeed to be feared—but not by anyone who follows the Dragon
Odinsson. They will use weapons surpassing your imaginations,
but they shall fight with us, not against us. Our enemy is Ethelred
the Weak, and all those who dare call him sovereign. Are you
with me, my men?"

Fenris whined eagerly. Loki patted his head while he waited
for the wind that bore his speech to make its circuit. Moment by
moment, a cheer went up from each ship. Finally, the wind dis-
persed, and Loki could hear his own words, jumbled and nonsensical, fading.

He called another wind, to fill the striped square sails. The
Force descended once again on the battered shores of Britain,
where its nightmarish allies waited for the Antichrist.

The final battle had begun.

19

The Andredesweald
December 999

Alwyn thought he was drinking honey, so urgently sweet was Kennag's kiss. For an instant he couldn't move. He simply sat, stunned, and let her do what she would with him. Then his body took control. He pressed hard against her as she clung to him, his virgin lips seeking the painfully sweet nectar from her open, eager mouth. He felt as if he were lost again in the Lady's well, drowning, but this time in heat and desire, not in the cold embrace of dark waters.

He had wanted her from the moment he laid eyes on her, without knowing just what it was he wanted. His body knew, though. It was young and strong, though its left arm was crippled, and it wanted to entangle itself in the soft flesh of this beautiful young woman.

She whispered his name, and the sound of her husky voice increased his passion. He trembled now, as he stroked her long legs with his right hand. Kennag gasped, and her eyes glittered. Teasingly, she flicked her tongue over his lips and he gasped in exquisite torment.

It was not only his body that was ready for her. His heart was as well. He felt joy flooding him like light, and the thought of union with her was—

Wrong.

He blinked. The thought flickered through his fevered brain with just enough cold clarity to make his hand pause in its passion-driven caresses.

"Kennag—"

She was on him again, kissing him passionately, but this time the embrace seemed smothering.

What was he doing? He was a sworn man of God! Back at St. Aidan's, Alwyn had heard whispered stories of licentious monks fathering bastards left and right, and even looking with lustful eyes upon one another. He had always been horrified by these tales. He had taken a prideful comfort that, even though a lowly cripple, he would never, ever be tempted by such vile things.

Until the moment had actually arrived, and the temptation had come in the form of a woman who stirred not only his body but also his soul. And it was not vile.

Kennag writhed on top of him. Despite his growing chagrin, his flesh still wanted her. But Alwyn was more than flesh and, his heart breaking with the effort, he pushed her off him.

She wiped a tress of fiery hair from her sweaty brow. Her lips were swollen and red, bruised from their kisses. "You want to take me," she whispered.

Tears filled his eyes. He edged away from her, suddenly aware of how cold and damp he was. "God knows that I do," he replied truthfully. "I love you. I ache for you. And had I been anyone other than who I am. . . . But I'm a monk, Kennag. I made a promise."

Her eyes narrowed. "You fear your god's reprisals," she spat.

He shook his head. "No. I fear losing faith in who I am."

Kennag stared, as if she couldn't believe what she was hearing. "Haven't you already lost that faith, Alwyn? Aren't you ready to give up, as I am? Come, my love." She reached to touch him again, but he jerked backward. "Come lie with me. Let us forget the madman's quest and enjoy one another."

Stubbornly, he shook his head. "I won't abandon our task, and I refuse to treat you so badly. How could you trust me if I broke so deep a vow for you? How could I bear to live? I would grow to hate you, hate us both, and I cannot endure the thought." He buried his face in his hand, feeling the hot tears of shame and regret slip through his fingers. "Leave me, Kennag. I am sorry."

There was no sound. She wasn't leaving. Finally, blinking rapidly to clear his vision, he looked up.

Rowena gazed back at him with her odd colored eyes. Alwyn looked around, confused. "Kennag?"

"Was never here," said Rowena softly. "I did not mean to intrude, but when I saw you run out of the church, I thought someone should keep an eye on you."

"I don't understand."

"It's simple. Ardith told you that this might happen."

He wiped his wet face and drew a shuddering breath. He wasn't sure what Rowena meant, but he understood now that the entire encounter with Kennag had taken place inside his own mind. Alwyn wondered if he should be ashamed that Rowena had witnessed his weakness. But she gazed at him with compassion. She might be a simple beast, but she was his friend.

"Ardith said nothing about anything like this."

Rowena cocked her head. " 'Everything you need to know, you know already. Search your mind, your heart. We cannot give you answers, but we can give you a place to think and a chance to rest a tired body,' " she quoted. " 'This holy place, this forest out of time—it may help you quiet your raging thoughts. Come, let us visit the church. Your journey inward will begin there.' "

Alwyn had to laugh. It eased the tightness in his chest. "That's twice you've quoted someone almost verbatim."

"Completely verbatim. It's a gift."

She had half-closed her eyes now, the feline equivalent of a smile. He reached out his right hand and stroked her. Rowena butted her head into his palm, purring loudly. Abruptly, she stopped and stared at him.

"You succeeded, you know. Here. With Kennag. You didn't let your own desires and fears stop you from doing what your heart knew was right."

The tears on his face were drying. Alwyn looked out from the mouth of the cave. The day was dry and sunny. It seemed as though even the storm had come from within him—a manifestation of the storm of doubt that had raged in his own heart. He smiled a little.

"I hope so, Rowena."

•   •   •

Kennag respected Alwyn's desire to be alone. But as the shadows began to lengthen, she grew concerned for him. She believed the Tribe when they told her that nothing in the forest would harm them, but who knew where Alwyn's despair had taken him? Perhaps he had wandered beyond the protective boundaries of the Andredesweald, out into the world where there was snow and ice and hounds from another world hungering for their blood.

She shuddered a little at the thought. She inquired, but no one, not even Ratatosk, had seen Alwyn since he had fled the church. Kennag began to wander, trusting her feet to take her where she needed to be, and ended up sitting beside the lake from which they had emerged that morning.

She hugged her knees to her chest and rested her cheek on them. One hand reached about for a stone, and silently she tossed the rock into the water, watching the ripples it made. They grew wider and wider, then subsided into nothingness.

"Like our lives," she said aloud. The thought was depressing. In the end, though the rock had made a loud splash and disturbed the mirror-smooth surface of the blue lake, it had meant nothing. The lake had swallowed it. Now, the rock that had sat for perhaps centuries on the shore was merely one of many on the bottom of the lake. No one cared. It didn't matter if the rock had continued to stay on the shore for another thousand years.

Except there would be no thousand years, if she and Alwyn failed in their task.

She frowned, found another rock, and repeated the process almost desperately, as if somehow she had to make a difference. This rock was bigger, and made more of a splash. In the end, though, the result was the same: the rock sank and settled, and the water calmed. After a moment, no one could have told that a rock had been tossed into the water.

Her thoughts drifted back to the horrors she had experienced during her brief time as Gwyn ap Nudd's prisoner. She had tried to avoid thinking about it, and had told Alwyn nothing of the ordeal. He seemed to have enough terrors to haunt his dreams, if the whimpering he made in his sleep at night was any indication. Poor Alwyn.

There had been millions of them in the hot, stagnant darkness. She could smell them, sense them, hear them moving about. Occasionally, she saw the gleam of a red eye, or from some unknown place a dim light showed her the unnatural curve of a foreleg or the sharpness of teeth as long as her arm. None of them approached, and she supposed she had Gwyn to thank for that. She was a special prisoner, to be used as bait if need be. It wouldn't do for her to be devoured in a gulp by some slimy, nameless denizen of the Unseelie Court.

Strangely, the horse had not been afraid, and none of the *things* would draw near the beast. The mare's warm, equine scent had been sweeter to Kennag than that of the roses that twined about her mother's cottage in midsummer. She had pressed against the horse, trying not to tremble, trying not to go mad as she heard slithers and scratches and whispers of what they would *do* to her if they were only permitted.

It had not been that long before her friends and the peculiar novice Cabal had come to her rescue. But, sweet Mother Brihid, it had been an eternity and more. A soft moan escaped her and she closed her eyes.

"I understand," said Alwyn's soft voice. Startled, Kennag opened her eyes to see him sitting beside her. He, too, picked up a rock and tossed it into the water. They were silent while the ripples crested, then faded. He laughed, a harsh bark of a noise. "Look at that. You can't even tell I threw a stone in. It's hardly worth the effort."

He turned his sad, brown eyes to her. "It's not worth the effort."

Her heart began to pound as she guessed at the meaning of his words. "Of course it is. It'll be the end of everything if we fail."

"Kennag, it is the end of everything already. Do you think for a moment that when we venture forth from this safe place, Hel's hounds won't be upon us in an instant? We still don't even know what it is that we have to do to stop Satan. There's no point in fighting anymore. We've lost everything already."

Her heart broke to hear those words from Alwyn, who had lashed out at her only a few days ago as they were traveling to Glastonbury. He had said then that he thought their quest hopeless, that he didn't want to be here, but that he would see his soul damned before he abandoned his duty.

"You once said you didn't want to look back a month from now and think that you hadn't done everything you could," she reminded him softly.

"Kennag, we have done everything we could—and we failed. What would be served by our marching straight toward our

deaths? This is a pleasant place, a good place. Let us stay here."
Shyly, he reached out his good hand and covered her left hand
with it. "Let us stay here," he repeated, his voice dropping to a
soft, shy whisper, "and take what comfort we may from each
other."

"Alwyn—"

"I know, my vows, but I don't care! I don't care about anything except you. I've been laughed at, scorned, insulted—surely
you won't turn me away, too?"

She closed her eyes. All her life, Kennag had been a healer.
Sometimes she healed wounds and sickness; other times, a discouraged spirit. The pain in Alwyn's eyes called to her with a
voice that elicited more than sympathy. And wasn't he right, anyway? Wasn't it true that it was too late? Wouldn't it be a good
thing to lie with this sweet-faced boy and give him some solace
before they faced their eternal torment? She could do nothing,
nothing. But she could comfort, could make a difference, in
Alwyn's life right now.

Kennag leaned toward him, kissed him tenderly, and pulled
his head down to her breast. There was more than mothering in
the gesture, and as his single hand tentatively began to stroke her,
she closed her eyes and opened herself to the passion his gentle
touch aroused.

Alwyn. Sweet, lonely, injured Alwyn, who had shown much
more courage than she in accepting this dreadful, heavy responsibility. Who had never known the gentle heat of a loving
touch—

Because he was a monk. Because he had made deep vows that
she was now tempting him to break.

She rested her cheek on his curly head, committing the unbearably sweet moment to memory, then gently disengaged herself. "I'm sorry," she said. "I should not have done this."

He went still. "You find me repulsive. Oh, I knew it. What
arrogance to think that you—"

"I find you beautiful." She reached for his dead hand and
brought it to her lips. "But I also know that you will despise
yourself if you break your vow of celibacy."

"What is there to lose? The world is ending, and we can't stop
it!"

"Then we keep trying!" cried Kennag. "We ride till our
mounts can go no farther, then we walk till our legs fail, then we

crawl, Alwyn! We keep going! Things may fall apart, but curse it, it won't be because *we* failed. That's all we've got left, Alwyn, and we can't lose it, we just can't!"

As the form before her shimmered, Kennag thought it was just the blurring of her vision from the tears that filled her eyes. But when it faded from view, she realized that it had all been an illusion. She glanced around wildly, but she was completely alone. Ardith's riddling words took on a new meaning. Kennag and Alwyn each had been alone, and given an opportunity to confront their fears and doubts—and, if Kennag guessed aright, their feelings toward one another. She had passed this strange test, and she knew in her heart that Alwyn would not waver.

She rose and went to find him.

They ate with the Tribe that night, each uneasy around the other. Ardith, Halig, and Rand seemed to sense their discomfort, and the evening ended early and quietly. Each of them had been given a blanket and pillow. The night was balmy, and the stars were out.

"Before we sleep," said Kennag, "we must speak, you and I. Something happened to me today—and I think to you as well."

They stood by the dying fire, their blankets and pillows bundled in their arms. Alwyn glanced down, and nodded. "But let us go away from here," he said. "I would not share such things with anyone but you."

In silence, they walked a distance away, then climbed a small hill with an open clearing at its top. Alwyn marveled at the brilliance of the stars set against the blackness of the night sky. When he had been at St. Aidan's, he had never been awake at this hour. The only time he knew the night was at matins, and then he was too bleary-eyed to fully appreciate God's glorious heavens. He wondered, too, if the stars shone brighter here, if the sky was more ebony where it arched above this special place.

"I faltered today," said Kennag, breaking the stillness. She, too, stood looking at the sky, then eased herself down on a blanket. She stretched out full length, her arms folded behind her head. Alwyn imitated her and waited for her to continue.

"I was tempted into forsaking the quest—and forsaking you. I thought you had come to me, your heart breaking, urging me to surrender to despair . . . and take solace in your arms."

He was glad of the cool night. He did not look at her, only up at the dazzling array of stars.

"I had the same temptation," he said quietly. "It was . . . the most difficult part of this entire journey."

"Yes." Kennag's voice floated to him. "It was."

Surprised, he glanced at her. Her words made his heart clench. She turned her head to look at him. Jesu, but she was glorious in the moonlight.

Without knowing what he would say, only that this was the time for confidences, Alwyn began to speak.

"I was born the youngest of seven. My earliest memories are of the looks of contempt and pity my family gave me. I could not help my family work, and consequently was told to remain in the house and tend the cookfire. My brothers and sisters teased me, and I took solace in my solitude. It seemed I could do nothing right. I was beaten, for what I did do and what I failed to do. I would not say I was unhappy, for I didn't know what happiness was.

"When I was five, I was brought as an oblate to the Abbey of St. Aidan's." At Kennag's quizzical look, he explained. "An oblate is a boy destined to become a monk. I was the youngest St. Aidan's ever agreed to receive. I underwent a ceremony designed to cut me off, irrevocably, from the world. I don't remember very much of it, but I have participated in it many times since, as an adult."

He paused, thinking of that time before the monastery. Images of torment and dislike and coldness filled his mind. "St. Aidan's was the answer to a prayer. The brothers were kind and wise, and no one ridiculed my deformity. Wulfstan—the man you healed at Ethelred's villa—was the precentor of the abbey at that time."

Kennag's frustrated glare made him actually laugh. "I'm sorry. None of these terms is familiar to you. I'll try to explain them. A precentor is the chief singer, librarian, and archivist. He decided who had the aptitude for working in the scriptorium— copying manuscripts. Wulfstan taught me to read and write, and encouraged me to continue with that work. For the first time, I truly had a place. I could contribute something instead of simply taking. And as Wulfstan rose in the church, becoming the cellarer—sort of a second-in-command to the abbot—and finally the abbot himself, he always found time to talk with me and encourage me in my work."

His voice caught. "There is no kinder, wiser man in this world. Kennag, if I owed you nothing else—and believe me, I know that I do—I would never be able to repay you for saving his life. I was rude to you when you were trying to help. I know better now."

Kennag smiled. "I am a healer. I followed my calling, that was all. But Alwyn—if you were so happy there—" She hesitated.

"Go on."

"It's your arm," she blurted. Alwyn felt his face grow hot and was grateful for the darkness. "You hide it, you apologize for it. I think you hate yourself for it. Didn't the monks tell you that you were whole enough?"

"Words," said Alwyn. "Nothing more. Sometimes words aren't enough. Sometimes I have to—to punish myself for my failing. I know I'm not a whole man, that I'm not fit for anything but a cloistered life. Not like you. You always belonged to this world."

"That does not mean I was happy in it," she said. "There were moments when I would gladly have laid claim to the peace that you have found. A few months before I was called, my life was broken."

Kennag again stared at the starry sky. The moonlight silvered her face. She looked very beautiful, and very wild. Her voice was calm despite her words.

"I had been married when I was young to a man much older than I. But we were of a similar spirit, Niall and I. I loved him a great deal, and when the ocean took him one day, I mourned him with all my heart. But even in the midst of my grief, I was still whole inside. I was Gleannsidh's healer, and I had duties. I still had a purpose. After a year had passed, I was ready to open my heart again. I did, and my heart was answered. His name was Bran. He was the son of the blacksmith, and he understood fire. On Bealtaine—"

Her voice had grown thick. She paused, clearing her throat. Alwyn propped himself on his right elbow and let her continue at her own pace.

"On Bealtaine, we pledged ourselves to one another. I won't apologize for our customs, Alwyn, though they may shock you. It is our way, and had been for hundreds of years before your priests of Christ ever came to our land. I knew I would conceive that night, and I did. But not Bran's child. That was the night when the Lochlannach descended—the Norsemen. They took Bran aboard their ship. He would have made them a fine, strong slave. I was violated and would have been taken as well, but I escaped. I hid in the village well while they ransacked Gleannsidh. They burned our homes, and fell upon the women, and took what they wanted."

Alwyn didn't feel any shock at Kennag's words—at least, not shock directed at her or her actions. He did feel sick inside to hear of the violence that had been perpetrated on this lovely, fiery woman, and was amazed anew at her strength.

"When I realized I was with child, I decided to miscarry. I know the ways of herbs, it is an easy thing to do." He watched her long white throat move as she swallowed, hard. "It was not so easy to watch my mother give birth to a child of rape—to deliver that child myself."

She turned to look at him. Her eyes were black pools in the moon's light, but they glittered with unshed tears. "He was two months early, Alwyn. He should not have lived. But he did. He was as whole as a full nine-month child, and I hated that baby. I hated him for the fact that he was here and alive, and Bran was gone. For the fact that my mother loved him, this living reminder of the brutality of that awful night. It was wrong to hate a life only just begun. That baby is my brother, and I ought to have loved him, regardless of whose seed he might have been.

"I held my hate and anger close. They were my friends, my comfort on dark nights. And when I was called, when I walked into the Faerie knoll the same night I delivered my mother's child, the Good Folk shamed me with my hatred."

"Kennag—"

She lifted a hand and pressed it to his lips to silence him. "I resented their judgment because I knew it to be accurate. I came on this trip not to help save my world, not really. I came because I couldn't bear to be in Gleannsidh anymore, not without Bran, not with that infant. I hated the Christians, because it was for the treasures of their church that the Lochlannach came that night, and I intensely disliked you. I thought you a crippled boy monk, as I called you, and deemed you too frail, too weak of spirit, to be any kind of a worthwhile companion."

Her hand moved from his lips to his beardless cheek. "I'm sorry, Alwyn. I've been so wrong about so many things. And now

it looks as though I'll never be able to put any of it right. I won't
be able to apologize to my mother and hold my baby brother in
my arms. Bran is—you remember, when I had the vision and I
refused to tell you about it?"

He nodded. Her hand on his cheek was soft. He ached to
touch it, but he kept his eyes on her face.

"I saw Bran's body. He's dead, Alwyn. I had hoped that somehow he had survived, even as a slave somewhere, but the Second
Sight doesn't lie. He died on the same shore as—" She stiffened,
withdrawing her hand. "Iona. The name of the little island where
the monks were massacred was Iona. That sounds familiar."

The faint stirrings of illicit desire were quenched at once, as
if cold water had been thrown on a hot fire. Alwyn sat upright.
The night was pleasant, but he suddenly felt cold.

"Iona," he breathed. "Iona. The Lamp of Faith. It's one of the
most holy places here in Britain." He buried his head in his hand.
"All along, Michael knew."

"Alwyn, speak in a tongue I understand," said Kennag, also
sitting up. "What are you riddling about now?"

He turned a face full of misery to her. "The night that Michael
appeared to me, he told me, 'Do not let the lamp of faith become
extinguished!' He tried to tell me. He knew how we could stop
Satan, stop the whole—God and Christ damn me for a fool!" The
ache inside him was overwhelming. Horror washed over him,
and he curled up into a tight little ball.

Failed. Failed. He had been given the key and had been too
foolish to recognize it. Michael had been wrong to trust him, he
had thought so all along—

"Midhir's balls, Alwyn!" Kennag shook him, not gently.
"Come to your senses! What do you mean? How could we have
stopped Satan?"

He was so ashamed, he didn't want to tell her. He had told her
things he had never confided to a living soul, things he had even
refrained from speaking at confession. And she in turn had
opened her spirit to him and showed him the dark, shameful cor-
ners of her heart. How could he not tell her? At the very least, she
would be angry with him, and oddly he thought that might help
him feel better.

He took a shuddering breath. "Iona has been called the Lamp
of Faith," he repeated, trying to keep his voice calm and his
words clear. "Michael told me, 'Do not let the lamp of faith be-

come extinguished.' In other words, if we had headed straight for Iona instead of floundering about here in the South, we could have stopped the massacre. The Lamp of Faith would not have gone out."

She was silent for a moment. Then, with a hint of the laughter he so loved in her voice, she asked him, "And just how could a pagan woman, a monk, a cat, a squirrel, a ghost, a donkey, and a horse have prevented several hundred Norsemen from slaughtering a monastery full of unarmed monks?"

He blinked. "Oh." He paused. "I do see your point. But—"

"And I see yours, Alwyn. Yes, if we had understood what he meant earlier, perhaps we could have warned someone and. . . ." Her voice trailed off. "Maybe that's not what Michael meant after all."

"I don't understand."

"From what I know from my religion, and what I've gleaned about yours, there's more to a faith than the place where a holy house is located and the people that pray there."

He nodded, starting to comprehend what she was trying to say. "That's right. There's much more to my faith than that."

"So, brutal though it might be—how could simply killing the monks and burning the buildings *truly* extinguish the Lamp of Faith?"

He stared at her with new appreciation. "It couldn't," he whispered. "Faith endures, unless it is somehow obliterated. Or forgotten." Alwyn's skin prickled beneath the soft fabric of the warm brown robe.

"The cattle," said Kennag.

"What?"

"The cattle. In my vision of the massacre, the buildings were destroyed, all the monks killed—but the cattle were deliberately left untouched. You yourself said when I told you of it that—"

"—It was too bizarre not to mean something. If only we knew what!"

" 'Iona of my heart, Iona of my love,' " came a soft voice from nowhere. They glanced around. " 'Instead of monks' voices there shall be lowing of cattle. But before the world comes to an end, Iona shall be as it was.' Dunstan told me about that, once, long ago. It seems I remember everything now."

Slowly, directly in front of them, the white shape of Neddy

began to materialize. "Hello, Kennag. Alwyn. I'm sorry I've been so long away."

"Neddy, I was worried about you. Are you all right?"

He smiled. He stood more erect than he had before, and there was a sad sort of peace on his pretty, boyish features. "It is your kind heart that makes you worry even about a ghost, Kennag. I am well. I—I would like it if you would call me Neddy, still. Though I know my real name now. I am—I was—Edward."

"That makes sense," said Alwyn. He, too, was surprisingly glad to see the boy-ghost. "Neddy is a common nickname for Edward."

The specter turned to regard him. A smile quirked one edge of his mouth. "King Edward, called the Martyr. But you don't have to bow, Alwyn. You're my friend."

Alwyn gasped. Impossible. The ghost was having delusions of grandeur, posing as a dead king—

But the guard had recognized him at King Ethelred's villa. And Neddy was the right age. . . .

"I was murdered by my stepmother's retainer, Angelo. He stabbed me here"—he placed his right hand in the small of his back—"when I was sipping the welcome cup." His lip trembled. "The *welcome* cup," he repeated, as if he still hadn't gotten over the sense of betrayal. Then he laughed, harshly. "I've put the fear of hellfire in *her*, all right! That's where I've been. But I came back. I thought perhaps I might be of some help."

Alwyn had started to recover from his shock at learning Neddy's true identity—and that of his killer. Now he recalled the strange quote with which Neddy had materialized.

"You said Dunstan told you the quote," he said.

Neddy nodded. "Yes. He said it was a prophecy spoken by Saint Columba on his deathbed. We were studying about great monasteries." He shook his head. "Now that I know who I was, it's as if I remember every word ever spoken to me."

"Did he tell you what it meant?" asked Kennag.

"No. I remember I thought it amusing, the idea of nothing but cattle wandering around bellowing on such a sacred isle." Alwyn noticed that his vocabulary was more sophisticated, as befitted the shade of a martyred king.

"Can you repeat it?"

Neddy did so.

"The Norsemen were ordered not to kill the cattle because

Satan wanted the prophecy to be fulfilled," said Kennag, reasoning it out slowly. "Alwyn—Iona must be silent save for the lowing of cattle before the world can end. Iona has to be as it was—before the monks came. If even one monk were alive on the island singing to his God—"

"—The prophecy would not be fulfilled," finished Alwyn. He struggled to contain his excitement. "The world *can't* end! Neddy! You may have saved us all!"

Startled, the ghost gave a shy smile. Heedless of Neddy's presence, Alwyn flung his right arm about Kennag and pulled her into a tight embrace. She was laughing in his arms, her warm cheek against his, her sweet breath in his ear. He felt her breasts pressing against his chest, her body forming to fit his. It was similar to his "memory" of her, but vastly different in an important way.

Other paths, other choices, other destinies. He loved her, and perhaps she loved him, but they had each chosen their own way. He knew his destiny now.

As if reading his mind, she drew back. "Are you ready?"

"The Witnesses are destined to be killed, you know," Alwyn reminded her.

"In a way, I died today, when I gave up hope. So did you. Anything would be better than that."

He felt a smile curve his lips. Lord, what a woman! More fit for the task than he had ever imagined.

Her face fairly glowed in the moonlight. "What are we waiting for?" she said in that strong voice he had come to love. "We've got a world to save!"

PART III

The Final Battle

And he gathered them together in a place called in the Hebrew tongue Armageddon.
— REVELATION 16:16

20

*Then Herod, when he saw that he was
deceived by the wise men, was exceed-
ingly angry, and he sent forth and put to
death all the male children who were in
Bethlehem and in all its districts.*
—MATTHEW 2:16

Ethelred's Royal Villa, Kingston
December 28, 999
The Feast of the Innocents

Angelo knelt with the others and received the sacrament, mildly
amused, as always, at the blasphemy it represented. God had
abandoned this world and all its creations, from man and beast to
wine and bread, for Angelo to play with as he saw fit. No doubt,
if Father Cenulf had known Angelo's true identity, he would have
thought that the king's adviser—only adviser, now that the Witan
had been dissolved—should go up in flames for simply being
touched by a "holy man." The solidity and simplicity of mortals'
faith was endearing in a pathetic sort of way. From time to time,
Angelo had grown fond of a mortal. But that had never stopped
him from using mortals to further his own ends.

Today it would all come together. He had thought that
Ethelred would struggle against this, the final solution. But the
king had only gazed at him with dull eyes and murmured, "If you
think it best, Angelo." It was as if the dissolution of the Witan
had taken all the fight out of the boy. Oddly, Angelo was sorry.
Ethelred hadn't been the most difficult man to sway at the best of

times, but Angelo had enjoyed crafting persuasive arguments to win him over.

After the service, Ethelred and his men, reeves and thegns and representatives from all over the country, retired to the feast hall. Ethelred sat in his heavy, carved wooden chair with no animation to his features or body. Angelo's poppet, utterly. His men stood at attention, awaiting his pronouncement.

Ethelred took a deep breath and began the speech Angelo had written for him last night.

"We have fallen upon troubled times," he began. "Many say that the Day of Judgment is fast approaching, and I fear this to be so. The earth has quaked, as if in fear or perhaps anticipation, of the footsteps of the approaching Christ."

Angelo smiled a little. He did have a way with words.

"The sun bakes us in December, but its face is hidden by dark clouds of smoke. Rumors of monsters engaged in battle with the forces of good have reached our ears. Those of us who know our Bible, as all godly men ought, can see the Signs being played out plainly before our faces. Secular traditions have their signs as well, and the foremost of these is the coming of the warlike races. We have encountered them in battle, on land and sea, and we know them: the Force."

Ethelred's voice was monotonous, but even so, the power of the words reached his listeners. Angelo had chosen this new set of "advisers" well. War-hungry, each of them, eyes glittering with greed and fingers itching to hold swords. It would be all he could do to keep them here in the room and listen to the speech in its entirety.

"An Antichrist is any man who is against Our Lord. Surely the Force is comprised of thousands of Antichrists. And their leader may indeed be the Dragon of which the Book of Revelation speaks. According to reports, he commands a mighty serpent and a beast whose brow is marked with the number six hundred sixty-six. These Danes have dwelt among us for years, like a snake in the grass, like Satan in the garden of Eden."

Angelo hadn't particularly enjoyed penning that line, but it fit, and it did make the whole stronger.

"They have tempted us to passivity, gulled us into paying money instead of fighting them like good, godly men. No more. The final battle against evil has begun, and all those who are not

saved must die. Let us take up the arms of God as well as those
of mere men."

Angelo winced at the lackluster tone of the king's voice. He
ought to be crying these words with passion, not droning on. Ah,
well. Judging from the restlessness of the listeners, the speech
was having the desired effect, regardless.

"Today, we have solemnly celebrated the Feast of the Innocents. This day honors the innocent boy-children slaughtered by
Herod in his cruel attempt to kill Christ our Lord. There could be
no more fitting way to honor the deaths of innocents than by destroying the guilty. I hereby decree that all the Danes who have
sprung up in this island, sprouting like cockle amongst the wheat,
are to be destroyed by a most just extermination."

The thegns roared their approval. Their hatred and fear had
now been given an outlet. Ethelred had sanctioned butchery—
nay, made it a holy cause.

Angelo smiled.

Oxford, England
December 28, 999

Gunhild was a striking woman, even among her own people, and
here in the land of the English she stood as a flaxen-haired goddess. Nearly six feet tall, with large bones and hair only slightly
threaded with gray, she cut an imposing figure. Gunhild was
quick to laugh, quick to anger at injustice, and quick with a kind
word to those in need of such. Oxford had been her home for the
last fourteen years, the home she had made with her husband,
Swein. From time to time, she longed for her native land of Den-
mark, but for the most part she was content.

But for the last fortnight, Gunhild, sister of Thorkell, had
known fear. It sat deep in her belly, a cold knot as dark and
twisted as the hate-filled dwarves who lived in Nidavellir. The
fear had first come when Swein's business as a metalworker
began to slow. Until the Force, as the English called the Norse
marauders, had begun truly hammering at the beleaguered island,
Swein had had to turn customers away. Now, he could not sell his
work for love or money, and their children often went to sleep
with empty bellies. There were the glances, the dark looks, the
muttered words, and the fear moved in Gunhild as if the dark
dwarf baby kicked.

Gunhild did not think of herself as a Dane, not anymore. She was as English as her neighbors. She attended the church services and had been baptized in the faith of Christ, as had Swein and all six of their children. She spoke the language with hardly an accent, and the concerns of the residents of Oxford were her concerns.

Her long fingers went to her throat and clasped the cross that hung there as she gazed out the window. Swein had made the necklace for her, as a gift on the day of her baptism. She had not removed it since, and now she held it tightly, as if it were a pagan talisman of protection. For the last two days, neither she nor her husband had dared venture forth into the streets. Swein was angry, though as usual, he hid it well. He now sat at the table, still working on his jewelry. At his left elbow was a large pile of exquisite brooches, necklaces, and bracelets.

"Would that Thorkell would leave the company of this Dragon Odinsson," Gunhild said to her husband, still gazing out the window. "Perhaps our friends would not be so angry with us."

Swein grunted, narrowing his eyes as he worked a particularly intricate curl of copper. "It is not just us, love. I spoke with Olaf before the fire-rain came, and he told me that no one would purchase his bread. It is not your brother they fear, it is our blood."

"That is foolish!" cried Gunhild, her voice catching on the last word. She blinked back tears. "As if you and I would run away and fight for the Norsemen simply because of where we were born!"

Now he looked up at her, and the dark baby fear kicked again at the resignation in his bearded face. "They are afraid. As am I. These strange signs—they fear the end of the world is near, and they may be right."

"But—we saw the fire-rain, true, and felt the earth tremble. But the reports of locust-monsters and Death riding on the earth—surely these are falsehoods!" The stories of battles, never in a specific place, always "just a day's ride or two from here," had vexed the very logical Gunhild. Monsters with the faces of men and the teeth of lions did not roam the earth, devouring mankind. Such things simply didn't happen. Swein was right. People were frightened, and fear engendered lively imaginations.

She snorted again. "If our little Gerda came to me with such a tale, I would spank her for lying! And that grown men would—"

A loud pounding came on the door, inches from where Gunhild rested her head against the wall. She let out a startled yelp, and clapped her hand to her mouth. Her heart pounding, she opened the door.

Fat, red-faced Olaf was there, panting heavily. Sweat dewed his forehead. "Come quickly!" he gasped. "There are orders . . . kill the Danes . . . we're going to the church for sanctuary. . . ."

Gunhild had recovered herself, and laid a hand on the baker's shoulder. "Speak slowly, Olaf," she said in a calming voice.

He swallowed, gasped, and began again. "King Ethelred has sent out an edict," he managed, "that all Danes in England are to be killed."

Gunhild felt relief wash over her. "That is absurd," she chided him. "You are listening to rumors."

"No! I heard it read! We're all going to the church at St. Fritheswide, to seek sanctuary! Hurry, or it will be too late!" He reached for her and tugged, as if he could pull her along with him.

"Mother?" Their eldest, Valda, stood by her side. Gunhild's heart ached suddenly at the beauty of their thirteen-year-old daughter. Large, calm, blue eyes gazed first at their old friend, then at her mother. "What is it?"

"Nothing," began Gunhild, stroking her daughter's golden hair. "Olaf is only—"

"Correct," interrupted Swein. "Listen, love. Listen."

Gunhild did, straining to hear. At first, she heard nothing. Then, like the distant hum of angry bees, she heard the sounds of voices approaching. A scent floated to her nostrils: the acrid smell of smoke. She crossed herself as the significance dawned on her. The frightened people of Oxford had been inflamed by the words of their king, whether or not those words were true.

They were coming to kill.

The fear almost crippled her for an instant, but she forced it down. "Get the children," she told Valda. "We're going to the church."

Valda, wise beyond her years, understood at once. With a calm resolution that brought tears to her mother's eyes, Valda turned and went to find her siblings. "Gerda! Erik! Come, we're all going to pay a visit to Father Godwine!"

They were among the last to arrive at St. Fritheswide's Church. Gunhild had wanted to take some of their more valuable possessions, but Swein had shaken his head. "Let the jewelry be," he said. "If they break into our house to steal it, at least we are not there."

Gunhild carried two-year-old Gerda, and clutched little Erik's hand tightly as they hastened down the road toward the church. The unnaturally hot sun beat down upon them, but shed little light. A strange black cloud hid the sun's illumination, but not its stifling heat. Swein went ahead, their two elder sons flanking him. Watching them lope toward the church, Gunhild was reminded of young deer. The thought stabbed her. Men hunted deer. . . .

Please, St. Fritheswide, turn away the wrath of these English. We are their friends. Calm their thoughts, so that they will remember this—

Prioress Athelgiva looked paler and more frightened than Gunhild had ever seen her. Beside her, still clad in the purple and white garments for the sacrament of today's holy ritual, Father Godwine waved them forward frantically.

"Hurry!" he cried. "For the love of God, make haste!"

Now Gunhild could hear the cry of the maddened crowd. They were only two streets away and headed right for the church. She could smell the smoke strongly now, and hear the crackling of flames. How many homes had they set afire in their fear and hatred? How many had they killed already? She broke into a run, fairly dragging Erik, whose stubby legs could not keep up. Valda rushed forward, the infant Torfi in her arms, and leaped for the safety of the open church door.

The instant Gunhild was inside, the door slammed shut behind her. One foot caught in her long dress. Gunhild stumbled and would have fallen had not several hands reached out to steady her. Gasping, she looked around.

The little wooden church was crammed with people. Dozens, perhaps hundreds of Oxford's Danes had sought sanctuary here. Everywhere she looked, she saw a sea of frightened, pale faces, fair hair, blue eyes. Erik began to cry, but she had no strength to offer him. Handing Gerda to Valda, Gunhild flung herself into her husband's arms and sobbed, the fear finally breaking her.

From outside, she heard Father Godwine's voice. "Listen to me!" he was saying. The hubbub of noise within the church quieted as everyone strained to listen. "These are your friends within!"

A roar greeted his words, and Gunhild winced at the foul words and the hate with which they were uttered. Now Prioress Athelgiva's voice rose above the din.

"It is a frightening time, that much is true. God's judgment is approaching. Perhaps you ought to look to your own sins, instead of those of others. Some of these families have lived here for a hundred years. They hate the Force, as we do. Please, think about—"

Her voice was drowned out. Then she uttered a short, desperate cry of pain, and was silent.

There came a loud pounding on the door. The Danes assembled inside gasped. Their protectors had just died for them, and now the mob outside was demanding admittance. Like rats, they scurried back from the door. Miraculously, the door held, and the cries of anger outside increased.

Gunhild screamed at the loud crash. The mob had broken the church's small windows and were tossing flaming brands inside. Swein ran and put one out with his bare hands, staying grimly silent as his flesh blackened and burned. Gunhild's heart broke. Never again would Swein's clever hands fashion delicate jewelry, or stroke her in all the intimate places she so loved him to touch.

More brands came. The imprisoned Danes tried to put them out, but there were too many. Clothing and hair caught on fire, and the screaming and panic deafened Gunhild. Her eyes fell upon the saint's shrine. Inside lay the body of St. Fritheswide. Anger flooded her, driving out the mindless terror, and she screamed at the dead saint, "Protect us! Protect us!"

But St. Fritheswide would work no miracle here today. Shrieking in fury, Gunhild snatched at the cross about her throat and snapped the delicate chain. She hurled it impotently toward the shrine and began to invoke the names of Frey and Thor and Odin, even the traitor fire god Loki. She didn't care who saved her children, as long as they were saved.

Her eyes began to sting. The black smoke scorched her lungs. She could hear Eric and Gerda coughing, see Valda, courageous to the last moment, trying to comfort her younger siblings.

Gunhild couldn't breathe. She coughed, struggled for air, failed. Pain seared her as her gown caught fire. The last thing she knew was the nearly crushing embrace of her husband as, weeping at his helplessness, he held her close and let the flames take them both.

December 30, 999
A Field in England

Loki Chaos-Bringer was in his element. The spawn of the abyss had been vomited forth, and now his brave Norse warriors fought side by side with creatures out of nightmares. They had seemed wary and frightened at first, but since the beasts seemed to share the same blood lust, the Norsemen had accepted them as perverse allies.

The little village whose name Loki had not even bothered to learn had fallen as if it had never been. In a short time only the blood and the burning houses would mark the site as being a dwelling place of men. The monsters, their humanlike faces grinning and laughing, went about the grisly business of devouring every bit of bone and flesh of the men, women, and children who lived here.

They moved from site to site like a sea. Angelo had told them not to attack major towns, not yet. He wanted the rumors to work their magic of terror first. The Force grumbled a bit—tiny villages offered little in the way of plunder—but they obeyed.

The creatures from the abyss could not care less whom they tortured and devoured.

The heat from the unnaturally close sun, along with that of the crackling flames, was uncomfortable. God of fire he might be, but his body was human, and Loki dragged a sleeve across his sweaty, sooty brow. Beneath him, the red horse pranced, its nostrils flaring happily as it inhaled the scent of blood and charred flesh.

Good. They were done here. Time to move on.

A howl rent the air; Fenris, singing for joy. Loki found the waterskin tied to the saddle and drank deeply of the tepid liquid as he pondered what he would do on the morrow. Night was approaching, signaled by a slight cooling of the stifling air. The dark clouds made it impossible to gauge day or night by any other means.

The first time the strange, dark allies had descended on a village in the middle of nowhere, they had burned precious supplies along with peasants. Human flesh might sustain the creatures from the abyss and Fenris, but Loki's human troops needed less exotic fare to survive. They had not made that mistake this time. Horses and oxen had been captured, and foodstuffs gathered for a later repast. Frightened poultry added their squawks to the cacophony that reached Loki's ears.

This little island could not hold, and would not even need to hold for more than another two days. Come January 1, 1000, according to the calendar used by these folk, Angelo would be triumphant. The world—his world—would end.

And Loki's rampage of personal destruction would begin.

He took another gulp of water. A few months ago, lying deep beneath the earth, when the only sounds were the dripping of poison on his forehead and his own screams of agony, Loki had been certain that his lust for vengeance would never ebb. He would kill, and kill, and kill some more, and never be sated, like a hole forever empty. Even when he slew Heimdall, the gods' champion, and took Heimdall's own blow in his belly and died from it, he had known that he would still hunger for blood and mayhem.

But that hunger was beginning to fade.

Loki frowned, troubled by the revelation. Ragnarok was yet to come—his hour of triumph and defeat commingled. Destiny. He had known it since the hour of his birth, and the inevitability of it had comforted him during the eons of imprisonment. But he had slain hundreds, beginning with the crew of slavers and continuing until this moment, when he had ordered the massacre of insignificant village dwellers. Any joy he had taken in such tasks had faded the moment the bloody work was done. He found himself longing for the quiet nights on the water, under the open skies.

But all that was left now was butchery, culminating in his own death. Loki shook off his moodiness, put away the waterskin, and called to his son. Fenris bounded up to him, his thick fur clotted with blood.

"We are in luck, Father!" panted the giant wolf. "A rider is headed this way!"

Loki frowned. "Coming, not fleeing? That is most unusual." He called the little wind that was his messenger and spoke. "No one is to harm the approaching rider until I have spoken with him! Capture him and bring him to me!"

With a gesture, he released the wind to do his bidding. His

pronouncement would reach the ears of every member of his army, human and nonhuman. "Show me," he told his son. He guided the red horse of war with subtle pressures of his thighs and followed the wolf as it bounded up a low ridge.

Sure enough, heading straight for the site of the massacre was a lone man on horseback. The horse seemed to have more sense than its rider, for it shied and clearly had no desire to draw closer. The man whipped it mercilessly, driving it forward.

"A madman?" said Loki to himself. "A fool, whatever else he might be."

The slope would have been tricky for the horse, so Loki dismounted. The beast would come when called. He and Fenris descended the slope, sliding a little from time to time. By the time they reached the bottom, the mysterious rider had already been halted and dragged off his horse. The beast, freed, bolted at once, neighing frantically. Thorkell and his men were interrogating the rider, using words and blows alternately.

"Cease!" demanded Loki. "He will be of no use to us if his mouth is too bloodied to speak." He turned his attention to the man, who sagged in the grasp of two of Thorkell's men. "You. Who are you? Why have you so brazenly approached us? Surely you could see our standards from a great distance."

The man turned haunted blue eyes to Loki. He licked swollen, bloody lips. "Are you the Dragon Odinsson?" he asked in a cracked voice.

Loki stood up straighter. "I am. Are you fool enough to come seeking me?"

Slowly, with an effort, the man nodded. "He is killing us! In my pouch . . . a missive. . . ."

With a quick jerk of his head, Loki indicated that the men should search the rider. One of them pulled out a piece of parchment—bloody and crumpled. Wordlessly, he handed it to Loki. Few of Thorkell's men could read at all, and none of them knew English.

Loki's human heart sped up as he read. "No," he whispered. "No . . . Angelo would never permit. . . ."

Savagely, Loki backhanded the man. "You come bearing lies!" he cried. "False documents! I will kill you with my bare hands—"

"No, great Dragon!" begged the man, his feet digging into the soil as he squirmed. "No, look—the seal—"

Loki glanced down again and saw that the man was right. This mad decree did bear the king's seal.

And Loki knew the handwriting to be Angelo's. No one else wrote such a perfect script, not even monks in a monastery.

"Great Dragon, what is it?" asked Thorkell. He was atop his glorious white horse that was no horse, and to Loki, that creature seemed to be grinning.

Loki didn't want to tell him. He didn't want to believe it. But the truth was there. Betrayal.

His throat closing as he spoke the words, he read the significant portion. "I, Ethelred, governing monarch of all Albion, do hereby decree that every man, woman, and child of Danish blood is to be executed. We must weed the field for the pure crops to flourish."

A dark red rage began to pulse through Loki's body. It throbbed at his temple, made his hand clench shut about the damning document. Angelo had assured him that Ethelred was nothing but a pawn. Therefore, this idea of slaughtering everyone of Danish blood—from warriors in battle to babes in cradles—had to have been Angelo's.

Angelo was deliberately murdering Loki's people. There was no purpose in this. What harm could an elderly farmer or his infant granddaughter do to Angelo or Ethelred? This was hate, pure and simple. Hate, and fear, and a sweeping solution to eliminate any who might stand against him in the end.

Dimly, Loki realized people were screaming at him. Thorkell, in particular, was frantic. Blinking, swimming up from his fury, Loki heard the words "They burned the church over their heads! Great Odin, was my sister Gunhild among them?" Tears sprang to Thorkell's eyes and poured down his face.

Loki reached out a hand and placed it on Thorkell's thigh. He had no desire to touch the white beast that the youth rode. "Thorkell, I must ask your forgiveness."

That startled the boy. "What? Great Dragon—"

Oh, this was hard. "While we have been fighting the English armies, I have been conversing with Angelo, Ethelred's chief adviser. I had thought he was our ally—it seemed to further his ends, and we have known traitors aplenty in the king's service ere now—but it seems that all along, this Angelo was only serving himself. This decree was his, not Ethelred's. He has turned against us and murdered our people."

The tears were still wet on Thorkell's face. His lower lip trembled as he listened.

"The beings we have allied with, have run with to the slaughter—they are servants of Angelo."

"But—"

"Do not ask me how, or why!" Loki cried. "Only hear me and believe! Spread the word among your men. When I give the signal, we will fight them."

Thorkell paled. "But, Great Dragon . . . they are monsters. How are we to fight such as they?"

"I have skills you have not seen me display, young one. Keep your faith in me a little longer, and soon we will, all of us, have our revenge." To Thorkell's shock, Loki reached up and pulled him off the white horse. In the boy's ear, Loki whispered, "As soon as you may, slay your steed."

A few moments later, after a stunned Thorkell had gone to tell his followers the awful, shocking news, Fenris and Loki sat on the top of a hill. Loki called fire, and stared into the hovering, blazing ball of flame.

"Angelo!" he demanded. "Speak with me!"

Loki half feared the king's adviser would not respond. But if he knew Angelo—and now, he believed, he truly did—then he would enjoy gloating. And Loki might learn something more.

Angelo's face manifested in the dancing ball of fire. He grinned fiercely.

"Don't tell me, let me guess," he purred. "You've learned of Ethelred's latest decree, and you don't like it."

"You would be correct," replied Loki, keeping his voice and mien calm with an effort. "Perhaps you can explain why you are murdering the followers of your own Antichrist."

"Quite simple. I don't need them anymore. And I don't need you, either. I do thank you. You did your job perfectly. But in a very few hours, as mortals reckon time, the world and all its delightful playpretties will utterly belong to me."

The rage welled up again, but Loki controlled it. "You wanted my help to end your world. Then I would have the chance to end mine!"

Angelo threw back his head and laughed. Beside Loki, Fenris growled softly. Whatever he might be, Angelo was lucky that he and Fenris were separated by many miles.

"Ah, Loki, Master Trickster, Lord of Chaos. How easily you

were duped. You should be embarrassed. Why would I want the world to be destroyed, when I can become absolute master of it?"

"*What?*"

"There will be no Apocalypse, my friend. No Ragnarok. Just eternal torment of these things called men."

"You and I had a bargain! You lied to me!"

Angelo smiled sweetly. "Poor Loki. I am the father of lies. And now you know it."

Loki was on his feet now, his powerful human's body taut with rage. "I will fight you on this, Angelo! I command thousands!"

"Thousands of men," Angelo reminded him. "I command millions of beings made of much stronger stuff. But by all means, struggle on, Loki, if it amuses you. It certainly amuses me."

And then he was gone.

Fenris threw back his head and howled his rage. Loki joined him, screaming his throat raw, then fell to the earth and wept. Treachery. And he had been a fool. Angelo had been right—he had been far too easily deceived. All those who followed him were going to die for nothing, and Ragnarok would never occur.

But he could still fight, despite Angelo's jeers. The bastard had given him dark gifts, and Loki planned to use them.

The battle that ensued was dreadful.

Fire lit up the sky—flame and lightning commingled, with the sound of thunder rumbling beneath it all. The first to die was Loki's demon horse, falling beneath a precisely directed bolt of lightning. If what Loki suspected was true, he did not truly kill the thing, only the form it had assumed. No doubt it would return again, in another body. But for the moment, it was no longer a threat.

The slaying of the Red Horse roused monsters from their feeding. Angrily, they descended on the lone man standing in the center of the open field. Loki laughed. The wind whipped his black hair. He arched his fine, strong human body and called his Gifts.

The lightning he summoned struck several, destroying them on contact. Their huge, distorted bodies were hurled several yards distant, to land as smoking, charred corpses. Trees grew at a staggering speed where there had been only silent acorns in the soil. Following Loki's commands, their branches reached with the animation of arms, seized and choked the falsely fair beings who followed Gwyn ap Nudd.

Still the hellspawn came, their numbers uncountable. More seemed to emerge from nowhere. But Loki was ready for them. Beneath their feet, claws, hooves, the soil suddenly turned to fire. Screams never before heard on the earth filled the air, and even Loki felt a shudder trace its way up his spine.

Then the fire that had been solid earth became water. The blazing bodies were extinguished, and those who yet lived floundered and gasped. With a wave of Loki's hand, the water froze. The nightmare things that had once been his allies and were now his enemies found themselves trapped in the ice. Some were still alive, and struggled to free themselves.

Fenris leaped forward, slipping slightly on the ice but not slowing. He bit and tore at the flesh that protruded from the ice, and at that moment, Loki signaled his men.

Thorkell led them. He had obeyed Loki's order without understanding it, and no longer rode the white horse given to him by the treacherous Angelo. Between Thorkell's legs was a plain roan mare, but she would do. Loki wondered if Thorkell knew he was riding to his death. He suspected the boy did.

Roaring, the remnants of the Force charged down the hillside. They carried axes and swords, and were filled with the fury of the wronged. The creatures trapped in the ice did not stand a chance.

And yet still more came, as if the earth vomited them forth. One sprang on Thorkell and his steed. Loki did not watch as the creature tore Thorkell to bits, though he silently mourned the loss of the Dragon Odinsson's first, best follower. It was time to call on his last, darkest miracle.

Loki had never tried this one ere now. He had hoped not to need to. This power disturbed even him, but now, he had to win at all costs. He closed his eyes and asked for the seventh Dark Miracle.

Several yards away, lying where they had fallen a few hours ago, the bodies of the hapless villagers began to move. Some of them were partially devoured, missing limbs and even heads. But they came when they were called. They shuffled as fast as their various mutilations would permit, and turned on their slayers with a methodical determination that life had not granted them. The villagers were joined by the more recently slain Norsemen, whose lethal wounds were still bleeding freely. Loki felt something akin to sorrow as he watched Thorkell's corpse, mangled almost beyond recognition, rise and fight.

The dead found weapons—sticks, rocks, in some cases the bones of their fellows. The Unseelie Faeries laughed at first. But a thing that is not alive cannot be frightened or hurt, and their implacable sense of purpose was their chief weapon.

The sight was ugly enough to turn Loki's stomach, but he forced himself to watch. He heard a cry that he recognized, and whipped his head from side to side, his eyes searching the carnage for the owner of the voice.

She rode the ugliest black horse he had ever seen. The thing was a skeleton barely held together by skin, and its nostrils flared with fire. Racing ahead of her, her hound Garm bayed. Hel charged down, eager to claim her victims.

"Hel!" Loki cried.

"Father! I have come to aid you!"

He waved her forward, an odd pleasure filling him in the depths of his despair. His family was together for the first time since the Aesir gods had banished them to their various prisons. He had many faults, and he knew it, but Loki did love his children.

The demon horse cantered up to him, Garm at its heels. Flushed and panting, Hel smiled fiercely, showing white teeth. "Father! It is a battle the likes of which I have never seen! Tell me of it!"

He did so, and watched the smile ebb from her face to be replaced by a scowl of fury. "Angelo," she hissed when he was done. She glanced back toward the field of the unnatural battle, taking in the sight of corpses battling monsters in silence.

"If you wish to defeat Angelo," Hel said slowly, "perhaps I have information that can aid you."

21

**The Andredesweald
December 999**

Kennag felt as if her feet had been given wings. Her heart certainly was light enough to fly. They had just decided to press on
until they were slain in a monstrous fashion, but a lamp glowed
in front of them: hope. They had a chance, slim though it might
be. Iona was a long, long way away, according to what Alwyn
had told her. Fortunately, they had spent only a single day here
with the Tribe. They still had twenty-seven days to make the
journey, provided they could elude capture.

Even better than her own hope was seeing it reflected on
Alwyn's face. When he told her that he had flogged himself because of his deformity, she had almost wept. It was good to see
him smiling again, his brown eyes full of renewed purpose. As
they hastened back to the Tribe encampment, the ghost of the
murdered king kept pace with them. She couldn't wait to find
Ratatosk and Rowena, Balaam and her strange, magical steed,
and tell them that, at long last, they had a solid, achievable goal.

Out of the corner of her eye, Kennag saw a white blur.
Quickly she turned her head, her rapid footsteps faltering in the
wet grass.

"Kennag?"

She ignored Alwyn's query. Her heart began to pound with slow, painful thuds.

Rider and horse were but a few yards to their left, glowing strangely in the darkness of the close-growing trees. For a moment, recalling when she had first encountered Neddy, she thought she was seeing the ghost of some dead noblemen, forever on his proud, spectral steed. But even as the thought flitted across her mind, she dismissed it. There was no hint of translucence about the pair, only paleness.

Her heart stopped.

She felt it abruptly cease beating in her chest, was aware that the blood flow was slowing. Cold knifed through her, and her lungs no longer drew air.

The Rider smiled, slowly. There were two dark holes in his face where eyes ought to be. His steed was still, calmer than any living horse Kennag had ever seen.

She remembered Alwyn describing the signs that would herald the end of the world in his Christian faith. Some of them, she had seen. Three horses—the white one with the standard, the red one formed of the blood of murdered monks, and the black one the goddess Hel had ridden.

Kennag was gazing at the fourth rider of the Apocalypse. Alwyn's words returned: *The Fourth Seal releases the Pale Horse. Its rider is Death.*

Death's smile widened, and he nodded, as if reading her thoughts.

Anger welled up inside Kennag. *Then read this, Death,* she thought fiercely. *Alwyn and I are not to be killed until the creature from the abyss slays us after forty days! If you are part of this plan, then you must respect that!*

She heard laughter in her mind. *It is not your appointed hour, true. But one day, we will meet again. You will not escape me.*

No mortal can, agreed Kennag, *but that day is not today.*

The pale rider turned and disappeared into the darkness of the woods. Kennag inhaled with a *whoosh*. The beating of her newly started heart made her chest ache, and she stumbled and would have fallen had Alwyn not rushed to catch her.

"Kennag? What is it? Another sign?"

Breathing heavily, she nodded. "Yes," she managed. "The Four Horsemen have arrived, Alwyn. They're all here now."

She saw the understanding dawn in his eyes, and he swallowed. He knew who this fourth and final horseman was.

All at once, the gentle illumination provided by the stars and moon disappeared. Kennag felt suddenly, uncomfortably hot, and smelled the acrid stench of smoke and burned flesh. It was a stale smell, as if the wind had borne it from a distant place. Blind in this abrupt lack of light, Kennag whimpered softly and reached out to Alwyn. She found him likewise reaching for her. They clutched at one another.

"What's happened?" asked Kennag.

"I think it's more of the Signs," said Alwyn. His voice floated to her ears in the darkness. "Remember? The stars going dark, the sun scorching people. What I don't understand is why it's finally penetrated here. The Tribe lives outside our time and place."

"Not anymore," came Rowena's voice. Even in the darkness, Kennag could make out the faint whiteness of her fur. She was suddenly very relieved to see the cat. "They're gone. The encampment is gone, as if it never was. Even the church is different."

"Sweet Jesu, protect us," whispered Alwyn. Kennag felt him move beside her, and guessed he was crossing himself. "Then the final battle has begun. Remember? They would be called to fight for the side of good in the final battle."

"That's all right," said Kennag, as much to reassure herself as Alwyn. "We don't need them now. We do need some light, though, and a way to figure out our best path to Iona."

"What about your Second Sight?" asked Alwyn. "Doesn't that—that ointment let you see in the dark?"

"It lets me see beings that are not of the mortal world. It doesn't turn me into a cat. We'll need some torches or lamps. Rowena, can you—"

"Yes," said the cat, anticipating her request. "I can lead you back to the church. This darkness is dense, but my eyes can see. Barely," she added. "Can you see me at all?"

"Barely," echoed Kennag. "Don't go too fast."

Slowly they followed the faint white shape through the trees, stumbling often. A branch caught Kennag in the face. She had been moving too quickly, and the force of the impact knocked her down. Alwyn was also having a difficult time of it, even more than she. She, at least, had moved through a forest at night before. Such a thing was utterly unfamiliar to the cloistered monk. Rowena was patient, never moving out of their sight and waiting for them to catch up.

It seemed to take forever to reach the church. The darkness pressed in on them like something tangible. Kennag felt her chest tighten as the minutes stretched on. She was familiar with the darkness. It was not something to fear. But that was natural darkness, the simple lack of sun's light, not this artificial, hot, smothering darkness.

"There it is," came Rowena's voice. Kennag literally gasped with relief. "Can you see it?"

"I can't see a cursed thing," muttered Kennag. "We'll need to find the torches and bring them out here. I can start a fire if I can get to my pack."

"We'll get it for you," came a voice. Ratatosk, probably accompanied by a few of his gray-brown soldiers. Kennag vowed that when this was over, if she survived to return to Gleannsidh, she would never, ever, eat squirrel meat again.

"Thank you, Ratatosk," she said with heartfelt appreciation. Her feet seemed rooted here. The thought of going through still more of the Andredesweald with no light suddenly brought a knot of fear to her belly.

Beside her, invisible to her human eyesight, Alwyn took a slow, deep breath. In her mind's eye, she could see him straightening, readying himself. "We'll have to go inside to get the torches," he said. His voice was admirably calm.

Kennag didn't want to leave. She wondered if she *could* leave, if her feet would even obey her. "Let's wait till I get a fire started. We can light a branch."

"All right, but we'll still need to find tinder and a branch to light," he said.

She frowned. He was right. Curse him!

"You two are going to have some nasty bruises in the morning," said Rowena. "Follow me. I think I can see some deadfall."

They followed the white cat again. Kennag said a quick prayer to any deity who might be listening, thanking him/her/them for Rowena's presence. She didn't want to think about where they would be right now without her.

More scrapes, bruises, and tumbles ensued. At one point, Alwyn thwacked his skull on a branch with such force that the dead leaves on the tree continued to rustle for several seconds.

Going to him, Kennag probed his head and felt a lump the size of a small egg beginning to rise on his temple.

"Ouch!" he yelped, jerking away from her. She tried to reach out again to help him but succeeded only in jabbing her finger into his eye. "Ow! Kennag, just leave me alone!"

She couldn't help it. She began to laugh. She recognized the laughter for what it was—a normal human reaction to a frightening situation. She'd heard this kind of laughter issue from the lips of gravely wounded men, from women who'd lost their children. Madness, some called it, but Kennag knew it healed. So she surrendered to it, reaching for the forest floor and sinking down on it, her body shaking with peals of mirth.

She heard Alwyn's shocked protests, and then, he, too, began to laugh. It felt good, and she wiped at the tear or two that ran down her face. That was good, too. At last her whoops subsided, leaving her with a wistful smile on her face.

"All right," she said, mirth still trembling in her voice. "Let's find that deadfall."

It took only a few minutes, but it seemed like hours. Ratatosk and several of his squirrels arrived with the pack. Kennag rummaged through it, locating her flint and tinder by touch. With skill born of long years of practice, she soon had a small fire glowing. Across from the tiny flames, she met Alwyn's gaze. They smiled at one another.

The branches were damp, and sullenly refused to catch for a long time. Finally, one of them sparked. They approached the church and, as one, paused before opening the large wooden door.

"It's different," said Kennag. She realized she was whispering.

Alwyn nodded. "It's still beautiful. It's still a holy place. But when the Tribe left, they took something with them."

They opened the door and stepped inside. At once, their eyes fell upon the torches that lined the wall. Relief washed through Kennag—at last, a steady, strong light to stave off the unnatural darkness.

"I feel like we're stealing," said Alwyn, holding the sputtering branch as Kennag nimbly plucked the torches from their sconces.

"Don't your churches exist to help those in need?"

"Yes, but it's God's house."

"Aren't we doing what your God wants us to do?"

"I suppose so—"

"Then we take the lamps and say thank you."

He stared at her, then laughed. She grinned back. The illumination provided by the torches calmed her more than she had expected. It was as if the light chased away more than physical shadows.

Thus fortified with a light against the darkness, they found their way back to Kennag's horse and Balaam. The donkey was nervous and pranced a bit, old as he was, when he caught sight of them. Kennag rubbed the beast behind his long ears and felt Balaam trembling.

"There is a small village at the edge of the forest," Ratatosk told them. "My squirrels know the way. It's about five miles or so. We can be there by sunrise if we leave now."

"Sunrise," sniffed Rowena. "I wonder if there will be a sunrise."

"Regardless, we should go," said Kennag. "We can purchase supplies and get a clearer bearing on our directions."

Alwyn nodded. "Then let us be about it," he said.

It was a quiet walk through the woods. Kennag trusted Ratatosk's little gray army of squirrels, but she was more than grateful for the steady light of the lamps to save their shins and skulls from roots and branches. They stopped to rest from time to time, and to partake of their dwindling rations. Ratatosk's fellows were able to tell them where to find fresh water to fill their waterskins.

The sky lightened, but as Rowena had predicted, the dark layer of smoky clouds prevented a true sunrise. When Kennag was able to see her hand before her face, she suggested extinguishing the lamps. They might need them again in a few hours, when the darkness closed in.

Forest gave way to farmland. Mud clutched at their feet as they picked their way. All the snow had melted under this unnatural heat, and Kennag saw the sad remains of burned, blighted crops that the ceorl farmers hadn't even bothered to harvest.

"I think I can see some houses up ahead," said Alwyn. He pointed, and Kennag nodded.

"Let's go carefully," she said, taking a moment to locate her knife and inserting it into the girdle she wore about her waist.

"What are you—" began Alwyn.

Kennag interrupted him. "Look around you," she said. "A poor harvest. Smoke in the sky, blocking the sun. Summer heat in early December. You said yourself that people believe the world will end on December 31. People know their Bible, or so you say—they will recognize the signs as surely as you did. And they will be frightened. Frightened people are sometimes violent. I want us to be prepared, just in case."

"Kennag is correct," said Rowena. "I've seen it myself."

Alwyn looked uncomfortable, but said no more.

A path, leading toward the small dots that were wood-and-thatch houses and barns, became discernible. They followed the muddy trail, alert for any sound or movement. There was none.

"This is odd," said Alwyn. "It seems deserted."

Something brightly colored amid the yellow and brown of the earth caught Kennag's eye. She turned her head, and horror ran cold through her.

It was a body. She reached to touch Alwyn's shoulder. "Alwyn. . . ."

He turned and gasped, crossing himself quickly. They stood for a moment, then slowly approached the corpse.

It was that of a young woman, not yet in her childbearing years. Her hair was as yellow as the dead crops; her dress, brown and modest. Only a bright swath of red cloth about her throat drew attention to her. The face above the cloth was bloated and purple, and the eyes bulged. Her tongue protruded, a sickly black hue.

The cloth whose bright color had caught Kennag's eye had been the instrument of her death.

"This girl was strangled," said Kennag. "Judging from the condition of the body, not that long ago. Maybe a day or two. I wonder if—"

A harsh retching sound interrupted her. She didn't turn around. Let Alwyn have a moment of privacy. Monks sometimes dressed the dead for burial, but she guessed that Alwyn had never before seen a murder victim in such a state.

A moment later, he was by her side, pale but resolute. "Poor child," he said, making the sign of the cross over her.

"This does not bode well for our welcome," said Kennag. "The body wasn't even buried—they left it where it fell."

"There are more over here," called Rowena from a few yards

away. "Two adult males, one boy. It looks as though they were stabbed with farming tools."

"Dear God in Heaven, what kind of monstrous—"

"You, there!" The voice was sharp and angry. They whirled to see a tall, dark-haired woman brandishing a scythe. "What is your blood?"

"I don't understand," said Alwyn, backing up a little.

"Your blood!" repeated the woman. "Are you good Saxon folk, or are you the Danish monsters?"

"I am from the Northlands," said Kennag, beginning to put the pieces together. "But I am no Dane. Neither is my comrade, Brother Alwyn, monk of St. Aidan's."

The woman's frightened eyes darted from Kennag to Alwyn, and finally she lowered the scythe. "You do not look Danish," she said. "But . . . why are you here? No one comes from the Andredesweald."

"We are travelers who have lost our way," said Alwyn, stepping forward. "We would be most grateful for some food and drink, if you can provide it. We will pay you for your trouble."

The anger and fear left the woman's face. Kennag realized that the woman was about her age, although she looked much, much older.

"You may help yourself to what you can find here," she said, her voice dull. "There are few enough left who will want it. They have all gone, fleeing to Canterbury right after the king's orders came."

"Orders?" asked Kennag.

The woman glanced sharply at her. "Oh, yes—you were lost in the forest. Orders came from King Ethelred to slay the Danes. It happened just the other day. Our priest announced it at the Mass for the Innocents."

Nausea began to roil in the pit of Kennag's stomach. "An order to slay the Danes?

Alwyn had gone pale, but not for the same reason. "The Feast of the Innocents?"

"Yes, just the day before yesterday. We did what we could, but some of them fled into the Weald." The woman stamped over to the girl's body and spat on it. "Cursed Danes. It's they who have brought about the end of things. Dying was better than they deserved."

Alwyn, however, was still harping on this Feast of the Innocents comment. "You're certain?" he demanded. "You're certain the order came on the Feast of the Innocents?"

The woman bridled a bit and turned to Kennag. "Is he always this slow?"

"Not always," said Kennag, glancing at her companion. "But he does seem to be having a little trouble understanding you."

"Kennag," said Alwyn, seizing her arm and walking her a little way away. "Listen to me. If this dreadful order reached this village on the day of the Feast of the Innocents—"

"Alwyn," hissed Kennag, mindful of the woman's listening ears, "you should be mourning the wanton murders of innocents, not worrying about some Mass for—"

"Be silent and listen!" He shook her roughly. "The Feast of the Innocents is always held on the same date. That date is December 28."

Kennag's legs suddenly felt weak as the full realization smote her. "Are you certain?" she whispered. "Some of your holidays move around—"

"Not this one. December 28, Kennag. Do you realize what this means?"

She nodded weakly. She had told Alwyn that Worth Church and its environs were not a Faerie knoll. She had been correct, but the sacred, special site had resembled a Faerie knoll in one important aspect. Time was different there. They had stayed there only a day and part of a night, but several days had passed in the real world.

Today was December 30. There was no way they could reach the island of Iona before midnight tomorrow.

They had failed.

22

We have made a covenant with death,
and with hell we are at agreement.
                              —ISAIAH 28:15

Ethelred's Royal Villa, Kingston
December 30, 999

Angelo hadn't felt this much excitement in eons.

It had been tricky, and he had been temporarily thwarted from time to time. But in the end, he would triumph, as he had known all along he would.

Panic and fear were his strengths. He could feel them now, surging from every corner of this island. The earthy, simple terror of the ceorls and theows, as they watched their world unraveling; the manic fashion in which the thegns waged their war, against the hated Danes and also against the beings not of their world; the horror that had shaken the unflappable Force under Loki, as they realized that they had themselves been betrayed; and the quiet, sick fear that emanated from King Ethelred like a bad stench.

Glorious, all of it. He was glad his enemy played by the rules. It made it all the easier for Angelo to cheat—and win.

He gazed into the fire in his room. It darted from scene to scene, depicting images of rape and anguish and murder and panic.

"Behold Your beautiful creation now," he murmured, as if addressing his old rival. "Made in Your image, true, but infused with my bitterness. Given the choice, they choose mayhem."

Which, he mused, made them perfect for his purposes. How better to use the things He loved most against Him?

Time was moving swiftly. The chances of anything happening to prevent his perfect plan from reaching its final stage were growing ever more slim. Only a few things to do, now, to put the final touches on his masterpiece of deception and triumph.

He passed his hand through the flame, making it shift. Four images manifested in smoke and shadow. Four angels who had chosen his side, who had fallen with him, who had endured unspeakable torment for just this moment.

Their fair features, fashioned by God, had disintegrated into monstrous parodies of their former beauty. Full lips were swollen and slick with spittle. Long hair had turned to ropes or snakes or manes of fire. Bright eyes now gleamed with madness and torment. They had followed Angelo when he promised them glory, and had gladly submitted to being bound thus.

They had not realized what the bondage would do to them.

For an instant, Angelo felt pity for them. Then that soft emotion was gone. All his troops served him and his ultimate purpose. Some served in harsher ways than others, that was all.

Four true angels, angels who had not forsaken their Creator, also waited. He could see them in the flames as well—graceful, beautiful beings, their mouths forming around songs of praise, tranquil in their waiting. They did not suffer in their bonds, as Angelo's angels did. For that, Angelo hated them even more.

Bound they were until the Day of Judgment, at the River Euphrates. The task of the true angels and Angelo's dark angels was the same—to kill a third of mankind. The difference was that God's angels would do it with love in their hearts.

He spoke the words and watched as the unbreakable chains he had coiled around his four servants snapped and fell. Angelo winced at the volume of the cries of freedom emitted by the newly released angels. They flapped their monstrous, leathery wings, howled their delight, and left their lightless homes for the Earth—and their task.

They were not alone. Others, waiting for this moment, leaped up, chittering and hissing and screaming their delight. They were the troops of the dark angels—all two hundred million of them. And they were, all of them, ravenous.

"Feed well, my poor, broken children," Angelo said, softly.

Again he passed his hand through leaping flame, and again

obscenely ugly images filled his vision. Three of them, identical in their hideousness. Large, bulbous eyes blinked. Soft, wet throats quivered, and their skin was damp and green.

"My three messengers," he said warmly to them. A chorus of ear-splitting noises greeted him. "Now you shall play your roles."

Before his eyes, the froglike creatures elongated, their bodies changing. Their faces formed into human visages, ones that many would recognize: Prince Vladimir of Kiev, Robert II, called "The Pious," of France, and Basil II, Emperor of the Byzantine Empire. Emperor Otto III and Pope Sylvester II were, of course, already firmly in Angelo's camp, though Otto, like Ethelred, was blissfully ignorant of the fact.

The demons would replace the men whose faces they wore. The most power humans could wield at this hour of the world's turning would belong to them—and they belonged to Angelo. The mortals, these men and women and children whom Angelo so despised, would be in the palm of his hand come midnight on the 31st.

"You are now three of the most powerful men in the world," Angelo told the demons. "Your deeds will be seen as miracles, and the people shall flock to you for their salvation." They squirmed with delight, and he corrected them harshly. "No! Behave as such, or I shall send you back whence I found you!"

For an instant, they quailed, then they stood erect and proud, as befitted leaders of this world. Angelo nodded his approval. They would fool anyone.

"Go, and bring the peoples of the earth to me."

Wearing the assumed faces of the most powerful men in the world, the demons hastened to do their master's bidding.

Angelo smiled. Now, he could relax and enjoy his—

The smoke curled, twined into the distorted shape of Moloch. Angelo's smile faded. The demon cowered and whimpered, its bovine ears flattening against its night-black head. Something was wrong.

"Master!" it hissed. "News, news!"

"Speak, Moloch."

"Your ally—the one who was called Antichrist—he is no longer our friend!"

Angelo's tension ebbed slightly. "You come with old news,

Moloch. I am done with him and have revealed my plan to him. There is nothing that—"

"But he can, he can!" Moloch's distress was palpable. "He has new allies! See, see!"

Moloch's image faded. Angelo found himself looking at a battlefield. The Force was still, somehow, on its feet, hacking away at the demons, dark Faeries, and monsters that fought on the side of the enemy of God.

"This cannot be," breathed Angelo. He peered closer, and noticed that not a few of the Norsemen were fighting without their heads. Suddenly he realized what had happened. Loki was more clever than he had thought. He was using the seven Dark Miracles Angelo himself had granted him, to fight against his former ally.

Angelo growled deep in his throat. Then, even as he watched, the tide of battle seemed to turn—not in his favor. A fresh wave of warriors spilled into the scene. They were human-looking, clad in brown robes like monks and brandishing their weapons with the air of those who knew how to use them. Uncommonly handsome they were, down to a man—or a woman, for they, too, fought in this battle. And before the onslaught of these totally unexpected players in the game, Angelo's forces were falling back.

"Impossible," he growled. "Impossible. . . ."

"And yet it is, it is!" burbled Moloch. "Oh, my Prince, what shall we do?"

Angelo took a deep breath. "Let them fight. We have only to hold out for a few more hours. There is nothing they can do after that."

Moloch opened his teeth-crowded mouth as if to say more, but Angelo was weary of the conversation. He wanted to think. Before Moloch could utter a word, Angelo waved his hand. The flames subsided and the coals glowed with only natural radiance once again.

He sat on his bed and rubbed his eyes, trying to think. All the Signs had been completed save one, and he knew that he would bring about a horrified silence in Heaven when the world passed into his hands for all time. Ethelred was but a jabbering, soulless poppet. Angelo's demons were even now alerting his allies, who would soon play their parts as masters of men even as he was masters of them. Time was racing by, and with each moment Angelo was closer to his victory.

But things had not gone completely according to plan. Loki had proved more resourceful, and more angry, than anticipated. The Witnesses were still missing. They—

He felt a prickling at the back of his neck, and his breath caught in his throat.

They were here, again. Wherever outside of this mortal world they had hidden, they had emerged, as he had known they would. Quickly he rose, went to the brazier, and called up his scrying smoke.

He could see them talking with a woman in a field blighted by drought. Here and there was the corpse of a hapless Dane. Their conversation was soundless to him, but he knew where they were—and what they would do next.

Angelo smiled. Foolish mortals! They would not escape him again. He would send no corpse-goddess or hell hound after them this time.

This time, Angelo would take care of the troublesome Witnesses himself.

Kennag had never felt so wretched in her life. Not when Niall had died, not when Bran had been taken, not when she had been raped, not when she had lain on her bed in the agonies of induced miscarriage.

"Alwyn," she said, but could think of no words to follow the utterance of his name. "Alwyn."

Tears filled his eyes. Her own were bone-dry. She longed for the release of tears, of hysterical cries, anything to ease the horrible, cramped pain in her chest that screamed *failure, failure*.

"What is wrong?" asked the woman. Kennag started. She had forgotten the woman was there. She stared at the villager for a long time, taking in the thin face of hunger, the eyes empty save for despair. Kennag's gazed dropped to the woman's rough, red hands. Those hands had perhaps killed, but surely they had also helped reap a harvest once, had cuddled a baby, had touched someone with love.

She swallowed hard. "Nothing," she told the woman. "But we are disoriented. Can you tell us the direction of northwest?"

"Kennag," said Alwyn, staring at her. "There's no time. We can't possibly—"

She turned on him. She could not see her expression, of

course, but she felt the hot blood in her cheeks, the tight knotting of muscles in her neck. He fell silent.

The woman's chapped hand went to her throat. "We could always tell by the sun, before," she whispered. Then, after a moment, she said, "There. That cluster of trees is situated due northwest. There's a trail that'll take you directly to Guildford. From there, you can take the London Way to Watling Street."

"Thank you." Kennag went to her horse and prepared to mount.

"Weren't you wanting some provisions?" asked the woman.

Kennag settled onto the horse's back and met her gaze. "No, thank you. I don't think we'll be needing them after all. Alwyn, come. We have a long way to go."

She turned the horse's head and began to walk toward the little copse of trees. After a moment, she heard the heavy hooves of Balaam.

"Satan will stop us," said Alwyn as he brought the donkey alongside the Faerie horse. Rowena was perched on his saddle, and Ratatosk landed with a thump on Kennag's shoulder. Up ahead, waiting for them in the trees, was Neddy. He had prudently not manifested in front of the village woman.

"Probably," agreed Kennag. "Or else we simply won't get there in time, which is more likely."

"That is true," said Alwyn.

"You know we've got to try," said Kennag. "We won't succeed, but we've got to try. We learned that in the Andredesweald."

"You're right. Of course we do." A pause. "I love you, Kennag. It is a privilege to die in your company."

Her heart hurt again. She did not look at him. "I love you too, Alwyn."

They did not speak for a long time after that.

Kennag was sick in spirit and exhausted in body, but she grimly pressed on. They pushed Balaam as hard as the old donkey could go. For once, Balaam was silent. They did not hear a single complaint out of him, though Kennag knew the pace they set had to be grueling. Her horse could go faster, but she did not have wings. Reaching Iona in time was a moot point. Simply continuing the journey in the face of its fruitlessness was the only thing that mattered, now. Perhaps, in some sort of divine reckoning she and Alwyn did not understand, such stubbornness would count for something.

They rode until they could ride no more, then rested their mounts, then rode again. They passed through the town of Guildford and made straight for the London Way, not stopping for food. Kennag didn't think she could tolerate anything in her stomach at the moment. It was in a knot that rivaled the ones Niall would tie when he went out to sea. Night fell, with its frightening, impenetrable darkness. They lit torches and rode by that light, until the torches gave out.

Exhausted, they fell from their steeds and slept almost where they dismounted. Before she fell into a dreamless sleep, Kennag felt something soft and warm cuddle into the hollow of her throat. A purr rumbled, and she reached to stroke Rowena once before sleep seized her.

Neddy woke them after what felt like moments. Kennag thanked him, shuffled to her horse, and hauled herself into the saddle. Alwyn looked as exhausted as she felt, and even the animals spoke in soft, subdued voices when they needed to.

Today was the final day of the year. Kennag wasn't sure where they were. Alwyn said he guessed they were at Aylesbury, with over three hundred miles to go—miles they couldn't possibly cover.

"It doesn't matter," said Kennag. Her voice sounded hollow in her ears. "All that matters is the trying."

The harsh cry of an eagle sounded in their ears. Kennag realized abruptly how silent everything was, that this one sound from another living being should stand out so starkly. She lifted her gaze, trying to find the bird. It swooped about, and its words made the hair on her arms lift with fear.

"Woe! Woe! Woe, to the inhabitants of the earth!" It repeated its sinister prediction, swooping so close Kennag felt the wind from its wings, and then it flew away. In a few seconds it was swallowed by the dark miasma that whirled in place of the sky.

"Cheerful fellow," said Ratatosk. He flicked his tail in annoyance and launched himself from Kennag's shoulder to run on ahead, navigating from branch to branch of the overhanging trees.

"I've never eaten eagle," mused Rowena. "Wonder what it tastes like." She flexed her claws. "I'd like to sample *that* one."

To Kennag's shock, Neddy suddenly let out an angry roar. He

threw himself on the earth and pounded the soil impotently with
hands that made no impact. "It's not fair! It's not right!" With a
final howl of rage he sat up and glared at her. "You are so wonderful, Kennag. And Alwyn—I knew many churchmen in my
day, and you are far more saintly than they were. And here you
are, trying so hard, and it's just not fair, it's not—"

"Neddy, be still," soothed Kennag. "I haven't yet given up
hope."

It was a lie, but a sweet one, if it stilled the phantom tears on
the insubstantial face. "R-really?"

She felt Alwyn staring at her but pressed on. "Really." Neddy
snuffled a little, his eyes fastened on her face, hungry for reas-
surance. The poor child! He was only sixteen, though he had
been dead for longer than he had lived. She floundered for words.

"Think about what we've seen so far," she said. "I've escaped
from the Underworld, we've met members of the Lost Tribes of
Israel, I'm riding a Faerie horse. Alwyn has spoken with angels.
Something will happen. I feel it."

"Do you See it?" asked Neddy.

Her heart broke. She licked her lips and glanced from Alwyn
to Neddy, wondering what to say. She did not want to lie about
her gift.

Ratatosk saved her the trouble. She heard a crashing of leaves
and glanced up, trying to see his gray-and-brown shape in the
darkness. She saw the branches quiver as he leaped from one to
another, and his high voice faintly reached her ears.

"They've found us!" he was crying. "Run!"

Run where? The horse tensed beneath her but stood her
ground. Glancing at her companions, Kennag saw them ashen
but resolved. There would be no more flight. It was time to
fight—or die.

Now she could hear the hoofbeats, thrumming with a strong,
heartbeat rhythm on the earth. And something else—something
that was not a horse, but was running. Her body went weak, but
she forced herself to sit erect in the saddle. She reached for her
knife. It was a paltry weapon against the likes of her enemies, but
she could bite with this single tooth.

The shape detached itself from shadows dark as itself. A
horse, gaunt and angry, with red eyes and flames for hooves.
Kennag trembled and clutched the hilt of her blade so hard her
fingers hurt. She recognized the rider, the beautiful woman with

features and hair so like her own, with a rotting body from the waist down. Hel, the squirrel had called the thing. The corpse-woman's hound was keeping pace, as monstrous and terrifying as the horse and rider.

Kennag hoped she'd be able to get in at least one good blow before they claimed her.

Something else was keeping the dark horse company—a wolf, gigantic beyond reason, at least the size of the horse and perhaps even larger. She recalled the vision of the wolf digging in the loch, throwing mountains of earth as carelessly as a child flings mud. And atop the monstrous wolf, riding it as easily as if it were a proper, equine steed was—

"*Bran!*"

Beyond any hope, it was he! She had Seen him, lying dead among the scattered bodies of the monks at Iona, had believed the vision without question. But surely it had not told the truth. Surely, that frightening vision had been of a possible scene, not one that would truly happen.

Bran. *Alive.* Joy flooded her, chasing away any fear, any anger. Later, she could not remember dismounting from the Faerie horse to fling herself into her lover's arms.

She cried his name over and over between kisses on his beautiful face. His hair was as thick and black as she remembered, and she tangled her fingers in the shiny mass and kissed it, too. Kennag could not hold him tightly enough, could not fold her woman's body into the clean, strong lines of his powerful male form sufficiently to assuage the longing that raced through her body.

Dimly she realized that Bran was not enfolding her as well, was even taking her wrists, oh so gently, and disengaging her frantic, needful body from his own. He was saying something, but for a wild moment she could not understand the words, couldn't even hear them over the overwhelming sound of her racing heart.

"No," he was saying. "I am not Bran. I'm sorry."

Kennag gasped for air. "W-what?"

Her beloved's face gazed at her with compassion. "You must be the mate of him whose form I wear. I am sorry. How much misery I have caused in my foolishness!"

Bran's voice, but not Bran's words. Bran's body, but not Bran's movements. Suddenly fearful, Kennag backed away. She tore her gaze from Bran to look wildly again at the Norse goddess of death. The woman sat quietly on the black steed, her hound at heel. No one was moving to seize them.

"You—you're not Bran?"

Bran-not-Bran shook his head. "No. I understand you both have had cause to fear my daughter." He indicated Hel with a wave of his hand. "No longer. She led me to you, but not on the Enemy's behalf.

"My name is Loki, and I have come to help you."

23

*And the children of Israel went into the
midst of the sea upon the dry ground;
and the waters were a wall unto them
on their right hand, and on their left.*
            —EXODUS 14:22

**Aylesbury
December 31, 999**

"It's a trick," said Alwyn. "It has to be."

Bran/Loki smiled sadly. "No trick, friend Alwyn. Not this
time. It is I who have been tricked."

"You are Loki, the evil god of the Norsemen!" cried Alwyn.
He was angry. It was not the reaction he had expected, and he had
no idea why he was so furious, but he was. "You have allied with
Satan and become his Antichrist! Look at the wolf—it bears the
mark of the Beast!"

"I do not deny it—although I do not think of myself as evil,"
replied Loki. He reached to stroke the lines burned into the animal's forehead as he spoke. "But this Satan of yours, this Prince
of Lies—he has lied to me as well. And the enemy of my enemy
is my friend."

The woman on the black horse—Hel—made a sound of anger
and disgust. "And to think I helped him, that my father and brothers and I have been so *used* . . . ! I am glad you escaped me."

Kennag stood, frozen with shock. Her face was very white,
and she was alarmingly still. Alwyn spared her a quick glance,
then returned his attention to Loki.

"Ratatosk," he said to the squirrel perched on his shoulder, "you know him. What do you think?"

The squirrel fidgeted. "I do not know what to think," he replied finally. "Loki is not to be trusted, but he is not without his merits. He loves his children, this much I know."

"Listen to me." Loki's voice dropped to a growl. "Your Satan freed me and my children if we would help him in his quest to bring about the end of his world. After he had won his battle, I would be allowed to fight mine—to bring about Ragnarok. I would finally have my vengeance on the gods who murdered one of my children and imprisoned the others. My body still lies fettered far beneath the earth, but my essence is in this borrowed form. I learned today that I have been tricked—that your greedy enemy plans not to destroy the world, but to enslave it. He turned on my people, the Danes, who aided him in his quest, and ordered them slaughtered like cattle. He has forever denied me the one thing I lived for—my vengeance, my hour of victory and death combined. He needs me yet, that much is certain. He must have an Antichrist on Earth to fulfill prophecy. But once the year has turned and he has won, he will have no more use for me. I and my children will be sent back to our prison *forever.*"

He had moved closer to Alwyn and now stood beside the frightened Balaam. His blue eyes snapped with intensity, and his body seemed to emanate rage. Alwyn stared back at him, unable to tear his gaze from the handsome man who had once been Kennag's beloved and now housed an angry god.

"You two are the only ones who can stop Satan. You are the single thing that threatens him. He is afraid of you. That is why he sent Hel and Garm to find you. You want to stop him to save your world. I want to stop him to save myself. Selfish, yes, but an understandable motive."

"If it's not a lie," said Alwyn, but his voice sounded weak and unsure in his own ears. Everything Loki said rang true. It gibed completely with what the Bible said about Satan. And Loki's words about Satan's desire to reign forever sent chills through Alwyn's body.

He looked over at Kennag. She still stood as if turned to stone. Poor Kennag—to have found her beloved and then learn what a dreadful thing had been perpetrated on him.

"Kennag?" he said, softly.

She blinked, almost as if coming out of a trance. "You wear

the body of my love," she said in a controlled voice that only hinted at the anger and hurt she must be feeling. "Did you kill him?"

Loki regarded her with sympathy. "Lady Kennag, in truth, I do not know what transpired. I was in my body, in chains, and then I was in this body. You would have to ask Angelo what he did with Bran's spirit."

"*Angelo!*" cried Alwyn. "The king's adviser?"

"The same," said Loki.

Alwyn's stomach churned. He had met this Angelo, had spoken with him, all unknowing that. . . . Quickly he crossed himself. Sweet Jesu! All along, the Enemy had been right here.

"Do you think there might still be a chance that Bran is alive?" Kennag pressed on, heedless of the revelation that had so unnerved Alwyn.

"I do not know. Possibly."

Kennag took a deep breath. Some color returned to her cheeks. Before Alwyn could say anything, she said to Loki, "We are trying to get to the island of Iona—the place where you and your Force murdered the innocent monks."

Loki did not appear ashamed. "I know the place. You'll not get there in time on such beasts," he said, indicating the donkey and the horse.

Balaam craned his neck to look at Alwyn. "Leave me behind," he said softly. "I will only hinder you."

Alwyn stroked the rough coat of the donkey's neck. "Balaam, you were not young when I came to the abbey as a little boy. I can't abandon you now."

Kennag's mare whinnied furiously and tossed her head. Not for the first time, Alwyn wondered why he could not understand the beast. Still, she was clearly intelligent, and it was simple enough to catch her meaning.

"You will look after him, then?" Alwyn asked. The Faerie horse bobbed her head up and down vigorously.

"If you don't succeed, I can't imagine this Angelo would be kind to an old donkey that had helped you," Balaam pointed out. "And if you do succeed, you'll come find me." His brown eyes widened a little. "Won't you?"

"Of course I will," soothed Alwyn, realizing that with the words he had committed to leaving the animal behind and traveling with the trickster god of the Norsemen. Reluctantly, but seeing no other choice, he slipped off Balaam and rubbed the donkey's soft muzzle with great affection. As he did so, he caught sight of the five-pointed star on the ring. Either way, succeed or fail, he knew he would not be allowed to keep the ring. It would be taken back, and he would never be able to understand Balaam's speech again. Suddenly, he hugged Balaam about the neck, hard, then turned away.

"It seems we are casting our lot with you," he said to Loki. "I would not have believed it, but it does appear that we are now fighting on the same side."

"Excellent," said Loki. "I want to see the look on the bastard's face when all his glorious plans begin to unravel." He smiled, and Alwyn cringed from it. He was very glad this being was now with them rather than against them.

"You belittled our steeds," said Kennag. "But none of yours has wings that I can see."

"Hel will not be accompanying us," said Loki. "She has other tasks to help hold Angelo's forces at bay. But my Fenris"—he rubbed the giant wolf's shoulder with affection—"my Fenris does not need wings. Down, my son, and let them mount you."

Obediently, the wolf dropped to the earth, his legs folded beneath him. Loki held out a hand to Kennag. She regarded it for a moment, then her eyes went to his face. Taking a deep breath, she accepted his help and climbed onto the huge, broad back of the great Fenris Wolf.

Alwyn did not wish to accept Loki's help but, as ever, his dead arm proved to be a hindrance. He, too, took Loki's hand, and found to his surprise that the touch of the god felt like solid, warm human flesh. He wasn't sure what he was expecting, but certainly not something so normal. With Loki's and Kennag's help, the monk mounted the soft, furry back of the wolf.

Ratatosk and Rowena joined them, needing no aid to leap the distance. The white cat made directly for Alwyn, and settled herself between his legs. The squirrel, seeming to have no fear, bounded along the length of the wolf's neck and perched between ears as large as himself.

"Neddy, are you coming?" asked Kennag.

The ghost was still on the ground. He smiled. "I travel differently than you do. I will wait for you on Iona."

"We will see you there shortly," Loki replied, swinging himself up in front of Kennag and Alwyn. "Now, my son," he said, stroking the beast, "grow."

Before Alwyn's astonished gaze, the wolf, already unnaturally huge, did indeed begin to grow. Larger and larger, until his head towered above the topmost branches of the trees. He whuffed excitedly, and Alwyn cried out and clutched his ears. Kennag did the same. Rowena dug her claws into Alwyn's thigh, and he winced.

Kennag glanced back at the two companions they had been forced to leave behind. She gasped, and shook Alwyn's shoulder.

"Alwyn! Look!"

Alwyn turned. His eyes widened. Standing beside Balaam and caressing his long ears with affection was the most beautiful woman he had ever seen. Her garb, a revealing, flowing dress in a style unfamiliar to Alwyn, was white, and her blonde hair evoked the sun that had so recently hidden its face from them. She hugged the donkey, rubbing her fair cheek against his, and her blue eyes locked with Kennag's. The woman smiled.

It was only then that Alwyn realized that her long, slim legs tapered into golden hooves.

"Epona," breathed Kennag. "No wonder Gwyn's dark Faeries were afraid to touch her."

Alwyn had thought he was beyond shock after what had happened to them on this strange journey, but he was in error. He trembled with awe. Even he, a monk of God, knew who Epona was. The Romans had adopted this Celtic horse goddess, and her image—that of a beautiful white mare—was still in evidence on buildings and in statuary this long after their occupation.

As they watched, Epona's grin broadened. She tossed her golden hair, and it became a mane. Her woman's body shimmered and twisted again into that of the Faerie horse. But this time, Alwyn saw her as she truly was. No ugly nag she. All along, Kennag had ridden an exquisite white mare with a mane and tail the hue of the purest gold.

The mare reared and bucked, nipping playfully at Balaam's hindquarters. The old donkey responded in kind, braying in delight. They whirled and cantered away, an image of beauty and lightness amid the darkness.

As they watched the goddess and the donkey race into the distance, Alwyn felt giant muscles tense beneath him as the wolf prepared to spring into motion. Then Fenris surged forward, stretching his neck out and making his body long and lean and swift.

Yards fell beneath his gigantic paws. Alwyn and Kennag found it easier to stay on than they had thought. The sheer size of the wolf added to their stability, but as the ground raced past, Alwyn still felt nervous and dug his right hand deep into the long, thick fur for a better grip.

He had no idea how fast they were going, but Loki had been right about one thing: Fenris did not need wings.

Time passed, but the wolf's pace did not slacken. The miles were devoured, and for the first time since the woman in the village had revealed to them the actual date, Alwyn felt a surge of hope.

They crossed rolling plains and farmland, skirted huge forests and lakes. The landscape changed, became more rocky, as the hours passed. Now they moved toward a more mountainous region, but even these mountains, jutting harshly above the earth's surface, seemed smaller than usual in comparison with the great beast upon which they rode.

As night came, with its utterly black darkness, the scent of the wind changed. Alwyn now could smell the briny tang that announced the ocean was nearby, and he marveled anew. God's ways were fearful in their mystery.

With barely a pause, Fenris cleared rivers and valleys that Alwyn could not see, moving steadily northwest. The ocean scent grew stronger. A mountain towered upward on their right, dark against the darkness, and Alwyn could finally hear the rhythmic, comforting sound of the ocean. This much, at least, had not changed. Yet.

Fenris slowed, then stopped. His sides heaved. Even for him, the run had clearly been an exertion.

"We have come to the end of the land," said Loki. Alwyn blinked against the darkness. There came a sharp crackle, and then a ball of fire manifested in Loki's hand. Gently, Loki tossed the ball into the air and it hung like a lamp, whirling and becoming ever brighter until at last Alwyn could see as if the entire shore were lit by torches.

Fenris began to grow smaller. The sensation of the beast shrinking beneath him unsettled Alwyn, but he remained silent. When the animal was no more than the size of a horse, his riders slipped to the earth. Ratatosk and Rowena followed.

Kennag crossed her arms against the cold wind and peered across the black water. The island of Iona could not be seen, but Alwyn could sense it.

A deep, haunting cry floated over the water. Kennag and Alwyn glanced at one another, but Loki seemed pleased.

"Jormungand!" he cried. "You have found us, clever one."

"There is no boat," said Kennag. "How are we to cross to the island?"

Alwyn knew. He smiled, and planted the Rod of Aaron in the soil. It felt good in his hand—warm, comforting. He had made great use of the Ring of Solomon, and now, finally, the task for which he had been given the rod had arrived.

"God has given us a means to cross to the holy island," he said. His companions looked up at him, then stepped back respectfully. As Alwyn strode forward on the rocky soil, Rowena fell into step beside him. She rubbed her white head on his ankle.

Standing a few inches from the ocean, Alwyn suddenly didn't know what to say. He felt that he should have words for this moment, but nothing came. So, in silence, he stepped forward and dipped the end of the rod into the waters.

For a moment, nothing happened. Then the pattern of Loki's firelight reflected on the water changed. It swirled and danced, and Alwyn heard a splashing sound. Like a bolt of lightning, a division appeared in the water. It ran in a straight line from the rod until it vanished from Alwyn's sight.

"God be praised," breathed Alwyn. As if invisible hands were pushing the water back, the ocean moved away from the rod along that clean, perfect line. The wet ocean bottom, littered with stones and weeds, was revealed, shining in the light. A corridor lay before them as tons of water obligingly parted, clearing a path directly to the island known as the Lamp of Faith.

Alwyn stared, drinking in the sight. He had always thought that such a vision must have filled Moses with a heady sense of power, but realized that was a foolish assumption. Alwyn felt no sense of power at all. This was God's handiwork, and Alwyn was a tool, as the rod was a tool.

"Alwyn, come on." Kennag, practical as ever, cut through Alwyn's sense of wonderment at the miracle that had just unfolded. He looked around with the grace of a drunken man to see his companions again perched atop the Fenris Wolf. Lurching forward, he scrambled aboard the wolf's back.

Once again, the great creature surged forward. In the distance, Alwyn heard the roar of the sea serpent that was yet another of Loki's horrible children. But he no longer doubted the tricky Norse god's intentions. He trusted in his own God, and surely the Rod of Aaron would not have wrought His miracles had their decision to ally with Loki been blasphemous.

A few times, the wolf lost his footing on the slippery ocean floor, and his passengers nearly fell. But he kept going, covering the few miles to Iona in the span of a handful of moments.

Abruptly, Fenris slid to a halt. Alwyn, Kennag, Ratatosk, Rowena, and even Loki struggled to stay atop their unusual mount. Alarmed by the sudden stop, Alwyn lifted his head to voice his anger.

The words caught in his throat.

Before them, towering far above even the head of the giant Fenris, was a wall of water that churned and boiled. It was more violent than those that stood tranquilly on either side of the corridor. It seemed almost angry.

"I don't understand," said Kennag. "The rod—why didn't it work on this?"

Alwyn shook his head. For a moment he simply stared, fighting back fear. Perhaps this barrier would require another touch of the divine rod. No one spoke. Finally, Alwyn slipped off Fenris. His feet squelched in mud that clung to his boots and released them reluctantly, with a wet, sucking sound as he made his way toward the wall of water. Praying silently, he adjusted his grip on the rod and thrust it forward into the water.

It was a mistake. At once, he felt something inside the wall of water clutch the rod and pull. Alwyn gripped it hard and stumbled toward the water wall.

"Help me!" he cried. At once, he felt strong arms going around him. He recalled Kennag saying that Bran had been the son of the village blacksmith, and was grateful for the power in those arms. Kennag, too, was there, tugging him back.

"This is no natural thing," cried Loki. "It did not respond to my commands either."

Whatever was on the other side of the wall of water was far stronger than any three mortals. Alwyn's feet slipped in the mud. He was hauled inexorably forward and fell, cutting his knee on a hidden rock. Mud and the smell of rotting vegetation assaulted him. He turned his face, suddenly afraid that the slimy ooze on the bottom of the ocean would fill his nostrils and mouth.

"Let go of the rod!" It was Rowena, half buried in mud, her white face shoved into his.

But he couldn't. It was one of two gifts bequeathed to him by Michael. He was supposed to take care of them, value them. He couldn't just let go of the rod as if it were a mere walking stick caught in the mud.

Closer he came to the churning wall of water. He could see into it now. Instead of fish and sea plants, he saw grotesque shapes he could not identify. They swirled, dancing in and out of his vision, but even the merest glimpse of them was enough to send terror shuddering through him.

Still he hung on. Loki's grip on his body was becoming painful. Alwyn wondered if he would be ripped in half.

Suddenly, a sharp pain stung his arm. Without thinking, he opened his hand. The rod sped between his fingers, burning them, and then it was gone.

Rowena had clawed him, forcing him to loosen his grip on the rod, and now it was gone. But there was no time to be angry with the cat. There was only time for Alwyn to stumble to his feet and gaze up in sheer terror as whatever dark and terrible power held the wall of water in place released it.

24

*Greater love hath no man than this,
that a man lay down his life for his
friends.*

—John 15:13

The Island of Iona
December 31, 999

With agonizing slowness, the wall of water collapsed. Alwyn
was vaguely aware of Kennag's scream, of Loki crying out
something, but he couldn't move to flee. He stared, unable to tear
his gaze away, watching the dark waters that housed darker
things fall slowly down on him.

Something struck him violently in the side, and he fell. Darkness slammed down on him, and for a moment he couldn't
breathe.

This was not what he had envisioned death by drowning to be.
For one thing, though his lungs fought for air, he felt dry, and
there was a clear sensation of something solid, soft, and thick beneath his body. No saturation of water, no sweeping current dragging him off to death.

Now the peculiar surface beneath him moved, and Alwyn
tumbled hard to his right. He heard yelps and meows and
grunts—how could that be, if they had all drowned?

The darkness was impenetrable. The earth beneath him continued to heave violently, and Alwyn rolled again. He struck his
head and came to a stop against something large and smooth and
hard.

Now his lungs sucked in air. He rubbed his throbbing head with his right hand, probing fingers feeling a lump already beginning to rise. He was definitely not drowning, but what had happened?

And then, only a few feet in front of him, the darkness parted to reveal the light of Loki's swirling flame. By that dancing light, Alwyn saw that the pillar against which he was leaning was a mammoth tooth, and the peculiar surface that rolled and moved so readily was a slick tongue.

"Don't be afraid," cried Loki as Alwyn drew breath to shriek. "My wonderful child, my Jormungand, has saved us!" The god hastened forward to the entrance of the monster's mouth and peered out. Kennag, Rowena, and Ratatosk joined him.

Alwyn gasped, trembling. He was in the mouth of a giant sea serpent! And yet—it was better than drowning before the wall of water, was it not? God was working in strange ways, indeed, on what could be the final day of the world as Alwyn knew it.

Slowly, the monk crawled toward his companions, trying not to acknowledge the slimy sensation of a cold, wet tongue beneath his hand and knees. There was a great deal of mud and stones in Jormungand's mouth. The creature had not had time to be delicate, but had simply lunged forward, seizing debris as well as five living beings, before the waters had come crashing down.

The creature was holding them remarkably steadily. Peering out of Jormungand's mouth, Alwyn realized they were a great distance from the surface of the water. Toward the left, standing partially out of view, was the gigantic Fenris. The water barely reached his belly. He splashed and pranced, yelping now and then with what was clearly frustration.

Below and to the right, Alwyn could see a small patch of dry land, and a small building that appeared from this distance to be a child's wooden block. It was the monastery. Alwyn didn't want to think about what the dozens of still, tiny brown lumps scattered about the island were.

He realized that the entire island was surrounded by a ring of water that fountained straight up several yards from the ocean's surface. The path along which they had come, the path made possible by the rod's parting of the sea, was also visible. It led directly to this encircling wreath of churning, angry water. This, then, was what had blocked them. Twice, Loki had come to their rescue. Fenris, the wolf, had taken them to Iona in time, and Jormungand, a monster if there ever was one, had snatched them up from certain death.

For an instant, Alwyn wondered why Jormungand didn't just set them down on the island. Then movement on the surface of Iona caught his attention.

Nothing of this world moved like that, not even a spider or a serpent—jerky, almost mad, spasming movements from something that had too many limbs and . . . and too many *heads*. . . .

They crawled up from the violent agitation of the water. These were the things Alwyn had barely glimpsed. Here were the soldiers of Hell, blaspheming the sacred island with their presence, prepared to do battle with anyone who would dare thwart their master's purpose. More things emerged, some bright and angry-looking, some dark and shadow-spawned, all of them sending a thrill of fear through Alwyn that all but paralyzed him.

"Midhir's balls," breathed Kennag. "Not even the Unseelie Court has beasts like that." Strangely, hearing Kennag utter one of her obscene phrases made Alwyn feel much better. She had been shaken by seeing Loki, but she had recovered. He could almost feel a solid strength emanating from her.

"The Unseelie Court are children compared to Angelo's creatures," muttered Loki, his handsome face twisted with hatred. "They have claimed the island. We must retake it, somehow."

In silence, Alwyn crossed himself.

Loki turned to him, his eyes glittering in the fluctuating light of the swirling fireball. "What is your task at this place?"

"I—I need to sing."

"*What?*" Loki's jaw dropped. "Do you mean to tell me I brought you all this way for you to sing a little song? How can that—"

"It is prophecy!" interrupted Kennag. "As long as a monk's voice is sounded on this island, the end of the world cannot come."

"That is the *stupidest* thing I—"

"Look down there!" Kennag pointed to the milling throng of demons that were clustering by the hundreds on the tiny, three-mile-long island. "Do you think Angelo thinks it is stupid?"

Loki glanced down. "You have a point."

"You're right I do." She peered out, and for a moment Alwyn feared she might fall. "If only there was a moon—I could get my bearings. Alwyn, does the moon go away as one of the Signs?"

Alwyn licked dry lips. "No. But it is supposed to turn red as blood."

"I don't care if it's as purple as a thistle, if I could only see it."

"That is easily accomplished," said Loki, a touch boastfully. Leaning out of Jormungand's mouth, he waved a hand. A wind appeared out of nowhere. Safe inside the sheltering cave of the monster's jaws, Alwyn could not feel the wind, but he could hear it.

Loki directed its path with delicate flutterings of his long fingers. After a few seconds, the thick barrier of smoke parted before the insistent wind, and the gibbous moon glowered down on them. Its red glow was almost more unsettling than the black smoke that had hidden it.

"We don't have much time," said Kennag. The scarlet glow from the blood moon, combined with the swirling orange of Loki's fireball, cast an eerie light on her pale features. "It is well into the night. Whatever we do, we've got to do it quickly."

"What are the exact words of your prophecy?" asked Loki. "I need to know so that we do not inadvertently play into Angelo's hands."

"They are St. Columba's deathbed words," said Alwyn. " 'Iona of my heart, Iona of my love, instead of monks' voices there shall be lowing of cattle. But before the world comes to an end, Iona shall be as it was.' "

"I believe you now," said Loki grimly. "I was instructed to slay all the monks, but to leave the cattle untouched. I can see them now, huddled down there. They do not know how lucky they are. 'Iona shall be as it was,' eh? With no monks' voices, and only cattle?"

"We think so," said Kennag. "Prophecies are notoriously vague."

Loki laughed aloud at that, throwing back his dark head and letting the mirth pour freely forth. The bright sound in contrast with their dire situation angered Alwyn at first, but Loki's laughter had a certain disarming infectiousness about it, and he could not remain angry for long.

"Kennag, you are right about that. Well, we shall simply have to do what we think best. I would prepare for battle if I were you." He glanced at them one at a time, taking in the woman armed with a knife, the brother armed with nothing at all, and the cat and squirrel armed only with their teeth and claws. He shook his head. "Your Gods alone know why you were chosen, but I will help you where I can. Fenris! Jormungand! Our guests need to visit the monastery!"

With startling speed and grace, the giant wolf went from a standing position to a leap. He bounded over the wall of water so quickly that it did not have time to adjust its height to prevent him. Mighty jaws clamped open and shut, closing down on one dark thing after another and hurling them miles distant. Alwyn had only a brief chance to grasp Fenris's actions before Jormungand also began to move.

Nausea gripped the monk as the serpent's head ducked downward. The island seemed to rush up at him. Without warning, Jormungand halted. Alwyn and Kennag tumbled sideways in the monster's mouth. Alwyn caught the briefest glimpse of a mighty tail covered with glittering scales lifting and then crashing down on Iona. At once they began to move again. Iona raced toward them, and then Alwyn found himself stumbling forward, his booted feet once again on dry land.

They were accosted by screams, shrieks, and a cacophony of other noises Alwyn had never heard before, and fervently desired never to hear again. The earth trembled, and he fell. He was uncertain whether the earthquake came from his allies or his enemies, but he didn't care. He lay where he had fallen, a huddled mass of terror.

The shimmering, white form of Neddy materialized in front of him. The dead king frowned terribly. "Alwyn, there's little time! It's nearly midnight! You have to sing!"

Alwyn blinked stupidly. Sing? He couldn't open his mouth. His throat had shut down, refused to cooperate. He could only stare, mute, at Neddy.

The ghost's features softened. To Alwyn's surprise, Neddy opened his mouth and began to sing in a soft, sweet voice. The song was not a particularly powerful one, one of the lesser hymns sung now and again with a congregation. But Alwyn found his lips moving, and to his wonder, his own voice floated out to join Neddy's.

Singing, he rose to his feet. The fierce wind snatched the words from his mouth as he uttered them. It did not matter. Alwyn was singing. Whether or not the words were heard by others was irrelevant. A monk's voice was sounding on the holy island.

He had thought the things on the island would come for him, but they seemed to be keeping their distance. He began the matins prayers, looking about for his comrades. Kennag, her little knife clutched in her hand, was running to him. Her red hair flew wildly in the wind. She clutched Ratatosk and Rowena in her arms. She mouthed something, the words of which he could not hear: *Keep singing*.

Over there, standing atop a large boulder near the desecrated monastery, was Loki. His hair, too, was the wind's plaything, but his body was as still as if it had been sculpted from stone. His eyes were closed and his lips were murmuring something; again, Alwyn could not understand.

Lightning exploded from the sky. It struck the nightmare creatures, slowing if not stopping them. Alwyn realized that the lightning, like the wind and the waters, obeyed Loki's commands. The thought unnerved him as he remembered the role that Loki, until recently, had been playing. Antichrist, with all the accompanying dark, evil powers.

The earth shook again, and Alwyn stumbled. He kept singing, working his way through the prayers he had sung every day for most of his life. There was comfort and strength in the familiar words.

Those words died in his throat, however, when the monks began to move.

Dead for twenty-nine days, they rose stiffly. Kennag was closer now, and brushed against one as she stumbled toward Alwyn.

Alwyn whimpered. Surely this was Angelo's doing. Christ could, and had, raised the dead back to life, but this parody of life was an insult, a mockery of a holy miracle. And yet, the corpses of the murdered brethren moved not toward Alwyn and his companions, but toward their enemies. Aghast, Alwyn looked at Loki, and saw the god smile grimly.

Christ could raise the dead. The Antichrist could only animate them.

"Keep singing!" Kennag's voice, close now, still faint. Swallowing hard, Alwyn began to rasp out songs traditionally sung at nones. *Dear God,* he prayed, tears of horror and fear stinging his eyes, *how long must this go on?*

"It can end right now, if you like," came a voice in his ear. Honey-sweet, smooth, and rich like cream. Alwyn turned, star-

tled, to see Angelo standing beside him. He was as gloriously
handsome as Alwyn remembered him, and the wind and heat that
scoured the island seemed to lay no fingers on his garments or his
body.

Alwyn moaned and stumbled backward. Terror flooded him,
and his voice fell silent.

"That's right," Angelo approved. "You don't have to do anything—just refrain from doing something. It's so easy, isn't it?"

Alwyn blinked. Yes, it was easy. His throat hurt. He didn't
want to sing. And the words were slipping away—

"Don't listen to him, Alwyn!" Kennag reached his side and
clutched at his arm. She shook him violently. "Don't you know
who this is? Can't you see what he's trying to do?"

Alwyn stared at her, dumb. She whirled on Angelo, growling
deep in her throat. "You can't kill us outright. You can't even
force us to be silent, because of the prophecy. We are the Witnesses, and we cannot die until the Beast from the abyss comes
for us!"

"Foolish child," murmured Angelo, his voice soft and gentle
as that of a parent speaking to a wayward daughter. "*I* am the
Beast from the abyss, and I *have* come for you."

Kennag went white at the words.

"It's a trick, Kennag." The voice belonged to Neddy, floating
several feet off the ground. "You haven't prophesied long
enough. He can't kill you, can't even silence you. Alwyn, don't
be fooled! Keep singing!"

Alwyn felt as if he were wrapped in heavy wool. The voices
reached his ears and he comprehended their words, but the
sounds were faint. He could no longer feel the heat or the wind,
was barely aware of Loki and his children using every bit of
strength they had to hold back Angelo's dark creatures. He could
only stare at the angelically beautiful being, and think, *I don't
really want to sing.*

"What did they offer you, Alwyn?" Strangely, Angelo's voice
sounded clear and strong to the young monk. "Saving the world?
What has the world done for you? Or, rather, done *to* you? A
lowly monk, crippled and shunned, laboring in a monastery."
The rich voice dripped disdain. Angelo stepped nearer. Alwyn
smelled the sweet scent of roses and honey.

"I can offer you a place in my new order," he murmured. His
breath was on Alwyn's face now, sweet and intoxicating. Alwyn

closed his eyes. He could no longer hear Kennag and Neddy's pleas. He could hear only Angelo.

"Do you want Kennag? I can give her to you. Do you want power, to be respected as Wulfstan is?" Angelo snapped his fingers. "It is done!"

Alwyn swallowed hard and opened his eyes. "I have faced such temptations," he managed. "I have conquered them. There is nothing you can offer me that would make me join you!"

"Oh?" Angelo hadn't moved. His handsome face melted into a smile. "Are you sure? Are you so very sure?"

He reached forward and touched Alwyn's left arm.

"*I can make you whole,*" he whispered.

Alwyn gasped. His arm tingled and burned. He looked down at it and saw it as strong and well-muscled as his right arm. No fingers curled in on each other like gray, dead twigs. This was a man's arm, an arm full of life, an arm that could move and touch and—

He flexed his fingers. Disbelieving, he made a fist. Tears filled his eyes, poured down his face. He was whole. He had never been whole in his life. He had prayed to God to heal his withered arm, had spent hours beating himself in repentance for whatever unknown sin had cursed him. God hadn't listened to him. Angelo had.

"Keep singing!" Kennag's voice was a raven's caw, rough and unpleasant to Alwyn's ears. He fell to his knees, ignoring her, staring at his beautiful new arm. He touched it with his right fingers, and could feel—could *feel*—the light caress.

Angelo snarled and made a quick, sharp gesture. Out of the corner of his eye, Alwyn saw Kennag lifted in the air and hurtled several yards distant. He did not see where or how she landed, nor did he care. All his attention was focused on his left arm.

Angelo laughed.

Storms raged about the monk. Demons fought, gods struggled, and Alwyn had no mind for them.

There was a blur of white, and Rowena was there. Before Alwyn realized what she was doing, the cat was on his beautiful new arm, clawing and biting. The pain was excruciating. Horrified at this attack upon his arm, Alwyn screamed and pounded the cat on the earth. She held on with her claws and freed her mouth enough to mew, "Keep singing!" before continuing the onslaught.

His hand, his new, perfect hand, was being mangled right before his eyes! Without realizing it, Alwyn had stumbled to his feet and raced over to a large boulder. Crying his rage, he slammed the cat against the stone again and again. He heard a crack, and Rowena went limp. He shook his hand free of her and cradled the bleeding arm against his chest, murmuring to it as if it were a distressed child.

He glanced up, and his gaze fell on something small and white and red. Alwyn blinked, his vision clearing, and he realized what it was.

Rowena. He had killed Rowena!

She had attacked him to distract him, to remind him of their battle. And he, with his new, diabolically strong and beautiful arm, had slain her.

Was this what it all came down to? The fate of the world resting on a monk's pathetic desire to have a good left arm?

Blood pooled beneath the white form of the dead cat.

Is this what it meant to have the use of his hand? That he would kill a devoted friend with it? That he would throw away all he believed in, all he fought for, and deliver the world up to Satan forever?

No.

The lump in his throat threatened to block his voice, but Alwyn fought it. His voice was squeaky with raw pain, but he lifted it and sang with all his strength. Clenching both hands into fists, he raised them to a Heaven he could not see but still believed in, and sang with all his heart.

Angelo's voice was a terrible scream. "Silence, monk! SILENCE!"

But Alwyn would not be silent. He sang for Kennag and her courage, for Balaam and his great heart, for Ratatosk and the Faerie horse who was a goddess, and for Neddy. Most of all, he sang for Rowena, friend and companion, who had given her life for this moment. He would not fail her, not now.

Angelo darted about the monk, dancing like an angry predator and twisting his human-shaped body into postures no human could make. Twice he reached out as if to throttle Alwyn, and twice he withdrew, snarling.

Finally something seemed to break in him. His eyes rolled back in their sockets and his mouth yawned open, impossibly wide. A voice much deeper and resonant than that coming from a human throat boomed forth:

"IF I FAIL, THEN YOU FALL WITH ME!"

The fair, human form Angelo had worn like a mummer's costume shattered into a thousand bright-hued pieces. A twisting monstrosity of shadow and darkness burst forth, as if hatching from the shell of a man. It screamed again, and from its glowing eyes a beam of red energy shot directly toward Alwyn's chest.

"Vengeance!"

The cry had come from a human throat, but the voice was that of a god. Moving so quickly he seemed but a blur to Alwyn's frightened eyes, Loki leaped several yards and landed directly between Alwyn and the deadly bolt.

Kennag screamed.

Loki's body arched and twisted, the handsome face contorted in a grimace of sheer agony. Then he collapsed. Alwyn smelled the acrid stench of burning flesh, and saw that the limp body of Loki had a huge hole in the center of its chest. Still, he sang on.

A bellow of rage jerked Alwyn's attention back to Angelo— or rather, the thing had been Angelo. It gathered itself again, preparing to deliver the final blow.

Alwyn shut his eyes and sang to his God.

The creature staggered. Its nightmare face mutated from rage to an expression of uncomprehending anger and anguish.

"No," it cried, whimpering, then, louder, "*NO!* I will not yield! I will not—"

There was a huge explosion of light and a sound that momentarily deafened Alwyn. The earth rocked and heaved, and Alwyn fell. Gasping for breath, he eased himself up and turned to look at Angelo.

The demon was gone. Where he had stood, the earth had been burned and blackened.

Alwyn's ears felt hot and full, as if he had stuffed warm wool in them. The sound of his own raspy singing thundered loudly in his still-ringing ears. There was no other sound. The ocean had gone still. The walls of water commanded by Angelo had vanished, and even the natural movement of the waves against the shore had ceased. The only sound in the world was that of Alwyn's shattered voice, a fragile melody against the almost incomprehensible quiet.

His words faltered, and he, too, fell silent. He could hear his heart beating painfully in his chest.

Silence, utter silence; a stillness not heard since the world began.

That was the final sign prophesied in the book of Revelation—a silence in Heaven.

Had they succeeded—or failed?

25

God shall wipe away all tears from
their eyes; and there shall be no more
death, neither sorrow nor crying, neither shall there be any more pain: for
the former things are passed away.
—REVELATION 21:4

The stillness came like something physical, and every being on
the surface of the earth, and above, and below it, paused for a
moment. No wind swirled, no wave beat, no wing or leg or arm
moved. The silence was utter, as the silence before the creation of
the world had been.

Then, slowly, the dead who had been forced to move and fight
instead of rest as they ought, fell to the earth. The power that had
animated them had gone. They were corpses once again, nothing
more and nothing less. The ravens continued their flight, wheel-
ing and then descending to feast on the lavish fare laid before
them.

The monstrous beings summoned by dark forces ceased their
hunting and withdrew. They melted into the shadows, into the
crevices of rock and hollows of hills, gone to their dwelling place
of nightmare and darkness until they would, again, be summoned.

The Four Riders surveyed the scene from atop their black,
white, red, and pale horses. Without a word spoken between
them, they turned their mounts and slowly cantered away from
the battlefield. Their parts had been played. They would ride
upon the surface of this world no longer.

Fair faces, those of humans and angels and Faeries, broke into tentative smiles. The Lost Tribesmen hugged one another even as they wept, and their embraces reached out to the spirits of wind and water, and to the divine beings who loved both man and God with a passion that was as pure as it was strong.

The year had turned. The fear was over. The Witnesses had succeeded.

The Island of Iona
January 1, 1000

Slowly, like the exhalation of a baby's breath, sound returned to Alwyn's world.

First it was the *shuush, shuush* of the waves against the island's shore. Then it was the distant cry of seabirds, and then a soft wind that caressed his face and played with his hair.

He heard footsteps crunching in the sand, and turned to see Kennag standing beside him. Wordlessly, she reached for his hand—his right hand—and clasped it. Tears filling his eyes, Alwyn twined his fingers about hers and held on tightly.

Without knowing what they were looking for, they lifted their faces to the sky. The laughing wind did its task well, and blew away the last traces of smoke and darkness. The moon emerged from behind the foul cloud, white and clean and pure, its gentle light filling the skies and keeping the twinkling stars company. Alwyn didn't think he had ever seen anything so beautiful.

And then the singing began.

From above and around it came, though Alwyn could not see the singers. He had never heard any sound that was sweeter, though Kennag's voice came close. There were no words that he could understand, but the meaning was clear: *Praise God, praise God, ye heavenly host; sing alleluia, now and forevermore.*

Kennag tugged gently on his hand. He turned to her, loving her face in the moonlight, and realized that she was weeping freely. He had never seen her cry before, but now she did not hesitate to let the tears flow down her cheeks.

"Do you see them?" she whispered. Her tear-filled eyes were wide and bright, and a smile such as might grace a child's lips curved her mouth.

"No," he replied, his voice hushed and respectful. "I have not your gift."

She smiled at that. With her free hand, she wiped the tears from her face, and touched the salty liquid to Alwyn's eyes. "Then share it, my friend."

Alwyn blinked. And then he could See as Kennag Saw, and the beauty and wonder of it broke his heart. The sky was full of angels in shining, wondrous hues, their faces unbearably bright. Pure Love shone from them, as they flew and sang in the crowded night sky.

And on the earth were beings of light and grace as well. A king and queen strode toward Alwyn, their crowns living, dancing light, and their faces as beautiful as the angels'. He knew without knowing how he knew that they were the King and Queen of the Seelie Court, the great Faerie Folk who had sent Kennag on her quest. With them in a place of honor was a young girl, her long black hair and green garb glistening wet.

"You have done well, Daughter of Magic, and you too, Son of the One. You have accomplished your task. Know that you have saved a multitude of worlds here tonight, for as there are layers in comprehending and manifesting the divine and the just, there are layers in all worlds as well. We are glad that we have this chance to thank you—and to say farewell."

"Farewell?" Kennag's voice broke, and Alwyn could feel her pain as his own. "But—but we won! We saved Faerie! Eireth, what about your well?"

"You saved Faerie from being destroyed, from being violated," said the girl. Her voice was like the murmur of a stream. "You have preserved its wholeness. My well is likewise purged of its blasphemy. But nothing, not even the Witnesses, can prevent a thing from passing when its hour has arrived."

"No," protested Alwyn. He hadn't planned to speak. These were Kennag's legends sprung to life; her gods, her folk, not his. But the thought of such beauty passing from the earth suddenly pained him. "So many do not know of you—please, you can teach us—"

"Your heart is good, man of the Christian God," said the king. His smile was kind, but his eyes were sad. As Alwyn watched, those eyes changed from blue to green to brown. "But you do not yet understand that this is no tragic thing, but rather the natural evolution of this and other worlds. Our time has gone. There is no place for the magic of the earth and streams here any longer. Other faiths are rising, other ways of thinking and believing and knowing that which is the divine. This is what your courage has saved, dear ones. A chance for the world to go on."

Kennag was sobbing now. They smiled at her one last time, nodded respectfully to Alwyn, and strode into the waves. A host of Faerie Folk followed them, dancing and laughing joyfully. Alwyn wondered if they were truly forever gone, or just changed, transformed into something more ethereal and magical. He hoped the latter.

"They're gone," she said. "The tears—I can't see them anymore. The ointment has been washed away. The Second Sight is gone."

"I have not seen you weep before," said Alwyn gently.

"I could not—not since that horrible night," she said, gulping. "The pain . . . the pain is gone, Alwyn. It's all gone away, both the magic and the pain. It's all gone."

Something white floated into their vision. "Neddy!" cried Alwyn. "You were strong where I was weak. I thank you."

Neddy smiled. "I thank you—both of you. The being who took my life away from me has been defeated. All his plans have come to nothing. There is no reason for me to linger here anymore. It's time for me to pass on, as well."

"Oh, Neddy," said Kennag, her voice thick. "I will miss you."

"And I you, Kennag. If only I—" He suddenly paused in his urgent speaking, and laughed a little. "Listen to me. I speak as man, rather than spirit. I still have much to learn."

He turned away from them and strode to the boulder. Something small and white and red lay crumpled in the sand beside it. Alwyn turned his face away, guilty and remorseful. His arm was as it always had been, dead and unfeeling. The monster who had given it life had taken it again when he vanished. Alwyn could no longer feel the physical sting of Rowena's claws, dug into his flesh in a desperate attempt to rouse him from unholy temptation. But the sting of pain in his heart would not fade.

"Alwyn." Neddy's voice was gentle, and despite his anguish, Alwyn had to look up. "Behold."

Neddy extended his arms. "Come, my friend. I shall not travel the road to my rest alone this night."

And on this night of miracles, Alwyn witnessed yet another, one that filled him with more wonder and hope and joy than anything he had yet seen. A lithe, transparent shape detached itself from Rowena's limp corpse and sprang, purring, into the ghostly arms of the martyred king. Neddy cuddled her close, burying his spectral face in her insubstantial fur. Alwyn remembered the first meeting of the two. Neddy had been friendly and hopeful, and Rowena had eventually overcome her fear of him.

Rowena, oh, Rowena, I would give anything to undo what I have done. . . .

The spirit of the dead Rowena opened her eyes and gazed affectionately at Alwyn. How could it be? She was a beast, a mere animal. Animals had no souls . . . had they?

"My dear Brother Alwyn," came a gentle voice at his ear. "Is it so difficult to believe that one who gave her life for the whole world could earn a soul?"

Alwyn turned to see Michael standing beside him. He was clad, as before, in the humble garb of a Benedictine brother. His face and form were ordinary, but this time, Alwyn thought he could catch a glimpse of light shining behind the eyes, hidden in the folds of the deceptively plain garb.

"No," he said, his voice thick. "Oh, no, it's not difficult at all. I only—"

"Forgiven, my friend," said Rowena, her husky voice soft and distant. Even as Alwyn watched, Neddy and Rowena began to fade from his view. "Forgiven."

"Good-bye, Your Majesty," whispered Kennag. "May your rest be untroubled."

"Good-bye, Rowena," said Alwyn, as the image of boy and cat finally disappeared altogether. "Thank you."

"Loki and his children have also gone," said Michael. "They have all willingly returned to their prisons, until the hour of Ragnarok truly arrives. Ratatosk has returned to the Tree of Life. Even now, I am sure he has a tale to bend the Eagle's ear." Michael smiled with a hint of mischief. Alwyn was startled, until he remembered that Michael was a warrior angel. Not for him the gentle, eternal songs of alleluia. He was made of sterner stuff.

"The rod!" said Alwyn, suddenly remembering it. "I lost it— I could not hold—"

"Fear not," said Michael, and the rod suddenly appeared in his hand. "The things of darkness might have the power to take so holy an object, but they have not the power to hold it." He extended his other hand, and as Alwyn watched, the Ring of Solomon disappeared from his own hand to appear in Michael's palm.

It was over, then. No more ring or rod, no more Second Sight or magical healing powers. Alwyn and Kennag were mere mortals again, the only living things besides a handful of cattle on this sacred island.

Impulsively, Alwyn turned to Kennag. He found her standing, staring at him. Slowly, moving as one, they embraced. Alwyn folded his single arm about her, the left arm hanging as it ever had. He pressed his face into the warm crook of her neck, breathed in her scent, and loved her. Not with the passion of man to woman, but with something deeper. They had endured trials no mortals had ever undergone, and they had done it together. No two people in the world could ever be closer than they, though they would soon have to part forever.

He broke the embrace first, stepping back and squeezing her arm. Her hand touched his cheek with a butterfly's caress. Slowly, she moved away, turning from him and walking to the body that had housed first her lover and then Loki. Alwyn watched as she sank down beside Bran's body. She sat silently for a moment, then reached to touch the huge black hole in the broad chest. Her fingers ran up Bran's throat to his cheek, his lips, and then she buried her face in her hands and began to keen.

Loki had given up his freedom to save Alwyn, to save the world. In doing so, he had destroyed Bran. Any chance that the essence of the Dalriadan blacksmith was alive and could be restored to his true body once Loki departed was now gone.

Abruptly, Alwyn recalled the vision that Kennag had described to him: that of her lover lying dead on the shores of Iona, surrounded by the bodies of monks. This was the image the Second Sight had granted her—and it had come true.

Alwyn was vaguely aware that the sweet choir of the angels had begun to fade. Only Michael remained, walking up to Alwyn and standing in respectful silence beside him. After a moment, Michael spoke.

"Your task was not an easy one, Alwyn. We all knew it. We were powerless to intervene and could only hope and pray that you would find the courage and wisdom to halt the Enemy. And you did."

"She had the courage," said Alwyn, still gazing at Kennag as she wept over the body of her dead lover. "Rowena had the courage. I nearly failed all of you."

"But you did not," said Michael. "You succeeded. You have

earned the gratitude of all mankind, Alwyn of St. Aidan's. And to thank you, I have been empowered to give you the one thing you have prayed for."

Abruptly, Alwyn could feel his left hand again. The scratches Rowena had inflicted were gone. He was hale and whole, and he lifted his arm up and touched it with the right one.

He glanced at Michael. "Is this another test?"

Michael smiled and shook his head. "No, friend Alwyn. It is the miracle for which you have prayed so long. God's mercies are marvelous."

Slowly, Alwyn lifted his left hand and pressed it to his heart. This was the hand that had killed Rowena. He placed his right hand atop it and squeezed. As if drawn, his gaze again fell upon Kennag. He saw her enraged, bitter, laughing, brave. Kennag, whose courage had shamed him throughout this whole ordeal.

"If . . . it is permitted," he said, "I . . . I have another request."

Epilogue

Wherwell Abbey, Hampshire
March 10, 1000

The soft sounds of women's voices raised in praise to God drifted to Abbess Elfthryth's ears. The musical drone was all but drowned out by the raspy sound of her own labored breathing. Smoke from dozens of candles and incense made the breathing worse, and tainted what air she could gasp with ash and a sickly sweet scent. She did not know if it was day or night outside the cold stone walls, and did not care.

Yet the abbess was content. The voices of the nuns were a plea to Heaven on her behalf. The candles and incense sanctified her little cell, and the thick walls shut out the world and encased her in this stone womb. She was safe here.

Over her protests, Sister Wulfgifu had removed the hair shirt Elfthryth had worn since the day she entered the abbey, never to leave it save in death. The gentle sister had replaced the painful hair with soft linens, and now tenderly bathed the old woman's hot brow with cool, herb-scented water.

Elfthryth wanted to thank her, but speaking was simply too much effort. She had lain here for a ten-day now, getting progressively weaker. Today, Elfthryth had not been able to sip the beef broth Wulfgifu had tried to feed her.

"Do you hear that?" Wulfgifu's voice was soft. In this reversal of roles, she had been gracious. Elfthryth wondered what had happened to the timid little girl she had brought from Shaftesbury. "The sisters are praying for you, Abbess. They are asking the saints to intercede on your behalf."

Saints. Saints like Edward the Martyr? A deep shudder of raw terror took Elfthryth. If the faith was divine, the clergy were human. Wherwell Abbey belonged to her, and enough money had bought her the position as abbess despite the fact that she had taken her vows a few weeks ago. She had put every penny she owned into Wherwell Abbey and its works, had even bathed the lice-ridden, filthy poor with her own delicate, royal hands. She had been here for only a few months. She had hoped to have years of service to bribe God into forgiveness. What if it wasn't enough?

"Are you cold, Abbess? How thoughtless of me not to notice. Let me get you another blanket and some fresh water. I won't be but a moment."

The dying woman could barely turn her head to follow Wulfgifu's girlish form out the door, and there was no strength to call her back. Suddenly, Elfthryth did not want to be alone. She closed her eyes, mentally reviewing her actions since that awful day when Edward's ghost had taunted her with visions of hellfire and torment. Had she done enough?

"You know," came a smooth, vibrant voice that she recognized with a spurt of horror, "you have to actually *repent* for it to work."

She opened her eyes and wanted to scream. She could not. Her face seemed to have no muscles, save for her eyelids. He sat in the chair Sister Wulfgifu had vacated, smiling down at her. He was as gloriously beautiful as she remembered—the golden hair, the perfect face, the elegant clothes, the smile such as would grace the face of a cherub. Only the malevolent gleam in the blue eyes gave any hint of his true nature.

He rose and extended a perfectly manicured hand to her, and his grin widened. She saw sharp teeth.

"I believe, Your Majesty," he said softly, "we had a deal."

**The Village of Gleannsidh
March 10, 1000**

Tink. Tink. Clang. Tink. Hissssss. . . .

Kennag's lips curved in a smile. The rise and fall of Bran's hammer from his shop was punctuated by occasional snatches of song. Bran's singing was about as pleasant as a raven's croak, but it was the sweetest music in the world to his wife. It meant he was happy, content, as she was.

Outside, the snow fell softly, almost apologetically. It would accumulate as the day went on. By nightfall, its downy blanket would soften all sound, wrap the two of them in its muffling embrace, help them shut out the world as they loved by the fire. Kennag did not begrudge the snow its falling.

She had a sudden, vivid memory of a dream she had had while in Glastonbury. In the dream she had been standing where she was now, in her little cottage, her belly big with child, hearing the clink-clink of Bran's hammer rising and falling as he worked the metal into things of beauty and service. Glastonbury's Tor had been filled with illusions, but always the Second Sight had been true.

Keenag blinked back tears of joy, returning her attention to the task at hand. She stirred the kettle, sniffed, and added a few more herbs to the concoction. Morag's youngest had taken ill again, and the little girl always responded to Kennag's ministering. A clean scent arose from the boiling water, and Kennag smiled.

There was breath of cold, crisp air as her mother bustled in. Snow dusted her gray hair and the small bundle she carried. "Sweet Brihid, but it's a chill day!"

"Welcome, I would think, after the strange heat and darkness." Kennag had not told anyone what had happened to her, nor was she likely to. Enough that strange things had been afoot, and now had departed. Enough that she and Bran were back, and the hate in her heart had melted like a lump of ice before a warm fire.

"Wherever you were, Kennag, it has made you even wiser," said Mairead. She sat in a chair by the fire, unwrapped her baby, and freed a breast for him to suckle. "Bran still won't tell us how he escaped from the Lochlannach," she said. The unspoken words, *or where you were all this time,* hung between them.

"Nor will he, I think," Kennag replied, the reply suiting both the spoken and the unspoken questions. Her gaze traveled upward, to the roof that now bore dozens of hanging plants. She let her eyes feast on the sight. There were some she had never seen before, but somehow knew how to prepare. She did not wish to use them, almost; they had been a gift, appearing the same night that Kennag had left on her quest. That night, too, according to her mother, a beautiful woman appeared to the door with a cloth that appeared to be spun of spider's web, so fine was the weave. Wrapped in this blanket, Kennag's baby brother—Bethag, named after their father—had slept for three days straight. Upon awakening, he was as hale and hearty as any nine-month babe.

Kennag reached for a plant, then crumbled it between her fingers. The fragrance almost made her cry.

There came a brisk knock on the door. The baby, startled, began to cry as loudly as any other baby might. While Mairead tried to soothe him, Kennag opened the door.

Standing there was the last person in the village she had expected to see. Father Edwy, the snow falling on his tonsured pate and melting almost at once. He had come while Kennag had been away, to fill the place of the priest who had been murdered by the Norsemen on that awful night. Kennag had not had much conversation with him. Standing beside the unusually somber priest was Ciarda, holding the hand of her little boy Padriug. The boy was pale and trembling.

"Father Edwy? What do you want with me?" asked Kennag, her eyes narrowing.

"I have been treating young Padriug here for a few days, but he doesn't seem to be getting any better," said Father Edwy. He looked a bit uncomfortable. "I thought perhaps you might be willing to help."

"Of course I am willing," said Kennag, startled. "But the Church has often told me that it would let a child die rather than ask for such aid as I might provide it."

His round cheeks, red with the cold, flushed even redder. "Here, I am the Church. And I know that my God loves His children, and would wish them healed by one who cared about them."

Amazed, Kennag smiled a little. She thought of Alwyn. Perhaps there would be a place for her, after all, in this world of the Christians.

The Abbey of St. Aidan's, Chesbury
March 10, 1000

The snow had stopped, and the sun streamed through the windows in the scriptorium. The small white kitten Alwyn had adopted, Pangur Ban, dozed contentedly in the sunbeam. Pangur Ban was not supposed to be here, but Alwyn had smuggled her up anyway. He liked having the little animal near him. The bright light made the colors drying on Alwyn's most recent manuscript seem even more vivid. A letter had been delivered to him this morning, and now, having completed an entire page, he permitted himself to read it.

He blew on his fingers as they fumbled clumsily with the letter. At one point, he took the parchment in his teeth to permit his fingers to slip beneath the wax seal and break it. Spreading it out, careful to avoid touching the drying ink, he read:

My dearest Alwyn,

News of your safe return fills me with delight. I know how difficult your trip must have been. I am also pleased to report that I myself am most well and healthy.

The Person who so sorely troubled our minds has departed—whither, I know not, but I do suspect. The bells continue to ring in celebration of the return of the sun and moon after so long away. Men seem to be more devout than hitherto, which pleases me as much as it amuses me.

Our Friend seems at a loss without this Person, and is more than eager to listen to what older, grayer heads might have to tell him. The Force seems to have retreated, but dear God, how many lives have been lost in this battle.

I pray this missive finds you well and happy, dear friend. Praise be to God, Who has delivered us from darkness—and to all those who speak His truth.

There was no signature, only a playful sketch of a paw print—the print of a wolf. It would be too dangerous for Wulfstan to have identified himself, even now.

Alwyn smiled as he folded the letter and carefully put it to one side. With Angelo gone, Ethelred was desperate for advisers. He could find no better one than Wulfstan. Ethelred "Badly Counseled" would have to find a new nickname.

He thought about the journey he and Kennag had made together, and the journey home as well. Balaam had waited for him, and seemed more energetic than he had in years. Epona's grace, no doubt. They had found the kitten right outside the abbey, as if she had been waiting for them. Alwyn had convinced Abbot Bede to free the old donkey from service, and now Balaam munched happily on hay and oats in the barn.

Bede himself seemed different at first, then Alwyn realized something that moved him profoundly. Bede was not uncomfortable with Alwyn's deformity. He had been uncomfortable with Alwyn's shame. Since his return, Alwyn had not kept vigil with the scourge even once, and, please God, he would never feel the need to do so again.

Alwyn reached for a fresh quill and dipped it into the inkhorn. Time to decorate the text.

The light from outside grew brighter. Puzzled, Alwyn glanced out the window. The sunlight on the snow nearly blinded him. He squinted, and realized the impossible: the light was growing, and the cold room had warmed to a summer temperature.

"Hello, Brother Alwyn," came a soft voice he knew. He turned, knocking over the inkhorn with his dead left hand in his haste. He blinked. His eyes dazzled by the light, colorful dots swirled in front of him. Finally, he could see again, and was not altogether surprised to find Michael, clad as a monk, standing beside him.

Awe and trepidation flooded him. "Michael."

Michael smiled. With a gentle wave, the spilled ink that had flooded over Alwyn's manuscript page disappeared. The quill floated up from the floor to lodge itself comfortably in the inkhorn. Little Pangur Ban rose, stretched, and began to circle Michael's ankles, purring wildly.

"As you have surmised, I do have another, final task for you," Michael admitted, "but one I think you will find much more pleasant. If, of course, you are willing."

Alwyn couldn't lie. The thought of undertaking another arduous journey so soon was almost more than he could bear. Yet he knew he could not refuse.

"I know it is useless to run away," he said. "I will do whatever it is you ask of me."

Michael turned and clasped his hands behind his back. Walking the length of the room, he began. "Elsewhere on this island, there are monks who are serving God in the same fashion in which you, Alwyn, are being asked to serve. Something secret, something wonderful, something that will help heal this wounded world more than you can possibly imagine. And they are performing this glorious task right here—in their scriptoria."

"I don't understand."

Michael picked up the quill and a fresh sheet of vellum. "Write the following words: 'It began, again, to snow.' "

Confused, Alwyn did as he was bid. The minute he finished the final word, the sky darkened. He stared at the white flakes falling from a sky that had, seconds before, been cloudless.

"Now write this: 'Ealdorman Leofsige killed Aefic, the king's high reeve, and the king banished him from the land.' When you are done, reread Wulfstan's letter."

Alwyn licked his lips and did as he was bade. His hands trembled so that he could not unfold the letter. With great kindness, Michael did it for him. Disbelieving, Alwyn saw that the text of the letter had changed. One passage clearly stated: *His Majesty was betrayed by Ealdorman Leofsige, who treacherously murdered the good high reeve Aefic. Leofsige no longer dares show his face in this land.*

"What you tell me happens," he said to Michael. "What I write—changes things. Changes history."

Michael clasped Alwyn's hand with his own. The archangel's touch felt warm and human, but there was something else. Alwyn felt confidence seeping into him through that heavenly touch.

"The words that you write will be collected into a literary work that will speak for over a thousand years," Michael said. "You and the others who will write this chronicle will reshape the world. What you write, will be. And you will write an account of this tumultuous time in your country's history."

"But why?" asked Alwyn. "We survived it—the world did not end."

"But mankind must not know just how close it came to a false Judgment," replied Michael. "There was too much death, too much terror. Mortals saw more than they ought of Heaven and of Hell. Mankind's spirit will be broken if this is allowed to pass into history without . . . gentling. When the true hour comes, then all will be made plain. There can be no deception then. Until that blessed hour, you, Alwyn, will write what will be known as the truth."

Alwyn recalled the body of the murdered Danish girl he and Kennag had found in the village outside the Andredesweald.

"The massacre and the Force—" he began, but Michael interrupted him.

"Some things are fate, Alwyn. They cannot be changed. Man must make mistakes in order to learn from them, and you do not know all that our Heavenly Father sees. This is a grave responsibility. I ask you, do you accept it?"

The kitten gave Michael's ankles a final rub, then sat at Alwyn's feet. In her little face, Alwyn saw the wise eyes of Rowena. His heart suddenly felt full, overflowing. He laughed, not knowing why, only that the joy in him needed an outlet.

He did not answer Michael with words. Alwyn, humble monk of St. Aidan's, simply reached with his single good hand and picked up the quill.

Author's Note

"So ... how much of this really happened?"

One of the pleasures of reading historical fantasy is separating fact from the author's imagination. For the reader's entertainment and education, here is a brief discussion of some of the events, people, and places depicted in *A.D. 999.*

The young King Edward was murdered at Corfe Castle in 978 by a dagger to the bowels as I have described. He was canonized during the reign of King Cnut (1016–1035), but even before then, miracles were said to happen at his tomb. His personality is recorded to have been somewhat less than saintly, however. To the best of my knowledge, his ghost was never seen.

Historians and public thought at the time both connect Queen Elfthryth with the deed in some fashion, but this was never proved. A tale has it that Elfthryth rode to Edward's tomb in an attempt to quash rumors that she murdered him, but her horse shied and would not approach. What is fact is that she did become an abbess at Wherwell, where she died in A.D. 1000.

Ethelred was in residence at Corfe and could conceivably have witnessed the murder, but history exonerates the ten-year-old boy from actual involvement. The great twelfth-century historian William of Malmesbury tells us that Elfthryth often beat Ethelred with candles, and that the king had a lifelong fear of them. Ethelred's name means "Wise counsel," and he had been tagged with the nickname "Unraed," which means "poorly counseled." The pun, translated into modern English, has forever dubbed the unfortunate king "Ethelred the Unready." He was a victim of bad luck and bad judgment. Traitors cropped up frequently. One such, a man named Aelfric, did indeed warn the Viking Force of an impending attack by the English. Ethelred banished the traitor and blinded his son.

The Vikings hammered at Britain throughout his reign. Rampages such as the one that devastated Kennag's fictitious village of Gleannsidh were common, and slaves were as valuable to the Vikings as plunder. Dreadful famines were reported throughout the land as well, and outbreaks of St. Anthony's fire, an actual disease, were reported. It was, all in all, a bad time to be in Britain.

Bishop Wulfstan, later Archbishop of York, became one of Ethelred's advisers. He also advised Ethelred's successor, King Cnut. His famous "Sermon of the Wolf" shows us that he was keenly interested in apocalyptic thought. He is remembered as a good adviser and an eloquent author.

The roof collapse at Calne, which resulted in the deaths of several members of the Witan, did occur in the year 977. However, it was Saint Dunstan who clung to the beam and survived, not my evil Angelo.

I have borrowed the name Thorkell, one of the great Viking kings, for my more youthful character, and made him the brother of the murdered Gunhild, instead of King Swein. Ethelred's order to execute everyone of Danish descent living in England, known as the St. Brice's Day Massacre, is tragically not fiction; the burning of the Danes who had taken refuge in St. Fritheswide's church in Oxford is likewise true.

The battle of Maldon is a famous one in British history. For the purposes of this story I have chosen to set it, and many other events, in the year 999 rather than in 991, the actual year in which it occurred. Another such real event, depicted here in the year 999 rather than its actual date of 1013, was the martyrdom of Archbishop Alphege, or Aelfheah, at the hands of the Vikings as I have described it. A third is the sacking of Iona, which actually occurred in the years 800, 825, and 986. I've no idea what the real Vikings did with the cattle.

Both Glastonbury and Worth Church are real places. Glastonbury is of course known for its mysterious Tor, which is thought to be an entrance into the Underworld, and for its tales of Avalon and King Arthur. The Blood Spring, known today as the Chalice Spring and Well, still survives, and its water still is tinged with red. Worth Church is a humbler place, one of the best-preserved examples of Anglo-Saxon architecture still standing. It, too, has an air of mystery about it. No one knows for certain why such a large church was built in the middle of a dense forest, and there is no record of it in the Domesday Book.

To those who know that Pope Sylvester II, Gerbert d'Aurillac, was an intelligent and good man, I tender my apologies and offer forth the fact that, during his tenure as pope, he was indeed accused of being the Antichrist.

As for the mythic characters, the squirrel Ratatosk, Loki, and Loki's children Hel, Fenris, and Jormungand are straight out of Norse mythology. I have tried to preserve their essences while fleshing them out into fully realized characters. Angelo can be found, under another name, weaving his dark way throughout the Bible. King Arthur needs little introduction; in the year 1191, his remains and those of Queen Guinevere were allegedly dug up in Glastonbury Abbey. Scholars remain skeptical, but regardless, the legends link Arthur with Avalon—Glastonbury—and say that there he sleeps, until the hour of his country's greatest need, when he will awaken and fight again. Gwyn ap Nudd, king of the Faerie Underworld, is traditionally depicted as less evil than I have cast him here.

The Anglo-Saxon Chronicle, from which I have drawn much information and of which I have young Alwyn become part, is a remarkable collection of documents. It is believed to have been begun in the early tenth century. Some portions were clearly written in hindsight; other passages are fresh enough to have been written from notes jotted down at the time. Four versions have survived, and are believed to have been written by several different monks over several years.

Finally, a word about calendars. In the year 999, calendars were pretty much whatever one wished to make of them. The Church had the year starting on Christmas Day. The Roman tradition, followed by much of the populace, had it beginning on January 1. Other dates were put forward at times. There is a droll comment in one of the versions of the Anglo Saxon Chronicle in which the editor laments the difficulty of actually reckoning the beginning of the year.

For simplicity's sake in this twentieth century, in which

A.D. 999 was written, I have opted to use the calendar with which my readers will be most familiar, and the year ends in this novel on December 31.

—Jadrien Bell, November 30, 1998, Denver, Colorado

About the Author

Jadrien Bell is the pen name of a well-known science fiction and fantasy author. Readers are encouraged to visit the author at www.jadrienbell.com.

P. N. ELROD

"Offers deft touches of wit, beauty, and suspense.
Entertaining." —*Publishers Weekly*

__DEATH AND THE MAIDEN   0-441-00071-1/$4.99

__RED DEATH   0-441-71094-8/$4.99

THE VAMPIRE FILES

"An entertaining blend of detective story and the
supernatural from a promising new writer."
—*Science Fiction Chronicle*

__BLOOD ON THE WATER   0-441-85947-X/$5.99
__BLOODLIST   0-441-06795-6/$5.99
__BLOODCIRCLE   0-441-06717-4/$5.99
__FIRE IN THE BLOOD   0-441-85946-1/$5.99